The Disabled Tyrant's Beloved Pet Fish

Canji Baojun De Zhangxin Yu Chong

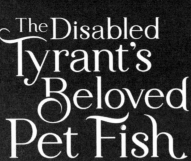

The Disabled Tyrant's Beloved Pet Fish

Canji Baojun De Zhangxin Yu Chong

WRITTEN BY
Xue Shan Fei Hu

TRANSLATED BY
Mimi, Yuka

ILLUSTRATED BY
Ryoplica

BONUS ILLUSTRATION BY
Kura

COVER ILLUSTRATION BY
Changle

Seven Seas

Seven Seas Entertainment

The Disabled Tyrant's Beloved Pet Fish:
Canji Baojun De Zhangxin Yu Chong (Novel) Vol. 2

Published originally under the title of 残疾暴君的掌心鱼宠[穿书]
(Canji Baojun De Zhangxin Yu Chong [Chuan Shu])
Author©雪山肥狐 (Xue Shan Fei Hu)
US English edition rights under license granted by 北京晋江原创网络科技有限公司
(Beijing Jinjiang Original Network Technology Co., Ltd.)
US English edition copyright © 2024 Seven Seas Entertainment, Inc
Arranged through JS Agency Co., Ltd
All rights reserved

Cover artwork made by 長樂 (Changle)
Original Cover by Fin Publishing Part., Ltd. (Thai edition, Thailand)
Arranged and licensed through JS Agency Co., Ltd., Taiwan
Interior illustrations: Ryoplica
Bonus color illustration: Kura

Seven Seas press and purchase enquiries can be sent
to Marketing Manager Lauren Hill at press@gomanga.com.
Information regarding the distribution and purchase of digital editions is available
from Digital Manager CK Russell at digital@gomanga.com.

Follow Seven Seas Entertainment online at
sevenseasentertainment.com.

TRANSLATION: Mimi, Yuka
ADAPTATION: Leah Masterson
COVER DESIGN: M. A. Lewife
INTERIOR DESIGN & LAYOUT: Clay Gardner
COPY EDITOR: Leighanna DeRouen
PROOFREADER: Jade Gardner, Kate Kishi
EDITOR: Harry Catlin
PREPRESS TECHNICIAN: Melanie Ujimori, Jules Valera
MANAGING EDITOR: Alyssa Scavetta
EDITOR-IN-CHIEF: Julie Davis
PUBLISHER: Lianne Sentar
VICE PRESIDENT: Adam Arnold
PRESIDENT: Jason DeAngelis

ISBN: 979-8-88843-309-6
Printed in Canada
First Printing: August 2024
10 9 8 7 6 5 4 3 2 1

TABLE OF
CONTENTS

Fish Sneezes

PRINCE JING MADE A NOTE of the carp spirit's name. "Li Yu" was quite fitting, he thought. It seemed he hadn't made a mistake when he decided to call him Xiaoyu.

But all the spirits in the storybooks he'd researched were at the very minimum hundreds or thousands of years old, and his fish was only eighteen. This made him basically an adult by human standards, but it was much too young for a yao.

Of course, he knew it was possible that the carp spirit was lying to him about his age, but this didn't stop Prince Jing's conclusion that the carp spirit's cultivation level must be quite low, since he could only transform for two hours a day.

The carp spirit seemed to be hiding why he'd come here, but Prince Jing wasn't in a hurry to ask. He didn't want to scare Xiaoyu away.

Prince Jing continued to write, *Why did you save me?*

Li Yu wasn't quite sure how to answer. After all, he didn't think the incident when he helped Prince Jing rinse out his eyes was such a big deal. On further consideration, he decided Prince Jing must be asking about the matter regarding the House of Cheng'en. Trying to be as concise as possible, he explained, "I found out the second prince's plot by a stroke of luck, and I wanted to let Ye-shizi know so he could put his guard up. All I did was write a letter! Everything else that happened was thanks to the plans Your Highness and Ye-shizi made, so I really don't think that counts as saving Your Highness."

Prince Jing was taken aback to hear Li Yu answer the wrong question, but he didn't bother correcting him. If Xiaoyu wouldn't even take credit for something as important as saving Ye Qinghuan, then there was no use mentioning cleaning his eyes, either.

Prince Jing was becoming increasingly pleased with this fish.

He wrote, *Where are you staying now?*

Wasn't he staying in Prince Jing's manor, seeing Prince Jing every day? But that would definitely make Prince Jing suspicious, Li Yu thought, so he lied and said, "I...don't have a fixed residence, so I just wander..."

Prince Jing was taken aback by his fishy audacity. He wanted badly to expose his secret. Unfortunately, a bunch of people—including the emperor and his concubines—were outside the warmed chamber, so he couldn't reveal his hand at such a critical moment.

It wasn't just that he couldn't expose Li Yu. He also had to do everything he could to protect him. It would be best to take this lying little humanoid fish back to his manor and stamp him with his seal. It was far too audacious and risky for him to just show up in the palace like this.

Since you have nowhere to stay, come to my manor, Prince Jing wrote.

Li Yu was startled. He couldn't believe that Prince Jing...was willing to give him, a stranger with no identity, a place to stay?

"Y-you'd really take me in?" Li Yu had to confirm it. "But why? We've only met a few times."

Prince Jing's expression was serious as he wrote, *You've saved me before, as well as the House of Cheng'en. I trust you.*

This was too good to be true! The issue of his suspicious human self was solved, just like that?

"But if I come to the manor... I-I'm very busy, so I may not have much time to do things for you..."

Li Yu looked a bit troubled. It would be great if he could exist as a resident of Prince Jing's manor, since then he'd be able to walk around freely, but if that happened, he'd have to actually help Prince Jing out. He couldn't just freeload. However, with his two-hour transformation limit, the most he could do was sweep the yard. Surely Prince Jing's manor had plenty of those sorts of servants already!

But no one knew this fish's daily life better than Prince Jing. All he did every day was eat and drink his fill, and occasionally accompany the prince while he was reading or drawing. Most of the time, he just blew bubbles, swam around, or slept under his water plant quilt. Prince Jing wasn't sure if this fish who had barely gotten any chances to suck essence recently was actually busy or just pretending to be busy. He felt a little disgruntled.

In any case, there was no way he could have the fish clean the yard. Prince Jing wrote, *Don't worry too much. You can stay in the manor if you just do one thing.*

"...What is it?" Li Yu asked expectantly.

I have a fish. When I'm not around, help me take care of him.

Li Yu gaped at Prince Jing like...well...a fish.

Prince Jing, afraid he wouldn't understand, pointed toward the crystal bottle. When they'd sat down earlier, Li Yu purposefully blocked the bottle with his body so that Prince Jing wouldn't realize the fish inside was gone. But it seemed that Prince Jing really hadn't noticed, or else he wouldn't point at it for him to look at.

So Prince Jing wanted him to take care of his fish?

Li Yu hastily nodded in agreement. Of course he'd accept such a generous offer! He didn't know how to do much, but taking care of himself was right up his alley! "All right! I can do that! I can help Your Highness take care of your fish!"

As they were talking, there was a knock on the door. Prince Jing glanced at Li Yu, who quickly covered his mouth.

Outside, Wang Xi said, "Your Highness, the emperor has started asking after you."

Prince Jing had come to this warmed chamber in the side hall with the excuse that he needed to change; he couldn't spend hours in here. Prince Jing looked at Li Yu again and wrote, *Watch my fish for me here. Someone will guard the room, so don't worry.* He patted Li Yu gently on the shoulder.

"Your Highness…"

A warm current flooded through Li Yu's heart, leaving him so touched that he sniffled a bit. Prince Jing had solved all the problems that plagued him and even told him to not worry. Since it was Prince Jing's promise, he truly believed it. No wonder he was so happy when Prince Jing said he'd take him in. Staying close to his tyrant master was what made him feel most at peace.

Prince Jing walked out of the warmed chamber and ordered Wang Xi to keep guarding the room for him. Nobody was to enter or leave. Wang Xi didn't quite understand it, but he did as he was told.

Meanwhile, the emperor had ordered the imperial physician to examine Concubine Qiu's arm injury again, but it was impossible to make any further conclusions. The emperor started to wonder if he'd overthought it and misunderstood her, and he was beginning to look at her more kindly.

Since all the concubines were present, Concubine Qiu couldn't stay lying in her bed the entire time, so she came out with the emperor after a while to see them.

Though Concubine Qiu was ill, Consort Qian saw she had still put on exquisite makeup and wore a thin, fragile-looking inner coat. She internally cursed Concubine Qiu for her slyness, but at the end of the day, she wouldn't embarrass her in front of the emperor. Since the emperor wasn't punishing Concubine Qiu, Consort Qian decided she should follow his example and stop targeting her, warmly calling her "sister" instead.

When Concubine Qiu was still a Noble Consort, she hadn't respected Consort Qian due to her mediocre appearance; now, however, she was smiling and laughing at her jokes as if they were close.

Prince Jing had been wearing a black robe before; now he had changed into a silver-hemmed sapphire one. It was rare to see him without the crystal bottle, so the emperor teased him and said, "You finally learned you can't take it everywhere! Got splashed a couple of times, did you?"

Wang Xi had been tasked with guarding the warmed chamber, so he couldn't accompany Prince Jing—for all that Prince Jing wanted to change the subject somehow, it wasn't easy to make the emperor understand his thoughts without his usual interpreter. Instead, he simply stayed silent and let the emperor misunderstand.

Prince Jing watched from afar as Concubine Qiu chatted with Consort Qian. He'd sent someone to pass the information along to the third prince, but it seemed like the third prince's progress was slow. Consort Qian was clearly plotting something, as she kept trying to lend an arm to support Concubine Qiu. However, Concubine Qiu was extremely careful, and her confidants wouldn't let the other consort get close, pushing her away every time. Consort Qian was anxious whenever she thought of her son's mission for her, but she couldn't be so blatant that Concubine Qiu would realize what she was doing.

The third prince was struggling too. He'd received the information from Prince Jing, but he only half believed it. He couldn't randomly suggest another examination of Concubine Qiu's arm before the situation was clear. Concubine Qiu was, after all, his father's former concubine. Instead, he sent his people to look for Huanhua in the Imperial Garden.

The sixth prince had the same idea and signaled to him to wait for more news. For now, all the third prince could do was try to subtly ask around about Concubine Qiu's injury—although even this much was beginning to irritate the emperor, who stared at him coldly. The third prince was afraid that he'd properly upset the emperor if he was being too suspicious, so he quieted down after a while.

Concubine Qiu, assuming her bid for sympathy was working, knelt and pleaded, "Your Majesty, Zhao-er knows he was wrong. He's been worried about my injury, and I haven't seen him since he left the palace. I would be immensely grateful if Your Majesty would grant me the favor of letting Zhao-er enter the palace to keep me company for a bit..."

Mu Tianzhao had dared to plot against the Duke of Cheng'en. This was a huge mistake, and Concubine Qiu knew it—she wouldn't be so brazen as to ask the emperor to pardon him, only for him to lift the ban. As long as he could still enter the palace, all was not lost. Though the emperor had hastily demoted the second prince to marquis, Concubine Qiu was sure she understood the emperor well enough: as long as his heart softened once, she could slowly and gradually cajole him, perhaps even to the point where he might change his mind and make the Marquis of An a prince again...

How could Concubine Qiu accept that even the mute fifth prince could hold the title of prince while Mu Tianzhao languished as a marquis?! Her Zhao-er was the emperor's eldest son!

Concubine Qiu had actually quite accurately predicted the emperor's usual thought processes. However, the emperor had already read the Marquis of An's letter, where he'd pleaded to visit his mother, so when she came to beg for the same thing, the emperor remained hesitant. Concubine Qiu had been hurt in the fire—did that mean she deserved an award? Why were they both asking for a favor?

The emperor told her mildly, "Recover from your injuries first. There's no need to speak of anything else."

Concubine Qiu was shocked that the emperor didn't relent. Even though she wanted to say a lot more, she didn't dare.

"Ah, right." The emperor really didn't want to talk about the Marquis of An anymore, so he changed the subject. "You've seen Prince Jing's fish before, correct?"

...Fish???

At the sound of this word, embarrassing memories flooded into Concubine Qiu's mind. She'd briefly forgotten the incident, but the trauma it had caused ran deep in her psyche. The terror of being slapped in the face by a fish made her bite her lip until it nearly bled, and she asked anxiously, "Why do you mention the fish all of a sudden, Your Majesty?"

The emperor chuckled. "That fish is no normal fish. It has grown golden scales—I believe it is an auspicious sign. You should come take a look too."

A fire in Zhongcui Palace was, after all, far from auspicious. The emperor considered Prince Jing's fish a good omen, and though he remembered that Concubine Qiu didn't seem to like the fish, he hoped she would stop driving herself into a corner. Wouldn't it be better to make up with Prince Jing than keep trying to cling onto the Marquis of An? It could also wash away Concubine Qiu's bad luck.

Concubine Qiu just barely managed to not look bewildered. She couldn't follow the emperor's train of thought at all. He'd already turned to Prince Jing, smiling, and ordered him to bring the little carp over.

Prince Jing's heart tightened. It hadn't been two hours, and he didn't know if Xiaoyu had transformed back yet. He couldn't take Xiaoyu out of the room right now, so he had to think of a way to stall. Since Wang Xi wasn't around, Prince Jing asked Luo Ruisheng to prepare some ink and a brush. He picked up the brush, writing slowly to take up more time.

When he saw Prince Jing's bold calligraphy, the emperor was quite happy. The gist of what Prince Jing had written was that while he was getting changed in the warmed chamber in the side hall, he had fed the fish at the same time. The fish was taking a nap at the moment to digest its meal.

The emperor found himself in a slightly awkward position. He knew that Prince Jing loved his fish, and now that it had started growing golden scales, the emperor considered it uniquely auspicious among fish. He had to be extra patient.

The emperor chuckled. "In that case, I'll punish Prince Jing with a couple of rounds of Go while we wait."

Prince Jing nodded in agreement, and Luo Ruisheng immediately rushed to bring over the Go board.

The emperor almost never lost at Go, but he lost two games in a row against Prince Jing. Prince Jing only won by a narrow margin each time, though. The emperor was smiling as he internally scolded him: *What a brat!* Even though he lost, the emperor didn't really mind.

While the games were in progress, the third prince came over to watch. He wanted to join in on the fun, but he was the worst at Go of all the princes. He still chimed in occasionally even though he didn't understand the game, but the emperor thought he was a nuisance and made him go away. When the third prince looked at Prince Jing again, his eyes were full of admiration, envy, and hatred. He'd wanted to win him over to his side in the past, but he was a bit more wary of Prince Jing now.

The sixth prince smiled and pulled on his arm. "Third Brother, one should keep silent during a game of Go. I don't quite understand the game either, so let's stand to the side and wait."

The emperor usually barely noticed the sixth prince, but seeing him come to help the third prince at just the right moment, the emperor's opinion of this son improved.

After those two rounds of Go, Prince Jing figured it was about time. He got up to go to the warmed chamber and find his fish. He found Wang Xi still diligently guarding the door to the room. Prince Jing had said nobody was allowed to enter or leave, and that was how it would be. The servants who showed up to serve tea were all stopped at the door.

When conversing with the emperor, every word and sentence had to be fearful and cautious. Meanwhile, Li Yu was hiding in this room, relaxed and free of worry. When Prince Jing went out, he'd left behind the jade box used to feed his fish. It was filled with fish food and the desserts that he knew his fish liked. Li Yu just held the jade box in his lap and ate out of it directly while he waited for his two hours to be up. It was very reassuring to know Prince Jing was outside, so much so that it felt as if time passed more quickly. When the system began its countdown, he closed the jade box and waited next to the fish tank...

Li Yu had just jumped back into his crystal bottle when Prince Jing came back into the room.

Ah, master! Li Yu flicked his tail. *Your fish fed himself just like he was supposed to!*

At first, the little carp was worried that when his human form "disappeared," Prince Jing would look for him. But he didn't—he came straight to the bottle and took the fish and crystal bottle away.

"Your Highness, the person who was in the room just now..." Wang Xi wanted to ask where the male concubine had gone, since he kept appearing and disappearing suddenly.

Prince Jing glanced at him. *He left already.*

Wang-gonggong was utterly and completely confused. But the little carp whom Prince Jing always carried around with him felt his anxious heart settle back down. It seemed Prince Jing was already used to him disappearing all the time.

Prince Jing brought Li Yu before the emperor. The little carp was quite surprised when he saw Concubine Qiu. Why was the Noble Consort still here? Had nobody slapped her in the face yet...? Or had the plot that he knew changed yet again?

The emperor asked Prince Jing to bring the fish closer, and asked Concubine Qiu to come closer as well. Her body was stiff, and she stared uncomfortably at the fish in the crystal bottle, her eyes almost bulging out of her head. Although the fish's stomach and tail had golden scales on them now, she was sure that this was the fish that had slapped her in the face before. She would recognize this damned fish even if he turned into fish bones and fish ash!

But here she was, with the emperor asking her to take a good look at the fish. Concubine Qiu was entirely unwilling, but she couldn't disobey the emperor, especially when it was clear from his words and actions that he really valued this fish.

Concubine Qiu forced herself to get closer, wrenching her trembling lips into a painstaking smile. She wanted to say something to praise the fish—but she had cussed this fish out ten thousand times in private, so when she was suddenly faced with the need to praise him, she froze up!

Li Yu trembled in fright at Concubine Qiu's rictus grin—and then he noticed the scent of cypress.

Huh? Was the Noble Consort still using her old tricks? Why hadn't the sixth and third princes done anything yet? Li Yu furtively glanced at the third prince. He looked extremely resentful, as if he wanted to throw himself in front of the fish. Li Yu suddenly understood—was it just that the third prince was useless and he couldn't find the right time to expose her? That was no good! Perhaps Li Yu really was fated to confront the Noble Consort himself. Now was the time for him to make his move!

It was boring to just float belly-up every time. Li Yu smiled naughtily. This time, he'd try something else.

Concubine Qiu stared at the fish without blinking. Suddenly, she had a bad feeling that the fish was going to try something devious again—

The fish kept flicking his tail at her. Speckled with golden scales, his black tail was alluring and beautiful. As Concubine Qiu watched, she became somewhat entranced. Suddenly, the fish shuddered, and with a pop, spit out a trail of bubbles. He paused, shuddered again, and spit out another long trail.

Concubine Qiu honestly had no idea what to think of this.

When the fish spit out the first set of bubbles, the emperor and Prince Jing were close enough to see it. The emperor was surprised. "Tianchi, what's wrong with the fish?"

Prince Jing knew that the carp spirit was up to something again, so of course he'd support him. With a dark expression on his face, he shot a pointed glance at Wang Xi, who had finally arrived. Wang-gonggong immediately spoke for His Highness. "Your Majesty, this fish often becomes uncomfortable when he smells something pungent. He's sneezing."

This again?! Although Li Yu supposed that should work as an explanation with his current goals... *Fine, Wang-gonggong! The fish won't get mad this time when you say he's sneezing!*

A Gift for the Fish

ONCUBINE QIU'S expression turned ugly. Was the fish mocking her for her body odor? How was that possible?! This thing definitely had a grudge against her. "Your Majesty, is Wang-gonggong implying that I have a strange smell and I'm suffocating the fish?"

The third prince, Mu Tianming, who'd been waiting for this moment, exchanged glances with Consort Qian. "Sister Qiu, why are you acting so nervous?" said Consort Qian, taking the hint. "The fish was fine with His Highness. What is it about you that's making it so...uncomfortable?" Unlike Wang Xi, Consort Qian couldn't just outright say that the fish was sneezing. She'd never heard of such a thing before, so she addressed the matter a little more tactfully. "Perhaps it really smelled something odd? You've just been injured, let's have the imperial physician take another look at it. It's best to be careful in case the injury has worsened somehow."

Concubine Qiu hesitated. She knew that Consort Qian was up to no good, so of course she wanted to refuse. However, the emperor was sure that Consort Qian spoke from a place of concern, and after a moment of thought, he said, "Consort Qian is right. Why don't we summon the imperial physician to examine it again?"

The previous imperial physician was called back. Mu Tianming made sure to remind him, "You must carefully examine Concubine Qiu's injury for any changes, especially if there's a peculiar scent."

The imperial physician agreed and examined her even more carefully than he had the previous times. Concubine Qiu was panicking, but she had no idea what could possibly be wrong with her injury. Each time he had examined her wound before, the imperial physician had just told Concubine Qiu to rest, but this time he knelt and begged for forgiveness. He told the emperor that while her injury was fine, the scent of cypress wood could be smelled on it, and that before he had only observed the injury itself and had failed to notice this.

The scent of cypress...?

The emperor didn't understand what this could mean at first, except that Prince Jing's fish really could notice unusual scents. The emperor's fish approval rating increased once again.

The sixth prince was usually restrained and pleasant, but something suddenly occurred to him. "Father, I don't recall that there are any cypress trees in Concubine Qiu's residence, Zhongcui Palace. The injury on her arm..."

The emperor came to a jolting realization. He rounded on Concubine Qiu. "Did you lie to me?" he said sternly. "Tell me, where were you actually injured?"

When the imperial physician had mentioned cypress, Concubine Qiu's legs began to tremble. Now, in the face of the emperor's glare, her mind went blank and she collapsed to her knees, quivering. How was she going to explain why her injury was stained with the scent of cypress trees that didn't grow in Zhongcui Palace?

A servant rushed in hurriedly and whispered something to Mu Tianming. The third prince's eyes lit up, and he immediately stood to say, "Father, I have news regarding the fire in Zhongcui Palace. I heard that Huanhua, a servant in Zhongcui Palace, has disappeared. My guards just found a female corpse in the imperial garden, and after investigation, we've determined that the corpse is Huanhua."

What???

The little carp thought palace politics were boring, so he was playing the rubbing-finger game with Prince Jing and having a great time. When he heard the news, he was shocked. Huanhua was a minor character who didn't die in the novel. How come she was dead now? No wonder it took so long for the third prince to make any progress and he'd needed Li Yu to make a move instead...

From what the third prince said, it wasn't clear if Huanhua had committed suicide or if she'd been murdered. If it was the former, perhaps she'd ended her own life because she couldn't explain how the fire, originally meant to be just a small fire, had grown large enough to burn down half of Zhongcui Palace. If it was the latter, then Li Yu had no idea who'd killed Huanhua based on just what the third prince said. Either way, Concubine Qiu was the prime suspect.

When Concubine Qiu heard this, though, a look of surprise flashed across her face.

The third prince, trying to hide the joy in his voice, said loudly, "I heard that Huanhua used to be Concubine Qiu's close personal servant. Fortunately, she wrote a note before she died, exposing her murderer."

Concubine Qiu knew the situation was bad. The emperor, with a grim face, said, "Bring it up."

Now the investigation began in earnest. The third prince's guards confirmed that Huanhua had been murdered and left a note before her death, which pointed to none other than her master Concubine Qiu. In her note, Huanhua mentioned that Concubine Qiu was the one who ordered her to set the fire, and that her master must've wanted to kill her to protect the secret.

Normally, if someone left a note before they were murdered, the situation was guaranteed to be complicated. Li Yu sensed that something was off, but everything Huanhua mentioned about Concubine Qiu in the letter was true.

As the note suggested, the emperor immediately ordered someone to search Yaxin Terrace, and one after another, they found cypress branches, handkerchiefs, and other physical evidence that did not favor Concubine Qiu. They even found witnesses who had seen Concubine Qiu at Yaxin Terrace.

No matter how Huanhua actually died, it was true that Concubine Qiu had ordered someone to set fire to the palace and that she deliberately burned herself to deceive the emperor. She might have even killed someone. With these crimes...if the emperor had felt any bit of pity for Concubine Qiu, it was evaporating completely. Before, he'd thought Concubine Qiu was arrogant and failed to teach the second prince correctly, and that she and her son had become greedy and ambitious because he let it slip that he planned to make the second prince the crown prince. But he'd never imagined she could be such a vicious, cruel person...

Concubine Qiu fell to her knees. With all the evidence against her, she didn't even have a chance to defend herself. In front of everyone, the emperor demoted her to a commoner, banished her to the cold palace, and sent Luo Ruisheng to the residence of the Marquis of An to reprimand him to his face.

Neither Concubine Qiu nor the Marquis of An could cause any more trouble now.

Mu Tianming glanced smugly at Mu Tianxiao. This was exactly what he'd wanted—for the mother and son duo to be permanently dealt with so his position could be secured. The sixth prince responded with a shallow, obedient smile.

Prince Jing couldn't stand Concubine Qiu's wailing, and so he bid goodbye to the emperor. The emperor was still interested in the little carp, but it clearly wasn't the time to examine this good omen, so the emperor asked Prince Jing to come to the palace another day to discuss it.

As Prince Jing left, the sixth prince kept his gaze fixed on him, as though deep in thought. Prince Jing noticed his gaze and also noticed that the sixth prince kept one arm down, his hand hidden in his sleeve. He hadn't taken his hand out of his sleeve the whole time.

Silently, Prince Jing raised an eyebrow.

Mu Tianxiao smiled, and both hands were revealed as he clasped them together to bow at Prince Jing. "Fifth Brother," he said gently, "take care."

Seeing nothing wrong with his hands, Prince Jing nodded at him politely in turn.

Li Yu went along with Prince Jing in his crystal bottle. Since Prince Jing had already taken him in and out of the palace several times, he recognized the path, and he realized that they weren't heading toward Prince Jing's manor after they left the palace. Prince Jing's determined profile was as sharp as a knife, and dozens of silent, black-robed guards followed him. Wang Xi looked solemn beside him, with the corners of his mouth curved downward.

What were they going to do? The little carp was confused. He recalled that in the novel, Concubine Qiu getting slapped in the face was mainly a plot point to showcase the showdown between the third prince and the second prince. Prince Jing wasn't actually present for it. In the novel, the fire only destroyed one room, and Huanhua didn't die. Concubine Qiu was demoted but wasn't sent to the back palace, so she was able to keep struggling for a little while longer. But in this new version of events, not only was Prince Jing there, he even passed news to the third prince, eliminating the nefarious Concubine Qiu by the third prince's hand. Her end was much worse now than it was in the novel...

On the surface, it seemed like the third prince and the sixth prince had won this bout, but the true winner was Prince Jing.

Li Yu suddenly thought of Huanhua's death and started panicking. If she didn't commit suicide, then who killed her? The little carp glanced sneakily at Prince Jing. Why did Prince Jing have a murderous aura about him again? Could it be that he was the one who'd secretly killed Huanhua?

He soon discovered the answer on his own.

Prince Jing walked, traveling late into the night, carrying the crystal bottle with him as he took many twists and turns. At last, he stopped in front of a residence and waved his hand. The black-robed guards disappeared into the night behind him. Prince Jing found a place to hide and silently observed the house from afar.

Loud sounds of cursing and reprimands came from the residence, as if someone was arguing. After a while, a man walked out angrily, surrounded by his assistants. Li Yu recognized him as Luo Ruisheng, the head eunuch.

Luo-gonggong couldn't keep his anger off his face. The servants beside him tried to placate him by saying, "The Marquis of An even dares to talk back to you when you came under the emperor's orders? He's truly a thoughtless fool. There's no way we can help him anymore."

Luo Ruisheng was quite angry, but he thought it was inappropriate for a follower of his to say something like that so bluntly. "There's no need to ridicule him like that. In the end, he is still a prince."

His followers didn't care. "Tsk, Luo-gonggong, you're so worldly and experienced. Who cares about a fallen phoenix? He's nothing but a chicken without the emperor's favor."

That was true. Luo Ruisheng laughed in cold contempt and didn't say anything else.

So this was where the Marquis of An lived, Li Yu realized. The emperor had just ordered head eunuch Luo Ruisheng to reprimand him, which was why Luo-gonggong was here.

Luo-gonggong and his assistants soon disappeared into the distance. Once they'd left, Prince Jing ordered his black-robed guards to surround the residence. He wrapped the chain of the crystal bottle tightly around his hand a few times, held it firmly, took a breath, and jumped onto the roof.

Li Yu was startled, unprepared to suddenly become a flying fish. His tyrant master actually took his pet fish with him up to crouch on the Marquis of An's roof! He tried to look around, but it was too dark to see very much. He didn't know what Prince Jing was going to do, but it wasn't as if he could get out of the crystal bottle, so he had to accompany Prince Jing, curious as to what might happen next.

Prince Jing kept holding the crystal bottle tightly with one hand as he gently uncovered a roof tile with the other. Dim candlelight from the house shone outward immediately. The little carp quickly swam closer. Was Prince Jing here to get a look at the Marquis of An at his lowest? He wanted to see too!

Whether it was intentional or not, Prince Jing moved out of Li Yu's way. The little carp, who had just been swimming around wildly to try and get a better angle, stopped—he could finally see what was going on inside the house.

The Marquis of An had been locked in his house for a long time. The floor was covered with a great variety of broken porcelain and tiles; there were no intact ornaments left. Mu Tianzhao sat in a red sandalwood chair, clutching his head in despair. Ever since he was banned from leaving his residence, he hadn't seen the emperor again.

Now, there was news that Concubine Qiu had been banished to the cold palace, and the emperor had even sent Luo Ruisheng just to scold him. Mu Tianzhao was born a prince—he'd never suffered like this before. His anger boiled up until he couldn't contain it anymore and he'd argued with Luo-gonggong. Unfortunately, it was too late to regret it now.

These days, he was not doing well. He often beat and scolded those around him, and his wife and children didn't dare approach him. There were only one or two servants with the courage to come and look after him. One of them, an older servant, brought over a bowl of soup and whispered some comforting words to Mu Tianzhao, but he only waved his hands, irritated, and started cursing at him loudly. The servant left quietly, not daring to stay for longer.

Watching what was happening below, Li Yu felt a bit gratified when he saw that the second prince's usually clean-shaven face now sported a five o'clock shadow. However, Prince Jing didn't plan on just watching. He suddenly reached into his robes and took out an object.

Li Yu was shocked when he glanced at it. That object...was his long-lost fish pillow!

The fish pillow was a reward for one of his quests and was made of special materials to make it look exactly like him. Most people couldn't even tell them apart unless they touched it. He'd already forgotten where he lost it; how did it end up in Prince Jing's possession?

Thinking about Prince Jing quietly keeping his fish pillow and not returning it to him, Li Yu was speechless.

Meanwhile, Prince Jing took out a string as thin as a strand of hair and tied it to the fish pillow's tail, then winked at the little carp who was watching.

The mischievous smile in Prince Jing's eyes clearly said he was about to pull off something fun, and Li Yu was just wondering what he was going to do when Prince Jing tossed the fish pillow into the room, keeping hold of the thin string.

...Whatever it was he was up to, it still wasn't clear.

Li Yu quickly looked back into the room, only to see the fish pillow drop silently into the soup bowl. Since there was a string to control its descent and Prince Jing's timing was impeccable, it made no noise, and Mu Tianzhao—still yelling and cursing—didn't notice it.

After he finished cursing his old servant, Mu Tianzhao moved on to cursing out Luo-gonggong. He felt a little thirsty, though, so he picked up the bowl on the table and took a sip without looking at it.

When he finished, he suddenly noticed a particular gray fish floating in the bowl...a fish that always brought him bad luck. Terrified, he dropped the bowl onto the ground.

"It wasn't me! It wasn't me! Don't come to me!"

Mu Tianzhao frantically shook his head, staring at the fish on the ground. The fish was unmoving, as if dead, and he was so frightened that he staggered backward. Realizing something, he started scratching at his throat violently, shouting wildly, "Someone! Anyone! Save me, please save me!"

Mu Tianzhao was too scared to look at the fish again and didn't dare stay in the room alone with it, blindly stumbling his way out of the room in a panic.

Why was his reaction so extreme? Li Yu didn't understand. He knew Mu Tianzhao hated him, but he was *horrified* when he saw the fish plush, frightened so badly he was screaming for help. This was way too dramatic—what, was the fish going to bite him?

Unless...

A light bulb went off in Li Yu's head. Looking at Mu Tianzhao's weird actions... Was he the one who had poisoned the fish food and almost killed Xiongfeng when Xiongfeng nearly ate it? So as soon as he saw the fish pillow, the Marquis of An thought it was a dead, poisoned fish coming back for revenge, and even thought...that the soup he drank was poisoned?

The Marquis of An was out of the loop. He didn't know that the carp meant for food was still alive and well.

Li Yu finally understood what the Marquis of An was thinking—and also figured out why Prince Jing carried him up to the roof of the Marquis of An's residence to let the fish pillow down. He took a deep breath. If the Marquis of An wanted to harm the fish, then Prince Jing...was probably getting revenge on his behalf.

The little carp looked at the Marquis of An, who was yelling crazily down below, and then at the quiet Prince Jing next to him and suddenly wanted to nuzzle his master.

What a considerate and thoughtful fish owner!

There was no way Prince Jing was the one who killed Huanhua. Prince Jing could easily deal with the second prince himself; there was no need to go and murder a palace servant who didn't need to die in the first place.

While the Marquis of An was hysterically running around, Prince Jing took the opportunity to reel in the fish pillow and put it away. Then he firmly grasped the crystal bottle and came back down from the roof.

"Your Highness!" Wang Xi rushed over. It was his job to meet up with Prince Jing once he came back from his fishing expedition.

The Marquis of An had completely fallen into disgrace. The time had come for him to repay the debt he owed to Prince Jing.

Prince Jing began by scaring him. He had learned his lesson from how frightened Xiaoyu was after he killed the female assassin—he knew he couldn't give Xiaoyu a front seat to any real payback. In front of his gentle fish, his only retribution against the Marquis of An would be a good scare, and hopefully this would be enough to make Xiaoyu feel justice had been served.

As for what followed... Prince Jing gestured at Wang Xi to do a clean job after he left.

After Wang Xi had received the order, Prince Jing took his fish back to the manor. When Wang Xi felt his master was far enough away, he ordered the black-robed guards surrounding the area to make their move.

Chaos descended the next day in the Marquis of An's residence. Apparently, after he was reprimanded by the emperor, he was in a terrible mood and drank to relieve his anger. After he got drunk, he wandered around by himself and accidentally fell into his own pond, and when a servant finally found him and fished him out, he was already breathing out more than he was breathing in.

The emperor was furious, as the Marquis of An clearly did this because he was upset with the emperor. Since he was still a prince, though, the emperor had the imperial physician treat him. The imperial physician was skilled, and the Marquis of An regained consciousness, but when he awoke, he seemed quite insane. Once in a while, he would alternately mutter "It wasn't me" or "It was me." Nobody could understand him.

The emperor was thoroughly disappointed with his son and ordered him locked up in his manor so he wouldn't go out and frighten others—though with Concubine Qiu banished to the cold palace, nobody would dare be so thoughtless as to mention the Marquis of An in front of the emperor.

Everyone had their loyal servants, and the Marquis of An was no exception. A servant from his residence went to head eunuch Luo with some money to ask him to beg the emperor for mercy. Luo Ruisheng agreed with a smile, but he just took the money without doing what he was asked. It was the Marquis of An's own fault for offending him.

A criminal should look like a criminal.

Meanwhile, Prince Jing had just returned to his manor with his fish when his servants brought him some good news. The new fish tank in the mansion had been under construction for a while, and after several days of hard work, the workers had finally finished.

Li Yu was a little sleepy, but that went right out the window when he heard the news. He kept acting cute and blowing bubbles toward Prince Jing; what kind of fish tank did Prince Jing make for him? He'd heard it mentioned several times already—he really couldn't wait! When the carp spirit flicked his tail now, Prince Jing knew exactly what he wanted. With this new awareness, he wasn't particularly in a rush to release him from the crystal bottle, and instead took him personally to see the new fish tank.

The barricades that originally surrounded the construction area in Prince Jing's manor were moved away, revealing what was hidden beneath. Li Yu made a little surprised fish noise, utterly taken aback.

He wouldn't have realized if it wasn't shown to him directly, but all the ponds around the courtyard had been dug out and connected. If there wasn't a pond there before, a pond was made, and it formed a huge fish tank that was nearly as large as the entire manor.

No, it could no longer be called a fish tank—the word "pond" was more appropriate. The fishpond was filled with clear, gurgling water. A small water wheel was built next to it, and there were guards every ten steps around its circumference to stop people from approaching.

Li Yu stared at his new fish tank, slightly stunned—it almost seemed endless! The rims of his eyes felt warm. Was all this just for him? He did grow larger, but Prince Jing had given him such a huge new fish tank...

Sob sob sob! He was so moved!

Prince Jing bent over and tilted the crystal bottle over to let the little carp swim into the new fish tank. But the little carp wouldn't come out of the bottle no matter what he did, so Prince Jing took him out himself. The little carp looked at him with his dark eyes and nuzzled his hand affectionately with his head. Prince Jing gave a slight smile, then put him into the water. This was his gift to Xiaoyu, and he hoped the little fish would like it.

Prince Jing had felt nothing when he dealt with the Marquis of An, but the thick, murderous aura he'd given off then was gone now. In its place was a slightly bashful mien.

The little carp circled at Prince Jing's feet a couple of times with initial reluctance, then slowly swam away, gradually increasing in speed. Behind the fish, the water bloomed into crystal clear waves.

This was the first time Li Yu had been in a pond since he transmigrated, and there was so much space for him to swim! He was a little cautious at first, but a breathtaking underwater scene suddenly caught his eye. This wasn't actually a normal fishpond; the meticulous and particular Prince Jing had ordered workers to dig out an underwater world just for his fish.

On the underwater stone wall, luminous pearls were embedded in circles, brightening what would have been dark water as if it were daytime. The rippling bottom of the pool was lined with rounded stones of different colors, and in the center was a group of buildings, mountains, rocks, and trees—they were carved from jade and scaled down from the real landscape.

The little carp was stunned. He swam over to take it in and slowly realized that it was the scenery outside Prince Jing's manor. The craftsmen were skilled, so the work was detailed—everything from the roads and stalls to the pedestrians, the carriages and horses, even the cats and dogs, were all depicted in jade. Since Prince Jing carried him around everywhere in the crystal bottle, Li Yu had always noticed the bustling, lively scenes outside the manor. He had been jealous with just the brief glances he was allowed. Now, his new fish tank had all of it, and it all belonged to him.

Li Yu meandered around, entranced, as he used his fish tail to admiringly poke and prod at everything he passed. He couldn't leave the residence, but his love for excitement and exploration was thoroughly satisfied by this.

At last, he swam to a lone building at the bottom of the pond. He thought it looked quite familiar; after some examination, he realized it was Prince Jing's quarters. He hadn't thought that his tyrant master would have his own room carved into the pond. Li Yu circled the building and found that the door could be opened outward. Clumsily, the little carp opened it with his mouth.

In the courtyard, there was a man carved from jade wearing a hair piece with neatly done hair, brocade robes, and a sword at his waist. The facial features weren't clearly carved, but Li Yu immediately realized that it was supposed to be Prince Jing. Among everyone he knew, Prince Jing was the only one who would dress like this.

Why are you alone? How sad. Li Yu knocked over the jade statue with a giggle, coiling around him unceremoniously. After he had his fill of playing around, he picked the jade statue up and put it back neatly.

He remembered that he'd seen a little ornamental stone in the shape of a fish on the stone wall underwater. There were actually a lot of stones like that, so Li Yu found one in no time, grabbed a corner of it, and yanked it off of the stone wall with all his might. It went well—the fish dragged the fish-shaped stone to the jade statue and placed it right next to it, then closed the door.

Done! The tyrant master wasn't alone anymore!

Li Yu swam in an excited circle, then went to find his real master.

The Fish Is Not for Sale

Prince Jing waited next to the fishpond, but he didn't see his playful fish return. Suddenly, he realized that his gift might have been a bit stupid. Would the carp spirit be so happy in the pond that he'd prefer to live there instead of staying by his side? After all, in the eyes of this fish, he couldn't even compare to a mouthful of food. There wasn't a chance he'd win against a new fish tank, right?

Prince Jing hesitated for a while before he decided to enter the water himself to look for his heartless carp spirit. But right then, the water rippled and a fish head poked out of the middle, followed by the little carp quickly swimming over.

...So, the fish did have a conscience after all.

Prince Jing wasn't upset anymore. As the little carp swam in circles happily below him, Prince Jing leaned over and patted his back. The little carp suddenly curled into a ball and rolled into his palm.

...What was going on?

Prince Jing picked the fish up and checked him all over, afraid that the fishpond might have been constructed too hastily and that he'd been injured by some rough unfinished edge. But his fish looked completely fine, lively and vigorous—unharmed. Prince Jing gave it some thought and decided to put the fish back into the crystal bottle. The carp spirit was very obedient, and he had no problem with the crystal bottle despite having just emerged from a huge, luxurious fishpond.

Prince Jing took his fish back to his room and placed him in the fish tank there. The carp spirit still didn't object, and Prince Jing took it as a sign that the fish still wanted to live with him. The slight disappointment from earlier turned into a secret delight. The fish couldn't speak or express his thanks, but Prince Jing wasn't looking for that anyway. It was enough as long as he was willing to stay by his side.

Since Xiaoyu had been busy the whole day, Prince Jing suspected he would fall asleep soon. But when he put his fish back, Xiaoyu was either pressed to the wall of the fish tank and gazing at him or swimming around to follow his every step.

Hurry, go to sleep. Prince Jing tapped the fish's head, and the obedient little fish actually clung onto his hand and wouldn't let go. Most of the time now, Prince Jing could understand what the carp spirit wanted, but occasionally, he still wasn't sure.

After a bit, the fish let go on his own and lay on his white stone bed.

Prince Jing was quite tired as well. He lay down on his own bed and soon fell asleep—but the little carp, who'd been pretending to sleep, had been listening to his breathing and started to move again as soon as he noticed Prince Jing had drifted off.

The tea bowls were still in his room, even though a new, huge fish tank had been built. Li Yu leaped in and out of them, following a familiar path to Prince Jing's bed. There was a red lotus tea bowl next to the pillow today, and the little carp carefully jumped into it.

He didn't know how to express his gratitude. The tyrant master was too good to him; not only did he avenge him, he built such a huge fish tank too. But there wasn't anything he could do for him in return. Li Yu gazed at his master's sleeping face for a while, but eventually his fishy senses started tingling and he just wanted to... nuzzle him. But if he jumped over directly, he'd get a bunch of water on his face. What should he do?

Perhaps, like a cat or dog, he could just carefully give his owner's face a friendly little kiss.

It wasn't as if he hadn't done this sort of thing before, after all. Since Prince Jing was lying on his back, Li Yu picked the most good-looking part of his face, slid out of the bowl, and tried to plant his lips on it. But Prince Jing shifted suddenly, and Li Yu had to dodge out of his way. Prince Jing turned over on his side, and the handsomest part of his face disappeared into the pillow.

Li Yu had lost his target and had to change course.

He smirked. Since that part of his face was hidden, he would have to nuzzle his master's nose.

The little carp opened his mouth and vigorously flapped his fins a couple of times as if he was about to take a big chomp—but in the end, he only gently brushed past Prince Jing's nose, his fishy lips pausing for a moment on the tip.

He he he, he did it! Li Yu felt great, as if he'd just eaten several pieces of peach blossom pastry.

Kissing Prince Jing's nose was a big move for Li Yu, and it was actually harder than kissing his face. Li Yu had to tilt his fish body while on the jade pillow to reach his master's nose, and if he missed, he would immediately slip.

He was just priding himself on taking such excellent care, but his fins were slippery and so was the jade pillow. There was no way to keep himself in that kind of position for a long time. His fin slipped as soon as he was finished, and he started to fall uncontrollably toward Prince Jing's face.

Aaaahhh, his triumph was about to turn into a disaster!

Li Yu couldn't stop himself, and in a last-ditch effort, he tried to push himself away with all the strength he could muster in his tail. When he was just an inch away from Prince Jing's face, his fish body stopped.

To be precise, it was his fish tail that stood upright like a sturdy base, supporting his fish body.

...Huh?

The little carp glanced at his own tail curiously. At such a critical moment, his tail became as hard as iron—most likely because of his new fish scales. He knew they were supposed to be strong, but he hadn't tried them out yet, and he was surprised that the tail could support his body like that.

Saved, Li Yu was just about to jump back into his fish tank when Prince Jing, just an inch away from him, started to shift in his sleep again, his face following him. Before Li Yu realized the danger, his slippery fish body was pressed against something burning hot and soft.

Uh oh!

He was sure he hadn't fallen onto Prince Jing, but Prince Jing's lips were now pressed against him. If not for the other party's closed eyes, it really did seem like his scorching lips were kissing his fish belly, fins, and...

Li Yu's tail, previously as hard as iron, suddenly turned limp as if it'd been burned. His whole body swayed as he leapt away, trembling. He was too panicked to clearly see where the tea bowl was, and for the first time, he somehow missed the bowl. Instead, he fell onto the ground right next to it, flopping frantically a couple of times before he made it back in.

Li Yu shoved his embarrassed head under his leaf blanket, his entire body almost smoking!

Hurry up and calm down! The master was just sleeping, and it didn't mean anything! the little fish kept telling himself.

Meanwhile, the person on the bed had been listening to the fish's movements the entire time. Only when the carp spirit finally made it into the crystal fish tank and stopped making any noise did Prince Jing reach out and touch the corner of his lips.

It was the fish's fault for not absorbing essence properly. He'd actually woken up as soon as Xiaoyu jumped onto the bed, but he became impatient waiting for him and took the initiative instead. But the charming failure of a fish spirit escaped in the end.

Prince Jing recalled the feeling of the fish against his face and slightly smiled.

The next day, a fish and a human, each with their own ulterior motives, were both feeling a bit guilty. For some reason, the fish was still a soft little carp—he hadn't had a chance to turn into a human yet before an uninvited guest arrived at Prince Jing's manor.

The heir to the House of Cheng'en had been wondering about the new fish tank in Prince Jing's manor for a while. When he heard that it was finished, Ye-shizi wanted to be the first to take a look and join in on the fun, so as soon as it was dawn, he brought Xiongfeng with him to visit. He was stunned by the sight of the manor's huge fishpond as soon as he entered.

From what Ye Qinghuan had seen on his previous visits, he thought Prince Jing was sectioning out pieces of the grounds in preparation for a few new ponds, but this was far beyond what he'd imagined. He didn't think that Prince Jing would make his entire manor into a pond for the fish.

Ye-shizi was impressed but also thought Prince Jing was a bit crazy.

Ye Qinghuan let go of Xiongfeng's leash so he could have a private talk with Prince Jing.

Xiongfeng had never seen such a large pond before, and he was running along the edge of it when he saw the little carp having fun in the water. Li Yu noticed Xiongfeng too. He remembered that he hadn't seen Xiongfeng since his scales started changing, so he was afraid Xiongfeng wouldn't recognize him, but not only did Xiongfeng not bark at him, he also curiously reached his nose out toward Li Yu like always, wanting to poke him.

Huh...

Li Yu recalled that his scales should be strong enough to resist a dog's teeth now, so he suppressed his fear and stuck his head out of the water, letting Xiongfeng gently nudge him. Finally getting his chance to poke the fish, Xiongfeng started wagging his tail out of happiness and scampered around the entire pond. Of course he recognized his little carp friend—dogs recognized things by scent. But just running around wasn't fun enough, so Xiongfeng jumped into the pond with a *splash* and paddled to the fish.

Li Yu splashed his face with water as a warning: You can come down and play, but you can't knock over the house my master made for me!

Fortunately, Xiongfeng was obedient and only played with the fish, with no intention of diving to the bottom. He wanted to race the fish in the water, but obviously the little carp swam faster than he did and soon left him far behind.

Ye-shizi and Prince Jing both watched these events unfold.

Ye-shizi clicked his tongue several times, and Prince Jing's face darkened a little. He thought Ye Qinghuan's dog was an eyesore and was about to ask Wang Xi to drag both Ye Qinghuan and his dog out of the manor. Completely unaware, Ye Qinghuan teasingly nudged Prince Jing's arm, his eyes sparkling like the water as he gazed at the pond.

"Are you not afraid you're going to lose him in such a big pond?"

Prince Jing paused. The question came out of the blue, so it took him a moment to realize what Ye Qinghuan was asking. He smiled slightly and shook his head. He might have been worried before, but he knew now that Xiaoyu wouldn't do that.

The fish and the dog were having fun in the pond. Prince Jing walked over, and the fish, who had disappeared to who-knew-where, immediately appeared on his own and swam over to Prince Jing's feet, flicking his tail toward him intimately. What flattery.

Unbelievable.

Ye Qinghuan refused to lose and walked over to Xiongfeng with secret anticipation, but Xiongfeng was staring at himself in the water and had no time to pay attention to him.

That's enough! he thought in despair. *I'm about to lose everything, including my underwear!*

Ye-shizi, who had come to see the fish tank and was outdone again, angrily led Xiongfeng away.

Ye Qinghuan had just left when the third prince, Mu Tianming, came knocking on the door.

Although he'd always wanted to win over Prince Jing, he didn't visit often, and Prince Jing treated others quite coldly. The last time Mu Tianming had visited was to attend the banquet that the emperor ordered Prince Jing to host. That time, he'd wanted to plant Chu Yanyu around Prince Jing, but until now he hadn't even dared step through the door for fear of Prince Jing's refusal.

Mu Tianming had a purpose for his visit this time too. He used to simply enjoy observing the fish Prince Jing raised as entertainment, but he was shocked to learn the fish had started growing golden scales—the emperor even called it an auspicious sign. That caught the attention of the third prince; since the fish also contributed a lot to the defeat of Concubine Qiu, Mu Tianming was willing to believe that the fish was a good omen. Mu Tianming, who desperately wanted to be named the crown prince, naturally wanted to take this good omen for himself to get in the good graces of the emperor.

Now that the biggest obstacle before him, the second prince, was gone, and the sixth prince was on his side and wouldn't compete against him, the throne would be his, sooner or later. Things were different now; the support of Prince Jing and the House of Cheng'en was no longer important to the third prince. Instead, he started to become wary of Prince Jing.

Despite wanting the fish, he didn't want to take rash action, leaving himself open to retaliation and a loss of reputation. Instead, he'd employ peaceful measures before resorting to force. It was just a fish, after all, so Prince Jing wouldn't make a fuss, right?

Once Wang Xi had received Prince Jing's order, he brought the third prince to Ninghui Hall, which was used to entertain guests. Mu Tianming brought a lot of his men—all carrying boxes and chests—and placed them in Ninghui Hall. At Mu Tianming's order, all the boxes were opened, revealing the gold and silver within.

Li Yu might have a huge fish tank now, but he still liked the crystal bottle Prince Jing took him around in. When he heard the third prince had come, there was no way Li Yu was going to miss the show. He jumped onto the crystal bottle as soon as possible and flopped around. Prince Jing granted his wish; it wasn't like the third prince could do anything in his own manor.

But when the third prince presented the boxes full of gold and silver, the shameless little carp sank right to the bottom.

Li Yu had never seen so much gold and silver in his life. What was the third prince doing?

Mu Tianming got right to the point. "Fifth Brother, I'd like to make a deal with you. Your fish is quite nice, and I like it. Are you willing to part with it?" Mu Tianming smiled and pointed at the boxes his people had laid out on the ground. "If this much gold and silver isn't enough, I can add more until you're satisfied. How about it?"

Holy shit, Mu Tianming wanted to buy him from his tyrant master? Illegal! Not allowed!

Li Yu found himself desperately praying in his heart: *Don't do it!* Gold and silver were great, but that didn't mean he wanted to be exchanged for them. Prince Jing treated him very well, after all—he didn't want to leave him.

The little carp quickly checked Prince Jing's reaction.

The veins on Prince Jing's forehead were visibly throbbing, and Li Yu could tell that the tyrant was really angry. Seeing this, the little carp calmed down right away and continued watching to see how his master was going to reject the brazen third prince.

Speaking of which, the third prince had never given him a second glance, so why did he suddenly want to buy him? It must be because the emperor said he was auspicious. The little carp hated calculating people who only acted based on what others said!

After the third prince proposed this deal, Prince Jing glanced at Wang Xi with a cold expression.

Wang Xi didn't care about any third or second prince. He only recognized His Highness Prince Jing. Prince Jing clearly wasn't happy, so Wang Xi loudly said, "There's no need to continue, Your Highness. My prince won't sell his fish."

Mu Tianming, surprised, said, "Perhaps you think the price I offered was not enough? What about ten thousand taels of gold and one hundred thousand taels of silver?" He was becoming increasingly uncertain. It was just a fish! Even if it was auspicious, this was way too expensive. But if it could help him become the crown prince, then so be it.

Li Yu didn't think he'd be worth so much. He disliked the third prince, but he couldn't help but wiggle around proudly.

If looks could kill, the third prince would have died a couple thousand times over already. Wang Xi glanced at Prince Jing's icy expression and said, "It's not a matter of price. This fish is His Highness's beloved pet, so even if you come with millions of gold taels or tens of millions of silver taels, His Highness won't sell him."

Li Yu was super moved! In the eyes of the tyrant, he was worth more than a mountain of gold? The little carp finally understood the full meaning of "Priceless Pet Fish."

Prince Jing definitely wouldn't give much respect to someone who tried to poach his fish, so he had Wang Xi kick the third prince and all his gold and silver out. Mu Tianming hadn't expected to be treated this way and left with a sour look on his face.

At last, the annoying third prince was gone!

Li Yu happily flicked his tail at his master, wanting Prince Jing to take him to the big pond to play, but Prince Jing turned his head to the side and wouldn't look at him.

What now?

The little carp wasn't sure why his master was suddenly mad at him, so he could only cutely wiggle at him...

Prince Jing wanted to be stone-hearted for once, but the little carp was too good at being cute and he couldn't resist pulling the cute fish over to pet him until he trembled. It had been upsetting when the carp spirit stopped swimming the moment he saw all the gold and silver the third prince brought!

In a fit of anger, Prince Jing ordered all the workers to replace the white stones that the little carp liked to sleep on with rounded silver stones, and the leaf blanket with a handkerchief made of gold silk, embroidered with aquatic plants.

Overnight, Li Yu suddenly found that his bed and blanket had become shiny!

Ah, master! I love you to death! the carp spirit yelled inwardly, hugging the blanket and refusing to let go as he rolled around on his bed!

Teaching Fish to Write

THE SYSTEM HAD BEEN GIVING Li Yu a break for a while now. But that night, as he rolled around in his gold-embroidered blanket, at last understanding what it meant to be treated like a "Priceless Pet Fish," it finally spoke up again.

‹Congratulations, user. The assessment of your main mission has been completed, and the user can enter the next main mission.›

Is it finally time to move on? Li Yu wondered.

He had never worried about the assessment—the tyrant master treated him very well, so he had full confidence that he could continue with the main mission. Although he had accepted the koi side quest, he'd been leaving it alone and hadn't made any progress because the prompt was so strange. It'd been a while since he'd done a main mission, and he actually kind of missed it.

Li Yu immediately entered the system to check. Just as the system said, he could click on the new main mission, called "Tyrant's Pet Fish for Revitalizing the Family." He thought the name of the mission was strange, but he did sort of remember it from the first time he ever entered the system. Didn't the system say the direction of the main missions would be determined by the assessment? He didn't see anything different from before.

Li Yu clicked on the "Revitalizing" mission. This main mission was similar to "Priceless Pet Fish" and had several steps to carry out.

The prompt was to improve the tyrant and fish pet's life. The first step of the mission was—

Indulge with the tyrant.

...Hold on, how come it felt like the fish-scamming system had become even more of a scammer after the vacation? What in the world was the connection between revitalization and indulging? And what was 'indulging' supposed to mean? Did that mean he had to go drinking with the tyrant? Li Yu had sampled green plum wine before, so he knew that he got drunk easily. He'd definitely do something he regretted if he got drunk again. He felt like he was getting scammed by the mission's drink requirement.

<Can't I just skip this mission?>

<Certainly,> agreed the System. *<Would you rather become fish bones or fish ash?>*

...Forget it. Neither of those options was appealing, so he'd have to just do as he was told and carry out his mission. To pump himself up, he looked at the reward first. This time, it wasn't doubled stats or a new skill but a mysterious reward: obtaining one of the tyrant's secrets. Li Yu's first impulse was to reject it entirely. He didn't really want to know any of Prince Jing's secrets. That was his private business. What's more, he was a transmigrated fish. He already knew a lot about Prince Jing from the novel, so this reward was a bit useless to him.

Li Yu decided to push his luck, despite the earlier threat. *<Is there no fish plush like last time?>* It would be nice if he could have another plush. He transformed often now, and it wasn't good to leave the tank empty, so he really wanted another one. Prince Jing hadn't returned the plush from before, and that one was different from his current size and shape anyway.

The fish-scamming system had probably never met a user who wanted to pick out their own reward like that. After a period of silence, the system replied: <*According to the user's suggestion, the main reward of 'Revitalizing the Family' has been updated. Please take a look.*>

Li Yu was surprised. Would the system really make changes because of something he said? He went to check the "Indulge" mission. Sure enough, there was a fish pillow listed as a reward now. He was extremely happy about this change. On a whim, Li Yu had a thought—since the rewards could be changed, could this "indulging" be changed as well? How was a fish supposed to indulge with his tyrant master? Sob sob sob, it was much too difficult.

This time, the fish-scamming system stayed silent.

<*...Okay, I can see right through you. You can change anything except things that involve scamming fish, is that it?*>

Li Yu was kicked out of the system and, still wrapped in his gold blanket, started to think about how he could indulge with Prince Jing. If they had to drink, then there had to be wine, right...?

While the little carp was wondering how he was going to get hold of some wine to complete his mission, chaos descended outside. A couple of thieves snuck into Prince Jing's manor in the middle of the night and made it to the wall before they were caught by Wang-gonggong and the guards.

Ever since the fishpond was finished, the security around Prince Jing's manor had tightened. When the third prince left with a sullen look on his face after his offer to buy the fish was refused, Wang Xi kept his guard up and reminded the guards to keep an eye out at night—but he didn't think thieves would actually come. He immediately reported it to Prince Jing.

Prince Jing glanced at the once again unconscious fish in the fish tank. He used to think that his fish was sick every time this happened, but now he surmised that the carp spirit was meditating.

Prince Jing decided it wasn't necessary to distract Xiaoyu with this information, as he would be protecting him anyway.

When the thieves were brought before Prince Jing, all tied up, they weren't willing to admit who they took orders from. The guards found a couple fishnets on them, though, making their purpose very clear. But the thieves hadn't been aware that the fish they were ordered to steal didn't sleep in the fishpond.

Wang Xi hated these thieves as much as he liked Master Fish. "It must be the third prince," he said, teeth gritted. "He wanted to steal the fish since he couldn't buy it..."

But the thieves refused to confess, and the fishnets alone weren't enough to prove that it was the third prince.

Wang Xi suggested torture. Prince Jing thought for a moment, then glanced at Wang Xi sternly and meaningfully. He immediately understood, ordering the guards to take the thieves to the imperial governmental office and interrogate them thoroughly.

If Prince Jing's manor was broken into, they should report the case to the government office and leave the interrogation to them. That was the proper way to do things. If they took matters into their own hands, someone might take the chance to retaliate. Of course, though, after the thieves arrived at the government office, Prince Jing's manor could give a few suggestions as to how to make them confess as soon as possible.

The sixth and third princes were discussing the latest issue at the third prince's manor. Mu Tianxiao knew that Mu Tianming had visited Prince Jing to try and convince him to sell his fish. Mu Tianxiao didn't agree with this move; instead of trying to make the emperor happy through grand actions, they should just do a good job on the tasks the emperor gave them. But even though Mu Tianming trusted him, he didn't listen to everything Mu Tianxiao said, so Mu Tianming made the final decision himself and Mu Tianxiao couldn't do anything about it.

Fine, Mu Tianming had sent people to steal the fish after failing to buy it. But then he failed to steal the fish, and his people were arrested as soon as they entered Prince Jing's manor. Mu Tianxiao was speechless. All that trouble for a fish that His Majesty might forget about tomorrow?

"Of course it's worth it."

Mu Tianming was stubborn. When Prince Jing rudely kicked him out of his manor, it became a bigger issue to him than a mere pet fish. The third prince thought Prince Jing was only making it hard on himself, trying to make an enemy out of him even though he was close to becoming the crown prince.

"Imperial brother, it's best to stop sending people. If Prince Jing finds out..."

Mu Tianxiao tried to convince him, but the third prince brushed him off. "What are you afraid of? My people won't incriminate me. They'll stay silent. Why are you so afraid? Even if Prince Jing suspects me, what can he do? If he does anything untoward to my people, I'll have the Censorate punish him for abusing his powers. Let's see if he can even keep his title of prince."

Incredible. Mu Tianxiao rubbed his temples in stress. "All the same, it's not good that Prince Jing caught them. You should stop trying to steal the fish."

Mu Tianming clearly didn't want to give up. "So you think a mute should have an auspicious sign instead of you or me?"

"...Of course not." Mu Tianxiao smiled and gave him a look. "Since it's an auspicious sign, I'm sure Father will ask the Imperial Astrological Bureau about it."

"The Imperial Astrological Bureau?" Mu Tianming's eyes shone. This could indeed be a way to get rid of Prince Jing. "But Father himself called it an auspicious sign. Even the Imperial Astrological Bureau might not refute him..."

"Why would they need to refute it?" Mu Tianxiao's warm expression didn't change as he asked, smiling, "Has Third Brother forgotten the theory of 'too far is as bad as not far enough'?"

Mu Tianming paused for a second before he understood what the sixth prince meant—and he started laughing wildly.

As the sixth prince predicted, the emperor summoned the Imperial Astrological Bureau officials not long after, and the third prince made his move according to the sixth prince's suggestion.

There weren't many Imperial Astrological Bureau officials, but they were so important that a single word from them could sway a situation. Prince Jing naturally had a few of his own people planted in such an important department.

Prince Jing also had selfish motives when he took his fish to greet the emperor. Xiaoyu had changed a lot, and he might change in the future too. News of it would reach the emperor sooner or later, and Prince Jing wanted to let him know preemptively so that he could find an excuse for Xiaoyu, to cover up the fact that he was a yao. If things didn't go well, Prince Jing was also prepared for the Bureau to speak with the emperor; however, the emperor himself believed that Xiaoyu's new golden scales were a good omen, which saved Prince Jing a lot of trouble.

Prince Jing had guessed that the emperor would eventually consult the Imperial Astrological Bureau and ask them to cooperate, so when the third prince made his move, Prince Jing caught wind of it soon after.

Mu Tianming was so vicious that he wanted the bureau to tell the emperor that the golden-scaled fish was showing signs of transforming into a dragon. In this dynasty, only the emperor could use the dragon pattern and call himself the True Dragon and Son of Heaven. If a fish raised by a prince looked like it might turn into a dragon, the emperor would definitely put his guard up. When that happened, not only would Prince Jing be in trouble, it would be hard for anyone associated with him to escape from disaster— especially Xiaoyu.

Luckily, he'd received the news beforehand and wouldn't let that happen.

The third prince ordered someone to invite a senior monk in case the emperor questioned the Imperial Astrological Bureau. That way, he'd have two separate forces speaking in his favor. But Prince Jing wasn't going to back down either; he wrote a letter and had Wang Xi send it out immediately. He predicted that another storm was coming, but he'd protect Xiaoyu no matter what.

After he dealt with the serious business, Prince Jing returned to his room, only to see a figure he'd been waiting for. Xiaoyu had transformed into a human and was wearing a blue silk robe embroidered with gold branches. He was humming an unknown melody as he bent over to smooth out the bed. Prince Jing stared at him from far away, wanting to approach but afraid of disturbing him—so he just appreciated Xiaoyu's figure as the young man hummed the tune.

Xiaoyu was still the same as when they first met, spirited and lively. Every young man and woman he'd met before all tied their waist sashes tightly, but Xiaoyu didn't seem to know how. His was tied casually in a messy knot, hanging loose around his hips. A bare hint of the outline of his slim waist was visible. Prince Jing could have easily wrapped one arm around it—it was like a delicate willow that could snap at any moment.

Prince Jing acknowledged this was a bit over the top, but his mind still automatically made this comparison.

Further down, concealed beneath the blue robe, was a slightly raised, round...

Prince Jing looked away immediately.

"Your Highness, you're back!" Li Yu had noticed the movement behind him and smiled as he ran over to bow to him. Since he got back from the palace, he'd been carefully watching how the servants in the manor greeted the prince, and he performed one that looked about the same. He'd turned into a human this time because he had promised to "stay" in Prince Jing's manor and help him take care of his fish, so he had to show his face in front of Prince Jing occasionally to show that he was actually working—even if he was just feeding himself.

Li Yu was extremely grateful that Prince Jing had made such a huge fishpond for him, but fish couldn't talk, so he couldn't express his thanks in any way other than giving him a little fish kiss. And even though he'd transformed into a human and could talk now, Prince Jing didn't know he was his fish, so if he casually thanked Prince Jing "on behalf of the fish," the prince might treat him like a monster. All Li Yu could do was tidy up the room after feeding himself as an expression of silent thanks.

But Prince Jing's room was always kept very clean. Li Yu looked around the whole room and couldn't find anything to improve. In the end, the only thing he could do was mess up the bed and make it again. He didn't expect to see Prince Jing after he'd completed this one single task.

Seeing the fish in its human form made most of Prince Jing's anger toward the third prince disappear. He stepped forward and grabbed Li Yu's hand, dragging him along with him. There was something he'd wanted to do for a long time.

Li Yu was startled to be suddenly whisked away but silently cautioned himself that when he was a fish, he couldn't go against his master, and when he was a human, he couldn't go against a prince. With Li Yu in tow, Prince Jing quickly arrived at his table and had him sit down. Li Yu was a little panicked. Was he going to ask him questions again?

To be honest, one of the reasons Li Yu transformed into a human this time was because he wanted to find out where the wine was in Prince Jing's manor. Green plum wine was hard to get your hands on, so if he was going to "indulge," he needed to find where the normal wine was first. Then he could grab a jar, mix it with some water, and somehow make Prince Jing drink it with him. If he diluted it first, he wouldn't embarrass himself too badly, right?

Li Yu had a plan in mind. He wouldn't contradict or debate with the tyrant, he'd just pretend he was still a fish, obediently listening to what Prince Jing wanted him to do.

Prince Jing laid out some paper and a brush, then handed an inkstick and inkstone to Li Yu. Li Yu laughed, startled. "Your Highness, do you want me to grind ink?"

Prince Jing nodded lightly.

So, he wants me to grind ink for him first before I answer questions! Hah! Li Yu was complaining internally, but he still ground the ink very seriously. Soon, the thick black ink appeared. Li Yu put down the inkstick and thoughtlessly rubbed his nose, leaving behind a smear of ink on the tip of his nose without noticing. This reminded Prince Jing of the time Xiaoyu was covered in ink stains, and he couldn't help the upward twitch of his lips.

After Li Yu ground the ink, Prince Jing gave him a brush.

...He doesn't want me to answer questions, he wants me to write something?

Li Yu rolled up his sleeves. He clutched the brush awkwardly, almost like he was holding chopsticks.

"Please let me know what you want me to write, Your Highness!" *And it'd be best if I could get a reward, like a jar of wine or something! I was just worrying about what kind of excuse I'd need to get one!*

His crude grip surprised Prince Jing. No wonder the brush he used last time had frayed. But Prince Jing didn't judge Xiaoyu for not knowing how to write. He got up and stood behind him. Confused, Li Yu stared at him curiously. Prince Jing tried his hardest to not look at Xiaoyu's pale, exposed wrists as he reached out to cover the hand that was holding the brush with his own. He gently encircled Xiaoyu in his arms and turned him slightly to correct his awkward posture.

Li Yu blushed, very flustered. He wasn't illiterate, but he didn't know how to use the brushes they had in ancient times. Prince Jing was probably just teaching him how to hold a brush and write...but this was way too close! Prince Jing's hand was holding his, Prince Jing's arms were supporting him, and he could feel his warm breath on his ears... When he looked back, all around him, up, down, left, right, Prince Jing was surrounding him.

One of Li Yu's ears went completely red. He thought uneasily, *This is just a normal lesson, don't think anything crazy! Prince Jing's calligraphy is quite good and he's willing to teach me—don't waste his time!*

Prince Jing held his hand just like that and taught him how to write a proper, correct "fish" character.

...Writing wasn't that hard after all!

Before long, Li Yu was completely immersed in his scrawlings. If he was in fish form, his tail would have confidently pointed up to the sky. He didn't realize until he turned back into a fish that he'd forgotten to ask for a reward.

But Prince Jing had been teaching him how to write the entire time, so it's not like he could ask for a reward!

Li Yu was a little embarrassed. It seemed that Prince Jing had expertly thwarted his plans.

Fish Protecting
His Master

THE EMPEROR SUMMONED Prince Jing to the palace again, and this time, he specifically insisted that Prince Jing bring his fish.

Li Yu didn't know about the third prince's plans, or Prince Jing's counterplans, but since it was his first time being mentioned in an imperial edict, he was quite nervous. He jumped onto the crystal bottle cooperatively, waiting to be put inside. Prince Jing's expression was a little dark, but he patted the fish's head gently. Whatever was troubling him, it wasn't Li Yu.

Li Yu recalled that the same hand had intimately held his own while teaching him how to write, so he hid away shyly. It wasn't long before his fishy nature took over, though, and he came back out, wanting to be pet again. He could tell that Prince Jing was in a bad mood. He didn't know why, but he hoped Prince Jing would feel better soon.

Xiaoyu asking for pets finally made Prince Jing smile a little. After he petted the fish, Prince Jing brought him into the palace as the edict commanded.

Outside of Qianqing Palace, they were greeted personally by head eunuch Luo. When they entered the palace, they saw the emperor sitting on the throne with several other people dressed like officials. Strangely enough, the third and sixth princes were also there. Li Yu was confused. Last time, when there was a fire in the palace, the third and sixth princes made a trip to the palace to check on the emperor. But why were they here now?

The third prince was rash, while the sixth prince was devious. Together, they couldn't be underestimated.

And as soon as Prince Jing walked into the palace with his fish, the two princes' gaze turned to him, making the fish a little nervous.

As a result, Li Yu couldn't stop darting glances back over toward them.

The emperor smiled when he saw Prince Jing. "Tianchi, good timing. Since your fish is growing golden scales, I had the Imperial Astrological Bureau do a reading."

So that's what was going on. Li Yu nodded to himself. The emperor had summoned him because of the whole auspicious thing. It would be difficult to convince the general populace that this fish was auspicious just because the emperor said so. After all, it would be a bit ridiculous for the emperor to declare a sign of auspiciousness for himself. But if the Imperial Astrological Bureau confirmed it, then Li Yu would be the real deal.

The emperor had just finished speaking when a solemn official came out, spouting a lot of official language that Li Yu couldn't understand, which ended with, "Congratulations, Your Majesty, a fish growing golden scales is truly a rare auspicious sign—we took this in conjunction with the celestial phenomena that has occurred recently, and the Ziwei star[1] is slowly rising and shining dazzlingly. This means that our empire is peaceful and the people content. Everything is progressing smoothly. This is all beneficial to both our empire and Your Majesty."

---

1 The Ziwei star (紫薇星), Polaris, represents the emperor in Chinese astrology.

The official was praising him with such refined language, the little carp couldn't help but raise his tail proudly. He'd always thought that astrologers must be highly adept at saying exactly what the emperor wanted to hear. His status as an auspicious sign was practically a foregone conclusion.

The emperor's unease over the fire in Zhongcui Palace had vanished from his heart, and he nodded, smiling. "Very good. Those are my thoughts as well."

The Imperial Astrological Bureau officials received a sizable reward and thanked him, satisfied.

"Royal Father, i-is that it?" The third prince had waited for a while, and this was the conclusion he got? Wasn't the Imperial Astrological Bureau supposed to say that a fish growing gold scales was a sign of an impending dragon transformation? Why didn't the people he planted in the bureau do what he wanted?

Confused, the emperor asked, "That's it...what else would there be? It sounds as if you believe there should be more?"

"N-no...that's not what I meant." By now, the third prince had realized that something had probably gone wrong, but he refused to just let go of this opportunity. He clenched his teeth and said, "Royal Father, I'm unfamiliar with how the Imperial Astrological Bureau operates. Does only one official do the reading or is it several? If it's just one person, is it possible for them to miss something?"

Mu Tianming thought the problem must just be that his people weren't given the opportunity to meet the emperor, so if they just switched the official making the announcement, everything would go as planned.

The person who had just congratulated the emperor was the director of the Imperial Astrological Bureau, named Sun Simiao. Director Sun smiled at Mu Tianming. "Your Highness, that's a strong accusation. Reading the stars for His Majesty and the empire is an event of utmost importance, and the result you just heard was the conclusion that the entire Imperial Astrological Bureau came to. If Your Highness doesn't trust me, the answer will remain the same even if you ask for someone else."

Li Yu was a bit startled by the third prince. Why did he suddenly ask for an alternate opinion when everything was fine? He felt like there must be sinister motives at work. Alarmed, his whole fish body shook, and Prince Jing reached into the crystal bottle to touch his back with his finger, stroking him from time to time as if to comfort and calm him down.

Li Yu, naturally, was easily soothed by his tyrant master. The third prince wasn't anyone important! He was just cannon fodder, while Prince Jing had the protagonist's halo and was destined to be the next emperor. He was already piggybacking off of Prince Jing, so he had nothing to worry about!!

One had to be skilled to work at the Imperial Astrological Bureau. Sun Simiao wasn't high in rank, but his words still held considerable weight in front of the emperor. When the third prince questioned Director Sun for no reason, he even managed to respond graciously. The emperor trusted Sun Simiao, so he felt the third prince was behaving immaturely. "Tianming," he scolded him sternly, "don't criticize when you don't remember how the bureau works."

Scolded, the third prince lowered his head and gave the sixth prince a pointed sidelong look. Mu Tianxiao immediately understood and stepped forward to speak up. "Royal Father, my brother isn't talking nonsense. We heard a commoner's child singing a nursery rhyme that contradicted what the Imperial Astrological Bureau said... We were afraid that we'd misunderstood the nursery rhyme, so we had some senior monks come and take a look."

When the emperor heard the words "nursery rhyme," his heart skipped a beat. He stared at the sixth prince. "What nursery rhyme?"

"There are words and phrases that are blasphemous, so I dare not repeat them. Please take a look at this instead." The sixth prince took out a piece of paper he'd prepared from his robes and handed it to Luo Ruisheng to give to the emperor.

When the emperor received the paper, he read it carefully. Though his expression didn't change, Li Yu could tell that a cold atmosphere had settled around him. What was on the paper? Why did it make the emperor so unhappy? It wouldn't be a false claim like "Three generations of the Tang Dynasty later, there will be a female leader with the last name Wu," right?

After the emperor read it, he calmly gestured at head eunuch Luo to pass the paper to Prince Jing. When the paper landed in Prince Jing's hands, he opened it and his eyes swept over the words. He read quickly, but historical characters were difficult for Li Yu to decipher, so he only saw the phrase, "Golden scales do not belong in the pond, but will climb into the sky as a dragon."

Wait, what?! He wasn't an expert at ancient Chinese, but he could tell that these words were just trying to scapegoat him, the innocent fish!

It wasn't just trying to blame him—it also implicated Prince Jing. On the surface, it was saying that the fish could turn into a dragon, but wasn't it actually referring to Prince Jing ascending to the throne?

Prince Jing would indeed ascend to the throne in the end, but where did this nursery rhyme come from? Were they afraid the emperor wouldn't make the connection to Prince Jing? The emperor was the head of state, after all. Even if he was sympathetic to Prince Jing, he couldn't ignore this provocation!

"Tianchi, what do you think?" the emperor calmly asked Prince Jing. Right now, nobody knew what the emperor was thinking. Mu Tianming and Mu Tianxiao only hoped that the emperor would become wary of Prince Jing.

Once Prince Jing had discovered the sixth prince's dangerous plan, however, he had someone secretly follow the sixth prince— and discovered by chance that the sixth prince had been sending people to teach children nursery rhymes. Even though they were just nursery rhymes, Prince Jing was prepared.

He calmly glanced at Wang Xi. Wang Xi stepped forward and said, in place of his master, "Your Majesty, this is complete nonsense. His Highness is also confused as to why such a rhyme was spread amongst the people with the intention of ruining the relationship between a father and a son. His Highness implores Your Majesty to conduct a thorough investigation to see when this rhyme was spread. If it was just the past few days..."

The emperor had only recently discovered that Prince Jing's fish was changing scales, so it was possible that someone was deliberately taking advantage of this incident.

The emperor gave it some thought and nodded. "What Prince Jing said is reasonable. I also intended to do this..." He didn't get angry at Prince Jing over the nursery rhyme. Instead, he ordered his imperial guards to investigate and find out when it was first heard and who it had originated from.

The attempts to frame Prince Jing continued to fail. The third prince anxiously glanced at the sixth prince, who looked calm on the surface but was sweating a little on the inside.

This was truly a devious move the sixth prince had come up with, but it backfired since the emperor didn't pay attention to the nursery rhyme itself—he was more interested in when the nursery rhyme first appeared, which was something that could be easily investigated and found out.

It was then that the eminent monks that the sixth prince had summoned arrived. When he saw the row of monks, Li Yu, who'd been caught off guard and wasn't operating at full capacity, remembered that there was a similar plot in the novel where monks were involved.

Thanks to a little butterfly named Li Yu flapping his wings all over the place, the original plot was now a mess. In the novel, when the sixth prince and Prince Jing were fighting for the throne, a monk was ordered to lie to the emperor to frame Prince Jing. However, the rumor in the novel was "Prince Jing was born a mute and is therefore inauspicious"—now, instead, it was "a fish growing golden scales will turn into a dragon"?

It was, of course, nonsense. It wasn't rare for fish to have golden scales—for example, koi almost always had golden scales. The emperor himself had many koi in his own lotus pond, so why would a carp that was meant to be food transform into a dragon before them?!

That was a logical argument, but it couldn't be used to convince the emperor.

Li Yu thought to himself. Since these were both rumors thought up by the sixth prince, they should be the same in principle. Would the same flaw appear here?

In the novel, the sixth prince framed Prince Jing too hastily and couldn't find any trusted eminent monks to help him. Most monks weren't foolish enough to get involved in a conflict between princes. Thus, the monks he "found" were all fake ones; they had been freshly shaven, and they didn't even have any precept scars![2]

---

2 Precept scars (戒痕) are ritual burn scars given to monks in some Buddhist practices after they have taken their vows and shaved their heads.

With this in mind, Li Yu stared at the monk in front of him unwaveringly, trying to see if anything was off. Since he was staring so diligently, he slowly noticed that the monk would use his neck to rub his collar occasionally. The movement stood out—

Li Yu suddenly realized that if he had shaved his head in a hurry, there would be itchy little hairs left behind, and they must be making him uncomfortable!

The sixth prince had brought fake monks this time as well!

As long as they could expose the fake monks in front of the emperor, no matter how eloquently they spoke, there was no way the emperor would believe them.

Li Yu had thought it through. He was going to splash some water onto Prince Jing again and get them both out of there—but the sixth prince didn't give Prince Jing any time to breathe at all. He hurriedly told the emperor, "Royal Father, the investigation into the nursery rhyme needs time, and it may be wrong. I invited these eminent monks, so why don't we have them examine fifth brother's fish instead?"

Though the emperor had ordered the imperial guards to investigate the nursery rhyme, a seed of doubt had been planted in his heart all the same. It wouldn't hurt to have the monks take a look at the fish, so he nodded in agreement. But the emperor didn't explicitly say that Prince Jing had to hand the fish over to the monks. Prince Jing's hand tightened on the crystal bottle's handle. Wang Xi knew what Prince Jing was thinking, and he boldly said to the monks, "You don't have to move. His Highness will hold the crystal bottle and show you the fish."

The emperor knew Prince Jing cared about his fish a lot, and the monks could see the fish perfectly well like this. The emperor felt a little bad for doubting Prince Jing, besides, so he silently allowed it.

Li Yu didn't have the time to find an opportunity to tell Prince Jing. The sixth prince would probably be the first to refuse if he tried to make a long-term plan as he did before. Besides, the fake monks were right in front of him. Still, there was no way Li Yu would let the monks alienate the emperor from Prince Jing by spouting nonsense about golden scales turning into a dragon.

Prince Jing could suggest the emperor investigate the nursery rhyme because it was the first time the emperor had heard of such rumors, and he might not believe it right away. But if the monks said the same thing here and now... Even lies could be believed if repeated enough times. Would the emperor still trust Prince Jing then?

Li Yu was with Prince Jing all the time, so he knew him well; Prince Jing had no disrespectful intentions. The father-son relationship they had was troubled and hard-won to begin with. It shouldn't be challenged like this! The most urgent thing was to expose these fake monks right here. As soon as they left the palace, they'd be hard to track down. There were opportunities, even if he had to take a risk!

While Prince Jing was walking toward the leading monk with his fish, letting them get a look, Li Yu ferociously slammed into the side of the crystal bottle facing the monk. His fish body's strength had gone through several boosts from the system and was quite a few times stronger than before. Li Yu put all his strength into it. There was a loud crack, and a huge hole was punched through the bottle. The little carp immediately flew toward the lead monk.

The monk never expected the fish to emerge from the crystal bottle like that. Shocked, he instinctively raised his hands to block him. But it was too late. The little carp soared over his hands and landed with a smack on his shoulder. In the chaos, the system made a noise, but Li Yu didn't care about whatever mission had been updated. He'd been waiting with his tail raised, aimed and ready. As soon as he landed on the monk's shoulder, his tail swept outward.

He intended to sweep off the monk's hat. If that happened, he was sure that Prince Jing would be able to realize that the monks were impostors. Li Yu was going to expose them! He no longer cared about the mission, or how blasphemous it was for a carp meant to be food to sweep a monk's hat off in front of the emperor. He didn't have any time to think—all he wanted was to protect Prince Jing by proving the sixth prince was trying to frame him.

The monk was so frightened by the threatening fish that his mouth gaped, his hat fell to the ground, and he forgot to cover his head.

"Royal Father!" the third prince and the sixth prince shouted in unison as they watched the fish break out of the bottle and knock the hat off the monk's head!

Prince Jing, meanwhile, had been keeping an eye on Xiaoyu. As soon as he approached the monk, the carp spirit had started anxiously swimming around in the crystal bottle, so Prince Jing assumed something must be wrong. Clearly, the fish wanted to communicate something important. Prince Jing had made his own assumptions, but he didn't think the carp spirit would ignore his own safety and leap directly onto the monk!

The carp spirit had broken out of the bottle, but Prince Jing wouldn't let anything happen to his fish. He had to deal with any loose ends. Most of the fragments of crystal were near his hand, and an idea came to him in this crucial moment: while everyone was still looking at the fish, he grasped a shard tightly in his hand, slicing it open until blood dripped down.

"Your Highness!" Wang Xi shouted in shock from beside him. But Prince Jing waved his hand dismissively. There wasn't much time, so this was the only way.

Wang Xi stamped his feet, hesitating between bandaging Prince Jing and protecting Master Xiaoyu. In the end, he chose to protect Master Xiaoyu, because Prince Jing's expression told him to. He couldn't go against Prince Jing's wishes. Having swept off the monk's hat, the little carp fell to the ground, flapping. Wang Xi quickly grabbed the spare crystal bottle and put the fish back into it.

Now that his fish was safe, Prince Jing focused on finding the monk's flaws—and he quickly realized that there were no scars to speak of on the bare head of the monk whose hat had been knocked off. This was a fake monk! This was what Xiaoyu wanted him to know!

"Tianchi, what happened? Your hand..." The emperor had blinked, and in that short amount of time, the fish had already leaped onto the monk. With another glance, he realized that Prince Jing's hand was injured.

Wang Xi desperately wanted to speak for his master, but Prince Jing stopped him. He instead wrote on the front of Wang Xi's robes—

Royal Father, please hear me out. I realized that the monk was an impostor who had not gone through the ordination ceremony. Desperate times call for desperate measures, so I threw the crystal bottle at him to force him to reveal his flaws.

The emperor had been on edge ever since he heard about the nursery rhyme. Now, he looked back and forth from the blood-stained robes to the crystal fragments on the ground, his heart in chaos. In a panic, the fake monk put his hat on again, but it was too late. The emperor ordered the guards to hold him down firmly and take his hat off to check his head. Their inspection revealed he really was unordained.

The emperor understood now. He'd seen the fish go flying because Prince Jing had broken the crystal bottle in his haste. Prince Jing was unable to speak and couldn't prove his innocence, so this was the only means at his disposal to expose the fake monks. Out of habit and narrow-mindedness, the emperor had suspected Prince Jing at first and was nearly taken advantage of by a bunch of fake monks!

Prince Jing's hands were still bleeding, and his face was pale. The emperor regretted his actions very much. He patted Prince Jing's shoulder and said gently, "Tianchi, my son, you've suffered. Quickly, go to the imperial physicians and have them take a look at your injury." He ordered Luo Ruisheng and Wang Xi to help Prince Jing to the side hall to wait for the imperial physicians.

The third prince and sixth prince, along with the kneeling and kowtowing fake monks, were all left to face the furious emperor!

Desire to Be Sucked
by the Fish

THE IMPERIAL PHYSICIANS rushed over to check Prince Jing's injured hand, but Prince Jing shielded the injury, shot a look at Wang Xi, and glanced at the crystal bottle Wang Xi had brought over. He had simply been cut by the sharp edge of the broken bottle, but Xiaoyu was the one who broke the bottle in the first place, so they had to check if he was all right first.

Wang Xi sighed, resigned, and asked an imperial physician to look at the fish. Only then did Prince Jing permit the other physicians to treat him.

The imperial physician who was examining the fish soon came over to report that the fish was unharmed. Prince Jing nodded, but his own injury wasn't nearly so simple. The imperial physicians had to take out the shards of crystal that were embedded in his flesh one by one, and that alone took half an hour. After that was done, the wounds needed to be cleaned, and medicine was applied. Bloodstained gauze was continuously applied and removed, making Wang Xi's heart twinge in pain. He couldn't help but ask, "Your Highness, does it hurt? Do you want this old servant to blow on it?"

Prince Jing wasn't in that much pain anymore, but Wang Xi's words were enough to make his expression darken.

After the imperial physicians had dealt with Prince Jing's injury, they reminded him to keep his wounds dry and went to report to the emperor. Wang Xi furrowed his brows and hurried to move the crystal bottle away, afraid that His Highness would immediately start playing with his fish again. Prince Jing had to signal for Wang Xi to move the crystal bottle closer. Wang Xi obeyed, but he still put the crystal bottle in a spot that was out of Prince Jing's reach. Frustrated, Prince Jing ordered him to go outside and stand guard. Wang Xi did comply, walking out of the room, but he was clearly unwilling to leave with how many times he looked back.

Shortly after Wang Xi left, Prince Jing left his seat and stood in front of the table where the crystal bottle stood. The fish inside was no longer as brave as he had been when he broke out of the bottle and stared at the prince pitifully. The little carp had needed to be scooped up from the ground after he showed off his abilities and knocked the hat off of the fake monk, but his new fish scales were truly quite powerful. After all this chaos, the fish was still lively and active, and he felt like he could have assailed even more monks without issue.

He did still feel a bit unsatisfied, even after all that, but unfortunately he didn't get an opportunity to slap the third and sixth princes. But those two had been willing to bring fake monks before the emperor, so at least there was no way the emperor would let them off easily.

After his attack, Li Yu had been smugly basking in his success with no thought for his own safety—when he suddenly heard Wang Xi shout in surprise, Li Yu had looked around, only to discover that Prince Jing was bleeding. He'd frozen, unable to work out how Prince Jing had been injured, since he broke out of the crystal bottle in the opposite direction. At most, Prince Jing should have only been startled.

What's more, he'd made a huge fuss in front of the emperor. When he slapped noble consort Qiu in the face, the emperor hadn't been there to see it, but this time the emperor had witnessed everything firsthand. It was surprising that he hadn't been punished.

Soon, though, the emperor's furious scolding had made him understand that Prince Jing had taken the blame for his sudden, strange behavior. He'd been so focused on exposing the fake monks that he jumped out while ignoring his own safety and any potential consequences. His special nature definitely would have been revealed by his actions—but because Prince Jing hurt his own hand on purpose and pretended that the fish flying out was a special plan, the fish remained safe. Prince Jing himself, though...

Li Yu, safe in his crystal bottle, had gazed at Prince Jing from afar. He didn't know how serious Prince Jing's injury was, only that the emperor's features were now twisted, and the imperial physicians were descending upon Prince Jing.

Despite all this, Prince Jing had still insisted that an imperial physician check his fish first. There really was no need for that, of course. He was fine, so there wasn't much to check. But he was touched by Prince Jing's protectiveness—and still had no way to thank him. The crystal bottle separated him from everyone else, and from his fishy perspective, he could only see the busy backs of the imperial physicians. Li Yu couldn't break another crystal bottle and give Prince Jing any more trouble, so all he could do was press against the bottle's wall and watch.

Now, as the two of them stared at each other, he severely regretted not thinking before taking action. If only Prince Jing hadn't gotten hurt.

One of Prince Jing's hands was injured, so he tried to open the crystal bottle with his other hand.

The little carp immediately swam to the mouth of the bottle. He wanted to get closer, but remembering the time he'd accidentally flipped the bottle over, he didn't want to be too hasty. Instead, he just looked up at Prince Jing and wagged his tail like a good boy.

Prince Jing placed his uninjured hand into the water, and the pitiful fish who had caused so much trouble swam over and rubbed his fingers. The imperial physician and Wang Xi had both said the fish was fine, but Prince Jing could tell that his fish was feeling a bit low.

Maybe he was frightened and sad. Prince Jing patted the fish's head. For his own part, he was somewhat sleepy from blood loss, so once he'd confirmed that his fish was fine, he sat back down and leaned to one side so he could take a little nap.

Li Yu was quite worried about Prince Jing's injury. He couldn't speak in his inconvenient fish body, and he and Prince Jing were the only ones in this side hall, so as soon as Prince Jing's back was to him, Li Yu transformed into human form.

He now had a proper place in Prince Jing's manor, and because Prince Jing took pity on him for not having any possessions, he gave him a lot of old, unworn clothes. Li Yu wasn't sure exactly what was appropriate or fashionable in this style of clothing, so he'd just picked two of his favorites and kept them in his inventory so he wouldn't have to worry about running around looking for clothes when he transformed.

Li Yu got changed quickly and then approached the side of the daybed, bending to look at Prince Jing's hand.

The imperial physicians had bandaged it well, so his hand was wrapped in thick gauze. It hadn't been very long, but some blood had already started to seep through. Li Yu felt so bad that he worriedly chewed his lip. When he noticed that Prince Jing was lying on his side without a blanket, he was afraid that Prince Jing would catch a cold on top of being injured, so he pulled a thin blanket over to drape over him, wanting to take good care of him.

Prince Jing had been secretly waiting for this fish for a long time. He even pretended to fall asleep to get the fish to transform. As soon as Li Yu came closer, he turned around and looked at him with a smile.

Li Yu suppressed the tearful heat surging into his eyes and said, embarrassed, "Did you not fall asleep, Your Highness? Does your wound still hurt?" Li Yu's heart ached so much—it must be even worse for Prince Jing.

The cream the imperial physician used had an analgesic effect, so Prince Jing had already stopped feeling the pain, but when he saw Xiaoyu's eyes full of worry, he hesitated. For some reason, he found himself nodding. If it hurt...would Xiaoyu rush to blow on it for him, the way Wang Xi did?

He didn't need Wang Xi to blow on it, but he would think about it if Xiaoyu offered.

He waited for Xiaoyu to say those words, but Xiaoyu wasn't thinking of that at all. He thought Prince Jing was still in pain, so he scurried over to the jade box that contained snacks and took out a couple of peach blossom pastries. "Your Highness, if it still hurts, eat something sweet. It'll stop hurting when you eat something delicious," the carp spirit said, forcing a smile.

Prince Jing lightly coughed, somewhat disappointed. Oh well. Since Xiaoyu wasn't going to blow on his wound, eating the sweets he gave him was fine too. But his right hand was injured, so he couldn't really move it.

It took a moment for Li Yu to realize the problem. "I'll help you," he said. He took out a pastry and broke it into bite-size pieces. In ancient times, princes wouldn't eat just anything someone offered them, so Li Yu tasted a piece first. "You can eat this—it's not poisoned, I feel fine. Please feel free to have some."

Prince Jing thought that was a bit excessive, as he trusted Xiaoyu, but it wasn't the time to mention that.

Li Yu brought the rest of the peach blossom pastry to Prince Jing's lips and watched as he slowly ate two pieces. He couldn't help but think that this used to be how his master fed his fish, but the fish was feeding his master now. Li Yu's eyes were still warm. At first, he managed to keep the tears under control, but once he got distracted, a couple of teardrops fell. Prince Jing was taken aback, and Li Yu panickily wiped at his reddened eyes. Prince Jing didn't know he was his fish, so it would scare him to see Li Yu shedding tears so suddenly!

Li Yu hurried to explain. "I'm sorry, Your Highness. Some sand got into my eyes, so—"

It was easy to say, but emotions were like floodwater bursting out of a dam. Once it found an opening, it couldn't be reined back—tears were just the same. Li Yu wasn't the kind of person who liked to cry, but he covered his face and his shoulders heaved for fifteen straight minutes before he finally managed to calm down, his face soaked.

He felt like he'd embarrassed himself immensely. *Sob sob sob! I wanted to take care of my master, but I let him see something so humiliating!* Li Yu's eyelids were slightly swollen, and his voice was hoarse. "My apologies. I was a bit scared after I found Your Highness injured."

Faced with such a clumsy lie, Prince Jing paused, then smiled and patted Li Yu's hand. Unfortunately, his own hand was still wrapped in gauze, so he couldn't hold a brush and had no way to say what he wanted to say. He felt unhappy that Xiaoyu was crying. In the end, it was his own incompetence that made Xiaoyu worry.

Prince Jing pulled out a clean cloth from beside the pillow and silently handed it to Li Yu. Li Yu wiped his face with it and smiled wetly. "Does it still hurt, Your Highness?"

Prince Jing sighed internally. *It's not like you're going to blow on it even if it hurts.* But, afraid that Xiaoyu would worry, he shook his head this time.

"Then you should get some more rest," said Li Yu. "Wounds heal faster when you're asleep."

Really?

Prince Jing had never heard of that before, but he did as Li Yu said and shifted his body to lie down.

Li Yu sat down on the side of the daybed, but soon got up, as if he remembered he had to do something—only for Prince Jing to grab his wrist.

"Your Highness," he said, distressed, "I'm going to get some water for you." Li Yu had noticed that Prince Jing's lips were dry and thought he might want some water to soothe his throat.

Prince Jing shook his head and refused. Helpless, Li Yu could only give in. Since Prince Jing was holding on to his arm, it was hard for him to step away. If Prince Jing wanted to sleep, then he could only watch from the side, but it wasn't as if sitting beside him was tiring.

Prince Jing lay quietly for a while, then opened his eyes. His deep gaze, heavy with emotion, fell on Li Yu.

Recently, Prince Jing was always looking at him like that. It was a different gaze from the one he used with the third prince, the sixth prince, or Wang-gonggong. Li Yu could always sense a slight smile in it. "Your Highness, is there anything else you want?" he asked worriedly, not realizing how gentle his tone was.

Prince Jing pursed his lips. He wanted to get closer, but this fish had no self-awareness, so he could only use some other tricks to accomplish that. So, Prince Jing, who was wrapped in a blanket and warm all over, pretended to shiver.

"...Your Highness, are you cold?"

Prince Jing nodded at him twice, earnestly.

Li Yu thought it was natural to feel cold after losing blood, and tyrants were no exception. But there were no more blankets on the daybed, so Li Yu said hurriedly, "Your Highness, please wait. I'll go find another blanket..."

Li Yu was about to go searching when Prince Jing bolted upright faster than he could, pulled him back down, and patted his shoulder, communicating that he should stay in place. Li Yu did as he asked, confused, and watched helplessly as the tall, large man wrapped in a blanket feebly rested his head on his thighs.

Huh? So sleeping on someone's legs while cold would help?

The human body *was* warm, so this might be more comfortable than wrapping another blanket around him...

Li Yu's eyes had just been hot, but now it was his face's turn. He convinced himself that since Prince Jing had been injured on his account, there was nothing wrong with him using his legs as a pillow! He tried his best to ignore the unfamiliar feeling on his legs.

Prince Jing closed his eyes, satisfied, and slightly smiled. Then he pretended to shiver again.

"Your Highness, are you still cold?" Li Yu asked cautiously.

Prince Jing nodded eagerly, three times this time.

Thinking of how His Highness was wounded because of him, Li Yu hugged him in resignation. "How about now?"

Prince Jing settled in, still somewhat disappointed. His Highness was soooo cold. He wanted someone to suck his essence!

Fishy Nursing

PRINCE JING *WAS* INJURED, so once he'd taken his medicine, he fell asleep after laying on Li Yu's lap for a bit.

Li Yu boldly stared down at the tyrant's handsome face, but after a while he found that being a pillow was hard on his waist and legs. Prince Jing had finally gotten to sleep, though, and Li Yu was too afraid he'd wake him to move.

But being tired wasn't the most pressing matter right now; he was forced to consider how much time he had left as a human. What if he just turned into a fish right here? Li Yu had a sudden thought—if he turned back while Prince Jing was laying on him like this, wouldn't he get crushed under Prince Jing's head? What if he was flattened?

Li Yu shook his head. He had to sneak away before he changed back, but Prince Jing was still sleeping...

In his moment of conflict, worrying about being stuck between a rock and a hard bed, the door to the side hall was cracked open. Wang-gonggong peeked inside.

Help had arrived!

Li Yu immediately blinked furiously at Wang Xi. Wang Xi immediately noticed that there was another person in the side hall and that His Highness was resting on that person's lap. He was stunned for a moment, then scurried over.

"You're...Li-gongzi?" Wang Xi quickly asked, his voice low.

Prince Jing had expended a lot of effort in his friendly abduction of the human fish to his manor, and of course made sure Wang Xi was informed of it. However, he didn't reveal Xiaoyu's real name. Wang Xi had at least managed to figure out that "someone else's male concubine" was just a beautiful misunderstanding. The young man was now a member of the residence, he was surnamed Li, and he worked only for Prince Jing. That was all Prince Jing explained, and nothing else. He didn't allow anyone to ask about him either, and he'd decreed that no matter who ran into Li-gongzi, they were to treat him with the utmost respect, as if they were greeting Prince Jing himself.

People couldn't just enter Prince Jing's room as they pleased; most of the manor's residents didn't get much of an opportunity to run into the fabled Li-gongzi. However, as Prince Jing's trusted confidant, Wang Xi had glimpsed Li-gongzi's back a couple of times. From what he could glean, this Li-gongzi probably lived in His Highness's room and his whereabouts were often unknown.

Because of Prince Jing's orders, Wang Xi wasn't particularly suspicious, but he did wonder if there was something going on between the prince and this Li-gongzi. Li-gongzi was definitely the person Prince Jing liked: Wang-gonggong had a good memory and recalled several occasions he'd come across Li-gongzi and His Highness entangled with each other. Now that Li-gongzi was a personal servant of Prince Jing's, he would often go into His Highness's room and not come out. Coupled with the fact that Prince Jing wanted them to treat him and serve him well...that seemed to be what was happening.

Right now, with Li-gongzi appearing next to Prince Jing and with Prince Jing sleeping in his lap, Wang Xi was even more sure of the relationship between the two. However, he didn't show anything on his face. His Highness had told him several times that if he saw Li-gongzi, he wasn't to be startled or speak nonsense but to treat him normally. Wang Xi kept that in mind and acted accordingly.

Li Yu nodded slightly to Wang Xi. Wang Xi softly inquired about Prince Jing's injury, and Li Yu told him what he knew. As Wang Xi was just about to exit and give the two of them some privacy, Li Yu stopped him.

"Wang-gonggong, please wait," Li Yu pleaded quietly. "I-I still have business to attend to, so could you help me?"

Wang Xi immediately understood what he wanted and helped him gently lift Prince Jing onto the daybed. Li Yu covered Prince Jing with a blanket, just as the system was already beginning to count down...

Li Yu didn't have any time to say anything else to Wang-gonggong. He ran toward the door and quickly hid behind a cabinet nearby, where he had placed a crystal bottle beforehand, just out of sight. Li Yu had lots of experience transforming by now, and aside from keeping track of the time, he had also gotten into the habit of placing a crystal bottle or a fish tank in a hidden area. When his time was almost up, he just had to hide nearby and transform, then jump into the crystal bottle or the tank. This time was no exception.

Li Yu quickly turned back into a little carp and gathered all of his strength in his tail. Jumping around all the time was a bit too noisy and noticeable, so ever since Li Yu realized that he could stiffen his tail and use it as a sort of base to support his fish body for a short amount of time, he would simply use it as a little skateboard. With a push, he arrived in front of the crystal bottle and jumped right in.

While he completed this series of dazzling moves, Wang Xi thankfully didn't even look around. Li Yu sighed in relief and started swimming happily in his crystal bottle!

Once Wang Xi had made sure Prince Jing was all right, he turned around to look for Li-gongzi but realized he'd disappeared. He thought Li-gongzi had perhaps left again, and since His Highness had forbidden asking after Li-gongzi's whereabouts, he obeyed. But when he passed by the door of the side hall, he found that the crystal bottle was on the ground for some reason, with Master Fish in it, wagging his tail at him. Wang Xi smiled and picked up the crystal bottle, placing it in front of the bed. When His Highness woke up, he'd definitely want to see his fish first.

While Prince Jing was resting in the side hall of Qianqing Palace, though, on the other side of the wall, in the main hall, most of the room was kneeling in front of the emperor.

Since the sixth prince had brought in those fake monks, the emperor thought the fake monks and the nursery rhyme were both very suspicious and ordered an investigation. However, the investigation into the nursery rhyme would require going out to question the common people, so the fake monks who'd dared sneak into Qianqing Palace were punished first. These fake monks were simply a random group of troublemakers. Unable to withstand the torture, they quickly admitted that the third prince had bribed them.

The emperor immediately started scolding the third prince, who'd thought his position as crown prince was all but confirmed. The sixth prince, who was rarely sighted but had made a rare mainstage appearance, was berated severely as well.

Since he was a child, Mu Tianxiao had always understood what the most beneficial thing to do was, and as soon as he realized that things weren't going well, he knelt in apologetic obeisance. "Royal Father, I was wrong, but I did not have any bad intentions. I heard the nursery rhyme sung among the common people, and was concerned, so I wrote it down to report to you. As for these monks,

I was not aware they were fake, as I didn't imagine they would have cause to lie. These were all lapses in judgment on my part, and I won't simply believe everything I hear in the future."

Mu Tianxiao was extremely devious and had always hidden behind Mu Tianming. His name wasn't directly involved with the fake monks and the nursery rhyme, while the third prince's was. He was never one to be an obvious schemer, so he was confident that no matter how far the emperor investigated, he wouldn't be implicated. Now that the emperor had exposed his plan, it was no big deal for him to admit his mistake. On the other hand, Mu Tianming was a little slower. By the time he started lowering himself to his knees, Mu Tianxiao had already finished his confession and said everything he was supposed to say.

"Royal Father, I didn't do it!" Mu Tianming said. "I just thought... there was something wrong with Prince Jing's fish." He was still in shock from the fish leaping out and knocking off the fake monk's hat. Prince Jing claimed he'd discovered the monk's flaw and threw the crystal bottle at him, but thinking back over it all, the third prince wasn't sure what had really happened first—Prince Jing's hand bleeding or the fish leaping out.

...But he felt like it was the fish.

Mu Tianming thought the fish was very suspicious. If he could convince the emperor of this, then the issue of the monks would be irrelevant.

"Tianming, you still don't think you did anything wrong?" After the monks' testimony, the emperor didn't want to listen to the third prince at all. The sixth prince had already admitted his wrongdoings, yet the third prince was still here trying to argue?!

The emperor knew very well that the sixth prince often followed the third prince and helped him out. Though the sixth prince was the one who'd mentioned the fake monks and the nursery rhyme, the monks only testified against the third prince. The sixth prince had mentioned the third prince several times in his speech too... The third prince had to have at least known about what the sixth prince did, but the sixth prince was willing to admit his mistake while the third prince wasn't. These contrasting attitudes meant that the third prince must have been the one behind all of it!

When the emperor had ordered the Imperial Astrological Bureau to read the skies for Prince Jing's fish, Mu Tianming jumped out to question them and was refuted by Director Sun. Later on, the sixth prince brought up the nursery rhyme and the fake monks—wasn't this an obvious attempt to overturn the Imperial Astrological Bureau's conclusions?

The emperor suddenly remembered something else. A few days ago, Luo Ruisheng told him that the third prince had gone to Prince Jing's manor to buy his fish, but Prince Jing chased him out. The emperor took it as a joke at first, but now that he thought about it, didn't the third prince think of the fish as an auspicious sign as well? Otherwise, why would he try to buy the fish? Why would he change his attitude in just a few days? The nursery rhyme, the fake monks...they were all attempts to use the fish to make him suspicious of Prince Jing.

But why did the third prince do this?

From what the emperor understood of the third prince, the third prince probably got jealous when he saw the emperor give Prince Jing's fish special treatment, and when the third prince failed to buy the fish from Prince Jing, he thought Prince Jing was rude and ordered the sixth prince to work with him to frame Prince Jing...

The emperor's head hurt.

He'd been keeping an eye on Mu Tianming, actually. Ever since he could remember, Mu Tianming was always competing with

Mu Tianzhao. Mu Tianming was inferior to Mu Tianzhao in terms of ability, but he had his strong points too. There was a period of time when he valued this son of his quite a lot, albeit not as much as he valued Mu Tianzhao.

The tragedy that befell Mu Tianzhao was ultimately because the emperor had prematurely and unofficially announced that he was to become the crown prince. Now, the second prince was no longer in consideration. Learning from his previous mistake, he had no intention of choosing a crown prince yet—he wanted to wait a couple more years and see how the other princes fared. When the seventh and eighth princes were a little older, he would compare all the princes and select the best of them to be crown prince.

But just because the emperor didn't have a crown prince in mind didn't mean that others wouldn't. Mu Tianming used to be quite humble, but without someone above him to compete with, his ambitions were quickly revealed.

It wasn't that the emperor was unaware of Mu Tianming's recent actions in court. He knew that the officials who used to have a good relationship with Mu Tianzhao had switched teams and that Consort Qian had also tried to intervene several times when he was dealing with Concubine Qiu. These were all expressions of their restlessness, but the emperor put up with it.

He didn't have many adult sons, so he hadn't made any efforts to control the third prince, hoping that even once he'd gained some power of his own, the third prince and his mother would behave themselves. That had clearly been a foolish assumption. If he'd really listened to the nursery rhyme and the impostor monks today, allowing himself to be alienated from Prince Jing, what would he have done to him?

He had already started to suspect Prince Jing...

The emperor was both upset and ashamed. He didn't want to shoulder the responsibility himself for almost falling for the trap, so he could only take out his anger on the two princes who were behind all this—the third prince especially. Since he'd already deposed the second prince, the emperor didn't want to take harsh action against any of his adult sons again so soon, so he simply relieved the third prince of his duties, as he did with the second prince.

The third prince was luckier than the second prince had been. Mu Tianzhao had received a title that meant there was no hope left for him, while Mu Tianming remained a prince and wasn't so thoroughly humiliated—but he wasn't much better off.

Since Prince Jing's hand was injured, the emperor ordered the guards to hit the third and sixth prince one hundred times with the plank, and he personally watched so they couldn't take it easy. After that, the sixth prince was fined and grounded, while the third prince was told that his presence was no longer required in court and that he was to go to the imperial study room to study with his younger brothers, the seventh and eighth princes, every day.

This punishment was only for bringing in the fake monks. If the investigation into the nursery rhyme concluded that the third prince was also behind it...then it would be up to the third prince to decide his own fate.

The third and sixth princes were the first and last of their standing to ever be beaten by the plank. It was a magnificent sight. The emperor ordered the guards to carry out the punishment right in Qianqing Palace. The two princes had their trousers removed in front of everyone and were held down over a stool to be beaten. The sixth prince bore the pain without uttering a single sound, but the third prince cried out every time he was hit. The sound could be heard in the side hall, where Li Yu floated in his crystal bottle, listening in satisfaction. The emperor was publicly punishing the third and sixth princes on behalf of Prince Jing, and Li Yu was appeased.

He was worried about Prince Jing, so he didn't enter the system even when he turned back into a fish. He felt like he'd heard the system chime while he was creating chaos in the main hall earlier, but he didn't know for sure what was going on with his missions. He decided he'd wait until Prince Jing woke up to check.

He didn't have to wait long. Prince Jing was soon woken up by the third prince's bone-chilling screams. When Prince Jing opened his eyes, he saw a little carp peeking at him from a crystal bottle.

Did he change back before he could absorb essence? Prince Jing wondered.

Well, the days were long, so there was no need to rush. Prince Jing smiled a little. He knew that Xiaoyu was worried about him, so he wanted to comfort him and pet him a bit. To the prince's great disappointment, though, before he could even lift his uninjured hand to reach out, the carp spirit's tail stretched out as he started to "meditate."

His tyrant master finally woke up!

Li Yu entered the system at once to check his main mission—only to find that the koi side mission he'd been ignoring had been updated!

The Joy of Petting Fish

L I YU CHECKED the koi mission. The original line was: *To become a koi, one must have the characteristics of a koi.* But it was different now; it said: *To become a koi, one must experience being a koi first.*

Huh?

Li Yu asked the system, *‹Why did the prompt change?›* If he remembered correctly, it had happened while he was creating chaos in Qianqing Palace.

The system patiently explained: *‹When the user becomes protective and risks his own life for the tyrant, that is when the user has the characteristics of a koi.›*

Li Yu suddenly realized: *So...“the characteristics of a koi” means being protective.* This whole damn time, he thought it was good fortune.

Actually, it made some sense. People hoped koi could bring good fortune, but wasn't that just a kind of wish for protection? Because of an unintentional move and a combination of strange circumstances, the koi mission had been accidentally updated. But the update wasn't complete—the mission was still in progress.

Li Yu was a little worried. *‹What does it mean to experience being a koi?›*

‹User, are you ready?›

‹Huh?›

Before Li Yu could react, the scene before him suddenly changed. The mental world of the system used to be wild and chaotic, but now, it was a vast, starry sky.

The system solemnly said, *‹User, please choose a target and experience being a koi.›*

Wait. The system wanted him to choose someone? He wasn't prepared at all. Li Yu had no idea what the system wanted, but with a closer look, he saw a new path in front of him that led into the dark.

Li Yu was still in his fish form. He cautiously gave it a try and found that he could still swim along the road without water. This would have been impossible in reality, so he must still be in the mental world.

The system urged him, *‹User, please carry out your mission with no worries.›*

No worries? As if! Every single time the system said that, it scammed him. Li Yu was so on guard, he thought about exiting the system first. He was completely unprepared! He'd only come in to check his progress. Prince Jing was still outside; what if he failed and couldn't turn into a koi?

But though he could normally exit the system easily, he couldn't now. The system had started scamming him already by not giving him a way out, trapping him in this mental world. If he wanted to escape, it looked like he would have to do as the system said and experience being a koi.

Since he'd caused a lot of trouble by changing scales, Li Yu wasn't terribly excited to become a koi, but such was the life of a fish…

Li Yu swam along the path in front of him. Eventually—he wasn't sure how much time had passed—a light shone from ahead, and his surroundings gradually became clear. He realized he was in the imperial palace, because the tiles on the walls were the gold ones that only appeared there. Since he could still swim around but couldn't leave the mental world, though—it was all an illusion.

The system didn't prompt him, meaning he would have to work everything out for himself. He was used to it by now, but what did it mean by 'pick a target'? He hadn't seen anyone yet.

As if in response to his confusion, he heard voices a distance away. Li Yu swam over and found two kids fighting in the grass. Of the two children, one, the older of the two, was taller and skinnier, while the other was shorter and chubbier, a little round boy with bulging cheeks and a plump body. The older one seemed to be about seven or eight years old, and the younger one about two or three. It wasn't clear why they were fighting each other.

The larger child was sly, pinching and twisting the flesh of the plumper boy, even kicking him in the stomach. Any other child would have started crying long ago, but not only did the plump boy not cry, he even clenched his teeth and greeted the other child's face with his fist, giving him a black eye.

Li Yu was close by, and it seemed the children couldn't see him. He tried separating them, but he couldn't touch them. So it was truly an illusion, and he could only watch. Did the system mean for him to pick someone out of these two children?

The fight ended quickly once the little plump boy chomped into the larger child's arm. The older child covered his wound and cried out, "Just you wait! I'm telling our Royal Father!" He howled and wailed the entire way as he ran.

The plump boy stared at his back coldly, then lowered his head and picked up a broken paper kite beside him, tidying it up himself.

From the mentioned "Royal Father," Li Yu guessed that these two boys must be princes.

But these ages didn't match the ages of the seventh and eighth princes he knew of. What's more, those two little radishes were on good terms, and the original novel never mentioned that they fought. So who was this little chubby boy?

As Li Yu watched, a servant ran forward in a hurry, hugging the plump boy. "Your Highness, why did you fight with the second prince again? Did you beat him into the ground?" Li Yu laughed with a *pfft*. The way the servant spoke was quite funny.

The chubby boy's dark eyes glittered, and he nodded. The servant turned around with the boy to wipe his face, and when Li Yu clearly saw the servant's face, he was shocked. His face was almost identical to Wang Xi's, just a little younger. Li Yu was stunned. Was this a mysterious relative of Wang-gonggong's?

Li Yu's interest in these two was piqued. The servant who looked like Wang Xi led the chubby little prince away, and Li Yu quietly followed, only to see them enter a building. Li Yu looked around and thought the place looked familiar, so he lifted his head and glanced at the plaque at the entrance. The words "Jingtai Hall" were engraved.

Li Yu stopped in his tracks. He was aware of only one prince who'd lived in Jingtai Hall, and the servant looked so similar to Wang Xi...

Having suddenly stumbled upon the truth, Li Yu almost screamed. *No way???*

No wonder the chubby boy didn't say anything when he was getting hit, and no wonder the servant looked so much like Wang Xi. A child's appearance would change a lot as he grew up, so Li Yu didn't recognize the chubby boy, but adults didn't change that much.

The silent prince who lived in Jingtai Hall and the young servant who resembled Wang Xi—weren't they Prince Jing and Wang Xi?

He knew the system liked to scam fish. Before, it had always been inconsequential things, but now not only was the system not letting him exit, it also put him in an illusion from more than ten years ago?

Huh. So Prince Jing was a little dumpling when he was a child.

Entering an illusion didn't seem like a big deal to Li Yu, since he'd already transmigrated into a book, but when he realized that he was seeing Prince Jing's childhood, he was a little happy. He swung his tail crazily, racing to follow behind the chubby boy. Baby Prince Jing and Wang Xi still couldn't see him, so Li Yu swam boldly in front of them and jumped into the familiar courtyard.

Wang Xi wiped Prince Jing's round little face clean, then left the chubby boy in the courtyard and told him not to wander around. It seemed he was going to get something. Prince Jing was very obedient and really just sat there with a straight face, unmoving.

Li Yu swam behind the round boy and swished his tail across his back a couple of times, but the little Prince Jing didn't react. Tsk, as expected, he couldn't feel Li Yu. So how was he to "experience" being a koi? Well, either way, now that Li Yu knew the chubby boy was Prince Jing, he'd definitely choose him. While he was thinking with his fish head cocked, the older prince that Prince Jing had chased away returned.

Li Yu remembered that Wang Xi had called him the second prince. So that must have been the second prince when he was a child.

The second prince ran over, and Prince Jing stared at him fiercely. The second prince said angrily, "Our Royal Father said I should teach you a lesson! He won't come to see you, and he won't care about you!"

Prince Jing was riled, and they started to tussle again.

To Li Yu, a fight between two children seemed like a fight between helpless baby birds. Even if he wanted to help, he couldn't. The two princes were tangled together in the fight again, and when they rolled over next to a pond, Prince Jing was unprepared. The second prince somehow mustered the strength to shove Prince Jing into the pond. The young Prince Jing didn't know how to swim, and when the second prince saw him struggling in the water, he ran away screaming.

Don't run! Come back and save him!

Li Yu swam back and forth anxiously, but Wang Xi wasn't there and nobody else was nearby either!

No, he had to save Prince Jing...

Even if it was an illusion.

Li Yu jumped into the pond without hesitation. The moment he hit the water, he felt a long-absent wetness... It seemed...he had fully entered the illusion.

There was no time to think. He swam straight to Prince Jing's side like an arrow.

The jet-black fish, with a golden belly and tail, suddenly appeared out of nowhere, surprising chubby little Prince Jing enough that he forgot to keep struggling.

He was just about to sink, but Li Yu opened his mouth and grabbed the hem of his clothes. He could touch Prince Jing now, as he'd suspected, but he was just a little carp. No matter how much strength the system gave him, he couldn't lift a two- or three-year-old child.

He needed to be bigger and stronger...

Li Yu prayed fervently. At that moment, his body seemed to answer his prayers and started to grow.

When he finally grew as long as the chubby boy's arm, Li Yu grabbed him by his clothes again. He could finally move him a bit, and he tugged and pushed him to shore.

The chubby boy's cheeks were flushed, and he looked excited. His eyes were wide open, and he stared at the fish without blinking. Li Yu was exhausted but still concerned for the boy. He couldn't leave the pond and swim in the air like he did before, so he stayed in the water and pushed his back against the little boy's hand. Chubby Prince Jing gave him a look of confusion.

...So dumb! He doesn't even know how to pet a fish! How did this kid turn into the man who petted me until my tail went soft?

Li Yu, resigned, pushed his body up to move through the little chubby boy's fingers. After Li Yu demonstrated how to pet him, the little guy reached a finger out and poked the fish's slippery back. Once he was used to how cold it was, the toddler put his whole hand on him and was soon petting the fish properly.

Petting fish makes one happy! There's a spot here, chubby boy!

As Li Yu enjoyed the chubby boy's unskilled petting, he put his head in the boy's palm and bumped it twice. He still didn't know what it meant, but Li Yu liked it a lot when Prince Jing did that. The chubby boy smiled and lightly patted his head under his guidance...

The smile on his plump face showed a glimpse of the handsome man he'd turn into. Li Yu flicked his tail audibly to encourage him.

He and the chubby boy silently played for a bit. There were numerous voices coming from close by, and since Li Yu could be seen now, he hurriedly turned around, flicked his tail, and hid among the aquatic plants in the pond.

The chubby baby Prince Jing was quickly surrounded by a flock of imperial physicians and a man wearing dragon robes—the young emperor—briskly walked over. To his surprise, he saw a pond of rippling water sprinkled with gold.

It was because the little carp was hiding among the aquatic plants. The emperor couldn't see the fish, but he saw the golden light that was reflected off of the fish's body and tail, imprinting its dazzling color into the depths of his eyes.

The emperor turned around and looked worriedly at the fifth prince that fell into the water. "How are you feeling? Are you all right?"

The chubby boy looked at the emperor and the pond. He couldn't see the fish anymore. He got up shakily, wobbled twice, and fell down again.

"Fifth Highness!" The imperial physicians hurriedly picked him up.

One of them felt the fifth prince's forehead with his palm and shouted, "The fifth prince has a high fever! It's hot to the touch!"

Li Yu hadn't realized the chubby boy's flushed face was an indicator of a fever, and he nearly lunged back out from the aquatic plants in worry. Suddenly, though, everything seemed to be separated by a layer of mist, and he felt himself gradually moving away.

The last thing Li Yu heard was the emperor's angry voice saying, "Cure him right now! If anything happens to Tianjing, there's no need for any of you to keep living!"

He was shocked. The chubby boy's name was originally Tianjing, not Tianchi? Did he have the wrong person? Was it not his tyrant master?

...Impossible. He'd read the entire book; the emperor didn't have a son named Tianjing. Wang Xi was his personal servant, and he couldn't talk—that was Prince Jing's character setting, but...

Why was Prince Jing's title "Jing"?

Did Prince Jing change his name when he was younger? Among a bunch of princes with names made up of characters that contained the radical "day,"[3] "Tianchi" didn't follow the pattern. If it was "Tianjing," then it would fit.

The only one who could change Prince Jing's name was the emperor, so that was likely what happened. But why? Li Yu couldn't think of a reason. But it wasn't really important; whether Prince Jing was called Tianchi or Tianjing, he was still his tyrant master.

The system's notification came right at that moment.

<User, congratulations on completing the "Becoming a Koi" side mission. You will become a koi and receive the abilities of a koi when you collect your reward.>

Li Yu's thoughts were still with the chubby baby boy who had fallen ill, and he kept having to remind himself that it was just something that happened in the illusion, not reality. Prince Jing was fine now and was just outside—he also wasn't a chubby little child anymore. So he wasn't actually sick, right?

But even though Li Yu knew it wasn't real, he couldn't help asking, *<System, the chubby...the child just now. What happened to him afterward?>*

<Afterward, he was sick. He recovered a few days later.>

Wow. How useful.

Forget it. He knew the system was good at scamming fish, so it was already quite impressive that he'd managed to find out this much.

Li Yu looked at his body. He had gotten larger in the illusion, but he was back to his regular size now. It was just an illusion, after all, so the effect didn't stay with him. He was satisfied with that. The koi

---

3   The princes' names all have characters that include the radical for "day" (日), such as 昭 (Zhao), 明 (Ming), 曉 (Xiao). Prince Jing's, 池 (Chi), is the only one that doesn't. However, the radical does occur in his title: 景 (Jing).

mission was now completed, most likely because he had helped the baby Prince Jing in the illusion just now.

The system had wanted him to experience what it was like being a koi. He knew that the characteristic of a koi fish was to protect, so experiencing what it was like to be a koi was for him to experience the feeling of protecting someone. Just like the way he chose the chubby boy and helped him.

He'd finally completed the mission and could turn into a koi...

Li Yu wasn't very excited, though, now that the long-awaited reward was right in front of him. If he turned into a koi, would his scales change color?

<Yes,> the system informed him. *<Your scales will be adjusted again.>*

<Then I'll leave it for later.>

He'd been forced to suddenly complete the koi mission. Last time his scales changed, he'd caused a lot of trouble. Prince Jing had only just finished dealing with it. If he changed scales again, wouldn't it be suspicious?

Even if he were a real koi, the change wouldn't happen so often.

<I'll get to it later...>

The system seemed confused...

Li Yu tried to leave the system again and succeeded this time. With a lingering fear, he returned to reality, where he found Prince Jing wrapping him in the gold blanket.

Li Yu wagged his tail, touched. Even though the illusion wasn't real, it was nice to meet you, chubby child!

Fish Mouth Hurts

RINCE JING REALIZED that the carp spirit was very friendly toward him after his "meditation." But the fish had clearly ignored him by "meditating" as soon as he woke up!

Prince Jing had read some new introductory books on cultivating, so he knew that when one meditated, one could gain insight on some things. So, what was it the carp spirit had come to understand?

Li Yu was quite proud of himself. *I found out Prince Jing used to be chubby! How surprising! How unexpected! He he he!* He knew that what happened in the illusion wasn't real, but the sight of that chubby little boy was something he could look back on in amusement for a long time.

Wrapped in the golden blanket, the little carp was laughing so hard that his tyrant master found it strange.

The emperor felt guilty that Prince Jing had been injured. He wanted him to stay in the palace until his injury healed, but Prince Jing only agreed to stay for three more days. The emperor was silent for a while, thinking about the way bad things seemed to happen to Prince Jing whenever he entered the palace, and ultimately relented.

After all this, the emperor remained somewhat uneasy. He wasn't suspicious of Prince Jing, but he wondered if there was something wrong with his fish that even the Imperial Astrological Bureau couldn't see. He sat silently in Qianqing Palace for two hours before ordering head eunuch Luo Ruisheng to bring the Zen Master Liao Kong from Huguo Temple.

This particular master was different from ordinary monks—that was why the emperor sent for him. In his younger years, he'd traveled the world, broadening his horizons, and was an extraordinary conversationalist. Now, he presided over the imperial family's Hugou Temple. If the emperor was said to trust Director Sun of the Imperial Astrological Bureau very much, then Liao Kong was the equivalent of three Director Suns. The only thing was that he had already lived through three different dynasties and was very elderly, so he didn't get involved in ordinary affairs. The emperor was the only one who could summon him; Liao Kong rarely answered to anyone else. Tangentially, if the third and sixth princes had managed to win over Liao Kong, they wouldn't have had to use any fake monks and things wouldn't have gone so poorly for them.

Head eunuch Luo rushed to Huguo Temple with an imperial edict, and Prince Jing, who was staying at Jingtai Hall over his few days at the palace, learned of it soon after. When Wang Xi gave him the secret report, Prince Jing glanced at his constant companion, who had been moved into a blue-white porcelain fish tank, then slightly nodded.

Li Yu was a fish, so it technically didn't matter where he lived—but at Prince Jing's manor there was the huge pond that Prince Jing had built for him, allowing him to swim around freely. He liked the manor more, but staying in Jingtai Hall for a couple more days wasn't a big deal.

When Wang Xi put him in the porcelain fish tank, Li Yu had been initially surprised. He'd assumed the fish tank in Jingtai Hall would be too small for him now—but Prince Jing had really updated and altered all the fish tanks he barely used too. He swam around inside, extremely comfortable. There was no one better at taking care of fish than his tyrant master, he thought proudly.

The first day they stayed in Jingtai Hall, the third and sixth prince's mothers sent people to visit.

Since the two princes were being punished for offending Prince Jing, the third prince's mother, Consort Qian, and the sixth prince's mother, Consort Zhang, wanted to ask Prince Jing for mercy. They had already asked the emperor, but Consort Qian had only recently gained a little favor from the third prince's brief advancement, and Consort Zhang, like the sixth prince, had never made much of a name for herself. Their words were useless in front of the emperor, and when he rejected their pleas, they were afraid to keep asking, lest he become angry and hurt the two princes further.

Consort Qian mulled over it and decided to take Consort Zhang with her to beg Prince Jing for forgiveness. Consort Zhang had no ideas herself. She had cried when her son was beaten, so she went along with Consort Qian. However, since they were concubines, it was not appropriate for them to visit a prince in private. Consort Qian wanted the emperor to be aware of their planned visit, so she sent several palace servants in advance with gifts for Prince Jing.

But those servants waited outside Jingtai Hall for several hours, and Prince Jing gave no indication that he would meet them. When the emperor heard the news, he was extremely dissatisfied to learn that Consort Qian and Consort Zhang were disturbing Prince Jing's recovery, so he had them added to the house arrest list, killing two birds with one stone by setting an example for the rest of the harem too. From then on, everyone started to avoid Jingtai Hall, and the surroundings quieted down considerably.

In the morning and evening, the imperial physician would come to Jingtai Hall to change Prince Jing's dressing and listen to his pulse. The first night, Prince Jing had a fever. When Li Yu woke up, he checked on Prince Jing out of habit—there was no one else around. Since he was in the porcelain fish tank again, it was difficult to see outside, so he swam to the edge of the tank, carefully placed his fins on it, and pushed himself up.

He saw Prince Jing lying down limply, as if he hadn't moved all night. Li Yu thought it was strange at first, and when he noticed Prince Jing's abnormally flushed face and short breaths, he knew that Prince Jing was running a fever. He immediately transformed into a human and rushed over to feel Prince Jing's forehead. It was very hot; the fever seemed to be quite high.

When the imperial physician was treating Prince Jing, he had mentioned that it was likely Prince Jing would get a fever, so cold water and handkerchiefs had been stocked in the room. Li Yu quickly dipped a handkerchief in the water and placed it on Prince Jing's forehead, then rushed out to find Wang Xi. Wang Xi was standing guard outside, so he came right away when Li Yu called for him. Upon seeing the situation, he immediately went to find the imperial physician, asking Li Yu to watch over Prince Jing.

...Obviously he would do his best, but he could only transform for two hours, so hopefully Wang-gonggong would be back by then!

In any case, he would just take care of Prince Jing for now.

Li Yu sat down next to Prince Jing, switching the handkerchief out when it warmed up too much. But Prince Jing was still burning up—he couldn't just continue like this. Li Yu thought back to the physical cooling methods he knew of from the modern world and decided to try one of them out. He undid Prince Jing's undershirt and wiped down several of his joints with warm water. It was quite effective, and the heat on Prince Jing's body soon receded.

But Li Yu himself was exhausted. The illusory events of the koi mission may not have been real, but the energy he'd used to save the chubby little boy was. After he exited the illusion and completed the mission, he still had to get up in the middle of the night to take care of a feverish Prince Jing...

Li Yu didn't want to complain. Deep down, he'd felt guilty that he couldn't help the chubby little boy with *his* fever, so he could make up for it now.

The imperial physician still hadn't arrived, but Li Yu had succeeded in lowering Prince Jing's fever. He covered Prince Jing with the quilt again and put a wet handkerchief on his forehead, afraid that the fever would come back.

The fish was too tired. He wanted to stay awake until he turned back into a fish so he could jump into the fish tank to sleep, but it was too difficult. Li Yu's eyelids were drooping, and before the transformation time was over, his body slowly slumped over.

Prince Jing was sleeping pretty deeply, and when he finally woke up, he felt weak, and his chest felt worryingly tight. The human-shaped fish was lying on his chest, fast asleep. Prince Jing thought he must be dreaming, and he was both confused and happy. He couldn't help himself—he softly touched Xiaoyu's face.

...He was real.

He didn't know what had happened, but since his fish was so defenseless, he found himself wanting to trap him. Prince Jing moved his injured hand without thinking, and the wound on his palm throbbed in pain. Maybe the wound had reopened, but it didn't seem to matter. He carelessly raised an eyebrow and used his other hand to pull the sleeping carp spirit into his arms.

Li Yu, who thought he was still a fish, squirmed and muttered, "Little Chubs, you're so heavy."

Little Chubs? Prince Jing was slightly upset. The fish was always under his watchful eye; where did this fat man come from to steal him away?! Prince Jing wanted to wake Xiaoyu and question him, but he'd only sat up a little bit when the handkerchief on his forehead slid off; the handkerchief had gotten warm, so he hadn't noticed it until now.

He held the wet handkerchief in his hand, Xiaoyu still sleeping soundly in his embrace. When he thought of how uncomfortable he felt when he woke up, he more or less understood what had happened. He must have had a fever, and Xiaoyu had been taking care of him until he'd fallen asleep from exhaustion. When he realized this, he was still a bit angry but felt reluctant to wake up his fish.

Who cared about some fat man? As long as he didn't let go, nobody could take Xiaoyu away.

Prince Jing was worried the carp spirit would catch a cold, so he tucked him under the covers and lay back down beside him. Xiaoyu snuggled into his shoulder sleepily, and Prince Jing suddenly realized what he'd done. He was sharing a bed with the carp spirit. Prince Jing's breath caught in his throat. Was it finally time for absorbing essence?

In the books, the snake spirits and fox spirits were always the ones to initiate, so Prince Jing could only wait. But this fish was an anomaly. No matter how long Prince Jing waited, he was still dead asleep.

Prince Jing's feelings were complicated. As if in revenge, he covered the carp spirit's mouth and nose. Li Yu whined and flailed a bit. Prince Jing let him go, and when Li Yu could breathe again, he settled back down. Prince Jing impulsively leaned in and kissed Xiaoyu's slightly parted lips.

Wang Xi jogged back to Jingtai Hall with the imperial physician in tow. Wang-gonggong wiped the sweat from his forehead and asked the imperial physician to wait. As always, he had to check the room before announcing a visitor. He peered in past the half-open door and saw no sign of Li-gongzi. He was a little surprised, but when he looked back at the bed, he froze. The two figures under the brocade quilt... Wang Xi knew immediately it was Prince Jing and Li-gongzi.

Wang Xi felt greatly conflicted.

His Highness had always been pure of heart and free of desire, so Wang Xi should have been happy for his master that something like this happened. But didn't His Highness have a fever? Why would they...at this time...

The imperial physician was already here; should he be announced or not? His Highness was finally enjoying himself, so if he ruined that, he'd be in huge trouble. But if he didn't announce the imperial physician, the still-sick Prince Jing and his weary body might not be able to handle it.

Wang Xi closed his eyes. Even if his master blamed him later, he had to do it! He knelt, and in a trembling voice, said, "Your Highness. The imperial physician is here."

As soon as Wang Xi spoke, the lips that Prince Jing had kissed several times suddenly disappeared out from under him. Prince Jing looked down. Xiaoyu had turned back into a fish in his arms.

He knew that Xiaoyu couldn't transform for very long, so he hadn't planned on doing anything else. But when he saw the black and gold fish on his chest, Prince Jing still paused for a moment, feeling like this scene was somehow familiar...

But he didn't have much time to think about it. He had to handle the fish first.

Prince Jing took out a jade bell from under his pillow and rang it.

Wang Xi let out a sigh of relief—His Highness was willing to see the imperial physician and asked him to wait outside. After all, with Li-gongzi there, he had to clean up first. He couldn't let the imperial physician in just like that. Wang Xi respectfully exited and closed the door for Prince Jing.

Once Wang Xi had left, Prince Jing stood up, fish in hand, already very experienced at carp spirit wrangling. He put the sleeping fish in the fish tank, wrapped him in the golden leaf blanket, and patted him on the head, slightly smiling. The fish, sleeping without a worry in the world, blew a bubble.

Finished, with nothing out of place, Prince Jing lay back down in his bed. He rang the jade bell again to let Wang Xi and the imperial physician in.

Wang Xi came in, his gaze wandering and his thoughts confused. His Highness was there—but where was Li-gongzi? There hadn't been much time, and he had been on guard outside. Where could Li-gongzi have gone? Prince Jing's gaze swept over to him, and Wang Xi immediately stopped his random guessing.

When Li Yu woke up, he was in the porcelain fish tank again. Recalling that he'd been so exhausted from taking care of a patient that he accidentally fell asleep, he was speechless. He'd been too careless. What if Prince Jing and Wang-gonggong found out? Thank goodness Prince Jing was asleep with a fever and hadn't seen him. He probably woke up in the fish tank because he'd turned into a fish next to Prince Jing's bed, and when Wang-gonggong returned and saw him, he must have put him back in the fish tank.

The imperial physician had already left, and Li Yu heard Wang Xi telling the other servants that Prince Jing's wound had opened again, but fortuitously, it was dealt with in time. There shouldn't be any serious issues if it was looked after carefully.

That was good. Li Yu's worries lightened considerably.

But... He kept shaking his head. Did his mouth get bitten by something? Why did it kind of hurt?

A Fish Follows
His Master

WHEN LI YU HEARD that the emperor had summoned Zen Master Liao Kong to the palace, he was perched on the edge of the porcelain fish tank, staring angrily at Prince Jing.

As soon as Prince Jing's injury improved, he started reading an old book on cultivation again, right in front of his fish. Li Yu didn't know what was wrong with him—how could the dignified male protagonist of a palace novel be interested in cultivation? And he was so focused when reading... Li Yu felt waves of danger crashing in his heart, afraid that Prince Jing would try to cultivate immortality when he wasn't watching.

Come what may, he'd deal with it. It wasn't the first time he'd interfered with Prince Jing's interest in cultivation! At first, he wanted to get Prince Jing's book wet as usual. He'd gotten many of them wet before, and Prince Jing had never blamed him, so he'd become fearless. But now, looking at the gauze on Prince Jing's hand, he hesitated. What if he got water on Prince Jing's wound when he jumped onto it? The imperial physician had reminded them countless times that the injury couldn't touch water. Li Yu didn't want his tyrant master to get worse and come down with another fever—that would make him exhausted all over again.

Maybe he could turn into a human and hide the book instead. Or tattle to Wang Xi? Wang Xi wouldn't want his master to cultivate, right?

Li Yu was just thinking of how to ruin Prince Jing's grand plan for cultivation when head eunuch Luo came to Jingtai Hall to convey a message from the emperor. Zen Master Liao Kong was here, and the emperor hoped Prince Jing would meet with him.

Head eunuch Luo whispered something into Prince Jing's ear, and Prince Jing glanced at Xiaoyu calmly before agreeing.

Meanwhile, Li Yu was a little panicked at the mention of Liao Kong's name. If his memory served him well, Zen Master Liao Kong was the head monk of Hugou Temple. In the novel, he was a monk with a transcendent status. When Prince Jing became a tyrant, Liao Kong had tried to persuade him to show more leniency. Though Prince Jing had already become quite the despot, he wasn't able to kill Liao Kong, which showed how powerful he really was.

But in the original novel, Liao Kong had only appeared to persuade Prince Jing. Why did he want to meet with Prince Jing now, when Prince Jing was fine?

Li Yu never considered his own role in all of this. Since Prince Jing had been reading a lot of books on cultivation...had he changed his mind about cultivation? Had he seen through the mortal world and decided to follow in Liao Kong's footsteps to become a monk? For a male protagonist of a palace novel who never played by the rules and wanted to cultivate all the time, it was totally possible!

Noticing that Prince Jing was about to go to Qianqing Palace, Li Yu jumped out of the fish tank and into the crystal bottle. He wanted to go too! Li Yu secretly decided that if Prince Jing mentioned becoming a monk to Liao Kong, then he would cause trouble in Qianqing Palace and ruin those plans!

Prince Jing wasn't planning on leaving him behind. As he put Xiaoyu into the crystal bottle, though, he felt that his fish somehow seemed to have a murderous aura today...

When Prince Jing arrived at Qianqing Palace, the emperor and Liao Kong had just finished with some small talk. Prince Jing greeted the emperor, and Liao Kong stepped forward and nodded slightly to him.

The crystal bottle was in Prince Jing's sleeve, so Li Yu peeked out. Liao Kong was at least seventy, his beard and hair completely white, but he was still energetic and healthy—very different from the sixth prince's fake monks. It was immediately clear that this was an advanced and eminent monk.

Li Yu only looked for a moment, but somehow, Liao Kong's fiery gaze turned toward him. Damn. This was a truly powerful monk; would he be able to tell that he was a transmigrated fish? Li Yu was shocked and didn't dare peek out again.

Prince Jing covered his sleeves instinctively, blocking Liao Kong's line of sight.

"Your Highness Prince Jing," Liao Kong said, smiling. "Long time no see."

Prince Jing frowned and nodded.

The emperor was quite excited; Liao Kong's arrival brought back memories for him. The emperor rubbed his hands together and said, "Tianchi, do you remember Liao Kong? You fell into the water when you were a child and you were in danger, as your fever wouldn't go down. The imperial physicians were helpless, and Liao Kong just so happened to be in the palace at the time. I didn't know what to do, so I asked Liao Kong to come see you. Thankfully, he knew an old method that could reduce fever. He also told me that you would be lacking water in your life, so I changed your name and prayed.

After that, your condition took a turn for the better and you made a full recovery."

Clearly emotional, the emperor added, "They say that those who survive a disaster will be met with good fortune in the future. I still remember the pond you fell into—at the time, it was glimmering with a dazzling golden light. Because of what Liao Kong said, I chose the name 'chi' for you."[4]

It was the first time Prince Jing had heard the emperor talk of such things. All he knew was that before he turned three, his name was Tianjing, and afterward, it was Tianchi. When he was given a title as an adult, the emperor gave him the word "Jing," returning his name to him. But he barely remembered his fever that year, much less the reason behind it.

Since he couldn't sneak any more peeks, Li Yu had opted to listen instead. He was stunned. Could it be that the illusion wasn't just an illusion but something that had happened to Prince Jing in the past? From what the emperor was saying, it seemed the plump little prince really did fall into the water and came out of it with a persistent high fever.

But in the illusion, Li Yu was there. In reality, Prince Jing had not been as lucky and probably had to drift to shore himself. Picturing the boy's round body floating alone, Li Yu found it quite tragic. At the time, it must have been very dangerous. If even the imperial physicians were helpless against such a high fever...it had to have been a life-threatening situation for a toddler. The emperor asked for a monk instead of a physician and changed his name in the hopes of changing his fate. Desperate times called for desperate measures...

---

4   The "chi" in Mu Tianchi is 池, meaning a pool or pond.

Li Yu hadn't yet realized what the golden light the emperor mentioned was. How could there be a light in a pond? It was probably reflected from something else.

Anyway, he had guessed right: Prince Jing's name used to be Tianjing. It was fortunate that Liao Kong had been around to prompt the emperor, Li Yu suddenly thought. If the emperor had gotten too creative, Prince Jing might have been called Tianguang or Tianjin—neither of which sounded as nice as Tianchi.[5]

Though Prince Jing didn't remember what happened back then, he still bowed to Liao Kong in thanks at the emperor's reminder.

Liao Kong modestly said, "It was but a slight effort. The Heavens help the worthy, Prince Jing."

"Great Master, please don't be humble." After a bout of pleasantries, the emperor finally got to the main subject. "I must trouble you to take another look today. Prince Jing has been raising a fish recently, and I think it's quite good."

Oh...Li Yu finally realized that Prince Jing didn't want to become a monk. The emperor wanted Prince Jing to meet Liao Kong because of his fish. The little carp was a bit troubled. He wasn't afraid of most people, but would an eminent monk like Liao Kong be able to tell that he was a transmigrating fish? Li Yu decided to hide as much as he could. He would try to look like a normal carp for eating and not cause trouble in front of Liao Kong.

Since the emperor had commanded it, Prince Jing calmly took the crystal bottle out of his sleeve and opened the lid in front of the emperor and Liao Kong. As soon as Liao Kong saw the black and gold fish in the crystal bottle, he became contemplative.

---

5   The "guang" in Tianguang (天光) means "light," and the "jin" in Tianjin (天金) means "gold." The positive connotations of these potential names are very on the nose—Li Yu probably thinks they would be tacky.

Under his gaze, the little carp was very obedient and barely swam. Prince Jing, afraid that the little carp was nervous in front of a stranger, lightly touched his fish's back with his uninjured left hand. Li Yu pretended he didn't feel it and wasn't cooperative at all. He coldly blew a bubble. Prince Jing really wasn't sure what to make of this.

Liao Kong witnessed every interaction between Prince Jing and his fish. He was silent for a moment before saying to the emperor, "Prince Jing's fish does seem quite extraordinary to me."

There was a pause, and before he could continue speaking, Liao Kong suddenly felt two burning gazes—one from the cold-faced Prince Jing and another from the little carp in Prince Jing's hand that was trying to act dumb. Pets really did take after their owners. Liao Kong smiled privately and said, "I've never encountered such a thing in my life. This fish..."

He stopped purposefully to create suspense, and, as expected, Prince Jing's gaze nearly bore holes into him. Liao Kong was over seventy, though. When he felt a chill on his neck, he chuckled and said, "This fish is the descendant of a koi. He doesn't look like one now, but he will as time passes."

Li Yu was dumbfounded. He didn't think a monk would have such good insight. He couldn't say that Liao Kong didn't see through him; how else could he know that he would look more like a koi in the future? But he couldn't say that Liao Kong had exposed him; otherwise, why would he not lay the truth bare?

Prince Jing gave Liao Kong a cold glance. As long as he didn't say Xiaoyu was a monster or would turn into a dragon, it was all the same to him.

The emperor hesitated before asking, "This fish really is a koi?"

Liao Kong nodded. "Yes," he said solemnly. "This type of koi is very rare. His Highness was very lucky to chance upon it."

The emperor trusted Liao Kong, and his words were consistent with what the Imperial Astrological Bureau had said. The emperor felt a burden lifted off his shoulders, and he smiled, saying, "No wonder I thought it was auspicious. Turns out it is at least part koi."

The third prince had even tried to frame a koi! The emperor was even more disdainful of him than he had been already.

Li Yu still tried his hardest to look like an ordinary carp, silently observing the emperor and Liao Kong's movements. Liao Kong had paused between his words, really giving off the air of a great monk, and he'd scared Li Yu several times. But in the end, he announced to the emperor that Li Yu was actually a koi. In the future, it shouldn't matter how much he changed, right?

Liao Kong looked scary to the fish, but he'd helped him in the end. Luckily, somehow without even trying, Li Yu had managed to get the approval of both the emperor and Prince Jing. Soon, he could accept the reward from the koi mission.

The emperor chatted happily with Liao Kong, while Prince Jing listened quietly. When Liao Kong left, the emperor ordered Prince Jing to see him off.

Surprisingly, Prince Jing didn't take the little carp with him this time and instead asked Wang Xi to take the crystal bottle back to his room first. He still had questions he needed to ask Liao Kong, and he didn't want the carp spirit to know.

Once they were alone, Prince Jing bowed deeply.

Liao Kong chuckled. "Thank you for trusting me, Your Highness. I hope I did not disappoint you."

Prince Jing looked up at Liao Kong and smiled. When Prince Jing had found out about Mu Tianxiao's plan to make up a rumor about "turning into a dragon," he'd predicted that things might get out of hand. The longer such rumors went on, the worse it would be.

The only solution was to stop the rumors quickly and thoroughly by finding someone who could convince the emperor and completely overturn the rumor.

But at first, Prince Jing wasn't sure who he should ask.

The emperor trusted Director Sun of the Imperial Astrological Bureau, but it was hard to guarantee that the emperor wouldn't be confused and swayed by the rumors. He couldn't rely solely on Director Sun. Prince Jing then thought of Zen Master Liao Kong from Hugou Temple. The imperial family had established the temple, and the emperor trusted Liao Kong's character. If he had any more doubts, he would definitely ask Liao Kong, so the prince might as well directly ask Liao Kong to help.

Everyone knew that Liao Kong was indifferent to worldly affairs and only took orders from the emperor, but they didn't know that Liao Kong had a deep, secret friendship with the former Duke of Cheng'en, Prince Jing's grandfather. Even though the emperor was the only one who could officially use him, Liao Kong would still run around for his best friend.

When Liao Kong responded to the emperor's request to help the fifth prince and his fever, it was partially for the Duke of Cheng'en's sake too. Prince Jing had known about this early on, and, with the former Duke of Cheng'en's assistance, he was able to ask Liao Kong for help this time. Prince Jing had made preparations with Liao Kong early on, and what had happened in front of the emperor just now was only a show to make the emperor's doubts dissipate.

There was no one else around, so Liao Kong kept praising him. "With such a mind, Your Highness, you have a bright future."

Prince Jing thought he was teasing, so he lowered his eyes and clasped his hands politely.

The conversation that followed was more secretive. Prince Jing took out paper and a brush from his sleeve that he had prepared beforehand and handed it to Liao Kong. The monk picked up the brush and wrote, *Your Highness, are you not afraid something will happen if you take him around with you?*

Liao Kong didn't say who "him" was, but they both knew.

Prince Jing wrote without thinking, *He wouldn't hurt me.*

Liao Kong nodded. He could tell that Prince Jing's carp wasn't an ordinary carp, but he sensed it was not evil or malicious. If he had, he wouldn't have agreed to do this for Prince Jing to cover up for the fish. "Your Highness, your heart is as clear and bright as a mirror," he said. "Is there anything else you need me to clarify?"

Prince Jing wrote, *Great Master, do you know why he came?*

Liao Kong took a long, thoughtful look at Prince Jing. "I may not be able to help with much else, but I do know a little about this. The day you fell into the water many years ago, I happened to be in the palace and had seen a black and gold fish swimming by in the pond you fell into."

What! Prince Jing's gaze swam with emotion, and his hands couldn't stop trembling. He wrote something in a hurry, then crossed it out. When he was finally able to calm down, he wrote, *What did the fish look like?*

Liao Kong said, "The same as your fish right now. It was completely black, except for golden scales on its belly and tail—only it was slightly bigger."

Prince Jing was silent. The size of the fish wasn't an issue; he'd seen Xiaoyu grow larger not long ago. The fish Liao Kong saw must have been Xiaoyu. Had Xiaoyu come to see him when he was younger?

Liao Kong went on, "The pond you fell into was extremely deep—it would have been impossible for a toddler to swim out on his own. Do you understand what I mean, Your Highness? Let me put it this way." Liao Kong smiled. "I don't know what 'he' is, but 'he' must have come for you."

Come for me?

Prince Jing was deeply moved. He suddenly remembered the familiar scene of Xiaoyu laying on his chest when he turned back into a fish, as well as the first time they met, when he'd picked up the fish on the brink of death that the cat had thrown away.

What was he thinking back then? Why did he stop for a fish?

Because he had heard something hitting the floor.

And it was...the sound of a fish's tail slapping the ground. He didn't know how he knew, but it seemed to have been etched into his memory. The sound of a fish's tail meant the fish was still alive. When the sound stopped, it meant the fish was about to die.

So, without thinking, he went to save the fish.

Prince Jing couldn't help but chuckle. He didn't remember the incident from the past, but the instinct left in him was probably a remnant of that time.

Fish Turning into a Koi

EVER SINCE LI YU was given the "koi" stamp by Zen
Master Liao Kong right in front of the emperor, he was
no longer an ordinary carp for eating. He'd completed
the koi mission, and the reward was waving at him, but Li Yu
still resisted the temptation. Though he was now part of the koi
family, he couldn't change so quickly in front of the emperor and
Liao Kong. It wasn't until a few days after he'd returned to the
manor with Prince Jing, once Prince Jing recovered from his injury,
that Li Yu figured that he wouldn't draw too much attention.
He picked a sunny day and sneakily entered the system to accept
the reward.

He'd asked the system before if the reward would change his
appearance this time too. Li Yu looked expectantly at the reward
and found that it was mainly divided into two categories. One was
the color of his scales: he could choose from gold, red, green, silver,
or purple. The other was a koi's good luck. The system was stingy
and wouldn't increase his good luck for every stat but was willing to
increase it for three random statistics.

It was all right, Li Yu thought. He was skilled at comforting himself by now. Increased luck for three stats was better than nothing,
right?

Since the reward was random and he couldn't choose the stats, he chose the color of his scales first. He'd chosen gold before, but the golden scales had just grown on top of his original inky-black base. Li Yu assumed that it would be like that this time too, so he thought about what color to choose for a long time. In the end, he chose silver, wanting to look like a cool koi.

After he made his selection, his body didn't change while he was still in the system. Li Yu assumed that it would only take effect after he left the system, just like last time. He wasn't really in a hurry, so he went to check the increase in luck. Since he accepted the reward, the stats had gone up, and the fish-scamming system had listed the stats that were chosen.

1. Slapping villains in the face, Luck +10
2. Well-fed and well-clothed, Luck +10
3. One-shot-and-done, Luck +20

What?

He could understand the first two stats fine, but something weird seemed to have been mixed in, and it had been increased a lot for some reason.

‹Excuse me, what does one-shot-and-done mean?›

‹It's a skill needed for special missions,› said the system mysteriously. *‹The higher the stat, the easier it is to complete the mission.›*

‹Why does it sound a little off... I guess since it helps with finishing quests, I'll accept it. I'll find out what it is when I use it.›

Li Yu accepted the reward and exited the system. He immediately looked at his tail in excitement, trying to see if he'd grown silver scales yet. With just one glance, he was shocked. His fish tail, which used to be black with a streak of gold, had turned silver with a streak of gold.

What had happened to the cool mix of colors he was expecting?!

Li Yu gulped. Was the color change this time not to add scales to his already-existing colors but to completely change his main color?

He immediately jumped out of the fish tank, used his tail as a skateboard, and rode it to the bronze mirror in Prince Jing's room.

A silver fish slid into frame and faced him in the mirror. From a distance, its silver scales shone like pearls, and its belly and tail still had gold streaks in it. Li Yu took a deep breath. He...he'd turned from a black fish into a silver fish!

And it wasn't just his new color. He'd become larger and more robust again, growing more and more like a koi. As expected for the rewards of the "becoming a koi" mission. Now he definitely looked like one.

This change was a lot more dramatic compared to the time he started growing golden scales. Even if Liao Kong wanted to cover for him now, he didn't know if Prince Jing would be able to help him out.

But when he thought about it, black wasn't an option among the choices given. That meant he was never destined to have a normal base color.

Li Yu was a bit worried about how Prince Jing would react. Would Prince Jing be able to accept it if his little black fish disappeared and was replaced with a large silver fish? He didn't dare swim around after his change, so he entered his cave and only left his mouth out in the open. He thought he would slowly reveal himself when Prince Jing came to him.

That way, it wouldn't be too shocking, right?

During this time, Wang-gonggong came over to feed him. It was the first time he'd ever seen Li Yu fail to swim around excitedly when he saw his favorite foods. Wang Xi thought it was a bit strange, but he didn't question it and used a jade ruyi[6] to move the food to the mouth of the cave, making it easier for the fish to eat it. Li Yu was hungry, so he appreciated this. Wang Xi saw the fish mouth flash a bit, and the fish food instantly disappeared. Wang Xi dazedly thought that the fish head seemed to be glowing.

Unable to make heads or tails of it, Wang Xi walked away.

When Prince Jing came over, he noticed that Xiaoyu had been in the cave for a long time. The usually lively carp wasn't moving at all—something was fishy. Prince Jing reached a hand in to pull him out. But even though he managed to get a hold of the fish, Prince Jing wasn't able to remove him.

Li Yu sobbed. *I'm stuck again...*

His fish had been stuck before, so Prince Jing guessed that the carp spirit must have had another growth spurt. He immediately ordered his servants to move the ornamental mountain and save the fish trapped inside. When the ornamental mountain was moved out of the way, a fish with glittering silver scales and a pitiful gaze swam out.

Prince Jing stared at him.

Li Yu was afraid his tyrant master didn't recognize him, so he blew some friendly bubbles and curled the tip of his newly silver tail around Prince Jing's finger. Prince Jing could see that his fish's color had changed a lot. Even if he was mentally prepared for this eventuality, he still needed time to process it. Li Yu was left with no other choice. He flipped over to show the golden scales on his stomach. He really was the same fish! It was just that his base color changed.

Prince Jing finally recovered from the shock and raised his hand, hesitating, then poked the fish's belly.

---

6   A ruyi (如意) is a decorative Chinese scepter. Its name means "as you desire" and is a symbol of good fortune.

Ack, this was to help you recognize me! Not for you to poke!

The silver fish turned back over under his hand, and Prince Jing stroked the smooth back of his fish again. Though the black had changed to silver, it still felt the same, and the fish's reactions were the same as well. It was definitely Xiaoyu.

The little carp spun around in the water twice. Seeing that his tyrant master had started petting him again, Li Yu let out a small sigh of relief—but at the same time, his suspicions increased. How come Prince Jing accepted it so quickly? It was just like last time, when he grew golden scales and got bigger... Wasn't Prince Jing a bit too calm as a fish owner?

He couldn't think of a better description than "calm." Maybe this was also part of the protagonist's halo? If Prince Jing gaped in surprise like Ye-shizi would, his image would be a little ruined.

Prince Jing picked the fish up without hesitation and measured him against his arm. His fish had indeed grown larger. Xiaoyu was as long as his forearm now.

At first, he was a palm-sized little black fish. Then he was a black and gold fish as large as two fists. Now, he was a silver and gold fish as long as his forearm.

What was going to happen in the future?

Prince Jing realized that his fish always exceeded his expectations, so he was quite looking forward to it.

Since his fish had suddenly grown again, the current tea bowls and fish tanks were no longer usable. Prince Jing took his fish and walked outside to put him in the large pond right outside the room while he ordered people to quickly bring out larger tea bowls.

Prince Jing had thought of this problem the last time his fish got bigger—he was a very farsighted person. When he was choosing new tea bowls last time, he acquired even larger ones as well, and all they had to do now was retrieve them. Li Yu soon received a red lotus tea bowl that fit his new body.

At the same time, Prince Jing warned everyone in the manor, including Wang Xi, that Xiaoyu was going to keep changing. Now that Xiaoyu was confirmed to be a koi—with Liao Kong's guarantee as well as the emperor's orders—no matter how much he changed in the future, it would just seem like his natural koi transformation.

One good thing that came out of this change was being able to confirm what Liao Kong said. Prince Jing weighed the pros and cons and three days after the fish changed to a silver koi, he finally wrote to the emperor about it, slightly editing the sequence of events. He obviously couldn't say that Xiaoyu had immediately completely changed color, so he maintained the excuse that Xiaoyu was still growing new scales. It was more believable, anyway.

While Prince Jing was working hard to cover up for his fish, Xiaoyu didn't have very many worries after Prince Jing readily accepted him. His tyrant master always protected him well, and he had an inexplicable confidence in him. With the koi mission completed, he had to start focusing on the "Revitalizing the Family" mission. But this main quest was still stuck on the first step, the "Indulge" quest.

To do that, he suspected that he needed some wine. One day, after his major koi transformation, Li Yu changed into a human when Prince Jing wasn't around. Remembering that Prince Jing liked to read cultivation books recently, the first thing he did was hide those books so they couldn't be easily found. Then he sought out Wang Xi to settle the wine matter as soon as possible.

"Wang-gonggong, may I ask where the wine is?" Li Yu politely asked once he located him.

He had a gift box in his hand; when asking for a favor, it was necessary to prepare something to show thanks, especially in ancient times. Li Yu didn't know what he could give as a gift—most of his belongings came from Prince Jing, so he couldn't give those away. After much thought, he packed up a couple of pieces of his favorite desserts and put them in a box, using a red ribbon to tie it prettily. Wang Xi smiled at him, and Li Yu shoved the box over.

Today, he was wearing a pearl-white robe. The collar and hem were embroidered with seemingly endless golden water ripples, and the cuffs were encircled with small jade beads, each the size of a rice grain. The belt was made of a loose, colorful fabric, and he wore silver-patterned white boots. Prince Jing would occasionally give him "old" clothes, and this outfit in particular was very similar to his current fish body. Shortly after he'd received it, it became his new favorite, and he wore it everywhere to show it off.

Li-gongzi obviously didn't know much about the clothes he was wearing, but Wang Xi knew all about it. He'd ordered these clothes overnight from the best tailor in the imperial city according to Prince Jing's wishes and gave them to Prince Jing after they were cleaned. For some asinine reason, His Highness would always call those new clothes "old clothes" and give them to Li-gongzi, and Li-gongzi didn't even notice. But every time Li-gongzi put on a new set of clothes, His Highness would hide and watch for a long time.

Wang Xi could tell that His Highness cared a lot about Li-gongzi, even though the way he showed it was strange. Even Wang Xi couldn't help but want to smile when he looked at the young man in white. Li-gongzi rarely came out of the room and didn't interact with others much, but he was always polite and didn't put on airs.

Wang-gonggong weighed the gift in his hand. It wasn't strange that His Highness would like such an endearing boy.

"Why are you asking me about wine?" Wang Xi asked, smiling. "Do you want to drink some?"

Li Yu nodded. His real goal was to finish the mission, and drinking wine was just a way to get there, but it wasn't wrong to say that he wanted to drink.

"His Highness has ordered that we are to get you anything you want. Please come with me, gongzi." Wang Xi held the gift box and brought Li Yu to the wine cellar.

Li Yu's eyes widened as he stared at the rows of wine jars in Prince Jing's manor. "That many?"

Wang Xi smiled. "There's wine from other manors and from the palace. What kind do you want? Do you know its name?"

Li Yu blinked. He wanted one that would allow him to complete his mission immediately.

Struggling, he said, "I don't know. Apart from green plum wine, are there any other kinds that aren't so easy to get drunk off of?"

"There is. There's one called Amber Light, made from grapes. Even women and children can drink it safely." Wang Xi patiently introduced it to Li Yu and chose a small jar of "Amber Light" for him.

Li Yu left excitedly, carrying the wine jar. Wang Xi was loyal to Prince Jing and immediately reported it to him.

Xiaoyu wanted some wine? Unsurprisingly, Prince Jing was worried. To his knowledge, the carp spirit's alcohol tolerance was quite low. To prevent his fish from transforming randomly when he was drunk, Prince Jing decided to stay with him. Wang Xi volunteered to lead Prince Jing to find Li-gongzi. After taking a few steps, Prince Jing noticed the gift box in Wang Xi's hand. His expression said he clearly wanted to know what it was.

Ten minutes later, Prince Jing expressionlessly put away the handmade gift box from Xiaoyu. Wang-gonggong held the money that His Highness had given him in exchange, feeling both ashamed and amused.

Fishy Smashed Cucumber

L I YU GOT THE WINE he wanted. The fish-scamming system's missions usually just had scary titles, and he could complete them on his own with no problems, so clearly they weren't actually too hard. "Indulging" could mean indulging in a drink; he didn't have to overthink it. He suspected that he only needed Prince Jing to drink a sip.

Considering his tyrant master's injury had just closed up, and one shouldn't drink too much when injured, Li Yu had no plans to get him drunk. He opened the jar of wine that Wang Xi had given him, took out just half a cup of the fragrant wine, and poured it into another clean jade container. He then added several cups of cooled tea, and after he mixed them together, the scent of wine was nearly imperceptible. This way, he could complete the mission easily without getting him drunk, and it wouldn't affect Prince Jing's injury.

He was probably the best in the world at completing missions.

Li Yu happily put away the mixed wine, but an important question arose after his preparations. How was he going to get Prince Jing to drink this diluted wine?

Prince Jing was a prince. Usually, a servant would test all his food with a silver needle and taste some in front of him. If the wine Li Yu had tampered with was tested first, it would be discovered before

Prince Jing could drink it. A servant would definitely not serve such wine to his master.

So he had to take charge of pouring the wine in front of Prince Jing and tasting it himself. Prince Jing seemed to trust him a lot—he even ate the snacks Li Yu gave him when he was injured. Li Yu thought it should work. But that meant he had to use his human form to complete the quest... Well, he supposed it was fine either way. The system had never specified whether he had to use his fish form or human form. He couldn't drink wine as a fish, even if it was diluted wine, so it was easiest to use his human body.

He had to invite Prince Jing over first. In order to drink wine, the excuse he would use was...to invite him to dinner?!

That was the only excuse Li Yu could think of at the moment. He had lived at Prince Jing's manor for a while now, and whether he was a fish or human, Prince Jing had always taken good care of him. It was reasonable for him to want to repay Prince Jing with dinner.

In the end, after an internal debate, it seemed the key was to invite Prince Jing to dinner. Li Yu suddenly remembered that the fish-scamming system had added luck points to his "Well-fed and well-clothed" stat. Did that mean he'd suddenly become an excellent cook? Why not use this chance to try it out? Li Yu rubbed his hands, feeling like the God of Cooking had possessed him.

Deciding that he still had enough time left in his human form, and that he didn't need to cook anything too complicated the first time, he decided a simple, home-cooked meal would be fine...

Li Yu ducked into the manor's kitchen. Prince Jing normally didn't keep him from going anywhere, but as Li Yu was afraid that he would run out of time in his human form, he hardly ever wandered around. He'd only come out a couple of times, but despite this, a lot of people in the manor already knew him. Among them were the kitchen staff who would make Li Yu's favorite food. When the kitchen servants saw him, they were surprised but welcoming. Everyone knew how much His Highness valued Li-gongzi, after all.

Li Yu had no intention of troubling them at first and asked them to continue with their work after saying hello. Auntie Xu, who had helped him before, was in the kitchen as well. Li Yu asked her for help, afraid that he wasn't familiar with the rules here.

Auntie Xu had been beaten as punishment because of Li Yu before. At the time, Prince Jing hadn't gotten to know Li Yu and still thought he was a fish thief. Auntie Xu was punished as a result, and Li Yu still felt extremely guilty. Once he was able to move freely around in the manor, he'd found her in person and apologized directly.

Auntie Xu knew that it was all a misunderstanding and was quite open-minded. She did violate the rules of the manor, so the punishment couldn't be considered unfair. She'd never held a grudge and didn't blame Li Yu. Later on, when Prince Jing realized the truth, he increased her monthly wage as compensation, and Auntie Xu said that it was a blessing in disguise.

Li Yu mentioned that he wanted to personally make a dish for Prince Jing. Auntie Xu stopped the work she was doing, and Li Yu decided on an easy cucumber and egg dish. Cucumbers and eggs were both available in the kitchen, and it was hard to mess it up. Auntie Xu helped him wash the cucumbers, beat the eggs, and told him where different condiments were kept. It was said that a nobleman stays far from the kitchen; for a man as noble as Li-gongzi to want to cook, he must be confident in his skills. Auntie Xu felt like she would be able to witness something novel today.

And she did witness something novel, but not because of any great talent...it was because Li-gongzi really wasn't cut out for cooking. In all the years Auntie Xu had been working in the kitchen, she'd never seen a newbie like him. It was just stir-frying eggs and cucumber together—how hard could it be? But Li Yu ended up somehow wreaking chaos on the entire kitchen.

Li Yu thought he was a cooking god before he stepped into the kitchen, but instead he was scrambling for his life the moment the oil began to sizzle in the wok.

He was frustrated and disappointed. He knew that the system liked to scam fish, so why couldn't he remember that? What 'koi's good luck'? He didn't feel it at all. The spatula felt strange in his hand any way he held it, and after he once again burned the eggs Auntie Xu had already beaten for him, there were no more eggs in the kitchen. There wasn't any time for someone to get more either. Li Yu finally learned a painful lesson: that some skills could not come from nothing with just luck.

But he'd already decided he was going to cook for Prince Jing, and he still had to complete his quest. Li Yu thought about it helplessly. Since there were no more eggs, why didn't he go for something easier? Instead of cucumber and egg, why not just smash a couple cucumbers and make cucumber salad? He should know how to do that, at least.

Li Yu pressed the back of the knife against the juicy cucumber and whacked it fearlessly. There were no big problems this time, but the cucumber shapes that resulted were extremely inconsistent. Li Yu, acting entirely on instinct, haphazardly dumped a few tablespoons of soy sauce and vinegar over it, making Auntie Xu very nervous.

The chefs of the palace had standards for not only the taste of the dish, but its appearance as well, in the hopes of impressing their masters. It would probably be very difficult for His Highness to enjoy Li Yu's cucumbers.

"Gongzi...why don't you make soup? How about fish soup?" Auntie Xu carefully suggested, watching Li Yu's expression. She really wanted to help him; it was clear that Li-gongzi wasn't good at cooking, so making fish soup would be better. She could handle preparing the fish, and Li-gongzi only had to put it in the pot to cook it. His Highness had also not had fish soup for a long time, so even if it didn't taste good, it wouldn't be a huge deal.

Auntie Xu had good intentions. Already stressed out, Li Yu was shocked by the words "fish soup."

Sob sob sob! It wasn't a bad idea, but he was a fish! How could he make other fish into soup?!

Li Yu politely declined. He was determined to finish the dish he'd said he would finish, even if he had to do it on his knees.

He didn't have much time left in human form, and he still needed to complete his mission. Li Yu took the plate of small cucumbers he ended up with and went to offer his treasure to Prince Jing. Auntie Xu was left to clean up his mess in the kitchen. The parts of the kitchen that Li-gongzi had used looked like the aftermath of a plague of locusts, and Auntie Xu wasn't sure what to say.

Meanwhile, Prince Jing had heard from Wang Xi early on and rushed over to find Xiaoyu, but he wasn't there. The jar of wine that Wang Xi had given Xiaoyu was hidden away, as if he had no intention of drinking it with Prince Jing.

What on earth was going on?

The carp spirit had tucked the wine jar under the bed, with a large, obvious bowl covering it as if to hide it. The fish was away, so Prince Jing secretly took it out to check and found that the wine was practically untouched. Next to the wine jar was another bottle of extremely diluted wine.

Prince Jing couldn't work out what the fish wanted to do. He had to put the wine jar and wine bottle back in their original spots so the fish wouldn't notice.

It was surprising that Li Yu wasn't in the room. Prince Jing let him roam around as he pleased in the manor, but when he left the room, he would have someone keep an eye on him in case of an emergency. Soon, a guard reported that Li-gongzi was in the kitchen, saying he was going to cook for Prince Jing.

Prince Jing was pleased—even if the wine wasn't for him, Xiaoyu still cared about him. He was afraid that Xiaoyu would encounter some sort of danger in the kitchen, such as turning back into a fish, so Prince Jing rushed there to keep an eye on him. While Li Yu was sweating buckets trying to conquer the pots and pans, Prince Jing was right outside the door. The servants all knelt on the floor, keeping him company as he quietly watched the young man bustling around inside. His fish was working so hard here just for him... It was impossible for Prince Jing to calm the warm ripples that spread across his heart.

Li Yu rushed back to the room, carrying his smashed cucumbers. To his surprise, Prince Jing was already sitting casually in the room, as if nothing was going on??? Li Yu smiled nervously. "Your Highness, are you free? I'd like to have a meal with you."

He was afraid that Prince Jing would refuse him. There wasn't much time left in his transformation, so if he declined, then he would have to wait until next time—and he'd have to smash the cucumbers all over again too. He was extremely nervous, but Prince Jing nodded without hesitation.

Sure.

Oh!

"Your Highness, please wait a moment. It'll be ready soon!"

Overjoyed, Li Yu quickly put down the cucumber salad. His "meal" was actually just one dish. It really was a bit of a sad sight.

This was where the wine would come into play.

Li Yu took the wine bottle out from beneath the bed and smiled sheepishly at Prince Jing. "Your Highness, it's not enough to just eat. Let's...pair it with some wine. This wine is very light, so it's not a problem!"

So, the wine was for him after all. Prince Jing smiled, showing that he didn't mind in the least. Li Yu had been waiting for this moment. He found two wine cups and filled them up with the mixed wine, then worked up the courage to take a sip.

Everything was in place. As expected, Prince Jing would drink the wine first and then eat the dish, and his "Indulge" mission would be completed! Li Yu's burning gaze followed Prince Jing's slender fingers as he held the wine cup. A moment later, he put the cup down and picked up a soft cucumber with his silver chopsticks.

...Yeah, he could eat the cucumber first too!

Li Yu sat there and waited for Prince Jing to take a bite of the cucumber.

And then kept waiting for a response...

"How is it? What do you think, Your Highness?" Li Yu nervously prompted. Apart from completing his mission, he also wanted to know if the cucumbers he smashed were tasty or not.

Prince Jing's expression didn't change. He swallowed the alarmingly seasoned cucumber and picked up another piece. Li Yu excitedly thought, was the system not scamming him? Was he actually a charmed koi in the world of chefs?

Prince Jing finished Xiaoyu's salad, lifted the wine cup, and took a sip of the diluted wine.

Li Yu waited nervously for the system's notifications, but time passed, and even when Prince Jing was almost finished with the cup of wine, the mission had still not been updated. Li Yu's clever plan seemed to have somehow failed. Why didn't it work? He pouted in frustration. If this didn't work, then how was he going to complete the mission?

Li Yu was dejected for a bit but soon realized that Prince Jing, who was sitting across from him and drinking wine, had been silent for a while. When he looked up, Prince Jing had his hand on his forehead and his eyes closed.

What? No way. Was the tyrant drunk on just the diluted wine? Wasn't this the man who drank several cups of green plum wine in a row? But he'd heard that alcohol tolerance was unreliable and possibly dependent on mood and the body. Perhaps Prince Jing actually couldn't hold his liquor that well.

If he fell asleep while drunk like this, he would catch a cold. Li Yu was quite responsible when it came to taking care of Prince Jing; he took the initiative to put Prince Jing's arm on his shoulder and lift him upward. He meant to help him to the bed, but Prince Jing was much taller than him, and it was difficult to support him with just his shoulder. Li Yu finally put him down and put a quilt over him, getting ready to leave, when suddenly his sleeves pulled and held him back—

Maybe his sleeves had been accidentally caught under Prince Jing when he put him down, or maybe he tripped a little. Either way, he was yanked back somehow.

Li Yu fell onto Prince Jing. He blinked, somewhat confused at what was happening.

Then he saw the person underneath him open his eyes.

A Fishy Falling Out

L I YU'S EYES MET the black ones below his, and he immediately tried to get back up.

"I'm sorry, Your Highness, I accidentally fell!" he quickly explained in a hushed voice. He'd reacted pretty quickly, and he probably didn't fall onto Prince Jing very hard. Hopefully if he apologized, Prince Jing wouldn't blame him.

But Prince Jing wasn't a petty person, and in either fish form or human form, Li Yu had bothered and teased him before. Li Yu was quite sure that Prince Jing wouldn't be angry at him...but Prince Jing didn't do anything to suggest forgiveness either. He just kept staring at him with his dark eyes. Being stared at for so long, Li Yu's fish intuition told him something was wrong.

He was about to get up in a panic, but the person under him was faster than he was. Prince Jing folded him into his arms. Li Yu's face was thus pressed against Prince Jing's chest. Prince Jing wasn't satisfied with just this; he held Li Yu's waist with his other hand, as if afraid he would run away.

What was he doing? The warmth of the hand on his waist made Li Yu a little uncomfortable, and Prince Jing was still staring at him, even though they were so close. It was giving him goosebumps. Although he couldn't read Prince Jing's thoughts with just a glance like Wang Xi could, between his understanding of the novel and his interactions with Prince Jing, as both a fish and a human, Li Yu could usually figure out a thing or two.

...But not in absurd moments like these.

With some difficulty, Li Yu asked, "Your Highness, wh-what are you doing?"

His Highness wanted to do you, of course. Prince Jing hugged Li Yu and tucked a loose strand of his fish's hair behind his ear as he thought about how to make the person in his arms understand what he meant. It was inconvenient that he couldn't speak, but if he let him go during such a good opportunity to look for a brush and paper, it would kill the mood, and the carp spirit might not let him hold him again.

Prince Jing had noticed that the fish hadn't come to absorb essence in a long time. He was concerned that the fish had gotten enough from him and intended to switch to someone else—for example, a certain Little Chubs whom the carp spirit couldn't forget. Prince Jing had ordered Wang Xi to look into it but still hadn't figured out who it was.

Everyone in the manor liked the carp spirit. Prince Jing was pleased, but he also felt like other people were coveting his treasure. Such conflicting emotions left him feeling dissatisfied. It wasn't enough that the carp spirit was part of his household. He had to personally claim the carp.

This fish had come for *him*, and he was his, not to be coveted by others.

The carp spirit apparently still had no intention of revealing his identity as a yao to Prince Jing. Prince Jing had asked Liao Kong several questions when he had the chance, and Liao Kong solemnly replied that the yao probably came to the mortal world to undergo a tribulation. It was best to not mess up his plans, lest the yao fail his tribulation and get hurt instead. Prince Jing understood, and he couldn't expose his true feelings to Xiaoyu in case it affected him.

When Prince Jing thought about it carefully, though, he felt it didn't really matter if he couldn't expose Xiaoyu's true identity. If Xiaoyu didn't want him to know, he would just pretend he didn't know...but that wouldn't stop him from claiming the human Xiaoyu as his own. Quite apart from his identity as a yao, Xiaoyu was a distinguished guest in his residence. There was nothing wrong with him liking Xiaoyu; before the scholars in the books found out, weren't they also living a good, normal life with their yao?

In his lifetime, Prince Jing had never cared about someone so much. He'd finally found the one. Since he was a child, he was taught that he should take in whoever he liked, but if the carp spirit refused to come suck his essence, Prince Jing felt like he was in danger. He'd tried his best to study the books on cultivation, but he still didn't understand a lot of it. He didn't know why Xiaoyu wouldn't come suck him; human life was limited, and he didn't know how much longer it would take him. He might as well make the first move himself.

Prince Jing had already come to this decision when he heard that his fish was going to invite him to drink—otherwise, he wouldn't have accepted the invitation so readily. He even used a little trick to pretend to be drunk, letting the fish approach him, unguarded...

"Your Highness, can you let go of me?" Li Yu asked weakly. Whether he was laying on Prince Jing or being held by Prince Jing... both positions made Li Yu feel guilty. Prince Jing was drunk, but Li Yu wasn't. It felt like he was taking advantage of him. How could an innocent boy do such a thing? He wanted to get off Prince Jing immediately—there wasn't much time until his transformation ended, besides.

The hand that was tucking Li Yu's hair behind his ears stilled for a moment. Prince Jing had no intention of letting go. Instead, he gently held Li Yu's jaw, running a thumb over the young man's plump lips. He wasn't going to go easy on the fish.

Li Yu was feeling very awkward about the "drunk" Prince Jing's teasing. As a fish, he'd already bitten Prince Jing several times, so now that he was being hugged so tightly he couldn't move, he decided to open his mouth and bite Prince Jing's finger, hoping to give the drunk man a little shock of pain to sober him up! But everything backfired. When he bit down, the look in Prince Jing's eyes changed. He flipped open the quilt without hesitation and wrapped Xiaoyu in it to prevent him from escaping.

Li Yu's eyes widened as he was suddenly engulfed by a blanket and darkness. *Fuck. What was he trying to do?*

Before he could protest, a warm, soft touch came over his lips, the motion tentative at first. He heard the other person's content sigh, and that softness touched him again, firmly caressing his lips. Trapped in the dark blankets, Li Yu couldn't see or hear anything. His head was about to explode; he was young, but he wasn't completely oblivious to basic human affairs. This touch on his lips was obviously a kiss!

It was evident who it was—bastard! How could he treat him like this? He'd obviously mistaken him for a lover!

Li Yu was fuming, feeling ashamed and angry, but he was wrapped in the quilt and his opponent was much stronger, so he couldn't break free. The more he struggled, the more excited the other party became. Li Yu could barely breathe, and his body felt like it'd been electrocuted, loose and soft. He whimpered a few times and pummeled the other person in embarrassed fury, but it only made the kisses more urgent. Li Yu felt like he would die of suffocation if this went on, so when the other person tried to pry open his teeth, Li Yu hesitated and pretended to give up his resistance. As Prince Jing invaded and gently prodded him, Li Yu ruthlessly bit his tongue.

He bit too quickly and too hard and immediately tasted blood. Still afraid Prince Jing wouldn't let him go, he somehow freed a leg and kicked upward without thinking.

In pain, Prince Jing unhanded Li Yu, who pushed the quilt away and jumped off the bed.

His white clothes had gotten messed up while he was thrashing around under the blanket. Li Yu was both aggrieved and afraid and angrily yelled, "You have the wrong person! I'm not some other lover!"

He lifted his head and saw Prince Jing frowning and covering his injured mouth. Li Yu understood immediately—he didn't look like a drunkard at all!

"So you weren't drunk!" Li Yu suddenly realized the truth. Prince Jing wasn't actually drunk, so he'd done all that to Li Yu on purpose. He wanted to bully and molest him. What a huge asshole! Was this the true face of the tyrant master who had always been so kind to him?!

He was stunned, feeling angry, embarrassed, and disappointed. He couldn't tell which one he felt the most, but his head was buzzing. And just then, the system started the countdown to his transformation.

Aaaahhhh, he was going to turn back into a fish!

Li Yu had never been so panicked before. He definitely couldn't change back in front of Prince Jing! Out of desperation, he followed his instincts and ran away.

Prince Jing hadn't expected him to react like this. After a moment of stunned silence, he started to chase after him. But his tongue hurt, and when he took his hand away, it was bloody. The carp spirit bit him so hard—Prince Jing didn't know how he'd offended him. In his own mind, he'd never thought that the carp spirit would resist. He hadn't assumed the carp spirit that always tried to please him would dislike being treated this way.

Li Yu ran outside in a flash, still shaking uncontrollably with emotion. His transformation time was up, and he turned back into a fish and fell to the ground. Not long after, Prince Jing came running after him and saw a flopping fish on the ground.

Coming to a halt, Prince Jing carefully picked up the fish. Li Yu saw him and was reminded of how he was bullied just now, and suddenly became sad.

What kind of asshole master was this? How could he bully even a fish?! Aaahhh!

Li Yu flapped vigorously in Prince Jing's hand, wanting to be left alone. Prince Jing could tell his fish was unhappy, but he wouldn't let him go. He held the restless, squirming fish and returned to his room, placing him gently back in his tank.

Maybe it would be better to put him in the pond. But Prince Jing could tell that his fish was angry right now, and he was afraid that the fish would hide down there and never return. So, stubbornly, he put the fish back into the crystal fish tank.

Even if Xiaoyu was unhappy, he couldn't let him out of his sight.

Having escaped from his asshole master, the little carp swam to the silver stone bed and lay under the leaf blanket edged with gold, refusing to come out. After laying there for a bit, defeated, he remembered that both the quilt and bed were gifts from Prince Jing. The bullied, indignant fish flicked the blanket away immediately and plunged headfirst into the ornamental mountain cave instead.

He knew he shouldn't be using his fish form to express his anger at Prince Jing. Prince Jing didn't see him transform and didn't know his true identity; as far as he was aware, he had bullied Li Yu the person, and it would be strange for the fish he was raising to suddenly be upset. But Li Yu's mind was already in turmoil. He was still the one who was taken advantage of and molested, so wasn't it normal for him to be upset?

Apart from his shock, shame, and fury, he couldn't figure out why Prince Jing had bullied him. He hadn't spent that much time with him in his human form. Did...did he seem like such an easy person to Prince Jing?

What a douchebag! To treat him like that!

Li Yu was furious whenever he thought of it, so he swam out of the cave, took the blanket, and tried to rip it apart, as if it were Prince Jing. But it was soon clear that the blanket was too strong. He swam headfirst into the pile of colorful gems and tossed the round stones as far away as he could. But that still didn't help him calm down at all. In the end, he slammed his head against the crystal fish tank—but he didn't dare do it too hard, in case the fish tank broke...

Oh, right. He was pretty sure he'd kicked Prince Jing earlier. He didn't damage him permanently, did he? Of course not. He kicked randomly, and probably not very accurately...

Aaahhh! He couldn't do anything! And why was he starting to worry about that bastard? Anger!!!

Li Yu was thumping the crystal fish tank again when a figure suddenly appeared before him. He looked up and saw Prince Jing standing in front of the fish tank, holding a jade box filled with fish food and peach blossom pastries.

Really?

Asshole! I'm ignoring you! Li Yu whisked his tail. *Hmph! I've decided! I'm going on a hunger strike!*

He immediately swam back into the cave, even hiding the tip of his tail. Prince Jing watched the fish, bemused. He sprinkled a handful of fish food into the tank, but the fish that was normally greedy for food didn't come out.

Prince Jing shook his head helplessly and left the food there. He hid far away and tried to peek at his fish, but there was no movement from the tank. Since his fish had thrown tantrums before but always recovered eventually, Prince Jing thought it would be the same this time. But after a few days, the fish continued hiding in the cave, refusing to come out, much less transform. Even if Prince Jing wanted to explain, he wasn't given a chance to.

Prince Jing suddenly realized that the situation wasn't looking good. The fish seemed to be determined to ignore him forever.

Good thing I didn't kick him there, good thing I didn't kick him there...sob sob sob, I hate you the most!

Fish on Strike

PRINCE JING WAS TROUBLED by the fact that Li Yu wouldn't eat, so he asked Wang Xi to feed him. In the past, when they fought, Prince Jing would have Wang Xi feed the little carp, but now, Xiaoyu wouldn't even humor Wang-gonggong.

Asshole! You're in cahoots with each other! I'm not stupid!

Li Yu stubbornly starved for two days. He felt like he was getting skinnier and like if he wasn't paying attention, he would float right up to the surface.

Prince Jing wasn't very good at coaxing an angry fish, and he didn't really know why Xiaoyu was upset in the first place, so he discussed strategy with Wang Xi. Since he hadn't told Wang Xi about Xiaoyu's true identity, he could only explain both situations separately, so Wang-gonggong thought His Highness had run into two difficult situations at the same time. Li-gongzi and His Highness had quarreled, so Li-gongzi disappeared, while Master Fish wouldn't eat.

In the past, the fish had been His Highness's favorite, but since Li-gongzi's arrival, Wang Xi had seen firsthand how much His Highness doted on Li-gongzi. He felt like he had to weigh both situations carefully. He first asked what happened before Li-gongzi's quarrel. Prince Jing had sent everyone away that day, so nobody knew what happened, and Wang Xi had no choice but to ask Prince Jing.

Prince Jing hinted with his eyes and wrote a few words, leaving Wang Xi so shocked that he couldn't speak.

Had Li-gongzi refused to sleep with His Highness?

If it were anyone else, Wang Xi would have dealt with it according to the rules of the manor, but this was Li-gongzi, and His Highness didn't seem to have any intention of blaming him either. Wang Xi decided to put the rules aside and said, "Your Highness, the most important thing is to find him first."

Prince Jing felt a little dejected upon hearing that. Xiaoyu refused to transform because he didn't want to see him. How was he going to "find" Xiaoyu?

Wang Xi knew that Li-gongzi was often evasive. Seeing Prince Jing's expression, he guessed that Li-gongzi was hard to find.

Wang Xi said, "Then why did he leave in such a hurry? Do you know the reason, Your Highness?"

Prince Jing shook his head.

Wang Xi was just a servant. Though he'd seen and gone through a lot, he wasn't very experienced with relationships. He couldn't think of anything with just the small portions of information Prince Jing had given him. But Wang Xi still wanted to help his master, so he tactfully suggested, "Why don't you ask Ye-shizi about Li-gongzi?"

Prince Jing paused. That was an idea. Ye Qinghuan was thus quickly invited to the residence.

"Tianchi, you finally have something to ask of me?" Ye Qinghuan was so happy that Prince Jing would ask for his advice that he grinned so hard it hurt.

Prince Jing looked sullen, and Wang-gonggong told Ye-shizi everything he knew. He was afraid that Li-gongzi would be embarrassed, so he didn't mention him by name. At Prince Jing's signal, he changed it to "the person His Highness likes."

Ye Qinghuan was confused. He scratched his chin and said, "It's rare for you to ask me for anything. I want to help, but you know me..." Ye Qinghuan smiled, embarrassed. "I'm about to marry the princess, and I don't know what to do myself. I'm afraid I can't help you."

Prince Jing gave his unhelpful cousin an unimpressed look.

"But my mother wants me to treat the princess well. If I have anyone else, I'm to send them away. After I'm married, I should focus my affection only on the princess. If I like her, then I have to let her know as soon as possible. Between a married couple, arguments shouldn't last overnight..." The Duke and Duchess of Cheng'en had been married for decades, and they had a strong relationship. The Duchess of Cheng'en had passed on a lot of her own experience to her son, and Ye Qinghuan kept these pearls of wisdom like treasures. "Though our statuses are different, the principle remains the same. If you really care about them, you should make your feelings known. Asking them to sleep with you immediately is too impatient, don't you think?"

Prince Jing listened intently.

Was he too impatient?

A little bit. But nobody had taught him this before...so that must be why Xiaoyu was angry, right? He needed to make it clear to Xiaoyu what his feelings for him were. But if Xiaoyu wasn't willing to transform and see him, then how was he going to save this situation?

Prince Jing sank deep into thought. Ye Qinghuan kept rambling on, excitedly prattling about the details of the wedding preparations in the Cheng'en Manor, so Prince Jing stopped listening.

He had to deal with both things at once. He had to explain things to the fish-turned-human, and he had to find a way to make the hunger-striking fish eat.

Wang Xi had no way of knowing Li-gongzi's heart, but he was still useful when it came to Master Fish. If the fish refused to eat, he couldn't pry open its mouth and force-feed it, so they could only keep trying. Wang Xi suggested that Prince Jing gather all the fish's favorite foods in front of the ornamental mountain cave so the fish might eat on its own after some time. But if the food was left in the water for a long time, the water would get dirty. Wang Xi and a servant experienced in raising fish discussed what to do and decided on cleaning out the food once a day and putting in fresh food the next day.

Prince Jing thought it made a lot of sense. To make Xiaoyu happy, he put out all kinds of delicious food. The fish really wanted to eat it, but he couldn't bring himself to do it. Every time the servants cleaned out the food, the fish was the one who struggled the most and felt the most pain.

So much delicious food wasted...

Li Yu held on for two days. His entire body visibly shriveled, and even his scales lost their luster.

Seeing Prince Jing summon many people to take care of him, anxious to please him, Li Yu couldn't stand it. Prince Jing didn't know that Li Yu was his pet fish; he might think that his pet fish was sick and refused to eat. But he couldn't help but be upset when he thought about what Prince Jing did to him.

Not eating made him feel a little better out of spite, but if he refused to eat for a long time, he would die of starvation... No, wait, Li Yu thought in abrupt hungry frustration. This wasn't his fault, so why should he starve himself? Would Prince Jing realize why he was upset because he refused to eat?

Probably not.

Li Yu suddenly realized that he couldn't torture himself just because he was angry. He was already skin and bones, and the food was right next to him. The last bit of his pride died out as he weakly swam toward the food when Prince Jing wasn't around, wanting to quickly eat a little. Just a little.

Li Yu finally approached the mouth of the cave. The scent of the food that he hadn't tasted in a long time made him so emotional that he wanted to cry, but before he could take a bite, a servant came by. Seeing that the fish hadn't touched the food, the servant sighed and took away the food for the day.

What?!

Li Yu was so hungry that he was dizzy and his eyesight was blurry. No! Did he have to wait until tomorrow?

Prince Jing, who'd been secretly watching the fish, came over and saw the fish had finally showed his face. Prince Jing gave it some thought and reached for a handful of fish food.

When Li Yu saw the huge bastard's face, he instinctively wanted to turn around, but he was about to die of starvation. The fish food in Prince Jing's hand was tormenting him, and he was so hungry that he had no more energy to swim away. He just gave up and watched as Prince Jing gently placed the fish food in front of him.

Fine. Men...no, fish could stretch and bend! He shouldn't torture himself! He should have fattened himself up and tortured his asshole master instead!

...Just like that, the fish changed his mind and finally started eating.

Prince Jing smiled, extremely relieved. He touched the fish's back with his fingers. But Li Yu was still on guard. He chewed on his food and moved his back away. *Don't think you can bribe me with just some fish food! You can make me eat, but you can't pet me!*

Prince Jing watched the fish gobble the food up, and the smile on his lips dulled a bit.

Li Yu was so hungry that he felt full after just eating a little bit.

Prince Jing remembered what Wang Xi had said—that it was bad for fish to be too full. As soon as Li Yu stopped swallowing, Prince Jing started to push him to swim.

After Li Yu's hunger was gone, a lot of his anger disappeared too. He let Prince Jing push him, thinking it was easier than swimming around himself. When his stomach became more comfortable, he flicked his tail proudly and swam into the cave. He didn't want to sleep on the bed that huge bastard got for him yet.

Full and not really angry anymore, Li Yu entered the Moe Pet System. When he was at his most panicked, he'd heard the completed mission notification, so he was confused and wanted to confirm things with the system.

Why was his carefully planned drinking scheme unable to progress the mission, and why was the mission completed when his bastard master bullied him instead? Did he misunderstand something? Was such shameless bullying what the system meant by "indulge"?!

<Give me a reasonable explanation,> he demanded angrily. *<If you can't give me one, then I won't complete missions anymore!>*

When the fish-scamming system kept scamming him, he endured it silently—but there was a limit to everything. The system better not think that it could keep scamming him just because he was easygoing and honest!

<Because the user has completed the main mission "Tyrant's Priceless Pet Fish," the path of the following tasks will be determined based off of that. The user is required to develop a deeper relationship with the tyrant. Simply drinking with him is no longer enough to complete that step. Please think about it, user.> The system was talkative for once. *<You're already his "priceless pet fish," so your relationship can only get better from here on out.>*

<Yeah, right!> Li Yu huffed coldly. *<Does a better relationship mean stuffing my human form under a quilt and kissing me by force? What kind of logic is that?!>*

<But it is a better relationship than "priceless," isn't it?>

The system revealed its talent for debate, rendering Li Yu speechless. He still felt like something was wrong… Hit with a sudden idea, he went through all the missions he'd done, only to find a huge problem.

The fish-scamming system's quests all had clickbait titles, and he'd gotten used to it, but if he put them all together…it didn't seem like he was a pet to be raised at all! It was more like he was in a dating sim!

Stop making excuses! It was the system's plan all along!

Li Yu's anger now was no less than when he was taken advantage of before.

What pet wanted to have a deeper understanding, intimate contact, and indulgence with his master?

<"Tyrant's Priceless Pet Fish" is a series of initial missions that only require the user to achieve the necessary results,> said the system. *<The user can choose how to complete the quest, and all missions were voluntarily completed by the user.>*

The system seemed to be beating around the bush. Thinking about it, Li Yu realized that the system meant that the tyrant master doing this and that to him was because he was asking for it?!

<Not that you were asking for it, but the tyrant's actions toward the user now were caused by the user's choices in the previous missions,> the system corrected.

Great. Why didn't the system warn him that completing the quests would have an effect on Prince Jing?

The system responded, *<Because the missions of the Moe Pet System must be completed with the user's own sincerity. If you were told beforehand, then your choices would no longer be your own.>*

<You make it sound nice, but it was just a trap from the beginning!> Li Yu complained. This made him even angrier than when Prince Jing trapped him under the blanket. His face dark, Li Yu asked, *<Is there any way to make Prince Jing stop taking advantage of me?>*

<Prince Jing is the male protagonist. The system is unable to control his actions, but the user has the option to reset once. Once reset, all missions need to be completed again.>

Li Yu was surprised. *<I can reset?>*

Naturally, Li Yu wondered what kind of results resetting would have. It wouldn't clear the tyrant's memories, satisfaction, and everything else to zero, would it? If that was the case, then there wouldn't be any more troubles for him. But would that be fair to Prince Jing?

Due to Li Yu's transmigration, Prince Jing was no longer a piece of text but a living person just like him. It seemed quite immoral to destroy other people's memories whenever he wanted just because he was unhappy.

<User, you've misunderstood,> the System hurriedly explained. *<The Moe Pet System can only clear the user's memory of being a pet fish to achieve the effect of a fresh start, but it cannot change Prince Jing.>*

<So it's clearing my own memory?>

It sounded quite impressive, but wouldn't that just make him a pushover? If his memory was erased, wouldn't he still fall into the same traps?

Besides, he didn't think he'd done anything wrong on his previous missions. Was he supposed to let the Duke of Cheng'en and Ye Qinghuan be killed or leave the chubby boy to drown? He was the same person even if he reset, so he'd make the same decisions!

Plus, if he reset, but Prince Jing didn't, wouldn't it be even worse?

<It would be better if I didn't!>

‹If there's no need to reset, then please accept the reward, user.›

The system notified him that the "Indulge" mission had been completed. Now that Li Yu knew some of the truth, his heart was in turmoil and he had no energy to accept it. But then he remembered that he'd specifically asked for a fish plush as a reward for this mission, which was actually useful to him.

Li Yu was annoyed and said, *‹Give me the fish plush and store the rest for now. Does the next mission have a timer?›*

‹It does not.›

Li Yu bitterly thought, *Then I'm not completing any missions now! I'll wait until I feel like it!*

With that, he took the fish plush and exited the system, returning to his crystal fish tank. He didn't know how he was supposed to face his fish life in the future. He'd always thought he was smart, but now, having been scammed by the system and bullied by Prince Jing, he felt defeated.

The fish plush lay by his side. Because he originally wanted to use it as a cover when he transformed, he'd asked the system for another fish plush. As expected, this fish plush was updated to his most recent look: a silver fish with gold scales scattered across its body. But he didn't want to change into a human and interact with Prince Jing anymore.

Make him into fish bones and fish ash if you must!

Li Yu angrily fell asleep. When he was fast asleep, someone suddenly spoke loudly in his ear.

...Was it Wang Xi?

Li Yu wanted to hide as soon as he was fully awake, but he could hear the noise more clearly now.

It wasn't Wang Xi. Li Yu soon realized that it was two voices that he'd never heard before.

One voice mysteriously said to the other, "Does His Highness have to make such a grand gesture?"

The other voice said, "Yes. His Highness is very fond of Li-gongzi, but I heard he went missing. His Highness feels that he will come back and take a look, so this is the only method he can use to pass a message to him."

Li-gongzi, a secret eavesdropping fish, was puzzled. What was the huge bastard up to now?

The first voice continued, "Write it on the wall. If Li-gongzi is still in the manor, he'll definitely see it."

The two voices slowly faded. Li Yu angrily thought, *What act were they performing right in front of me?* Prince Jing most likely ordered these people to perform this little play to spread the news around the manor.

But it did pique his curiosity. Could a person who couldn't speak really leave a message? What message was it, and...why on the wall?

Li Yu took advantage of the situation and hopped over to the windowsill to get a glimpse outside.

Everywhere he looked, he saw the white walls of Prince Jing's manor covered with extra-large, flamboyant characters:

There are no other lovers. I adore you.

Stealing Prince Jing

I YU WAS DUMBFOUNDED for a full fifteen minutes.

That big asshole writing such nonsense on all the walls in the manor made Li Yu so embarrassed that he wanted to dive right back into his fish tank. Weird slogans from the modern world flooded his mind, along with the confession walls from school.

Others might not know why those two sentences were put together, but Li Yu knew that it was because he'd accused Prince Jing of treating him like one of his lovers and that this was his belated response. Prince Jing didn't have any other lovers, and he acted so out of line because he liked him.

Adore...adore...

He chewed on this word for a while, and suddenly his heart ached a bit.

If he and Prince Jing were ordinary people, he might have been a little touched right now. Whether or not he'd accept the confession aside, most people liked being confessed to, deep down—especially in such a brazen way, broadcasted to the whole world.

Li Yu didn't feel happy, though, and his mood grew heavier. He knew Prince Jing didn't have anyone else; he'd reacted as he had because he thought Prince Jing thought he was easy. Li Yu felt humiliated and hadn't wanted to face Prince Jing for a while.

But Prince Jing was using this method to tell him that it wasn't disrespect but love.

It was a bit of an old-fashioned way of saying it, but the meaning was clear—Prince Jing had fallen for him, which was even worse than if he'd disrespected him. Li Yu knew that he was Prince Jing's pet fish, and the "Li-gongzi" Prince Jing loved was nothing more than a fish clumsily trying to complete missions.

Such feelings came from scheming and planning—they weren't naturally formed. If things progressed like this, what would the next mission from the system be? According to the system's logic, it would require a relationship even deeper than what they had during the "Indulged" quest. If he wanted to complete the mission, then he might have to do things that would encourage Prince Jing to sink further into this misunderstanding.

Eventually, maybe he'd end up together with Prince Jing. A lot of transmigration novels ended that way.

But he didn't want that. His feelings were valuable, and the way the system was pushing him was uncomfortable. He could let some things go, but he wouldn't budge when it came to romance. He didn't want his feelings to be manipulated or calculated.

He always showed concern and worry for Prince Jing, perhaps because he'd been his pet for so long, but that was just the love of a pet toward his master, not the love experienced by two equals. There was no way he could accept Prince Jing's feelings and give him his heart in return. Prince Jing didn't know Li-gongzi was a fish, but Li Yu did. The fish didn't love Prince Jing, and neither did Li-gongzi.

If he accepted the confession without loving Prince Jing, it would hurt everyone involved.

While Li Yu was pondering all this, several servants came up to the white wall in front of him and gestured at the writing on it.

Li Yu knew Prince Jing had written those words and that he was trying his hardest to explain things to him. Since he wasn't turning into a human, Prince Jing couldn't find him, and since Prince Jing couldn't speak, he could only write his words anywhere that Li Yu could see. No matter how childish his methods were, this still represented Prince Jing's feelings toward him, which was why Li Yu felt a bit sad after he realized Prince Jing liked him.

He'd known Prince Jing for a while now, and he'd seen many sides to him. He knew that Prince Jing was a good person, since he treated both fish and people well. In the original novel, Prince Jing was cruel to others but affectionate to the one he loved. Li Yu was well aware of this, but he couldn't force himself to fall in love with Prince Jing.

Li Yu thought that as long as he didn't give Prince Jing any hope, if he didn't respond or transform into a human, Prince Jing would gradually forget about him. Just like the words written on the wall—they shocked the whole manor at first, but they would eventually be erased by the servants, right?

"The other walls are about done. Let's start carving this one next. His Highness told us to hurry up—even if Li-gongzi doesn't come back for now, he'll definitely see it when he finally does, come rain or shine."

The servants encouraged each other, and soon began to carve Prince Jing's words directly into the wall. When the carving was finished, a special permanent ink was applied.

Li Yu, who'd assumed the servants had come to erase the words, was shocked. Didn't this bastard know the meaning of shame? It was one thing for everyone in the manor to see it, but in the future, all his children and descendants...

Thinking of Prince Jing's future, Li Yu felt a lump in his throat, and his eyes started to sting again.

Li Yu jumped down from the windowsill, telling himself it was because the servants were making too much noise working on the wall, and scooted back into the fish tank. He wanted to sleep again, but he couldn't. Normally he could sleep even when he was extremely angry, but the few words carved into the wall seemed to be carved into his heart too, emanating waves of pain and sadness. He wanted to rest, but he was restless.

The room was silent, until there was a sudden soft click. The door bolt fell to the ground, the sound piercing the room. Since Li-gongzi came in and out of the room often, Prince Jing didn't let anyone lock the doors, so all the bolts hung loose. Maybe the person who pushed the door hadn't expected to enter so easily.

A figure quickly flashed in. The footsteps didn't sound like Prince Jing or Wang Xi... Li Yu became alert immediately. The person who entered the room stood at the door observing, with his back to the crystal fish tank. Li Yu immediately forgot about his conflict and stared at the person.

After confirming he hadn't been followed, the person gave a sigh of relief, turned around, and walked forward a few steps. Li Yu caught a glimpse of the person's beautiful, ethereal face.

This person—wasn't it the delicate concubine from the original novel, Chu Yanyu?!

Li Yu was stunned. Ever since the banquet at Prince Jing's manor, he hadn't seen Chu Yanyu again. He thought Chu Yanyu was with the third or sixth prince, but he was still at the manor? How come he hadn't known?

Chu Yanyu was wearing the same clothes that the servants at the manor wore. It was a bit plain, but it wasn't enough to hide his aura. Li Yu didn't think that someone as weak as Chu Yanyu would be able to enter the manor from the outside, which meant that he must have been in the manor the entire time.

Prince Jing was in charge of everything in the manor, so there was no way Chu Yanyu's existence could be hidden from him. That meant Prince Jing let him stay, just like he kept Li Yu. But when the third prince had presented Chu Yanyu to him at the banquet, Prince Jing had clearly refused. Did he change his mind?

He'd said "There are no other lovers," Li Yu thought bitterly. There might be no lovers, but he had a delicate concubine all along and didn't tell him. That was too much. Since he had someone, why did he confess? Hmph! He hated it when people kept their eggs in multiple baskets! Li Yu drew a big X over Prince Jing in his heart.

Chu Yanyu walked to the crystal fish tank and looked curiously at the fish swimming back and forth inside. Everyone in the manor talked about how Prince Jing was raising a koi. Chu Yanyu had seen Prince Jing's fish from a distance before, but he wasn't able to get close. He only remembered that the fish was black—but now, he could see that the fish had a silver body with gold on its belly and tail. With that appearance, it could only be a koi. It wasn't unreasonable for Prince Jing to dote on that kind of fish the way he did.

Chu Yanyu observed the fish for a while, and then he picked up one of the jade boxes on the table and opened it. He found red dry food in it, and when he checked, the other one had snacks that were broken into small pieces.

Chu Yanyu closed the box with the snacks, picked up the dry food, and smelled it. He guessed that it was fish food and frowned slightly, as if he didn't like the smell of it. But he still picked up a handful and walked back to the fish tank. Li Yu thought Chu Yanyu was bored and wanted to feed him, but Chu Yanyu lowered his head and whispered, "Be good. This is a rare opportunity I managed to get…"

Huh? Was Chu Yanyu talking to him because he knew he could understand? Li Yu was a little shocked—was that possible? But he quickly realized that Chu Yanyu couldn't have known that he was a transmigrated fish; he just thought he was alone and was talking to himself.

But he could hear everything. So awkward.

Li Yu pretended to not understand and stupidly blew a bubble.

Chu Yanyu wasn't suspicious and continued, "I've been in the manor for so long, but I've only seen His Highness a few times. I'm incompetent. I heard that there was a Li-gongzi who was doted on, and I can't figure it out…"

The doted-on Li-gongzi tried not to look too obviously confused. *What do you not understand?*

Chu Yanyu paused and looked down, chuckling, "I don't understand how he's better than I am. I've seen him from afar, and I'm quite confident I'm fairer than he. Why does His Highness like him but treat me like air? But I finally understand."

Chu Yanyu prattled on excitedly, almost as if he was in a daze. "The biggest difference between Li-gongzi and me is that he's the one who helps His Highness take care of his fish. He's managed to get close to His Highness because of the fish, so if I took over this job instead, I'd easily be on his level.

"And now, the opportunity has come." Chu Yanyu gently smiled, saying, "Li-gongzi is arrogant because of the favor shown to him, and he left without saying goodbye. He's playing hard to get and hoping His Highness will fall more in love with him, but he's not the only one in the manor who knows how to raise and feed fish— I can as well. I can completely replace him, and I'd do a better job."

Chu Yanyu threw the fish food in front of Li Yu, his slightly smiling face distorting for a second and his eyes becoming cold.

The scales on Li Yu's body were about to stand on end. He thought Chu Yanyu had lost his mind and was acting weird. From what he said, it seemed he wasn't doing well in the manor and was ignored by His Highness. Since he was never summoned, he wanted to steal Li-gongzi's job!

Hmph! Stealing?! He's acting like I have something special with the bastard. He wants to get my affection and then set his sights on Prince Jing!

The fish food Chu Yanyu threw in followed the current and landed in front of Li Yu. His ice-cold eyes were fixed on the fish. Li Yu couldn't help but shrink back a little. People had many sides—how come the proud, noble, delicate concubine from the novel turned out to be such a bad person on the inside?! Li Yu thought Chu Yanyu was dangerous, so he obviously refused to eat the food he was given. The fish food sank down near his mouth, but he didn't go to pick it up.

Chu Yanyu looked vicious for a second. He was having a hard time in Qingxi Garden these days. Shortly after he came to the manor, he was beaten within an inch of his life. There was no doctor to treat him, and everyone else in Qingxi Garden was too busy with themselves and didn't care whether he lived or died. Chu Yanyu secretly sent a letter to the sixth prince. The first few times had failed, but at last, there was a response. The sixth prince wanted him to stay with Prince Jing and gain his trust.

Chu Yanyu stroked the letter the sixth prince had sent him, feeling like his heart was being stabbed with a knife. His beloved sixth prince still put such faith in him, but he couldn't even see Prince Jing. How was he going to help the sixth prince in the future?

Chu Yanyu mulled this over, day and night, as if possessed. After much thought, he decided that he would do anything, even if it meant he had to abandon all dignity. He had to earn Prince Jing's favor!

Chu Yanyu didn't have much money left, so he had to use the method he disliked the most—he flirted with a guard for a couple days and promised him a lot of benefits, which earned him the opportunity to sneak into the inner courtyard. He'd heard that Prince Jing's new favorite, Li-gongzi, was throwing a tantrum and had run away from the manor, so he made up his mind and decided to use this opportunity to win over Prince Jing.

He suspected that Li-gongzi was favored because he was always around the fish, giving him an advantage. As long as he could take care of the fish too, then Li-gongzi wouldn't be needed anymore. But even though he was here already, the fish wasn't eating the food he gave him?

Whatever. Chu Yanyu sneered coldly, then poured a packet of brown herbal powder into a tea bowl and started mixing it.

Li Yu couldn't believe it. Delicate concubine, are you really intending to drug Prince Jing? That was a tea bowl used for the fish to travel around, not for Prince Jing to drink out of!

Nothing to Do
with Fish

L I YU STARED AT Chu Yanyu, bewildered.

All the tea bowls were extremely large now, since he'd grown larger. Did Chu Yanyu not find that strange?

Well, he couldn't exactly blame him. As a fish, Li Yu usually only jumped around inside the room and rarely did so outside. But Prince Jing kept ordering new bowls to be prepared, which created misunderstandings. Chu Yanyu assumed Prince Jing was used to using tea bowls that were several times larger than normal.

The brown herbal powder dissolved immediately into the water, leaving no trace. Li Yu was frightened since he didn't know what medicine Chu Yanyu had just dissolved. It shouldn't be arsenic— Chu Yanyu had touched it with his bare hands, so Li Yu knew it couldn't be anything so dangerous as that. Even if it was, he'd put the medicine in the wrong water, so it should be fine...

Li Yu tried very hard to reassure himself, but then Chu Yanyu got up and realized that there were more tea bowls of similar styles all around the room.

Oh well. He'd put all this effort into breaking in, so he couldn't leave any room for error. He'd just have to put the medicine in every bowl.

Li Yu watched him drugging everything and thought, *How much medicine did you bring, delicate concubine?*

There was a huge red lotus tea bowl on Prince Jing's desk, the size of a large regular bowl. Chu Yanyu didn't miss that one either, nor the smaller, colored glaze cup next to the tea bowl...

Li Yu didn't dare make a sound. The delicate concubine didn't know it, but the colored glaze cup was the only one Prince Jing actually used. Somehow, he'd still managed to get it right.

Chu Yanyu finished pouring medicine into the cup and looked at the final packet of medicine in his hand uncertainly. There were some noises outside the door, signaling that someone was coming. Chu Yanyu stopped hesitating and quickly downed the last packet of medicine himself.

Li Yu was now sure that Chu Yanyu wasn't using poison! If it was poison, he wouldn't have taken it himself. Then what kind of medicine was it, that Chu Yanyu needed to take it too?

Li Yu was flustered. In a palace novel, if it wasn't poison, then it was an aphrodisiac, right?

The delicate concubine who barely paid Prince Jing any attention in the original novel was now trying to give Prince Jing an aphrodisiac, and his fish just happened to be here to see... What an improbable and shocking series of events!

Chu Yanyu coughed a couple of times, wiped away the powder on his lips, and smoothed out the wrinkles on his outfit, before grabbing another handful of fish food and rushing over to stand in front of the fish tank, pretending to feed the fish.

Prince Jing entered the room.

Chu Yanyu pretended to be surprised, put down the fish food, and greeted Prince Jing. "Your Highness."

Li Yu was in the fish tank behind him, watching the tall figure approach step by step. When he thought of how this guy shamelessly confessed his plot to him, Li Yu's heart beat faster for some reason. He backed up a little, sticking close to the ornamental mountain.

Prince Jing didn't even look at Chu Yanyu, who was still kneeling. He went straight to the fish tank.

Aaahhh! The bastard is really coming! Li Yu instinctively wanted to dive into the cave, but then he remembered that Prince Jing didn't know he was Li-gongzi. What was there to be afraid of? *I-I can't hide! It has nothing to do with me!*

Oh, but the medicine Chu Yanyu just put into all the water...

It had nothing to do with him, but should he somehow let Prince Jing know?

But all Prince Jing cared about when he came in was seeing his fish. His dark, deep eyes seemed to penetrate his fish skin to reveal the human heart beneath. Li Yu felt chills from his gaze, and he felt a little guilty. He immediately ducked behind an aquatic plant near the ornamental mountain.

"Your Highness..." Chu Yanyu felt a bit aggrieved since he'd been kneeling for a while. Why was Prince Jing bent on seeing his fish instead of him, even though he was kneeling before him? But at least now he knew for certain that he had no status compared to this fish. It also meant that he was right to put his effort toward the fish instead.

Chu Yanyu took a deep breath and smiled, saying, "Your Highness, I was passing by when I noticed the fish was hungry and hadn't been fed... I came in brazenly. Please forgive me, Your Highness."

Chu Yanyu thought that he was beaten last time because he failed to figure Prince Jing out—perhaps Prince Jing didn't like it when others were too forward, so he'd apologize and admit his mistake first this time while emphasizing that he did it for the fish. As long as he acted the way Prince Jing liked, Prince Jing would definitely notice him.

Sure enough, when he mentioned the fish, Prince Jing glanced at him just once. But Chu Yanyu knew that since Prince Jing didn't chase him out of the room, it meant he could stay—he felt like he was getting closer to Li-gongzi's position!

Li Yu was uncomfortable with the fact that Prince Jing wasn't making Chu Yanyu leave, because there were usually no outsiders when Prince Jing was in the room. Was he finally treating the delicate concubine differently?

...What an asshole!

Li Yu thrashed his tail in irritation and accidentally snapped the aquatic plants he was hiding behind. Whoops...

Prince Jing had great hearing. He heard the sound of the aquatic plants snapping, so he looked over. Li Yu immediately curled up the tail that had caused the trouble. Fine, do what you want! Important things must be said three times. He was just a fish, and Prince Jing could keep whoever he liked. It was none of his business!

Prince Jing looked at the fish for a bit, but seeing that the fish didn't swim over, he didn't reach his hand out either, so as not to annoy the fish. Instead, he walked to the table and sat down. Chu Yanyu guessed that the medicine he took was about to start working, so he softly said, "Your Highness, let me pour you a cup of tea."

Li Yu couldn't help but swim to the front of the crystal tank. The delicate concubine was so proactive this time; were sparks finally going to fly between the original couple of the novel?

He should have been happy. If Prince Jing was with Chu Yanyu, then he wouldn't think of him... But was he supposed to pretend not to know that Chu Yanyu had drugged all of the tea bowls in the room?

Li Yu hesitated, unsure. On one hand, it would be helpful to him, but on the other hand...was Prince Jing, the big asshole.

He was a fish, not some saint. He was totally capable of caring only about himself and choosing things that only benefited him. Prince Jing and Chu Yanyu were a couple in the original novel, and Li Yu wasn't the one who put the medicine in the water. At most, he was just a bystander. If his conscience couldn't take it, he could ask the system to reset him so that he wouldn't feel any guilt and he could be a happy fish...

There was no need to feel so conflicted.

"Your Highness, I don't know which cup you use." Chu Yanyu's sweet voice sounded again. This Chu Yanyu was completely different from the arrogant, proud young man at the banquet. Li Yu's heart shook. Chu Yanyu was asking in order to minimize Prince Jing's suspicion. He knew Chu Yanyu was about to make a move.

Prince Jing cocked his head, as if he was about to reply.

You bastard! Ignore him! Li Yu thought in a panic.

But Prince Jing couldn't know what a fish was thinking, and his eyes landed on the glazed cup next to the lotus bowl.

Chu Yanyu understood and held the glazed cup with both hands, directly in front of Prince Jing. Giving it some thought, he knelt down obediently. From where Prince Jing was sitting, his figure should be displayed to best effect from this angle.

Chu Yanyu's face started to feel hot. He thought it must be the medicine. He'd never tried seducing anyone so boldly before, so it was normal to be worked up. It was different from flirting a little with the guards.

He would soon conquer the man in front of him.

"Your Highness, please have some tea." Chu Yanyu calmed himself down and coaxed Prince Jing softly.

Prince Jing took the cup, his slender fingers caressing the edges. Li Yu knew his habits and that he might drink it in the next second.

Why was Prince Jing so unguarded today? What happened to testing all of the prince's food and drinks with a silver needle? Okay, well, an aphrodisiac might not show up on a silver needle, but where was the servant who was supposed to try the prince's food?

Prince Jing was about to lift the cup. Li Yu had no time to think. At such a critical moment, he felt like he had to do something! No matter who Prince Jing liked or who he ended up with, there was no way Li Yu would allow them to drug him. If Chu Yanyu could make Prince Jing sincerely like him, then Li Yu wouldn't stop them, but using drugs—what was the difference between that and using force?!

He wouldn't accept either!

Chu Yanyu had already put medicine in every tea bowl for the fish. He couldn't jump over using the tea bowls to knock the cup out of Prince Jing's hands. If a person touched an aphrodisiac, they'd be hot with desire, but if a fish touched it, he might turn into boiled fish. Li Yu could only rely on himself now. He had to turn into a human and warn Prince Jing that way. He was still mad, but at such an important moment, he had to put his temper aside and prioritize other things.

Li Yu quietly took out the fish pillow that he kept in his inventory, threw it into the crystal fish tank, positioned it, and chose an angle to jump out from that Chu Yanyu and Prince Jing wouldn't be able to see.

Prince Jing seemed interested in what Chu Yanyu was saying, but he was actually following the fish's movements out of the corner of his eye. He realized the fish had jumped out and landed with a clear slap, which caught Chu Yanyu's attention. With no other choice, before Chu Yanyu could turn around, Prince Jing gently flicked the rim of his cup with his nail.

Chu Yanyu's attention was immediately diverted. "Your Highness, is something wrong?" Why wasn't he drinking the water with the medicine?

Prince Jing smiled, picked up the cup, and calmly brought it to his lips. Chu Yanyu watched him expectantly. Prince Jing looked past him and saw the fish on the ground, standing on its tail and sliding in a fancy arc to end up behind the cabinet. Prince Jing had never realized that a carp spirit's tail could be used that way…

He was distracted for a second and sneakily glanced at the fish tank again, worried that Chu Yanyu would realize that the fish was gone from the fish tank…but just as he was working out how to grab Chu Yanyu's full attention, he saw a silver fish in the huge crystal fish tank, facing head-down on the stone bed, strange and motionless.

Prince Jing had seen another fake fish that looked exactly the same as the carp spirit before. He was sure this one was fake too, because the real carp spirit had just jumped out of the tank. Perhaps it was a cloning skill… Prince Jing, who knew a little about cultivation, rubbed his eyebrows. With the fake fish, there'd be no need to worry about Chu Yanyu finding out.

He picked up the cup again and tried to predict how long it would take Xiaoyu to turn into a human. Xiaoyu was faster than he thought. He jumped out quickly, shouting, "Your Highness, you can't drink that!"

He was finally here. Prince Jing pursed his lips and put the cup fully aside.

Chu Yanyu was shocked by the sudden appearance of this young man, his fingernails digging into his palm. The young man who'd disrupted his plans was dressed in green robes, with bright eyes and white teeth. This slim young man was Li-gongzi, who had supposedly run away from the manor.

Chu Yanyu frowned, feeling irritated. Li-gongzi had left already, so why did he come back? Was he not happy that his position was being threatened and was now trying to take him down?

Or did Li-gongzi find out that he put medicine in the cup?

That was impossible. Chu Yanyu knew that he was the only one in the room when he did the deed.

"What do you mean? Why can't he drink it?" Chu Yanyu asked indignantly. The medicine had been used already; if he hesitated for a moment, Prince Jing would suspect him!

Li Yu didn't have time to deal with him. He stepped forward and grabbed Prince Jing's sleeve, loudly saying, "Your Highness, you can't drink this! It's been drugged!"

Chu Yanyu looked at Li Yu in surprise. No sooner than Li Yu had finished speaking, Wang Xi came in with a group of guards. Li Yu was stunned, and Prince Jing took his hand immediately. Prince Jing nodded to Wang Xi, who ordered the guards to grab Chu Yanyu.

Chu Yanyu, still hopeful, struggled and said, "Your Highness, I didn't. You can't just listen to Li-gongzi's side of the story!" He was trying to stay calm, but he realized something was wrong when Wang Xi took away all the tea bowls in the room. How did Wang-gonggong know that he had tampered with all the tea bowls?

And the medicine he'd taken just before—Chu Yanyu looked down at his uncontrollably trembling legs. That was what finally made him sink into desperation.

What was waiting for him?

In any case, it definitely wasn't what he wanted, which was Prince Jing's trust and favor.

Wang Xi took the wicked Chu Yanyu away like a gust of wind. Prince Jing and Li Yu were the only ones left in the room. Wang-gonggong understood that there was a lot that Prince Jing wanted to tell Li-gongzi, so he even closed the doors thoughtfully on his way out. While Li-gongzi was upset, Wang Xi and His Highness were both struggling, so Wang Xi hoped that Li-gongzi would have a change of heart.

With the door closed, the room returned to silence. Li Yu looked at Prince Jing coldly.

Prince Jing was happy beyond words and immediately wanted to hug him. Li Yu knocked away Prince Jing's outstretched hands and said icily, "Did Your Highness know that Chu Yanyu was going to drug you?"

A few things were strange about everything that had just happened—he was distracted at the time because of how worried he was, but he should have figured it out early on.

Prince Jing hesitated and nodded.

Since the last incident with Chu Yanyu, he'd been high on Prince Jing's alert list. Prince Jing knew what was happening as soon as the trouble started; otherwise, how could Chu Yanyu have so easily made it into the inner courtyard?

The medicine that Chu Yanyu had worked his hardest to get had been replaced long ago by soybean powder. Prince Jing had also confirmed that Chu Yanyu had no sharp objects on him and couldn't harm the fish, otherwise he wouldn't have let Chu Yanyu enter the room. He didn't care who was behind the delicate concubine's plans; he just wanted to use Chu Yanyu to lure Xiaoyu out.

In the words of the ancients, one day apart seemed like three years. Prince Jing hadn't believed it before, but now, he knew what it felt like. Xiaoyu had avoided him for the past couple of days, and a darkness had started brewing in Prince Jing's heart. He could do all kinds of crazy things for him—using a human pawn was nothing.

He wrote everything he wanted to say to Xiaoyu on the wall, but still he didn't appear. He was afraid that Xiaoyu would avoid him forever, so he felt he had no choice but to resort to this.

Chu Yanyu had schemed against him in front of Xiaoyu. Prince Jing had bet that Xiaoyu still cared about him and would show up to save him. And when he did...he could tell his fish how he felt in person.

The plan was risky, but he trusted Xiaoyu with his life. Fortunately, he was right, and he finally got to see Xiaoyu's human form again. Prince Jing was so elated that most of his anger disappeared. But once Xiaoyu confirmed that Prince Jing had known about the plan from the get-go, his expression kept changing. Prince Jing could tell that Xiaoyu was upset again.

The youth in front of him lowered his head, wiped his face, and muttered, "You lied to me again..."

Li Yu turned into a human for Prince Jing because he didn't want him to get hurt, but now that he knew it was all part of Prince Jing's plan, he guessed that it was probably to make him show up. Li Yu's heart hadn't recovered yet from being humiliated and deceived, and this time, his anger reached its peak.

"I hate it when people lie to me!" he spat out coldly.

He broke away from Prince Jing's arms, punched him in the chest, and ran out of the room without looking back.

Sick Fish

L I YU RUSHED OUT of the room. He knew that Prince Jing, as a prince from ancient times and a tyrant male protagonist, had his own way of dealing with things, but he couldn't stand the fact that he had been so full of passion while the other party was just acting—acting on purpose just for him to see.

He'd truly hated being lied to these past few days. His rebellious heart was like dynamite that exploded at a touch.

Wang-gonggong and a group of servants were waiting outside. Seeing him come out, he called out in surprise, "Li-gongzi!"

Li Yu's lips twitched. He didn't know what to say to Wang Xi, so he decided to ignore him. He turned away and ran toward one of the gardens behind the fake mountain.

Wang-gonggong ordered people to follow him, but Prince Jing came out after Li Yu and shook his head at Wang Xi, who understood at once that he wasn't to interfere.

Prince Jing gave chase himself. Wang Xi was afraid that Li-gongzi would run away again later, though. Prince Jing had stopped him from chasing Li-gongzi, but it would be fine for him to surround the garden, right?

The garden wasn't very large, and Prince Jing soon found Li Yu standing, dazed, in the middle of a pavilion.

Prince Jing didn't know why the carp spirit was upset again. Ye Qinghuan wanted him to learn how to make someone happy, but it seemed like he just couldn't help making mistakes. He didn't understand. And it was so inconvenient that he couldn't express himself when he wanted to, since he couldn't speak.

Prince Jing held a note in his hand. He intended to hand it to Li Yu, but Li Yu assumed he was still trying to catch him and smiled desolately.

Li Yu had a feeling that it would be hard for him to escape if he was caught. And he was still upset with Prince Jing, besides. He didn't want to see him, much less talk about love. He'd thought he had to transform to save Prince Jing, but since Prince Jing was apparently perfectly fine without his help, now he wanted to disappear as quickly as possible.

He remembered that the large fishpond Prince Jing constructed connected all the bodies of water within the manor—and under this pavilion was a pool. If he just entered the water, he could swim away and shake off Prince Jing.

Li Yu made his decision. Prince Jing had just stepped into the pavilion when Li Yu loudly said, "Stop chasing me!"

Prince Jing hesitated for a moment, nodded, and even stepped back to show his sincerity.

As he stepped back, Li Yu turned his back to Prince Jing, facing the pool under the pavilion, and leapt over the railing into the pool!

Prior to transmigrating, he didn't know how to swim, but after he turned into a fish, he found his human form could swim too—though there were few opportunities for him to do it.

He wasn't planning on swimming around, though; he just wanted to hide in the water until he turned back into a fish. That was the consequence of his reckless transformation, and it was safer to hide as a human than wander around. But his sudden plunge into the cold pond as a human sent chills racing through his body. Li Yu shivered as he tried his best to adapt to the water.

Prince Jing was completely taken aback. He had just started to wonder what Li Yu was up to when he jumped into the pool. His pupils contracted as he lunged after Li Yu, grasping at air. Looking down, he noticed a figure moving in the water and realized that Xiaoyu must have swum away.

Prince Jing knew that he couldn't compete with the carp spirit when it came to swimming; he could never match his speed in the water. However, all the pools in the manor were connected, so he could roughly guess where Xiaoyu was headed and rush to the next pool or pond to stop him.

Prince Jing left the pavilion and ran straight to where Li Yu might show up!

But he waited there for a while, and Xiaoyu never appeared. The carp spirit had escaped again.

Wang Xi came over to ask him where Li-gongzi was. Prince Jing shook his head, his face ashen. Xiaoyu couldn't maintain his human form for long, and Prince Jing couldn't ask his servants to go into the water to find him. The fewer people that knew the identity of the carp spirit, the better.

The pond he'd built was huge, but luckily, it wasn't connected to the outside—only the pools and ponds within the manor. There were guards on shore too, so Xiaoyu was at least safe in the water and couldn't leave the manor.

Prince Jing ordered his people to constantly keep an eye on all the water in the manor. He then went back to his quarters and waited outside, where Xiaoyu often came out of the water to play with him, hoping that perhaps Xiaoyu would come out after swimming around for a while.

Prince Jing waited for two hours, but Xiaoyu didn't show up.

When Li Yu entered the water in human form, he couldn't breathe like he was a fish, so he couldn't swim very fast. Since he'd turned into a fish, he could recognize a lot of aquatic plants now. He found one with a hollow stem, broke it, and held it in his hand. If he was about to run out of air, he could poke it out of the water and sneak a breath.

He'd guessed that Prince Jing would wait for him at the next pond, so he tricked him by hiding after he got there, tucked away in an unseen corner. Even after Prince Jing gave up and left, assuming Li Yu must not be there after all, Li Yu still didn't show his face. He stayed hidden until he turned into a fish again, and then he put his clothes into his inventory and started swimming around. Because of his current color, he'd be easily spotted if he got close to the water's surface, so he only swam in deeper waters.

The bottom of the pool was the same. Prince Jing had built miniature cities for him, and Li Yu felt uncomfortable when he saw them now. He wanted to swish his tail and destroy everything—out of sight, out of mind. With his current tail's strength, he might not be able to shatter them in a second, but he could ruin a good portion. But even though he raised his tail, he couldn't bring it down.

It was...Prince Jing's present to his fish, and he couldn't bring himself to take his anger out on it.

Li Yu coldly harrumphed and glanced indifferently at the underwater city. He couldn't strike anything with his tail, so he turned and swam toward the building at the end of the pool.

This building was made to resemble the one Prince Jing lived in, and the jade statue of Prince Jing and the fish-shaped stone Li Yu had placed inside were still there. In the past, when Li Yu came down to play, he would pull off the moss growing on the statues, but he wasn't in the mood for it right now.

Li Yu swam over angrily and shoved Prince Jing's statue with his mouth. It tilted, as if stumbling. He couldn't use his tail to destroy Prince Jing's statue either, since he wouldn't be able to play with it afterward. He pushed the statue several times, and it swayed and finally fell. Li Yu then pressed his whole body onto the statue, as if he was sitting right on him.

Prince Jing, you big bastard, aaahhhh!!!

Li Yu had saved him out of the goodness of his heart, but he had been deceived.

He rolled into an angry ball. The fish-shaped stone was lying off to the side, and Li Yu picked it up in his mouth and put it on the jade statue's back.

After messing around with it for a while, the fish got tired and fell asleep on the jade statue. His body felt lighter as he slept like that.

He didn't know how much time had passed, but Li Yu suddenly woke to the sound of human voices. Why were there people at the bottom of the pool? Li Yu drowsily wanted to see who was there, but he couldn't bring himself to wake up even after trying a couple of times.

Since he'd been sleeping at the bottom of the pool the entire time, Prince Jing was getting anxious and didn't want to wait for him to come out on his own.

So, he decided to go into the water and take a look. Wang Xi tried to persuade him that the pool was too big and it might be dangerous, but Prince Jing's gaze told him: Move aside. Wang Xi realized that His Highness had made up his mind, so he backed off and asked Prince Jing to take a few servants who were good at swimming to go with him. But Prince Jing shook his head, declining. He didn't know what Xiaoyu's condition was underwater, and he was afraid that Xiaoyu's identity would be revealed if there were other people around.

It would be best if he went alone. Prince Jing was good at swimming too; he changed into clothes that were suitable for swimming and entered the water.

The guards had been staring at the water for a long time, but they didn't see Xiaoyu. It was clear that Xiaoyu was still at the very bottom.

Prince Jing started searching the bottom of the pool but ran out of breath a couple of times and had to breathe before going back down again. He had searched almost everywhere when he came to the building at the end of the pool—and to his surprise, he saw his fish curled up there.

Prince Jing's heart clenched. He touched the fish's head, but the fish didn't move. He lifted the fish up gently, but the fish remained unconscious. Something rolled out from under him; Prince Jing looked and saw that it was his jade statue.

Hm.

Prince Jing guessed that the carp spirit was "meditating" again—though it was preferable in this case since it prevented him from throwing a tantrum and leaving. Prince Jing thought for a moment, opened his robes to carefully tuck the fish inside, and swam toward the surface.

"Your Highness, Your Highness! What happened?"

Wang Xi rushed over and found the fish in Prince Jing's arms. Wang-gonggong was bewildered—wasn't the fish master in the crystal fish tank in the room? Wasn't His Highness looking for Li-gongzi? Why did he...show up with the fish master?

Prince Jing gave him a warning glance, forbidding him from speaking further.

Wang Xi racked his brain. "Did I...get it wrong? Master Xiaoyu went into the pool to play, and Your Highness was looking for Master Xiaoyu, not Li-gongzi?"

Prince Jing nodded without a hint of guilt.

So that was what happened! Wang Xi immediately accepted it. He'd been wondering how Li-gongzi had managed to stay in the water this whole time and not come out, but it turned out that he'd misunderstood. His Highness was looking for Master Xiaoyu. Li-gongzi must have left long ago.

Wang Xi followed Prince Jing into the room. Prince Jing moved the fish pillow in the crystal fish tank to the side and put the little carp on the silver stone bed instead. Only then did Wang Xi notice that the fish that had been sitting in the fish tank was fake. Wang-gonggong wiped the sweat off his forehead and felt a bit ashamed. His Highness must have made it to deceive Chu Yanyu and protect the fish master. Why didn't he think of it before?

The fish master must have been put in the pool instead, which was why His Highness was looking for him—it all made sense now.

Wang Xi wanted to help Prince Jing change, but Prince Jing stared at the fish anxiously and waved his hand. Wang Xi brought over a dry cloth instead, and Prince Jing absent-mindedly patted himself dry, watching, but the fish never "woke up."

In the past, when the fish "meditated," he would return within half an hour, but Xiaoyu hadn't moved since he was brought back.

Prince Jing realized something was off and ordered his servants who were good with fish to take a look at him. But the servants weren't able to tell him anything new; they assumed Xiaoyu had just fallen asleep again, the same as always.

If it was the same, then why wouldn't he wake up?

Prince Jing didn't believe them and ordered Wang Xi to summon Imperial Physician Xu. Imperial Physician Xu wasn't exactly an expert on fish diseases—he simply had a lot of koi at home. He couldn't find any issues either, no matter how intently Prince Jing stared at him.

Prince Jing was extremely worried now. He was the only one who knew that this was a carp spirit that wasn't "waking up." Did something go wrong with his cultivation?

Prince Jing decided to take his fish to see Liao Kong. When Wang Xi heard of this, he anxiously advised, "Your Highness, please give it some more thought. Almost nobody knows about the relationship between you and Liao Kong, so if you take Master Xiaoyu to the Great Master privately..."

The emperor might notice it.

If Liao Kong was involved with any prince, the emperor would no longer trust him, and the words of advice Liao Kong had offered in the past would come under suspicion as well. Prince Jing understood this, but saving the fish was more important. Liao Kong knew some medicine, and he knew Xiaoyu's identity. He might be the only one who could help.

Even if it made the emperor suspicious, he had to go. Xiaoyu had saved him when he was younger, so it was natural that he should risk his life for Xiaoyu too!

But Wang Xi did have a point.

Prince Jing wrote, *Help me deliver a note to the palace. My fish is sick, so I'm requesting to take him to see Liao Kong.*

Wang Xi's eyes lit up. There would be no need to worry if he had the emperor's permission.

Wang Xi ordered someone to come and help Prince Jing prepare clothes for the palace. Prince Jing put Xiaoyu into the crystal bottle and began to write the note. It was already late into the night; if Prince Jing wanted to enter the palace, then they needed someone in the palace to deliver the message.

Everyone was busy for a while... The chaos finally woke Li Yu up. Or, more accurately, Li Yu had become aware of it multiple times, but couldn't force himself to wake up no matter what he did.

This time, he used all his strength to force his eyes open a crack and found that he was in the crystal bottle. His body hurt, and he didn't know what was wrong with him. He couldn't even flick his tail.

He thought that the system must know his situation, so he tried to call out to it. He didn't know if the system would respond since he talked back to it last time, but it was clear that he was in a bad state.

The system immediately said, *<User, hello. You're sick.>*

Li Yu realized that the pain and weakness he felt was from being sick. Was being sick as a fish similar to being sick as a human?

<You caught a cold because your human form stayed in the water for too long,> the system corrected him.

What should he do, then? If he was sick...would the system be responsible for curing him?

<The Moe Pet System only oversees the missions, not treating illnesses,> said the system solemnly. *<You are in critical condition, user. If necessary, please turn into a human and ask for help.>*

Li Yu finally felt the gravity of the situation. The fish-scamming system never asked him to turn into a human on its own. Was he seriously ill? He kind of guessed that he was sick when he couldn't wake up and felt weak all over. Though, actually, there was another surprising part of the request.

The system said he should turn into a human. Was it already the next day?

Li Yu looked around. Prince Jing needed to change clothes to enter the palace, and Wang-gonggong was busy following him around. There wasn't anyone in the room, and the crystal bottle wasn't capped. This was an opportunity!

Li Yu braced himself, then swam to the mouth of the bottle and tumbled out of it with great difficulty. This was already more painful than he wanted. He weakly pressed on his scale to transform.

As soon as he turned into a human, he felt much worse than he did when he was a fish. His whole body trembled, and his teeth kept chattering. His fish form seemed to be able to offset some of his discomfort, but it couldn't cure him, which meant he'd be in pain again when he took human form. But it was the only way he could be given medicine.

Li Yu used his last bit of strength to take out clothes from his inventory and sloppily put them on. He wanted to ask for help, but from who?

Meanwhile, Prince Jing had quickly changed his clothes and finished writing the note. He planned on heading directly to Hugou Temple as soon as the emperor gave permission, even though it was late at night.

He pushed the door open to get the crystal bottle when he saw someone on the floor, completely drenched.

It was Xiaoyu!

Recognizing Li Yu, Prince Jing quickly stepped forward to embrace him. When he unintentionally brushed against Li Yu's bare arm, he found that he was burning up.

Li Yu lay in Prince Jing's arms. He was angry with Prince Jing and didn't want to see him, but when he was trying to wake up, he'd heard Wang-gonggong attempting to persuade Prince Jing several times. The servants and imperial physician all said the fish was fine, but Prince Jing insisted that he wasn't feeling well and wanted to take him to see Liao Kong.

He knew everything, including the fact that Prince Jing came into the water to look for him and took him out in his robes. He could hear the strong heartbeat from the chest he was leaning on... Even though he couldn't wake up, the heartbeat stayed with him in his dreams and made him feel at ease.

"Your Highness, I feel...terrible..." Li Yu sobbed hoarsely. All of his grievances from the past few days... The pain made him want to forget about everything.

When Prince Jing heard this, he picked Li Yu up tenderly and kicked the door open. He knew Xiaoyu had a fever and wanted to call for someone, but he couldn't make any noise beyond a couple of coughs. Prince Jing was so anxious that he was sweating profusely.

"Your Highness!" Wang Xi finally heard him and rushed over.

Now that Xiaoyu was a human, the imperial physician could cure him. Prince Jing had Wang Xi clear the way, and he personally carried Xiaoyu to see the imperial physician.

Fishy Reconciliation

L I YU HAD A FEVER, but he didn't fall asleep again—he just felt weak. Prince Jing carried him all the way to the imperial physician's, unwilling to wait for him in his room. Li Yu, though touched, was also shocked to find out that he, a man, could be carried around so easily.

Sob, wasn't this the princess carry that he hated the most when he used to read novels? But he'd already gotten on this ride, and he was too weak to complain.

Wang-gonggong was staring at him with a burning gaze, along with many servants and guards. Li Yu numbly gave it some thought and couldn't think of a solution, so he just turned his head to hide.

He wasn't used to it, but he also wasn't against such an embrace. He slowly put his weight on the person who was holding him and let out a long sigh of relief, leaning into them until he wasn't nervous anymore. He wondered if he'd found someone he could rely on. The symptoms of his fever were still uncomfortable, but they no longer felt so unbearable.

Earlier, he was afraid that he might even die, but now, he was even managing to keep track of other people's reactions. Li Yu was feeling much more optimistic about his illness being cured.

Imperial Physician Xu hadn't left yet when an anxious Prince Jing suddenly rushed over with a young man in his arms. Imperial

Physician Xu had felt bad that he couldn't help Prince Jing with his fish, but now there was someone he could actually cure. He helped Prince Jing put the young man down, took out the medical kit he carried with him, and checked the patient's pulse. Then he examined the young man's pale face again, thinking that he'd have a better understanding of the situation if he could see his throat, but the patient was unconscious, so it was a little inconvenient. Just as Imperial Physician Xu was about to ask Prince Jing to open the young man's mouth, the young man, who'd been fully asleep just a moment ago, opened his dark eyes.

"Imperial Physician, I accidentally stayed in the water for too long," Li Yu quietly said, his voice rough. He already knew the cause of his illness, and he was afraid that he might actually fall asleep and delay the diagnosis, so he "woke up" to quickly tell the imperial physician.

Imperial Physician Xu had never seen such a proactive patient before. He couldn't help but smile as he said, "This gongzi is suffering from a cold, yes. The high fever hasn't subsided, but his energy levels are fine—it seems the illness is severe, but there is no danger to his life. He needs to be carefully taken care of."

Much more confident now, Imperial Physician Xu wrote a prescription. Prince Jing ordered Wang Xi to make it at once. The servants had finished cleaning up his room already, so Prince Jing stubbornly carried Li Yu all the way back.

Li Yu was getting carried around so much that his anger had deflated completely.

Prince Jing put Li Yu down on the bed and was about to change Li Yu's clothes, but Li Yu opened his eyes and shook his head fiercely until he made himself dizzy. Helpless in the face of his protests, Prince Jing didn't want him to feel uncomfortable, so he didn't insist on changing his clothes. Imperial Physician Xu had told him that Li Yu had to stay warm for the next few days, though, so Prince Jing turned around and found a gold-embroidered green quilt to wrap tightly around Li Yu.

Li Yu was wrapped up like a spring roll. He was still muttering internally to himself, *How did Prince Jing know that I liked green blankets?* But the fever had turned his brain to mush, so even if he thought it was suspicious, he couldn't figure out why.

Wang Xi scurried into the room with the medicine ready, but before he could put the medicine bowl down, Prince Jing snatched it out of his hands. Wang Xi's eye twitched, and he handed Prince Jing a silver spoon. Prince Jing glanced at Wang Xi, and Wang-gonggong immediately understood. "Your Highness, I'll be waiting outside. Please take care of Li-gongzi."

Prince Jing nodded, and Wang Xi walked away to guard the door. Li Yu's head was still dizzy from all the shaking, and he fell into a light sleep for a while until he felt something touching his face. With some difficulty, he forced himself awake, and saw a tall young man standing at the bed, holding a small jade bowl in his hand. His eyebrows were knitted in confusion, as if he didn't know what to do with the medicine, and he'd completely lost the domineering aura he'd had when he snatched it away earlier.

Li Yu wanted to laugh, but he held it back. "Your Highness, is it time for medicine?"

He didn't know how much longer his transformation would last.

Prince Jing nodded, a stiff expression on his face, and Li Yu made to sit up. Prince Jing paused, understanding what he was trying to do, and supported him before he was able to exert any of his own strength. Li Yu sighed and decided not to expend any energy fighting Prince Jing, letting him help instead.

Prince Jing took the soft cushion on the bed and placed it behind Li Yu's lower back. Li Yu leaned on the cushion, whispering, "Thank you, Your Highness... Please give me the bowl. I can do it myself." He held out his hand for the medicine.

Prince Jing understood what Li Yu wanted, but how could he drink the medicine by himself when he was sick? Prince Jing had been sick when he was younger too, and in his memories, Wang Xi had always fed him medicine by the spoonful. Prince Jing knew that he ought to feed Xiaoyu now, but Xiaoyu seemed to be resisting him. If he handed the bowl over... The medicine was fresh out of the pot and still hot. It would definitely be inconvenient for the sick Xiaoyu.

Prince Jing shook his head, rejecting Li Yu's request. He scooped up some medicine himself with the silver spoon, and blew on it gently. He was afraid Li Yu was still angry, so instead of sitting down on the side of the bed, he bent down to bring it to Li Yu's lips.

Li Yu had finally come to understand how stubborn this man was when he wouldn't put him down earlier, and he was actually afraid that if he didn't drink the medicine, Prince Jing would stand over him, waist bent, until he did.

I'll just drink it.

Li Yu lowered his gaze and took the medicine, his face instantly scrunching up from the bitterness.

When he saw this, Prince Jing put down the medicine and took out a peach blossom pastry from the jade box. He broke it into pieces, placed it on his palm, and handed it to Li Yu, gesturing with his chin.

...He wanted him to drink some medicine and then eat something sweet, right?

But isn't that how I took care of him?! How'd he remember to do this?!

At first Li Yu glared at Prince Jing and refused to eat it, but the medicine was too bitter. After a few more sips, Li Yu had to admit defeat and resignedly took a few pieces of peach blossom cake from Prince Jing to stuff into his mouth.

Prince Jing made no moves other than to keep giving him medicine and reminding him to eat the pastry.

At last Li Yu finished the bitter medicine, and Prince Jing took out a plain handkerchief. Before Prince Jing could get any closer, Li Yu took it and wiped his mouth ferociously with it. Prince Jing stayed silent and handed him another note.

Li Yu was worried he'd see another "adore." He was tired.

Prince Jing did treat him well. When he was carrying him around, looking for a physician, Li Yu was a little touched. When he suddenly fell ill, Prince Jing saved him in spite of the way he'd been sulking. He kept being cold to Prince Jing, but Prince Jing took good care of him and didn't seem to be affected by his temper at all.

Li Yu was a little curious how far Prince Jing was willing to go for him...

When he found out that Prince Jing liked him, he'd felt shocked and panicked, as well as angry at the system. Those intense emotions had made him feel lost for a while. He'd been angry for too long—he kept throwing tantrums, making trouble, and even got himself severely sick. Now as he was lying weakly on the bed, he finally calmed down enough to think and realized that he'd gone way too far overboard.

Prince Jing had fallen in love with him while he was completing his missions. Could he blame Prince Jing for that? He couldn't. If he really thought about it, Prince Jing was affected by the system too. Wasn't he innocent?

He kept resisting and resisting, saying that he hated this huge bastard, but when he really asked himself... How much did he really hate him?

When Prince Jing used Chu Yanyu to force him to come out, was he angry that Prince Jing tricked him? No. If he was more clearheaded, he would have realized that everyone in the palace schemed and tricked others. Prince Jing had always been such a person. He was more upset that his concern had been for nothing, not that Prince Jing had deceived him.

And wasn't he, the one Prince Jing was always protecting, the biggest liar?

His identity was fake, the fish was fake, everything was fake. Hadn't he lied to Prince Jing just as much? He would invent stories at every turn, for missions or anything else. And then after all that, he'd gotten upset and hypocritically criticized someone else just to vent his own dissatisfaction.

What it all came down to was really just that he'd suffered too many blows in succession and couldn't control his emotions. He'd heard that people usually regretted the choices they made when emotions were high. He should calm down before he decided what to do about himself and Prince Jing.

Li Yu didn't open the note for a long time. Prince Jing seemed to understand him and patted the back of his hand, as if encouraging him. Emotions aside, Li Yu realized, Prince Jing always managed to make him feel at ease. He stopped hesitating and opened the note to read: *Rest and recover well.*

Li Yu's eyes were warm again, and he nodded imperceptibly. Prince Jing tousled his hair, helped him lie down, and tucked him in the quilt.

"Your Highness, can you...leave me alone for a bit?" Li Yu asked.

Prince Jing had expected this. He'd been looking for a physician so urgently earlier because he knew Xiaoyu's two hours were almost up and that he would need to transform back into a fish. When it came to Xiaoyu's identity, he'd already come to the conclusion that if Xiaoyu didn't want him to know, then he would pretend to not know. So Prince Jing responded to Li Yu's request by picking up the bowl and getting ready to leave the room. Li Yu, on the bed, bit his lip.

He'd asked Prince Jing to leave because his time was almost up, but if he sent Prince Jing away like this, would he think that he was still mad?

He wasn't, actually. His anger had dissipated when he saw how dedicated Prince Jing still was to him even while he was upset. It was better to not be mad. It was too tiring and troublesome to be mad, and it hurt both himself and others.

His body was sick, but his emotions were cured.

"Your Highness, I-I feel a lot better after taking the medicine. Please don't worry. But I still have something important to do, so I can't stay in this room. I'll still come tomorrow, though, and I won't run away. So...can you come see me again tomorrow?"

Li Yu said it all in one breath, and his face turned a little red. He... he wanted to say sorry to Prince Jing for his behavior and hoped Prince Jing wouldn't take it to heart, but why did he end up saying...

...That he hoped Prince Jing would come see him?

Sob, why doesn't my mouth listen to me? It must be because I'm sick!

Prince Jing paused, turning around in disbelief. Li Yu hid his head under the quilt and pretended he hadn't said anything. Prince Jing spotted some of his hair sticking out of the blankets, smiled happily, and closed the door for him.

Li Yu counted Prince Jing's quick steps as he left and thought distantly that he really did still prefer getting along well with that big jerk.

Feeding the Fish
Medicine

L I YU TOOK A BRIEF NAP. When it came time to transform back to a fish, the symptoms of his fever had improved quite a lot, and his head felt a lot clearer too.

Back in his tank, Li Yu noticed that his fish plush was no longer lying on the silver rock bed.

How had it fallen?

Perhaps he had accidentally thrown it there when he was in a rush to transform. What a clumsy mistake... Prince Jing hadn't noticed that it was a fake fish, right? Well, it was fine even if he did notice. He'd had a fish plush before too. Prince Jing hadn't suspected anything then and had even used it himself to fool the second prince.

The real fish decided it wasn't a big deal and put the plush back into his inventory. He laid on the silver rock bed listlessly, taking note of when he'd be able to transform again. Perhaps being sick had made him weak; sleeping on a bed as a human felt a lot more comfortable than a rock bed. Besides, as a human, Prince Jing took care of him, but as a fish...

Wait, didn't Prince Jing say he wanted to take the fish to see Liao Kong?!

Li Yu leaped up from the silver rock bed. Wait, Prince Jing had noticed that the fish was sick and wanted to treat the fish, but then Li Yu had turned into Li-gongzi and passed out in his room, so Prince Jing took Li Yu to see the imperial physician instead. But what about the fish?

Uh, also, the fish got sick because Li-gongzi had jumped into the water to escape. Prince Jing jumped into the water to find Li-gongzi, but ended up finding the unconscious fish, so he took him back, but what happened to Li-gongzi?

...Li-gongzi appeared in Prince Jing's room, completely drenched.

Li Yu went over it again and again in his mind. The more he thought about it, the more something felt off. That was way too many coincidences. Did Prince Jing know Li-gongzi was the fish?

Li Yu came to the abrupt realization that his cover was so full of holes it was basically a sieve!

He had to think of a plan quickly. If Prince Jing realized the person he'd taken a liking to, Li-gongzi, was actually a fish—

A small voice in his head piped up, *So what? Prince Jing would never accept that, so he'd stop pursuing you.*

Li Yu said to himself, very seriously, *If Prince Jing really finds out, then I can no longer be his pet fish, and I won't be able to complete the Moe Pet System's quests, which means I won't be able to turn back into a human. I'll just be a fish for eating, without anyone to rely on. Even if I'm a real koi now—with no one to take care of me, I'd die very quickly, right?*

He couldn't let Prince Jing find out his secret, and he couldn't thoughtlessly make a stupid fuss just because he didn't know what to do with Prince Jing's feelings. After all, he'd already caused a huge ruckus. Li Yu swished his tail miserably. Taking care of the aftermath of this ruckus was now a huge fishy headache.

As Li Yu was sunk in thought, someone knocked on the door. Hearing no response, Prince Jing pushed it open. He'd promised that he would wait until Li-gongzi left before returning.

Li Yu immediately swam to the front of the crystal fish tank, well-behaved. The current matter at hand was to make sure Prince Jing didn't notice any similarities between him and Li-gongzi. For example, Li-gongzi was sick, so the fish couldn't be sick. As long as the fish was lively and energetic, Prince Jing wouldn't connect the sick Li-gongzi with the fish.

But...hang on...a few days ago, the fish was on strike, not letting Prince Jing pet him...

What had he done while he wasn't thinking clearly?! In front of Prince Jing, Li-gongzi was Li-gongzi and the fish was the fish—he couldn't mix them up! If even he himself was getting the two mixed up, Prince Jing would be able to see it too!

Li Yu hurriedly swished his tail at the prince as he swam in complicated patterns in the water.

Prince Jing did care about his fish the most, after all. Every time he came into the room, he always made a beeline to the crystal fish tank. Noticing that the fish wasn't so lethargic anymore, Prince Jing's expression improved a lot. But as he watched his fish swim around excitedly, he kept his hands to himself.

It didn't make sense. Usually, when he showed such affection, Prince Jing would always pet him, or at least pat his head. But now, no matter how cute he acted, Prince Jing's hands remained at his sides. He seemed to be deep in thought and had no intention of touching the fish.

Li Yu suddenly grew nervous. Prince Jing hadn't actually noticed anything, had he?

Li Yu's concern grew as Prince Jing stared at him with his brows furrowed. Then, he reached into the water, put the fish carefully on the silver stone bed, and covered the fish with the leaf blanket. At the end, he patted the fish on the head.

Prince Jing was thinking, *The imperial physician said he can't be cold.*

The fish was once again wrapped up like a spring roll!

Li Yu vaguely recalled that the blanket Prince Jing had wrapped around Li-gongzi was a grass green color edged in gold. And the way he'd touched Li-gongzi's head, had Prince Jing...

Had Prince Jing...really found out?

If he hadn't, why did he treat the fish and the human the same? He even knew that both the fish and Li-gongzi were fans of underwater plants!

As soon as this possibility surfaced in Li Yu's mind, he felt like the water in his fish tank had suddenly frozen solid.

At that moment, Wang-gonggong walked in briskly and clasped his hands together to greet Prince Jing. "Your Highness, the carriage is prepared, and everything is ready at the palace. Does Your Highness still wish to enter the palace?"

Prince Jing shook his head.

He'd wanted to go to the palace because no one was able to treat Xiaoyu, so he had to ask for the emperor's permission to seek out Liao Kong. Imperial Physician Xu had already diagnosed Xiaoyu with a cold and Xiaoyu had woken up and looked a lot better after drinking the medicine, so there was no need to rush to the palace in the night. Xiaoyu could recover quietly for a while, and he'd decide what to do after that.

Of course, he still wanted to send a message to Liao Kong afterward. He would feel a lot better after consulting Liao Kong.

Prince Jing's thoughts were a little complicated, so he wanted to write them down for Wang Xi. From the corner of his eye, he spotted the fish tumble off his silver stone bed, still wrapped up like a spring roll. He pressed his little fish face against the crystal, his eyes like dark grapes, staring at him pitifully. Prince Jing smiled. Xiaoyu was probably afraid of seeing Liao Kong. Yao were typically afraid of monks.

Prince Jing's brush flew across the page. After he was done, his expression told Wang Xi to read it out loud.

Wang-gonggong truly didn't know what was going on, but read loudly, under his master's orders, "Xiaoyu's fine. There's no need to go to Liao Kong."

Having eavesdropped successfully, Li Yu thought, *Oho! It was clearly the right choice to greet Prince Jing energetically. See, now he thinks the fish isn't sick. He's looking way too calm to have found out Li-gongzi's true identity!*

After all, if he had realized the truth, wouldn't he be asking Liao Kong to come and exorcize the yao? Li Yu was sure he was still safe, with a firm grip on his teetering cover. As for Prince Jing covering both Li-gongzi and the fish in a similar blanket... Li Yu glanced at the leaf blanket that he had draped over himself like a cape. Perhaps Prince Jing was affected by the fish's tastes and had also started to like green blankets?

That was a bit more likely than Prince Jing working out Li-gongzi was his fish. Really, when it came down to it, who would ever assume a human could turn into a fish?

Li Yu stopped thinking about it. Prince Jing obviously didn't suspect him, and Li Yu was happy to rest and recover. The next day, he transformed right away, and Prince Jing had already ordered his medicine to be made and was waiting for him.

Li Yu had thought taking care of a patient just meant feeding them good food and tucking them in...

Apparently getting sick caused fish to lose brain cells too! He forgot he still had to take his medicine after transforming!!

The medicine Imperial Physician Xu had prescribed him was way too bitter. Li Yu had clearly blocked out the taste due to how awful it was the first time.

In the end, though, when he wasn't being stubborn, he was quite reasonable. Even though the medicine was disgusting, he knew it was good for his recovery. His fever had broken, and he was no longer feeling any discomfort, which meant the medicine was working. Prince Jing brought over the new bowl, and Li Yu accepted it readily and drank all of it at once.

Prince Jing was holding a silver spoon, ready to feed Xiaoyu just like yesterday, but in the blink of an eye, Xiaoyu had already finished the bowl.

Li Yu grimaced from the bitterness. When he put down his bowl, he realized Prince Jing was still standing there silently. Completely oblivious, he asked, "Is there anything else you needed, Your Highness?"

Prince Jing put away the spoon and shook his head slowly.

As Li Yu watched him, he suddenly realized that the prince probably wanted to feed him the medicine—but he'd already finished it. Li Yu's thought process was very simple. Drinking the medicine was such a painful experience that he might as well just rip off the Band-Aid. Dragging it out would only make it worse! Except he'd accidentally messed up Prince Jing's plan. He didn't mean to!

Li Yu rushed to save the situation, saying, "Th-though I've already drunk all the medicine, it's still just as bitter…"

Prince Jing nodded. If it was bitter, then he should eat something sweet. He would feed him as many peach blossom pastries as he did yesterday.

Prince Jing broke apart the pastry with his head down. This time, Li Yu had learned his lesson, and didn't mention anything about eating it on his own. But Prince Jing kept standing there beside him, bending over him. Every time Li Yu spoke, Prince Jing would look down at Li Yu gently.

There was no way he could keep that up for a long time. "Your Highness, why don't you sit down?" Li Yu said, considerately.

What Li Yu meant was: Prince Jing should go find a chair to sit in. There were quite a few chairs in the room made of red sandalwood, so there were more than enough. But Prince Jing nodded and sat down on the edge of the bed with a whoosh of his robes.

The way Prince Jing had kissed him forcefully was still fresh in Li Yu's mind. Having him so close all of a sudden made Li Yu uneasy. But would he be making too big a deal of it if he asked him to stand up? Li Yu didn't want to be mad at Prince Jing anymore, so he could only scoot inward a little to put some distance between him and Prince Jing.

Luckily Prince Jing didn't notice. Or if he did, he didn't let it show.

Li Yu quickly finished the peach blossom pastries and wiped his mouth. Prince Jing then brought over a white-glazed lotus petal bowl. There was a dish flipped on top of it, covering what was inside.

"What is this?" the curious fish baby asked.

Prince Jing looked a little smug as he opened it for him. Li Yu realized it was a small dish of smashed cucumber. Delighted, he asked, "Did Auntie Xu make this?"

He'd guessed it immediately. Smashed cucumbers didn't exist in ancient times; he'd only made it once in front of Auntie Xu, so she must've made this. The one he made had all gone into Prince Jing's stomach, and it seemed to taste all right. What did Auntie Xu's taste like?

Prince Jing came a little closer and handed him a pair of chopsticks.

Li Yu picked up the chopsticks and tasted a piece first. Then, he ate faster and faster. As he ate, he gave a thumbs-up. After eating so many sweets, he wanted something savory. Auntie Xu's smashed cucumber was surprisingly comparable to the ones he'd eaten in the modern world.

Prince Jing's lips twitched upward. Just like that, he'd managed to close the distance that Xiaoyu had tried so hard to put between them.

Li Yu had drunk his medicine, then stuffed his stomach full of pastry and cucumber. Having eaten and drunk his fill, he felt a little sleepy. Prince Jing moved the jade pillow next to him, signaling that he should sleep a while. Li Yu wanted to but was afraid that he'd turn into a fish in his sleep. He wondered how much Prince Jing was willing to do for him.

"If I only want to sleep for an hour...will Your Highness wake me up?" he asked pitifully.

Waking someone up was a servant's job. Would Prince Jing do that for him? Li Yu was a little curious. But Prince Jing looked at Li Yu and nodded easily. This was something he could do. It was much easier than ordering cucumbers from Auntie Xu.

Seeing that he didn't even hesitate, Li Yu's heart pounded once again.

Wang Xi had important news to report to Prince Jing, but Prince Jing had specifically warned him before that when he was taking care of Li-gongzi, he did not want to be disturbed. Wang Xi peeked in through the crack in the door and waited until Li-gongzi had fallen asleep to call out to Prince Jing quietly...

Prince Jing walked out and stared at him with cold eyes, listening to what he had to say.

Wang Xi immediately understood. "He's at Qingxi Garden, awaiting Your Highness's punishment."

Prince Jing reached up to flick some dust off his robes. He pulled something out of his sleeve and handed it to Wang Xi. Wang Xi took it, confirming that it was some sort of medicine. His heart went cold. His Highness was much too harsh, but...this man had brought this on himself.

Inside the room, someone started sleep talking. At the sound of Li-gongzi's voice, Prince Jing's ominous aura immediately dissipated as he hurried back to look after Li-gongzi.

Now that he had his orders, Wang Xi immediately told the servants to do as Prince Jing instructed.

When Chu Yanyu was dragged back to his quarters, he suffered another beating. Perhaps because this wasn't his first time, he didn't pass out, but he wished he had. He never expected that after all he had to do to sneak into Prince Jing's rooms to drug him, he'd end up being discovered immediately...

It wasn't even just that his plan had failed. In order to entice Prince Jing, and in order to numb himself, he had drunk the aphrodisiac himself. He'd felt strange, and he'd assumed he was burning with desire. He cried and begged nonstop for the servants carrying out his punishment to take him to Prince Jing, hoping that Prince Jing would feel a little pity for his current state.

The drug was meant to help him forget about shame and do what he had to do, but in the end, Wang Xi told him coldly that he hadn't even taken the drug—all of the aphrodisiac had been switched with bean powder. That was when Chu Yanyu realized that what he was feeling was only the product of his guilty conscience. Everyone knew, but nobody told him. They all just watched as he made a fool of himself begging lewdly for affection.

Chu Yanyu lay on the ground quietly, wishing he was dead.

Now Wang Xi was here with a bunch of servants. Before Chu Yanyu could react, a guard had grabbed his throat and forced him to drink a cup of tea. Chu Yanyu knew it couldn't be anything good. He put his fingers down his throat and coughed loudly. But even though he coughed until he cried, he still wasn't able to throw up the tea.

Chu Yanyu glared at Wang Xi, tears streaming down his face. "What did you give me?"

Wang Xi's smile didn't reach his eyes. "Chu-gongzi wanted to drink this but wasn't able to. Have you forgotten already?"

Was this—real aphrodisiac?!

Chu Yanyu was shocked and alarmed. He turned to run, thinking that if he could escape to the sixth prince, there would be someone to protect him, to save him. But he was in Prince Jing's manor, and he was injured. There was no way he'd be able to get very far. Wang Xi walked forward to throw him down on the ground himself and tied up Chu Yanyu's hands and feet.

Chu Yanyu felt the true effects of the drug very quickly. He was trembling all over, eyes bloodshot. Every single rational thought had been swallowed up until nothing was left. Who he was, who the sixth prince was—none of that mattered. He just wanted release, or else for someone to kill him.

He thought Wang Xi had put him in this state so he could find someone to defile him, but nobody came. After Wang Xi tied him up, he gagged him and locked him in the room.

"Chu-gongzi wanted others to experience what it feels like to be consumed by desire," Wang Xi sneered. "Why don't you try it out yourself? Except no one will be coming to help you. Get a good taste of what this feels like, Chu-gongzi. This is Prince Jing's punishment for you."

Chu Yanyu couldn't move or shout. All he could do was whine pitifully.

Wang Xi disappeared into the distance. All that awaited Chu Yanyu was suffocating heat and endless darkness.

Greetings to the Fish Consort

LI YU RECOVERED from his cold quite quickly. In the days during his recovery, he would spend two hours every day with Prince Jing in his human form, drinking his medicine, eating pastries, and calmly observing him.

He wasn't even really sure what he was looking for, but once he'd calmed down, he thought it felt quite nice to be taken care of like this. Thinking back, Prince Jing hadn't just been kind to him these last few days, it had started back when he first appeared as Li-gongzi. Was that when the prince first fell for him?

If he got this question right, he'd score major bonus points...but although Li-gongzi was curious, when he looked at Prince Jing's distinguished, gentle side profile, he couldn't seem to ask it.

I think...I...should be able to work it out if I keep watching him, Li-gongzi reassured himself.

Imperial Physician Xu checked his pulse for him a few more times and adjusted his medication before finally pronouncing him fully recovered. Li Yu smiled from joy, but after he thanked Imperial Physician Xu, he found himself feeling strangely disappointed. He had recovered, so there was no need for Prince Jing to spend time with him anymore. He was once again just a servant in the manor tasked with taking care of the fish.

Li Yu ignored the discomfort in his heart and managed a bright smile as he said, "Thank you, Your Highness, for taking care of me all this time."

Prince Jing smiled gently and nodded.

Li Yu had recovered now, but he didn't know what had happened after Chu Yanyu tried to drug Prince Jing. He didn't dare ask the prince directly, so he tried to ask Wang-gonggong instead.

Wang Xi smiled at him. "Chu-gongzi made a big mistake," he said, not revealing anything. "He's been given the time to reflect on himself in his room. How do you know him, Li-gongzi?"

Li Yu couldn't explain, so he said vaguely, "I've heard Chu-gongzi's name before, when I was outside."

It wasn't entirely a lie. The delicate concubine was famous for his looks and talents in the original story, and had already been very well known back when he was under the sixth prince.

"Perhaps this old servant had heard of him too," said Wang Xi. "But that's all in the past now. Once someone has entered the manor, they ought to focus on being a good person, rather than crafting filthy plots. Personally, this servant thinks Chu-gongzi brought this upon himself. Li-gongzi, you shouldn't feel bad for him or ask for forgiveness on his behalf."

Wang Xi really was good with people. He even anticipated that Li Yu would ask for leniency. Li Yu paused. "Of course not," he said.

He wasn't that naive. Chu Yanyu had the nerve to try to drug Prince Jing. Now that he'd been caught, it was already benevolent of Prince Jing not to kill him. Wang-gonggong just said he was self-reflecting, so there was no need for Li Yu to ask Prince Jing for leniency over that.

There was no way he could know, though, what Wang Xi actually meant by "reflecting on himself," so he didn't give it any further thought.

So much for Prince Jing and Chu Yanyu's relationship. From what he knew of Prince Jing, the chances of the two falling in love must have dwindled to practically nothing. It seemed like he was stable in his position as the one Prince Jing liked, and there was no need to try to set Prince Jing up with anyone else anymore.

Reaching this conclusion, Li Yu felt a sense of relief.

He didn't want to find out what would become of Chu Yanyu. Prince Jing had already rejected Chu Yanyu back during the banquet. He could've lived a life completely different to the one he had in the book. But Chu Yanyu remained adamant on entering Prince Jing's manor—Li Yu only found out how exactly Chu Yanyu got in after Wang-gonggong explained. It turned out the third prince had just jammed him in there in a desperate bid for favor. Li Yu didn't know whether to laugh or cry.

Chu-gongzi had no status in Prince Jing's manor, even to this day. He couldn't even be considered a servant. Everyone in the manor knew to keep their guard up against him, and when they called him "gongzi," it was with a slight sneer—unlike Li-gongzi, who was someone Prince Jing cared for with all his heart. All the servants treated him with respect, careful not to offend him in any way.

Although Li Yu's appearance had messed up Prince Jing's canon pairing, he hadn't forced Chu Yanyu to drug the prince. Since that had been Chu Yanyu's own decision, it really wasn't Li Yu's problem.

Li Yu stopped talking about Chu Yanyu. Prince Jing didn't like that Xiaoyu kept asking about other people, so he signaled to Wang Xi with his eyes to stop talking about it.

Wang Xi, who had been given a great responsibility, immediately changed topics. "Your Highness, Li-gongzi, a new market opened up in the city recently. Um, this old servant heard that the emperor organized it alongside the King of Jinjue to celebrate the marriage between our empire and Jinjue. Many merchants there are from Jinjue, and they're selling little trinkets we've never seen over here..."

As soon as he heard "market" and "trinkets," Li Yu's ears perked up. Wang Xi held in his laughter. "His Highness was planning on going to take a look. If Li-gongzi is interested, why don't you ask His Highness about it?" Wang Xi blinked at Li Yu, then gestured toward Prince Jing with his lips.

Since his transmigration, Li Yu hadn't once had the chance to go shopping as a human, so he hurried to ask, "Your Highness, I want to go. Can I?"

That was what Prince Jing was waiting for. He nodded with a smile.

Li Yu could finally go out and walk around! If he stayed in Prince Jing's manor any longer, he was going to grow mushrooms! Li Yu was thrilled—until he realized that by modern standards, he and Prince Jing strolling around the markets would be considered a date, right?

...So, it was a date.

Li Yu snuck a glance at Prince Jing, blushing slightly. That asshole was employing his sneaky tactics again. Since Wang Xi was the one who'd brought it up, he almost didn't notice.

Since it was a date, did that mean Prince Jing was pursuing him?

This asshole used force before, Li Yu complained silently, *and now he's worked out how to woo me? He's getting too good way too fast!*

But Li Yu didn't have the heart to say no to the market. He bit his lip. It wasn't like he had a partner. He...might as well just let this big asshole pursue him for a bit. He didn't have anything to lose by it.

Li Yu nodded, officially agreeing. Wang-gonggong almost offered his congratulations. Now, if the masters were going out, it wasn't as if they would leave immediately. They had to see when the market was open and when Prince Jing had time. Besides, Xiaoyu needed "suitable" clothing for going out. Prince Jing chose a few more styles in private and asked Wang Xi to handle it. Really, Wang-gonggong was so busy lately that he barely had a moment to breathe.

In order to completely dismiss any remaining hesitation for Xiaoyu, fish-lover Prince Jing kindly suggested they take the fish out with them. Taking care of the fish would fall to Li-gongzi.

Li Yu couldn't have asked for a better opportunity. If Prince Jing wanted him to look after the fish, then when the time came, *he'd* be the one to determine which was the real fish and which was the fake.

Soon, the day arrived. Li Yu and Prince Jing had already agreed on a time to leave. Once he'd transformed, Li Yu immediately went to go meet the prince. He wore a new long robe that Prince Jing had given him—it was rose red and embroidered with silver lotuses. He tied a string of pearls casually around his waist. Wang Xi said he should dress a little more cheerily, since he had just recovered. Li Yu didn't quite understand the customs of ancient people, but it sounded good, so he put it on. He still wasn't very used to the belts people wore in ancient times, but the clothes that Prince Jing gave him always came with very thin belts, so he didn't have to give himself a headache trying to tie them.

Red was an auspicious color and made one's skin appear paler. Li Yu felt like he looked a lot more hale and hearty wearing red. In the bronze mirror, his cheeks looked like he was wearing rouge. He didn't normally wear such bright colors...

Prince Jing stared at him for a long while before he was able to look away.

Li Yu smiled, pleased. He understood that the clothes made the man, but Prince Jing's old clothes fit him too well, like they were actually made for him. Since he'd transmigrated into a fish, he didn't get to spend much time as a human. He was already incredibly grateful to have clothes to wear, so he never gave it much thought, but this time, he did: Why did Prince Jing have such a huge pile of old clothes that all fit Li Yu?

And why were these clothes all in colors Prince Jing would never wear?

Li Yu suddenly came to a realization. "Could it be that...these aren't old clothes at all, but ones Your Highness had made for me?"

Prince Jing hadn't expected to be found out like this, and his expression betrayed how awkward he felt. He didn't actually admit to anything, but his uneasy gaze said it all. If this had happened before, Li Yu might have been annoyed, but now that he'd adjusted his perspective, he could see Prince Jing's feelings toward him and the careful and thoughtful way he treated him.

Li Yu felt like his heart had been pounced on by a little kitten.

"Thank you, Your Highness. The clothes are very pretty. I-I'll continue to wear them..."

Li Yu tried to tell himself he was just wearing clothes Prince Jing had made for him, there was nothing weird about that, but Prince Jing's embarrassment seemed to be contagious. After looking into Prince Jing's eyes for a while, he started to become embarrassed too.

Li Yu looked down, playing with the gold chain on the crystal bottle. Because Prince Jing had given him the task of looking after his pet fish, Li Yu was the one who put the fish in the bottle. He put the fish plush in early on and tried to keep the bottle covered with his sleeve. When the time came, he'd swap it out and put himself in the bottle. He'd make it hard to tell if it was real or fake.

He remembered that Prince Jing would wrap the gold chain around his hand to prevent the bottle from slipping. In order to make it seem like the fish was really in there, Li Yu did the same thing. But he had only wrapped the chain around once when Prince Jing took the gold chain and bottle away from him.

Li Yu was confused. His heart leapt into his throat, afraid Prince Jing would take a look at the fish in the bottle and notice the difference. But Prince Jing only unwrapped the gold chain from his hand and wrapped it around his own instead.

...Huh??

Prince Jing couldn't speak, so he had to guess a lot of what he meant. Li Yu thought about it for a while. Prince Jing hadn't scolded him, so it probably wasn't because he wasn't taking good enough care of the fish. Perhaps he thought the chain would make him uncomfortable.

But Prince Jing's hand had been injured—and injured to protect him too...

Remembering what Prince Jing looked like when he was bleeding to protect him made Li Yu feel like he was going to drown in all his emotions. He'd originally planned to take a bit of time to calm down, but it was like Prince Jing had an invisible string tied to him, reeling him in bit by bit.

"Your Highness, gongzi, it's time to go." Wang-gonggong came to ask for further instructions.

The market was some way from the manor. Wang-gonggong had arranged for a carriage, and Li Yu had to make the most of his precious time. When it was time to get on, a servant bent down so Li Yu could use his back to step up into the carriage, but Li Yu politely refused. He really wasn't an aristocrat, and it wasn't hard to just hoist himself into the carriage.

Prince Jing's carriage was a little on the small side. When Li Yu was in there alone there was just enough room, but then Prince Jing got on from the other side, and with the two of them together it was a bit cramped. They had no choice but to sit face-to-face with their legs touching. When the carriage turned a corner or changed speeds, Li Yu would inevitably bump into Prince Jing or lurch against him. It never hurt, but Li Yu couldn't be any more flustered. He felt like he was taking advantage of Prince Jing. Every time he touched the prince, he would apologize. Prince Jing listened to his endless apologies, but his eyes were full of smiles.

Sob sob sob, you big asshole! When you smile like that, why does it seem like you're taking advantage of me?!

The carriage soon arrived at the market, and Prince Jing helped Li Yu down. Li Yu had climbed up onto the carriage himself, but when it was time to get down, his legs trembled at the height—it was clearly a bit taller than he was. He had no choice but to swallow his embarrassment and let Prince Jing help him. But Prince Jing really knew how to take advantage of the situation. As soon as he saw Li Yu give in, not only did he take his hand, he even put an arm around his waist. Thanks to the difference in their heights, Li Yu couldn't refuse, and he had to endure being half carried, half hugged off the carriage.

Having heard that nobility was coming, a lot of commoners had gathered at the market. It was a large, bustling crowd. Li Yu had just stepped foot on the ground and escaped from Prince Jing's arms when he heard the people whispering among themselves.

"Who is that noble?"

"The carriage looks like it's from Prince Jing's manor. Have you heard of Prince Jing?"

"Of course I've heard of His Royal Highness Prince Jing. I'm asking about the young gongzi next to him."

Li Yu's ears immediately perked up at a mention of himself.

"Who's that gongzi?"

"I don't know, perhaps His Highness's younger brother?"

"Do you hug your brother like that? Look at the way His Highness is fussing over him. He must be either a consort or a concubine."

"No way. A consort can come to the market too?"

"A consort wouldn't be able to, so maybe he's a beloved concubine instead?"

A concubine…!

Prince Jing also overheard the inappropriate conversation, and his expression darkened. Li Yu thought it was understandable that the people would gossip if they didn't know the truth, and it was unavoidable that Prince Jing would get angry too. It would be good if he could clarify the situation here…

The thought had just popped into his mind when Prince Jing's sharp gaze swept toward Wang Xi like he could hear Li Yu's thoughts. With a start, Wang Xi immediately ran over and pulled the uninformed commoners to the side to talk to them.

Once he'd done as the prince asked, Wang Xi returned to the group smiling. The commoners also came back smiling, yelling excitedly, "Welcome, Prince! Welcome, consort!"

Li Yu had naively thought Prince Jing was going to explain the situation!!! One mistake and he'd regret it forever. How had he become a consort? What was going to become of his reputation?

Well, never mind, a fish didn't need a reputation. Li Yu had lost count of how many times he'd comforted himself like this by now.

Fishy Shopping

NOW THAT THE PEOPLE had all started calling him consort, Prince Jing's expression relaxed a bit. But it didn't seem like he had any intention of correcting them, nor did he express anything further to Li Yu.

Li Yu thought if Prince Jing mentioned anything about it he could deny it, since they weren't actually married. It would be no good if people misunderstood. But Prince Jing never brought up the topic, and he couldn't very well mention it himself, lest it seemed like he cared about the title of "consort." So he just had to endure a bunch of people calling him consort and couldn't say anything to deny it.

Li Yu was starting to regret leaving the house. Sob sob sob, why did he have to be forced into this situation just because this big asshole wouldn't say anything?!

Wang Xi had come to this market beforehand to take a look around, and he quietly introduced everything to Prince Jing and Li Yu. If the masters were interested, he could lead the way. The manor's guards protected Prince Jing, while Prince Jing protected Li-gongzi. Although there were plenty of onlookers, no one came over to bother the group.

Prince Jing handed the simple map Wang Xi had drawn to Li Yu, clearly wanting him to take the lead. Li Yu only had two hours.

He couldn't waste his time on needless pleasantries, so he accepted the map without any hesitation.

Wang Xi's map was simple and easy to understand. You could see how everything was laid out in a single glance. The market had two entrances: north and south. Right now, they were at the north entrance, and all along the main road were plenty of stalls and shops. There was even a restaurant, and acrobats from Jinjue were performing inside. Li Yu knew he couldn't explore every nook and cranny of the market, so he headed for the busiest area. The restaurant was said to be the largest in the area, and although it was owned by a local, all the chefs were from Jinjue. Apparently, the people of Jinjue excelled at cooking beef and lamb, so the restaurant's specialty was barbecued whole lamb and all kinds of kebabs. All of this made Li Yu extremely excited, and he couldn't help drooling at the thought.

"Your Highness, let's just follow the main road slowly south. We can take a look at the stalls along the road, then have a meal at the restaurant and watch the acrobats. Then once we've reached the south entrance we can leave. How's that?"

It was a straightforward plan, and Prince Jing had no objections, so he ordered Wang Xi to make it happen. Wang-gonggong immediately ordered a guard to jog to the restaurant to reserve the best private room. A whole lamb would take quite a while to cook, so they could ask the restaurant to start preparing it right away. Li-gongzi and His Highness would walk around a bit, and by the time they made it to the restaurant, it would be about time to eat.

And so Li Yu and Prince Jing started to browse the market, as planned.

Just as Wang Xi said, there were plenty of Jinjue goods on sale. Li Yu had only read a few lines about this in the original novel: the people of Jinjue liked thick, sparkly, impressive gold accessories, especially bracelets and masks. They would often be carved with Jinjue's three-legged crow motif. Li Yu loved sparkly things too. Every time they passed by a stall with these golden accessories shining in the sun, he would always stop and take a curious look.

Prince Jing noticed a white jade hairpin with a rare fish design on the end. A piece of inky jade was used for the fish's eyes. Prince Jing thought the hairpin was made quite nicely. Although the materials used were a little rough, it looked rather like Xiaoyu. He asked for the hairpin to take a closer look.

Li Yu was delighted that Prince Jing was looking at the hairpin. It turned out this big asshole also liked sparkly accessories! While Prince Jing was examining the hairpin, Li Yu snuck off to a different stall. Prince Jing noticed immediately and handed the hairpin off to Wang Xi to take care of. He led the guards himself, following Li Yu from a distance. Ever since Xiaoyu arrived at the market, his eyes had been practically glued to all the little trinkets along the side of the road. There wasn't anything wrong with letting the carp spirit enjoy himself for a bit.

Most of the stalls along the main road were surrounded by people, but after a while Li Yu found one that was a little quieter. This one sold bracelets and masks. Li Yu's appreciative gaze paused at each mask hanging up on display. The masks at this stall all had a thick layer of gold powder, and a three-legged crow stood on the forehead of each one. Every crow had a beautiful peacock feather at its tail, making the masks seem ancient and mysterious.

After looking at the masks, Li Yu went to look at the bracelets. Imitating Prince Jing, he picked up a gold bracelet and observed it carefully under the sun. A three-legged crow was carved on the inside, just like he'd heard. Li Yu felt the bracelet with his fingers, feeling like it had been polished very smoothly. Other than the crow on the inside, there were no other embellishments. Trying it on, the thick, heavy gold on his thin wrist really gave off a feeling of new money. Li Yu thought it didn't suit him and tried to take it off.

But the merchant saw that Li Yu was alone and he didn't know who he was, so he said with a smile, "Since you've already put it on, customer, that means the bracelet is fated to be yours. This is a custom of ours in Jinjue. Please don't try to go against fate. Buy it."

The merchant was thick and muscular, with a dense mustache, and, like many Jinjue people, his eyes were slightly deep set. He was trying to force Li Yu to buy the bracelet immediately, and he wanted fifty taels for it. Li Yu was a little panicked. He'd only tried it on once, and it was so expensive. Had he run into an ancient version of hard selling?

Prince Jing, who was a distance away, was about to intervene as soon as he noticed something was wrong, but then he saw Li Yu scratch his cheek and smile mischievously. Prince Jing's footsteps stopped. It seemed he had accidentally come across Xiaoyu making mischief. Xiaoyu was a carp spirit, after all. As long as there was no danger, he could do whatever he wanted.

Meanwhile, Li Yu was thinking it over carefully. The merchant hadn't warned him he couldn't try the wares on. He then glanced at the other stalls. Everyone was trying things on, but the other merchants didn't say anything. This was the only stall abiding by this Jinjue "custom." Li Yu immediately understood he was being scammed.

Li Yu wasn't worried at all when faced with such a person. He said slowly, "Sir, when I first put it on, you didn't say I would have to buy it if I tried it on. Why are you only telling me now?"

"Now's not too late." The merchant threw all shame out the window. "My bracelets are imbued with spirit. Now that you've put it on, you've sucked away the spirit inside. If you won't buy it, how will I sell it to someone else?"

How could he make up such a stupid story?!

Li Yu weighed the bracelet in his palm. It was quite heavy, so it was probably worth a lot, but definitely not fifty whole taels. Li Yu had heard Wang Xi mention before that ten taels was enough to support an ordinary family for a whole year. How could he buy an accessory that was worth five years of expenses?

Besides, he didn't have any money. He was in charge of taking care of the fish at Prince Jing's manor. His "work" was very easy, and Prince Jing took care of all his meals and clothes. Li Yu never thought to ask for pay. He was just a transmigrated fish—why would he need to care about such material goods? Sure, he had an inventory, but it was better to save that for something important. Although he slept with a gold embroidered blanket and on a spacious silver rock bed every night, he actually had nothing to his name. He had no savings; he was a fish pauper. There was no way he could afford this gold bracelet, and he didn't want to waste money to support such scammy practices. It would be best if he could teach this merchant a lesson.

"Sorry sir," Li Yu said easily, "fifty taels is too much." *No matter what you say, I'm just not gonna buy it. What are you going to do about it?*

The merchant stared, eyes wide. There was no way he was mistaken. The youth's robes were made of top-quality ice silk—even the pearls casually tied around his waist were each a good size. Thus, he determined this youth must be a rich gongzi. But how could a member of the aristocracy not be able to afford a mere fifty taels? Plus, he looked like he had the time to haggle all day.

The merchant's expression was dark. "The least I can do is forty-five taels. I can't go any lower."

Li Yu sighed. "Sir, I can't afford forty-five taels either."

The merchant held on to hope. Each time, he would go down by five taels. They'd haggled down to twenty-five taels, but this gongzi still wasn't planning on paying. The merchant was starting to get angry.

"Then how much can you afford?"

"Sorry, sir, I forgot to bring my wallet today." Li Yu stuck his tongue out and smiled.

The merchant nearly passed out from rage. "Why are you shopping if you don't have money?!"

Li Yu said innocently, "You never told me I had to buy the bracelet if I tried it on!"

The merchant was so angry he wanted to chase him away. He was just about to curse Li Yu out when, out of the corner of his eye, he saw a tall youth with a bunch of servants standing behind the young gongzi. This tall young man looked over with a cold expression and met the merchant's eyes. The threat in them was obvious.

The merchant realized this must be the young gongzi's backer, and he trembled. His mouth gaped open and shut, but he swallowed his curses back down.

Meanwhile, Li Yu had no idea someone was supporting him in secret. The merchant fell silent, and Li Yu put the bracelet back on his arm.

The merchant was baffled by his actions. Quietly, he said, "Y-you won't buy it, so why are you still wearing it?"

"Sir, didn't you say I sucked away the spirit of this bracelet?" said Li Yu simply. "I'm wearing it for a while so it can suck some of my spirit back into it! That way you can sell it to someone else!"

The merchant had just said his bracelets had spirit. If he denied it now, he'd basically be slapping himself in the face.

The merchant's uneasy gaze floated over to the youth not far away. Perhaps he was imagining things because of the danger he could sense, but the youth's icy expression seemed even colder. There was nothing he could do as he watched Li Yu play with the bracelet, fiddling with it in all sorts of ways.

Passersby stared at Li Yu curiously, and there were some who were interested and also wanted to play with the bracelet. The merchant thought business had arrived, but Li Yu leaned in and casually said, "Did you guys bring enough money? This merchant has a rule that if you try it on, you have to buy it."

Once everyone heard that, they all left quickly. The merchant was furious and frustrated, but he couldn't show it. In the end, he could only ask Li Yu to return the bracelet and go somewhere else.

Li Yu was all smiles. "I hope your business does well," he said. "I'll be back next time!"

Please don't come back again, the merchant prayed silently.

Li Yu thought he'd only left for a short while and that Prince Jing was probably still looking at the hairpin. But when he turned around to go look for Prince Jing, he saw the prince standing behind him with a smile, as though he were a solid, metal wall.

"Y-Your Highness!"

Li Yu's tongue was tied. This asshole had been here the whole time? Then wouldn't he have seen him haggling with the merchant and messing around with him?! As the one that Prince Jing fancied, he must have completely shattered Prince Jing's image of him, right?

Li Yu was a little hesitant, but Prince Jing was smiling as he walked up to him. He patted Li Yu on the head, pulled out a white jade hairpin shaped like a fish, and carefully put it in Li Yu's hair.

When Li Yu had first transformed into a human, the system had made some adjustments to his appearance, making his hair longer so he'd fit in. Nobody had commented on it, and so Li Yu didn't give it much thought either, assuming he was doing enough to follow the customs. Every time he transformed, he was always in a rush. Having clothes to wear was good enough; he never had time to braid his hair or put on a hair piece. Usually, he left it loose behind him. Prince Jing thought he liked it like that and never said anything.

Now that he had a hairpiece, Li Yu stared at the round little fish, lost in thought. Did Prince Jing give him a fish hairpin because his name was Li Yu?

Prince Jing really did like fish a lot.

Li Yu's earlobes were a bit red. Was he supposed to learn how to tie up his hair now?

Fishy Eats Barbecue

L I YU SAW MANY MORE trinkets as he continued down the road—although his mood had taken a bit of a hit from that con artist merchant, so he really was just window shopping.

When they arrived at the restaurant he'd been looking forward to, Wang Xi was already waiting in front of the elegant two story building.

The restaurant was called "Dream of a Spring Breeze." Li Yu thought it was unique, especially since this was basically a barbecue restaurant. Wang Xi had booked the best private room upstairs ahead of time, and told Prince Jing and Li Yu that all of the restaurant's signature dishes were waiting for them upstairs. Thinking of the hot barbecued lamb and skewers, Li Yu sped up.

Prince Jing observed all of this.

When they arrived at the room, the rich smell of meat came wafting toward them. Li Yu inhaled deeply. How lovely, exactly the same as in modern times! But no matter how excited he was, he should let Prince Jing go first. Snatching back his gluttonous soul that was about to fly out of his body, he shifted to the side.

But Prince Jing walked over to him so they could walk in together. Before Li Yu could react, there was a warmth surrounding his hand. Prince Jing was already pulling him toward the head seat. He couldn't let go, but he couldn't continue to hold Prince Jing's hand either. This was the first time the restaurant had welcomed such an esteemed guest. The owner and several other workers were right in front of them. If he shook off Prince Jing's hand right now, would that embarrass him?

By the time he realized Prince Jing's pride had nothing to do with a fish, Prince Jing had already sat down. Tugging on his hand a little, he signaled that Li Yu should sit down too.

Li Yu immediately noticed something was off. He was sitting right next to Prince Jing. They'd sat together before, when they were drawing, but now that he knew Prince Jing liked him—and after the shock of being called "consort" outside—Li Yu very quickly realized the position next to the prince should be for the consort.

He hadn't even managed to deny the title properly yet. If he sat down now, wouldn't it really be true?

Li Yu was still hesitating when Prince Jing took a leg off the barbecued lamb and put it in the little bowl in front of him. Li Yu's eyes immediately lit up. *Oh, it's sooooo big, and it smells sooooo good.* He'd never eaten a lamb leg that was roasted so golden brown and crispy! Li Yu didn't waste any more time thinking. He just sat down in front of the bowl. Next to the bowl were several silver plates holding seasonings like chili powder, cumin, peanuts, and fermented black beans. "There are so many!" Li Yu exclaimed, surprised and delighted.

"This is the custom in Jinjue," the owner explained. "You can eat the meat by itself or dipped in the seasonings."

Li Yu liked this custom. He immediately began to make his own dipping sauce, starting with a lot of chili powder and cumin, then a little bit of sesame. He then looked up at the owner to ask, "Do you have sesame oil and minced garlic?"

He really wanted to ask if they had oyster sauce, but he thought they might not have oyster sauce here in the past, so he asked for sesame oil instead, which was also very fragrant.

The owner knew right away that this was someone who knew how to eat and hurried to respond, "Of course, of course."

A lot of the nobility didn't like to eat these two condiments, so the owner didn't usually bring them to the table for fear of offending the guests. He immediately asked a server to bring them both out.

Li Yu finished mixing his dipping sauce in no time, feeling very proud of himself. When he glanced at Prince Jing, however, he noticed there was nothing in his bowl.

Did Prince Jing...not know how to eat this? After all, princes mostly ate steamed or boiled foods, rarely ever barbecue. Although Prince Jing had given him a leg, he himself only grabbed half a slice of white meat.

"Your Highness, can I help you?" Li Yu asked quietly.

Prince Jing had been waiting for him to ask. Smiling, he put his bowl next to Li Yu without any hesitation.

As Li Yu put seasonings into his bowl, he asked carefully, "Does Your Highness eat garlic?" or "Does Your Highness eat peanuts?"

Meanwhile, His Highness was too busy watching him. He randomly nodded or shook his head, not knowing what he was answering to. Before long, a bowl of sauce was presented to him. Prince Jing vaguely remembered the smashed cucumber Xiaoyu had made him.

"All right, I made that according to Your Highness's tastes," said Li Yu. "Try it! It's definitely much better than just eating plain meat."

Prince Jing nodded. Under Wang-gonggong's worried gaze, he grabbed a piece of meat, dipped it into the sauce, and ate it without a change in expression.

Delicious. The prince smiled, satisfied.

Li Yu quickly ate nearly half of the lamb leg, drank some lamb soup, and tried to cut a plate of braised beef. Though his knife skills were lacking and it didn't look very good, it was at least edible, and nearly all of it went into Prince Jing's stomach.

They'd been eating for a while when someone suddenly announced that Ye-shizi had arrived, looking for Prince Jing.

Li Yu lowered the lamb leg, which he was holding in one hand. The ever-observant Wang-gonggong handed him a clean cloth. Li Yu wiped his oily fingers and mouth, then looked toward Prince Jing suspiciously. What was Ye-shizi doing here? Did Prince Jing ask him out to the market and invite Ye Qinghuan as well?

Li Yu was thinking too much. Of course Prince Jing hadn't invited any "unrelated" parties. Ye-shizi had just heard Prince Jing was eating at Drunken Spring Breeze and wanted to join the fun.

As for how Ye Qinghuan found out... Prince Jing's gaze cut across to Wang Xi, who rubbed his nose guiltily. He was Prince Jing's weather vane. If Ye-shizi asked where Wang Xi was, he would know where Prince Jing was.

Prince Jing ordered Wang Xi to let Ye Qinghuan in. Ye-shizi usually had his dog with him, but today he was finally here with someone else for once. He had brought a small, skinny young gongzi along. This gongzi had a kind of feminine beauty that could rival Chu Yanyu's, with a pair of glistening, peach blossom eyes, an upright nose, and small cherry lips. Both of his hands were wrapped tightly around Ye Qinghuan's arm.

Li Yu was shocked. In the original book, Ye Qinghuan was an only child, so this youth couldn't be his younger brother. But he was so close to Ye Qinghuan, it was a little weird. Besides, wasn't Ye-shizi about to get married to the princess? Why was he this close with a young man?

Unless...

Something occurred to Li Yu. He glanced at Prince Jing suddenly. Was being gay contagious?

Ye Qinghuan had never treated Prince Jing as an outsider. Now that he'd brought this young gongzi here, though, he seemed like he was hiding something. He hadn't said anything, but he kept giggling.

Li Yu thought it was even more suspicious.

At first the youth next to Ye Qinghuan was surveying the surroundings. Li Yu didn't have any reaction, but when he saw Prince Jing, the youth suddenly covered his mouth and said something in a murmur.

But as soon as he spoke, the jig was up. Because what came out of his mouth was a beautiful girl's voice. Prince Jing and Ye Qinghuan stared at each other for a while. It was clear who this person was, but Li Yu was still stuck on "this youth is actually a girl in disguise," "why would Ye-shizi take a girl dressed as a man shopping," "does Ye-shizi have someone else," and other melodramatic guesses.

Without realizing, he'd spoken his thoughts out loud. Ye Qinghuan chuckled. "I don't have anyone else. This is the princess."

Huh???

Li Yu had been thinking that perhaps Ye Qinghuan had done something unforgivable to the Jinjue Princess—but it turned out the youth next to Ye Qinghuan was the princess herself. Li Yu was even more shocked than before. He'd once glanced at this princess from far away at the banquet held in Yangxin Hall. At the time, the princess had spoken out on the fish's behalf and talked back to the second prince. But he'd been inside a fish tank back then and hadn't gotten a good look at the princess. Now that she appeared again, disguised as a man, Li Yu didn't recognize her at all.

"Hello." The Princess of Jinjue nodded at both Prince Jing and Li Yu kindly.

In terms of status, Prince Jing wasn't below the princess, so he had no need to bow to her, but Li Yu suddenly considered his own status. He quickly pushed his chair back, but Prince Jing suddenly put his hand on Li Yu's shoulder, not letting him stand up.

Ye Qinghuan laughed and said, "Li-gongzi, don't worry. We'll all be family sooner or later."

The last time Ye Qinghuan went to Prince Jing's manor, he'd found out Prince Jing had someone he liked already: Li-gongzi. Prince Jing usually kept Li-gongzi well-hidden, so Ye Qinghuan had never seen him. He'd wanted to meet him for a long time, so today, when he found out Prince Jing had taken Li-gongzi to the market, Ye Qinghuan immediately decided to take the princess along too.

The Jinjue people were more open, so a couple could feel free to meet up and go on dates even before marriage. At first, Ye Qinghuan was very afraid of getting married, but slowly he'd come to accept the idea. He went to the King of Jinjue himself, asking if he and the princess could see each other more to develop the relationship. The King of Jinjue had high hopes for Ye-shizi, so of course he agreed.

On the other hand, the Princess of Jinjue initially didn't like this husband that the emperor had called "steady and mature." But after she found out Ye-shizi had a dog, the princess started seeing Ye Qinghuan in a new light. This princess had many pets growing up, such as cats and bunnies. She thought when she got married, her husband's family wouldn't let her have pets anymore, but to her surprise, her fiancé shared the same interest as her. Besides, Ye-shizi was someone who stood out amongst his peers. Now, the little princess's feelings for Ye Qinghuan were growing by the day.

Like Ye Qinghuan, this was the first time the Jinjue Princess had met Li-gongzi. At first she was very reserved, not knowing what to say. But the princess still remembered the little carp at the banquet, so when she saw the fish's owner, she was extremely excited.

"Prince Jing, did you bring the fish this time?" she asked, curious.

Prince Jing's fish was actually right next to him.

Li Yu and Prince Jing were both thinking the same thing, but Li Yu was contemplating whether or not he could bring the crystal bottle out and let the princess see it without somehow getting close.

While Li Yu racked his brains, Prince Jing just smiled, giving Wang Xi a lazy glance. Wang-gonggong immediately lied for his master without blinking. "Unfortunately, Princess, His Highness didn't bring the fish out this time."

The fish who had been left behind sat in his chair and kept glancing uneasily at Prince Jing's hand. The golden chain of the crystal bottle was clearly still wrapped around his hand, but when he ordered Wang Xi to lie, he didn't even blink.

Why wouldn't this asshole let the princess see the fish? Though he guessed not letting her see did help him out. He he, Li Yu didn't need to worry about the princess noticing anything.

Faced with a gentle rejection, the princess was just like her fiancé, Ye Qinghuan. She paid no mind to Prince Jing's coldness and said, smiling, "Can I see it next time?"

Clearly, the princess not only wanted to see him, she wanted to pet him as well.

This princess's beauty was unmatched, and when she smiled, she looked even more stunning. Unfortunately, Prince Jing wasn't someone who would give in just because they were a girl or a relative. He shook his head decisively.

No, no way! Go pet yourself!

Although Prince Jing wouldn't let the princess pet his fish, two chopsticks were still added to the barbecue squad.

Ye Qinghuan wanted to bring the princess to join in on the fun partly because he thought the princess might be homesick, since she had been away from Jinjue for a while. This market and restaurant were filled with the feeling of Jinjue, so he thought the princess would like it. As expected, when the little princess saw a table laden with beef and lamb, her eyes curved into crescent moons, and she happily talked and laughed with him.

The princess elegantly ordered a servant to cut off a lamb leg and nodded toward Ye Qinghuan. He happily gestured for her to go ahead. The princess immediately rolled up her sleeves and grabbed the leg. With astonishing speed, the princess demolished the lamb leg like a whirlwind. Then she wiped her mouth, put the bone on a plate, and elegantly asked her servant to cut another.

Ye Qinghuan looked toward Prince Jing, lips trembling, only to see Prince Jing's Li-gongzi also gnawing on a leg of lamb. He had one hand on a leg, and one hand on his chopsticks. There was a smear of sauce at the corner of his lips. Li-gongzi was just about to lick it off when Prince Jing suddenly leaned over, obscuring Ye Qinghuan's view.

It was a while before Prince Jing sat back down. Li-gongzi's fair face was bright red. But most importantly, the sauce on his lips was gone, and his lips were a lot redder!

Prince Jing licked his lips happily.

...

Ye Qinghuan turned to look at his fiancée, who remained just as elegant. He screamed in his heart: in terms of shamelessness, he'd lost again!!!

Getting Revenge
for the Fish

L I YU HAD BEEN FOCUSED on gnawing on his lamb leg when Prince Jing suddenly stole a kiss. Now he was both embarrassed and annoyed.

He felt like the original book was full of lies. Otherwise, how could Chu Yanyu end up being so secretly evil while the tyrant was actually a huge asshole that liked to take advantage of him whenever he wanted to? Why did he have to kiss him while they were eating? Couldn't a person be allowed to live?!

And it was right in front of Ye-shizi and the Princess of Jinjue! Li Yu couldn't calm himself down fast enough to keep up with Prince Jing's bullying. The princess was focused on eating just like he was, so perhaps she didn't see, but Ye-shizi's eyes were wide open, looking like he'd been struck by lightning. He definitely saw. Sob sob sob, how was he supposed to face anyone after this?!

What a huge asshole!

Li Yu raised a hand, furiously wiping at his mouth where the asshole prince had kissed him. His eyes were round with anger, and sparks seemed to fly from them. He'd already regretted the times he kicked and hit Prince Jing when he got worked up. He had to remain calm. He couldn't act rashly. Besides, to be honest, fighting was no use. Prince Jing was taller and stronger than him. He could easily pick him up like a little chick, sob!

Prince Jing couldn't help but chuckle when he noticed him holding in his explosive reaction. Perhaps Xiaoyu himself hadn't even noticed that he was getting more and more used to being close to him.

Neither the Princess of Jinjue nor Ye Qinghuan knew Li-gongzi very well. In order to ease the mood and lessen the awkwardness, Ye Qinghuan tried to smooth things over by asking Li Yu to introduce himself.

Li Yu's face was still red as he gave his name and age.

When Ye Qinghuan found out Li-gongzi's name was literally just "fish," he finally understood. Prince Jing didn't just like fish, he even found someone whose name was fish. Not only had Prince Jing won, Ye Qinghuan wasn't even competing in the same bracket! He smiled, but privately, he wanted to grind his teeth.

The Princess of Jinjue was delighted to learn that Li-gongzi looked after Prince Jing's fish for him.

"Xiao-Yu, Li-gongzi, why don't you bring the fish over next time?" she said. She might not be able to convince Prince Jing, but the clever princess could tell Li-gongzi was easier to ask!

Li Yu awkwardly chuckled a few times. She wanted him to bring himself to the princess's manor? No thank you! Someone else's house of gold or silver was nothing compared to Prince Jing's doghouse. Li Yu didn't want to go anywhere.

Because there were two additional guests, there wasn't quite enough food on the table. Ye Qinghuan quickly ordered a daikon stewed beef, while the princess ordered a lamb meatball soup. Soon, both dishes were brought upstairs.

Two plates of bright green cilantro and spring onions came along with the dishes. Prince Jing and Ye Qinghuan liked neither, while the princess and Li Yu liked cilantro and spring onions respectively.

The two of them divided up the condiments without discussion. They stared at each other in understanding, exchanging a knowing smile, and their food buddy relationship was decided just like that.

Prince Jing suddenly felt like he couldn't keep a firm grip on the crystal bottle...

The Princess of Jinjue was a warmhearted person. Due to her relationship with Ye Qinghuan, she already considered Li Yu part of her family. As they chatted, she found out Li Yu had run into a con artist. Her eyebrows shot up as they twisted together and she said angrily, "How dare they?! How could someone like that come from Jinjue!"

At her dainty call, two guards dressed as servants immediately entered the room. The princess ordered them to knock that merchant down a few pegs. Li Yu thought there was no need. He thanked the princess for her kindness hurriedly, then recounted how he'd already messed with the merchant.

"That's not good enough," said Ye Qinghuan, who also wanted to get revenge for Li Yu. "That scammer tried to pick on you because you were alone. We should teach him a lesson to prevent him from doing that to others."

"Yeah, exactly." The princess smiled and clapped her hands together. "Li-gongzi, my people will take care of it. Don't worry about it."

Li Yu knew he wouldn't be able to convince the two so easily, so he turned his gaze to Wang Xi, seeking help. Wang Xi also wanted to teach the scammer a lesson, but Li-gongzi was His Highness's precious beloved, so he couldn't just say no to him. A light bulb went off in Wang Xi's head as he said, "This old servant will listen to the master."

Wang Xi's master, Prince Jing, was currently leisurely sipping on a cup of tea. He heard everything Ye Qinghuan and the Princess of Jinjue had said, but he showed no reaction. Li Yu was a little surprised. Prince Jing had even intervened when he was wrapping the gold chains a bit too tightly around his hand; why was he so impassive now?

As soon as he thought that, Li Yu felt embarrassed. Was he under Prince Jing's spell? Did he think it was natural for Prince Jing to want to stand up for him now? Prince Jing was Prince Jing, and he was himself. If Prince Jing wasn't going to step in, he couldn't force him to do it just because Li Yu felt he was in the right. Prince Jing clearly didn't want to trouble himself with this, and Li Yu wasn't able to convince Ye-shizi and the princess, so all he could do was watch helplessly as they gave their guards the order.

Soon after, the guards returned with some news, their expressions strange. Just now, the merchant had suffered a grave injury and was being taken away. They'd asked around, and apparently the merchant had been kidnapped with a cloth bag thrown over his head. He was taken to a dark alleyway and beaten up, left with a swollen face, all of his teeth missing, and a dislocated jaw. He couldn't speak anymore, so it seemed like he wouldn't be able to scam anyone anymore either.

"...Someone must have taken revenge because he'd scammed too many people." Ye Qinghuan was very satisfied, but the princess was a little confused. After all, it wasn't her people who had done it.

After a bit of thought, the princess said, "Next time you run into a scammer like that, you must tell me right away."

Feeling grateful, Li Yu bowed slightly with his hands clasped. "Thank you, Princess, Ye-shizi."

Prince Jing's gaze never left Li Yu. When Li Yu thanked the other two, Prince Jing's face looked like it had been struck by a blast of cold wind. He got up and pulled Li Yu's clasped hands down.

Ye Qinghuan had known Prince Jing since they were little and was more or less used to Prince Jing's temper. He chuckled. "Tianchi, don't be so selfish."

Prince Jing gave him a side-eye and turned to leave, still holding Li Yu's hand.

Li Yu estimated it was about time for him to transform anyway, and he had to allow some time for the trip back. He knew he couldn't stay out much longer, so he reluctantly bade goodbye to the princess and Ye Qinghuan.

"Li-gongzi, Ye Qinghuan and I will soon be married," the princess said, smiling. "When the time comes, you should come drink our marriage wine."

The Princess of Jinjue and Ye Qinghuan's marriage wine—

Li Yu's heart suddenly skipped a beat, thinking about the princess's ending in the book. The princess had married the sixth prince, and in the end, the sixth prince's entire family was killed. The princess had been implicated as well and was exiled to a place that was bitterly cold, never to return to Jinjue.

At the time, it was because Prince Jing was angry at the sixth prince. Now that Ye Qinghuan was fine and the little princess was about to marry Ye Qinghuan, she wouldn't anger Prince Jing and be punished anymore, right?!

He was really making a difference as a transmigrated fish.

But for some reason, Prince Jing had never told Ye Qinghuan that Li Yu was the one who had written the letter. Either way, Li Yu didn't care. It wasn't like he needed Ye-shizi to be grateful toward him. Seeing two people he had directly and indirectly saved get married was enough for him; Li Yu couldn't help but feel proud.

Li Yu smiled and nodded seriously. "Sure, thanks for the invite. I'll definitely come."

The carriage traveled quickly back to Prince Jing's manor with another bout of shaking and jolting.

Li Yu was no longer the unprepared little fish from earlier. As soon as the carriage began to shake, he decided to hold tightly onto the gaps in the wood of the carriage. This way, he wouldn't knock into the person sitting across from him, no matter how hard the carriage shook. But when Prince Jing noticed he'd rather grab onto the carriage than touch him, his expression darkened.

There were some things that needed to be said.

Li Yu gathered his thoughts. "Your Highness, can we have a talk?"

Prince Jing went stiff, his jaw tightening. But before he could refuse, Li Yu continued, "I know that Your Highness asked Wang-gonggong to plan this trip to the market. I thanked the princess and Ye-shizi, but I should thank you too. Thank you for bringing me out to take my mind off things, for always taking care of me, and everything else. I..." Li Yu looked down, trying to control his emotions. He said, as calmly as he could, "I've been trying to carefully think about your feelings for me for a long time. But you keep interrupting me."

Li Yu smiled lightly, feeling like he was being silly.

"You've truly been good to me and made me happy. But you've also made me afraid of losing you. I wasn't like this before..."

Li Yu didn't know what had gotten into him lately. He was an open-minded young man, even more sensitive than girls could be. He thought his feelings toward Prince Jing were limited to that of a pet toward its owner. Those feelings weren't romantic, but now that Prince Jing was doting on him in his human form every day, he was starting to have trouble telling the difference.

So although he'd tried to calmly think things through these last few days, he hadn't reached any real conclusion. Should he keep trying to think things through? Would that get him anywhere?

Li Yu thought he might just be running away.

Because the issue between him and Prince Jing wasn't as simple as "whether or not he liked him."

He was a modern person on the inside. He could understand a man liking another man, and he wasn't against spending time with Prince Jing—sometimes, he even liked it. He was happy to be bi, or even gay. His sexual orientation wasn't the problem. The problem was that Prince Jing was a character in a book, while he was a person from the modern era. Prince Jing was a tyrant, and he was a fish. Though it had nothing to do with sexual orientation, the distance between them was enough to fit a thousand mountains and rivers.

But those mountains and rivers weren't so easy to turn away from.

"I'm sorry, Your Highness." Li Yu struggled for a while and decided just to say it. If he kept hiding it, he'd just seem like a dick. He wanted to give himself some more time. He hoped time could force him to make the decision he couldn't make today. "You treat me very well. Can you give me a little more time to figure out the relationship between us? I-I don't know, I—"

Prince Jing looked deeply into his eyes. Before Li Yu could say any more in rejection, he suddenly sprang forward.

With a slam, Li Yu was pushed against the wall of the carriage. The carriage shook once, but Li Yu didn't feel any pain. Prince Jing's arm was wrapped around him, cushioning his back and taking the impact for him. The man's handsome face was reflected in Li Yu's pupils, getting closer and closer. Li Yu swallowed the words he wanted to say, feeling sure he knew what the other person wanted to do. He shut his eyes helplessly.

But after a long time, Prince Jing only held him in his arms, unmoving. When Li Yu opened his eyes again, he realized Prince Jing was smiling.

Li Yu was furious. This asshole was playing with him! And he thought he was going to k-kiss him! Li Yu's face burned. He wanted to get away, but Prince Jing held him even tighter. When he was about to turn his head away, Prince Jing left a gentle, comforting kiss on his forehead.

Li Yu remembered something he'd heard once: a kiss to the forehead represented a love that was pure.

Prince Jing...likes me. Li Yu's heart was racing.

Prince Jing turned Li Yu to face him. Once again, he was so close. His inky black eyes seemed to be enchanted. Li Yu thought he was going to be sucked in, with no chance of escape.

After kissing his forehead, Prince Jing's lips passed over his nose, and stopped an inch away from his lips.

The two of them held each other in the tiny, cramped carriage. They could hear each other's breathing, and even each other's fierce heartbeats. Li Yu knew what Prince Jing wanted to do. If he wanted to, he could avoid it.

But he didn't. In that moment, he realized with a start that he was hoping he would kiss him.

When those lips finally landed on his, Li Yu felt like his heart sighed.

When Prince Jing did something so intimate with him, his first reaction wasn't to get out of there—it was just a bit of shyness. If he was annoyed, it was because he was afraid other people would see and say things, afraid that...

He was afraid of a lot of things, and he got angry easily, but he was never truly mad at Prince Jing. In fact, he looked forward to it. What was he supposed to do? It seemed like he really did like him a little bit.

When Prince Jing kissed him, it felt like there was a little boat floating around in his heart. That was the feeling of love, right?

Fish Likes You Too

THAT WAS PROBABLY their longest kiss. Li Yu did regret it halfway through. After all, he'd only just accepted that he liked Prince Jing, but they weren't officially together yet. They couldn't just kiss until the world ended at any tiny spark of hope.

But every time he wanted to interrupt, the man holding him would smile and keep kissing him. He'd never seen Prince Jing so happy. This was the first time Li Yu had accepted his kiss and didn't push him away; he couldn't help himself.

Prince Jing had his eyes closed, his lashes trembling. It was like they had little hooks, constantly tugging at his heart. With this one kiss, it was like his heart finally opened up. His heart kept beating and beating as sweetness oozed out. He thought he must like Prince Jing. What else could this burning hot feeling be?

Li Yu's heart trembled, and he suddenly accepted it.

So, he liked Prince Jing after all. It was his own fault for not realizing sooner, for not realizing what was in his heart. His eyes were a little wet. With a shaking hand, he touched Prince Jing's lips.

After they stopped kissing, Prince Jing kissed his fingers devotedly, then put his arms around his neck. Before, Prince Jing was holding him. Now, they were hugging each other. Prince Jing wrapped his arms lightly around the skinny figure in his arms. He hesitated for a moment, but he decided not to touch the string of pearls on the youth's waist for now.

The entire world quieted down. All that was left was this tiny space in the carriage, where they could kiss tentatively, clumsily.

At some point, the horses had stopped. No matter how they enjoyed that brief moment of warmth, it wasn't enough.

All of a sudden, Li Yu let out an alarmed noise—the transformation countdown had exploded in his head.

He was out of time! He had to leave now!

Just a second ago, Li Yu had been pouting, unwilling to leave. Now, he pushed Prince Jing away, pulling Prince Jing's hand off of his string of pearls, and glared angrily at Prince Jing.

But what he said wasn't very threatening at all. "I-I still have things to take care of. I need to leave now. N-next—no, I'll tell you tomorrow!"

Li Yu rushed to jump off the carriage. Prince Jing immediately realized Xiaoyu was about to transform, but—

Prince Jing took a quick glance at the crystal bottle right next to him. The carp spirit's other form was floating inside quietly.

If the crystal bottle was here, where was Xiaoyu going to go?

He couldn't let the carp spirit transform outside, confused and disoriented! Prince Jing immediately grabbed Li Yu. He could see that the fish was very confused; he clearly wasn't ready to come clean yet. But Prince Jing was already very satisfied with Xiaoyu's kiss.

He patted Li Yu lightly on the shoulder, pointed at himself, and then pointed outside. Then he got off the carriage!

Wang-gonggong, who was waiting outside the carriage, caught Prince Jing's gaze and immediately started explaining for his master in a loud voice. "His Highness has urgent business and has to rush back right now. We're leaving the carriage and fish to you, gongzi!"

"...All right."

So Prince Jing needed to leave too. That meant he could stay in the carriage.

Time was of the essence. Li Yu didn't have time to keep thinking about it, so he hurriedly made a noise of agreement. Watching Prince Jing disappear into the distance, though, Li Yu paused and gathering all the courage that he didn't even know he had, he yelled at Prince Jing, "Your Highness, I-I wasn't angry just now!"

Hearing that, Prince Jing's heart stuttered. Then he turned back to smile at him.

Li Yu waved wildly, then put the curtains down. He opened up the crystal bottle—in the next second, he was already a fish.

That really was too dangerous. He almost got caught just now!

Li Yu immediately put his new clothes and plushie into his inventory. With that taken care of he was about to jump into the crystal bottle when a hairpin rolled by. He couldn't lose the hairpin Prince Jing gave him! It was a gift. Li Yu couldn't bear to just put it away, so he grabbed the hairpin and jumped into the crystal bottle with it.

In the water, Li Yu curled around the jade hairpin, running his mouth along it in delight. There was a fish just as cute as him at the end of this hairpin. When he first received it, he hadn't had time to play with it. To be honest, he'd been thinking about it this whole time.

Li Yu only put the hairpin in his inventory after he'd spent a while fooling around with it. Now, it was time for him to think about him and Prince Jing.

He never expected he would catch feelings for Prince Jing. Although Li Yu's reaction time was a little slow, he knew how he felt now. It was as if a stone that was weighing down heavily on his heart had suddenly flipped over.

But it turned out that after some conflict came relief and comfort. It turned out all of his unusual behaviors were because he liked Prince Jing too.

Li Yu was giddy with happiness, realizing this truth was a little sweet. It was so sweet Li Yu blew a whole string of bubbles. There was nothing to play with in the crystal bottle, nor was there an ornamental mountain for him to wreck, so all Li Yu could do was swim in circles in excitement until he nearly broke the bottle.

No, no, I can't think about this. Li Yu immediately stopped.

He liked Prince Jing, but what was he supposed to do now?

He'd been so conflicted about *why* Prince Jing had started to like him that he never even thought about the possibility of returning his feelings. He'd just assumed there was too much distance between the two of them, and there was no way they could be together. After all, he was a fish and Prince Jing was a human. He was a transmigrator and Prince Jing was a character in a book.

Li Yu still remembered all the reasons he had given himself. But looking at them now, weren't they all just obstacles to his feelings? He'd convinced himself with these reasons before, saying they weren't suitable, and there were countless dangers waiting for them. If he really decided to be with Prince Jing, then he was no longer a bystander in this book. He was a participant, part of the book itself. This meant he was now completely part of this world, part of Prince Jing's life.

But he was someone from the modern era. There were many things he and Prince Jing differed on. They might quarrel or even fight.

Most modern people understood that just because someone caught feelings for someone else, it didn't mean they'd last forever. Because of people's hearts, their environments, society—there were so many factors that determined whether a relationship would end in happiness or tragedy. Not everything could be solved just by liking the other person. When modern people fell in love, if things weren't going well, they'd break up quickly. But if he truly entered Prince Jing's life, things would no longer be up to him.

In ancient times, the emperor's word was final. His life would be in Prince Jing's hands. They were in love now, but once he was stamped with Prince Jing's seal, there was no way he could just leave if they were no longer good for each other. There was nowhere to run.

He knew and understood all this. They were all reasons to stop himself. There were millions of reasons standing in his way, and only one that made him want to walk toward Prince Jing—but just the one was enough.

They liked each other.

Li Yu remembered that in modern times he'd once heard someone say: what luck it must take to meet someone that you like, who also likes you back.

He was a youth who'd just experienced his first love. He really couldn't give up when he'd only just gotten a taste.

"Li-gongzi, Li-gongzi!"

Li Yu had been a fish again for a while now. Wang Xi, on Prince Jing's orders, had come to help Li Yu after waiting about fifteen minutes. But obviously Li-gongzi couldn't respond.

Wang Xi opened the curtain to the carriage, only to find a crystal bottle sitting on the floor. Next to it was a letter. Wang Xi grabbed it and took a look. "Did Li-gongzi leave again?"

Every time Li Yu transformed, he'd just leave without saying anything. He was afraid it'd start to get suspicious, so this time, he'd prepared a letter before they left the manor. The contents basically said he had something urgent to take care of and had to leave.

Wang Xi was used to it by now. His only concern was giving Li-gongzi's letter to Prince Jing. Wang Xi put away the letter, picked up the crystal bottle, and chuckled to the little carp inside, "Master Xiaoyu, I'm the only one left. Let me take you home right now."

The carriage started moving once again. Behind it, just a few meters away, was a tall figure riding a horse. It kept following the carriage, quietly protecting the person inside.

As soon as Li Yu was back in the manor, he entered the system.

It'd been a while since he last entered the Moe Pet System. The quest menu was still open.

As he faced the screen, Li Yu's emotions were complicated. After all, he was the one who didn't want to do the quests anymore, but he was also the one who was now back looking for the system.

<System, how long until I can go back to being a human for good?> Li Yu asked.

<After you complete the "Revitalizing" quest line, the reward will allow the user to return permanently to human form,> the system replied.

So that was it.

Li Yu was glad the system was an emotionless program that couldn't feel awkward. It didn't ignore him back or make fun of him for avoiding it. He had to reluctantly admit that if he didn't have the Moe Pet System, he might have become the Noble Consort's thousand carp soup long ago.

Now that he understood his own feelings, he couldn't help but acknowledge that, despite the fact that the system had made him complete all those tasks, his feelings toward Prince Jing and the way Prince Jing treated him were all real. He couldn't lie to himself anymore.

<...Fine. As long as I can turn back to a human. I'll...continue with the missions.>

Now that he liked Prince Jing, he no longer had any hesitations about completing the quests. Plus, they'd let him go back to being a human, so why wouldn't he do them?

Unexpectedly, now that he'd changed his perspective, terrible news became great news.

<Then does the user want the reward for the "Indulging" quest?> asked the system.

Li Yu hesitated, then remembered the reward for the "Indulging" quest was one of Prince Jing's secrets and a fish plush. He'd already gotten the plush. As for Prince Jing's secret—did he have any secrets that Li Yu didn't know about? Now that his attitude had changed, he couldn't help but want to know more about the person he liked.

Li Yu cleared his throat. It was a reward—there was no reason not to take it.

The system opened a window in front of him, and Li Yu realized the reward was a multiple-choice question. There were four secrets to choose from, set up in a square grid. The squares representing the options weren't filled in using the system's usual color scheme. Instead, a different scene was playing in each square.

The first was in the palace. It looked unfamiliar to Li Yu, so he skipped it. The second was a house. This one looked a little familiar. Then of the last two, one was an endless vortex, and the last one was a face.

With a jolt, Li Yu recognized himself. Prince Jing had a secret related to him? Then—what could it be?

Recalling the confession Prince Jing had carved into all the walls of the manor, Li Yu felt like his brain was about to start smoking. He figured the last secret probably wasn't a secret to him anymore.

He had to make good use of this chance, so he thought it would be better if he could see a secret that he might already have some context on and chose number two.

Once he'd confirmed his choice, Li Yu was suddenly surrounded by smoke.

Did he enter an illusion again?

Li Yu looked around and realized this was different from the time he met the chubby little kid. In that illusion, he could swim around as a fish, and everything seemed incredibly real. But this time, no matter how he struggled, he couldn't move. This was Prince Jing's secret, he realized—he was just a bystander. These really were just memories.

The house he'd chosen was right before his eyes. Now he got a good look at it, Li Yu realized with surprise that this was the second prince's place. No wonder it looked familiar!

He soon saw Prince Jing approach, carrying the crystal bottle. This was when Prince Jing had taken him along to scold the second prince. What happened then that he didn't know about?

Li Yu watched Prince Jing put the fish plush into the second prince's soup again. Rewatching the scene, he still felt incredibly gratified. He recalled they left quickly after Prince Jing was done with the second prince. Did something happen after that?

As he continued to watch, he noticed Prince Jing shift the crystal bottle to his other hand and make a gesture toward Wang Xi. Wang Xi then led a group of people to force the second prince to drink himself into a stupor. Once the second prince was in a daze, Wang Xi pushed him into the pond.

...The second prince hadn't fallen into the pond by accident. Prince Jing had ordered it.

The memory stopped abruptly, and Li Yu returned to the system.

It was a secret because it was something he didn't know. He could understand Prince Jing taking action against the second prince. After all, the second prince and Prince Jing had a lot of personal grudges, and he'd tried to harm the House of Cheng'en. But Xiaoyu was just a fish. Prince Jing was allowed to handle anyone however he wanted—why did he specifically take the fish elsewhere first? Was it that Prince Jing didn't want him to see it?

But he'd already used the fish plush to teach the second prince a lesson, and the fish was there for that.

But h-he—

Wait!

Li Yu suddenly realized that Prince Jing hadn't done anything violent in front of the fish for a very long time.

Now that he thought back on it carefully...ages ago, Prince Jing had killed a female assassin in front of him, which had frightened him quite badly. After that, he'd never seemed to beat or kill anyone again.

Perhaps that was the real purpose of the secret.

He thought Prince Jing's personality had changed, but the reality was that those things never stopped happening. Prince Jing was a product of these ancient times and had his own ways of dealing with things. There were some things he had to do. But just for the fish's peace of mind, he'd started doing them secretly.

Li Yu didn't know if he should be angry or moved.

...No, wait. Why did it feel like this huge asshole treated Xiaoyu better than Li Yu?

The Fish Chooses Love

NOW WAS NOT THE TIME to dwell on these things—
Li Yu hurriedly forced himself back on track and focused
on the next step of the "Revitalize" quest.

The next step: *Be inseparable from the tyrant. Hint: None.*

Li Yu had intended to be motivated and seriously try to tackle
the main quest, but now, seeing this next step...

Come out, System, I promise I won't kill you!

Li Yu could interpret "indulging" as drinking, but how was he
supposed to become inseparable from the tyrant? They hadn't even
started dating yet!

Besides, this main quest was probably going to keep going for a
while. If they had to be "inseparable" now, how were the steps going
to progress? Li Yu's eye twitched. He had a bad feeling about where
this was going. This "Inseparable" quest...let's wait a while.

Li Yu exited the system like his tail was on fire.

While he was in the system, his fish body would temporarily lose
consciousness. By the time Li Yu came to, he was facing an enlarged
handsome face. Prince Jing, who'd had to take care of urgent business, had already returned. He was holding the box, about to feed
the fish.

He hadn't felt it when they were kissing in the carriage, but Li Yu
felt a little embarrassed suddenly seeing the object of his affections!

In his embarrassment, his brain and fins both shut down, and he sank to the bottom.

Prince Jing hurried to steady the fish. Li Yu stared at him in a daze. His heart felt like a pool of spring water, with waves of affection rippling in the wind. No wonder he always thought this person was good-looking. It was because he liked him!

...That was what that feeling was.

Li Yu suddenly leapt up like he was startled. He swam a few anxious laps, then dove headfirst into the ornamental mountain, leaving only his tail visible. This all happened much faster than when he got mad or ran away. It was a good thing the fish was covered in scales, otherwise his entire body would have visibly blushed.

Prince Jing was a little worried that the fish was hiding in the mountain again. He was afraid the fish might be stuck or perhaps mad at him.

He tried to flick the fish's tail. It flapped dramatically, then disappeared into the cave as well.

Hm...

The lesson Prince Jing had learned from the last few days was that he had to coax the fish slowly. He couldn't rush it. He smiled, thinking back to the kiss in the carriage. Although Xiaoyu hadn't been able to finish what he wanted to say, Prince Jing was still in an unexpectedly good mood.

Li Yu hid in the mountain, occasionally listening to the noises outside and thinking about his future. Before he was aware of his feelings, he'd felt conflicted and indecisive. But now that he knew his heart, like anyone experiencing their first love, he was a soldier striding bravely forward. No matter how treacherous the path was ahead, it was all insignificant to him now.

He'd only found out how deep his feelings ran when he realized he liked Prince Jing. This day was just like any other, but now that he knew, merely seeing Prince Jing overwhelmed Li Yu with emotion. He liked him so much, he had to keep pursuing this relationship. Even if this path was hard, if he didn't at least try to walk it, how could he think about the future?

But he couldn't date Prince Jing as a fish. Currently, he only had two hours a day to be a human. That wasn't even enough time to be flustered and embarrassed.

He had to permanently turn into a human as soon as possible. Before that, he shouldn't get too close to Prince Jing. He should try to maintain some distance, even if he liked Prince Jing. He couldn't let the prince find out about his secret.

...Oh! He could set up some rules with Prince Jing! From what he'd seen over the last few days, Prince Jing likely wouldn't deny him. They could hold hands, go out on dates, kiss... They'd already kissed plenty of times, so that should be fine.

Then...what about...bedroom activities?

Li Yu had secretly read porn before, and there was a slight itch in his heart. He was a typical young man—of course this was something he was anticipating. To be honest, he was no longer against the idea of Prince Jing getting close to him. It had all just been a misunderstanding before, since he hadn't been able to recognize his own feelings in time. Now, he wasn't just not against such acts, he was privately looking forward to it a little. They were both adults, and things should naturally progress as their relationship developed.

Li Yu's face was red as he imagined himself suddenly turning into a fish during a certain rigorous activity... Such a scene would most certainly be so beautiful, one couldn't bear to look at it. If that happened, both him and Prince Jing might gush blood.

In order to prevent such accidents from happening, Li Yu temporarily put an "x" over bedroom activities. Men should really do their best to keep it in their pants, he thought regretfully. Once he finished the main quest, he wouldn't have any more reservations!

Li Yu was thrilled and filled with anticipation. He was using a small rock inside the mountain as his pillow, and he kept rolling around on top of it. By the time he barely managed to fall asleep, the rock had almost become smooth.

When he woke up, Prince Jing was gone. As it turned out, bright and early that morning, Prince Jing had received the emperor's request for him in the palace. He had something important to discuss.

When Prince Jing returned last night, the fish was embarrassed and stayed in his cave. When Prince Jing received the emperor's edict, the fish was still snoring away and didn't notice anything. Prince Jing touched the fish's tail where it was poking outside the mountain and thoughtfully entered the palace by himself. He didn't want to wake the fish.

Li Yu was sensible. He knew that seeing the emperor was important. But the original plot was now in shambles, and he had no idea where they were currently at. The third and sixth princes had both been punished, and were now trying to keep a low profile. Perhaps the emperor just happened to be feeling sentimental and wanted to catch up with Prince Jing...but it was also possible there was an update on the investigation of the nursery rhyme and fake monks, and the emperor wanted to make things up to Prince Jing.

Li Yu didn't think this trip to the palace meant any bad news, so he gradually calmed down.

Calculating when Prince Jing would be back, he transformed into a human. Putting the plush into the tank, he picked a set of silver robes that he liked very much and adjusted the collar.

He still had the jade hairpin Prince Jing had given him, but in order to use a hairpin, one first had to put their hair up. Li Yu didn't know how, and Wang-gonggong had gone to the palace with Prince Jing. He was too embarrassed to ask anyone else, so he had to just do his best. He found a silver hair ribbon, pulled his hair up into a ponytail, then stuck the hairpin into it, leaving the little fish at the end sticking out.

Li Yu nodded at himself in the bronze mirror. He thought he looked quite beautiful.

Prince Jing hadn't returned yet, so Li Yu sat at the table, smoothed out a sheet of paper, grabbed a brush, and wrote everything he'd thought of last night down while he waited for him.

Just as Li Yu thought, the emperor's imperial guards had found out that the third prince was the one who first spread the nursery rhyme implicating Prince Jing. They even found multiple witnesses and brought them before the emperor so he could question them personally. The emperor had once again been driven into a fit of anger thanks to the third prince. It was then that the director of the Imperial Astrological Bureau, Sun Simiao, just so happened to report that an investigation had revealed that officials of the Bureau had been bribed. And the person who had bribed them was the third prince, Mu Tianming!

The emperor finally understood why the third prince had kept questioning the Imperial Astrological Bureau out of the blue. He was creating an opportunity for the people he'd bribed!

The third prince had tried to frame Prince Jing with the nursery rhymes and impostor monks, and he even had his own people in the Imperial Astrological Bureau. He'd broken all of the emperor's taboos in one go. The emperor was planning on punishing the third prince again when he found the opportunity, but the third prince beat him to it by doing something else stupid.

These days, the third prince's injuries were improving, so he'd started reporting daily to the Imperial Study Room under the supervision of the servants to study with the younger princes. The third prince was very unhappy about this. It sounded nice when the emperor told him to go study, but he wasn't a child anymore. In the royal family, adult princes were supposed to share the emperor's burden and help him solve issues, but he was stuck studying with his little brothers. If the emperor never said anything, when was this supposed to end? Didn't that mean he'd never be involved in court?

When the second prince was first punished, he'd been put on house arrest. He was kept on house arrest until he was no longer able to think clearly, but the emperor never let him out again. And after that, there was no need to mention the second prince anymore.

A little too late, the third prince found himself both afraid and full of regret. He asked the sixth prince for help, but the sixth prince, who'd suffered the same beating he had and was trying to recover, asked him to settle down and try to keep lying low. But the third prince was unwilling to continue wasting time like this. His mother, Consort Zhang, was in regular contact with the wives of several officials. Mu Tianming used this connection to ask these officials to beg for his leniency in court, asking the emperor to give him back some responsibilities. He wasn't hoping for anything glamorous. He just wanted to appear in front of the emperor so the emperor didn't forget he existed.

After some discussion, the officials wrote a document to the emperor, saying the third prince regretted his mistake and was willing to help the emperor. They even asked an academic at the Hanlin Academy who was very good at writing to write it, so that he could describe the third prince's recent situation as pitifully as possible and hopefully take advantage of the emperor's fatherly affection to move him to tears.

When the emperor received the document, it wasn't clear whether he felt touched, but he was furious that several officials would write for the third prince together. He'd just discovered the third prince had bribed the Imperial Astrological Bureau, and now several courtiers were begging for his forgiveness on his behalf. The emperor was especially wary of princes getting too close to officials. Was the third prince trying to put pressure on the emperor even though he wasn't even anywhere close to the position of crown prince? All he did was order the third prince to study for a few days to teach him some patience. The third prince couldn't even understand that—how could he trust his son to self-reflect?

The emperor made a note of all the officials involved. The third prince never received the emperor's forgiveness, and now, not only did the emperor order him to study with the seventh and eight princes, he also had him copy the *Classic of Filial Piety* every day, before handing it in to the Grand Secretary for review.

The third prince was thoroughly humiliated, and all the officials involved were either fired or moved to other positions. It took the third prince a long time to realize what he'd done. When he went to look for the sixth prince again, the sixth prince no longer had any words of advice.

It is easy to lose something but hard to get it back. I told you to lay low, but you wouldn't listen. You just had to go dig this hole deeper for yourself.

After he'd dealt with the third prince, the emperor considered his sons. None of his adult sons were focused on the right things, and his two younger sons were still too young to tell how they'd fare in the future. Although the guards had already proved that the sixth prince was working for the third prince, and the emperor was currently disgusted with the third prince, the sixth prince might still turn out all right with a bit of warning. But he just couldn't get over his anger enough to fully commit to training the sixth prince for the throne.

As a result, the emperor couldn't help but think of his other son, Prince Jing. Thinking of Prince Jing's calligraphy, as well as his skill in playing Go, he knew Prince Jing was very capable. But he was born mute, and in order to protect him, the emperor had never heavily depended on him. But what had all his painstaking efforts truly accomplished? The second and third princes were shortsighted, taking action against Prince Jing and the people around him. They probably thought Prince Jing was an easy target since the emperor didn't seem to value him.

Since they didn't care about respecting him, the emperor also didn't want to consider their feelings. If Prince Jing wanted to stand strong before the new emperor, he didn't necessarily need the new emperor's pity. He could stand tall on his own.

Either way, the emperor didn't have to pick a crown prince any time soon. After all the third prince's dirty antics, he needed to reassure Prince Jing.

Once he'd summoned Prince Jing to the palace, the emperor said quite a lot to him, letting out sigh after sigh. In the end, he ordered Prince Jing to assume a position in the Ministry of Works.[7]

Prince Jing just wanted to go home, but instead he was smacked by a job falling into his lap...

The emperor continued, "Many things have happened in court recently, and everything requires my attention. Tianchi, why don't

---

7   The Ministry of Works was in charge of things like units of measurement, government construction projects, and natural resources.

you help me? I remember Tianzhao, Tianming, and the others started attending court at twenty years old. It's already a little late for you."

It was just boring busywork. Prince Jing nodded, expression blank.

The emperor got the impression Prince Jing wasn't very happy about this. Could there really be a prince who was unhappy with being given responsibilities? But Prince Jing was just like that. He always remained unmoved in the face of humiliation or reward. If Prince Jing was anything like the second or third prince, he might as well be facing a crisis soon.

It was a good thing he still had a capable son, it was just—

It was just, no matter how capable he was, it wasn't enough to outweigh the biggest issue.

He remembered how not long after Prince Jing was born, the imperial physicians had already deemed him mute, unable to speak for the rest of his life. At that time, the physician had told the emperor something sincerely: it was likely this muteness would be passed on to his children.

No matter how capable Prince Jing was, he couldn't carry on the heavy burden of the throne. The emperor couldn't select Prince Jing and doom the Royal Family.

He thought about how, after his ascension to the throne, he had always placed an emphasis on a di son. He kept hoping a di son would be born, but of the di princes that Empress Xiaohui had given birth to, all three had faced disasters and bad luck. Perhaps it just wasn't part of his fate... The emperor sighed.

Prince Jing accepted his new job, bade the emperor farewell, and returned to his manor. The emperor had probably given him this job to try to make up for doubting him. Though Prince Jing knew this, he wasn't particularly pleased. But when he pushed open the door and saw Xiaoyu, who had a weird lump of hair on his head, Prince Jing couldn't help but smile.

"Your Highness, look!" Li Yu pointed to the hairpin in his hair.

Prince Jing saw. The hairpin was a symbol of his feelings. Now that Xiaoyu was wearing it, did this mean...he accepted his feelings? Prince Jing stood there, his emotions running wild.

"Your Highness, there's more!" Li Yu sat down on the edge of the bed and waved him over.

Thinking back to the time inside the carriage yesterday, the overwhelming tenderness, Prince Jing went a little red. Li Yu was calling to him from the bed. It was the middle of the day right now—was he about to absorb essence?

...As long as Xiaoyu wanted it, anything was possible.

Prince Jing sat down.

Li Yu was blushing too. Before Prince Jing could grab his hand, Li Yu pulled out a piece of paper from his sleeve and said, smiling, "Let's lay down some rules, Your Highness!"

Fish Boyfriend

"I THOUGHT ABOUT IT," Li Yu said in a small voice, his face red. "I like Your Highness too... I want to be with you. But can you agree to a few things? If you can, then we can...try to be together."

Although he had times when he was lost or difficult to deal with, or shy when he liked someone, being forthcoming was one of his virtues. And, well...the transformation was forcing his hand. He only had two hours a day, so he couldn't afford to hesitate. If he wanted something, he had to mention it now. Once they'd come to an agreement, they could start dating!

Li Yu thought of the way Prince Jing took care of him and felt unusually confident. He held the page of writing up high, so Prince Jing wouldn't miss a single word.

He'd edited this "agreement" many times. Prince Jing taught him how to write before, so this time, Li Yu tried not to make any mistakes and keep the paper clean. Even though he was using this to "negotiate," he still wrote it very carefully and sincerely.

Meanwhile, hearing that Li Yu liked him back, Prince Jing's heart was blooming furiously. Although what Xiaoyu wanted wasn't exactly what he wanted, that didn't matter. Never mind a few things—he'd agree to dozens or even hundreds of things.

Prince Jing reached out and grabbed Li Yu's hand. He carefully rubbed away the ink Li Yu had accidentally gotten on his fingers. This small gesture made Li Yu's heart warm. He tickled Prince Jing's palm with the fingers Prince Jing had just rubbed clean. Gathering his courage, Li Yu held Prince Jing's hand and looked up at him, smiling.

Prince Jing was trying to confirm, over and over, that Xiaoyu wouldn't run away again in a fit of anger. He'd felt it in the carriage, but now that they'd said everything out loud, he still felt like this didn't seem quite real.

Was he also afraid of losing him?

Prince Jing burst into quiet laughter, patted Li Yu's hand, and accepted the paper.

The first line that he saw was: *Do not ask Li Yu to stay the night.* He rubbed his forehead. Xiaoyu accepted him but still wouldn't absorb his essence? He was fine, but would it have an impact on Xiaoyu? All the ancient cultivation books spoke of being diligent, but Xiaoyu...really only worked three out of five days.

Li Yu was afraid of Prince Jing thinking he was putting up a front and hurried to explain, "It's not that we can't, we just have to wait for an appropriate time..." He suddenly realized what was coming out of his mouth and immediately shut up. He blinked, his face red, trying to play dumb.

Even so, Prince Jing immediately understood it wasn't completely impossible...

"Either way, I said no, so no!" said Li Yu hastily. "If Your Highness doesn't agree, then let's not be together."

When he heard Li Yu say "let's," his heart swayed. He quickly snatched the paper back. It was too bad Li Yu couldn't absorb his essence, but he had Xiaoyu, and that was enough.

Li Yu made a triumphant gesture when he wasn't looking. Everyone said whining to your boyfriend was very effective. Clearly, it was a pretty good trick.

Prince Jing agreed to the first condition. Continuing on to the second one: *Do not ask Li Yu where he's going.* This one Prince Jing understood immediately. Xiaoyu only seemed to be able to maintain his human form for about two hours. Every time, he had to explain why he "disappeared." Watching him fumble for all sorts of excuses, each one faker than the last, Prince Jing struggled not to expose him. Xiaoyu was probably also tired of thinking up all those excuses as well, so he didn't want him to ask. It took too many brain cells, and keeping track of the lies wasn't easy.

Prince Jing nodded, agreeing to this one too. Finally, the last condition: *Do not get mad at Li Yu.* Prince Jing chuckled. Xiaoyu was too worried. When had he ever gotten mad at Xiaoyu?

Prince Jing agreed to all of them.

"One more," Li Yu said slyly. "Your Highness said you didn't have any concubines before. Can you please maintain that?"

In the book, Prince Jing wasn't someone who would like multiple people at once. But the original plotline was already a mess, and Chu Yanyu turned out to be secretly quite sinister. What if Prince Jing turned out to be unfaithful? Although it wasn't likely, Li Yu didn't want any accidents to happen, so he steeled himself. If Prince Jing turned into a pig, then he'd break up with him!

He hadn't written this condition down because Prince Jing had already said it himself and even engraved it onto the walls of the manor. Li Yu thought it was unnecessary to write it again and take up space in his agreement. So really, he'd taken advantage of Prince Jing a little bit.

But Prince Jing nodded without any hesitation.

"Then, Your Highness, you have to remember them," Li Yu said, giggling. "Can you memorize them?"

Prince Jing nodded again. He handed the paper back to Li Yu, went to the desk, and got out paper and a brush.

Li Yu followed him over, rolled up his sleeves, and prepared to grind some ink for him.

Prince Jing glanced up at Li Yu. Considering Xiaoyu's comprehension skills, he smiled and wrote down a silly little poem.

Your decision to stay the night,
Leave whenever you delight,
With you I will never fight,
I'll love only you in this life.

Li Yu froze and immediately threw the inkstick to the side. His Highness was amazing! Especially that last line! Now that he'd committed them all to memory, the next step was to kiss, hug, and shower him with affection, right?

Li Yu threw himself at Prince Jing. Prince Jing was surprised but still managed to catch Li Yu. With eyes full of tenderness, their lips slowly met.

They wanted to put all of their gentleness but also all of their passion into that one kiss and melt into each other until they were one. Prince Jing felt something lick the seam of his lips, and when he opened his eyes, Xiaoyu was smiling mischievously at him.

"...Does it still hurt?" Li Yu touched his lips. Because of a misunderstanding, Li Yu had recently bitten Prince Jing's tongue. He wanted to make it up to him now. To be honest, doing that felt very exciting. The curious fish wanted to try. It was his boyfriend anyway, so kissing with tongue...was very normal.

Realizing what he wanted, Prince Jing picked Li Yu up excitedly. *Holy crap, I just want to french kiss, wh-wh-what do you want to do?!*

Li Yu's heart was thumping in his chest, afraid Prince Jing was about to break the rules they'd only just set. But instead, after holding him tightly for a while, Prince Jing put him down gently on the desk, then leaned in and kissed him carefully.

Li Yu kissed him back enthusiastically. As he kissed him, he realized Prince Jing was much taller than him. Usually, when he kissed Prince Jing, he had to tilt his head up, which was slightly uncomfortable. Now that he was on the desk, they were eye to eye. As a result, kissing was also a lot easier.

Prince Jing wanted him to relax...

Li Yu suddenly realized that although Prince Jing couldn't speak, and he constantly had to guess what his intentions were—sometimes even guessing wrong—the way Prince Jing doted on him never changed. Li Yu felt both moved and warm. He held onto Prince Jing's neck tightly, happily pressing his lips to the other man's. Very quickly, he was defeated by the warmth.

As Li Yu latched onto Prince Jing like a koala, Prince Jing handed him something wrapped in bright yellow cloth. Li Yu opened it and took a glance. It was the emperor's orders for Prince Jing to go to the Ministry of Works for a job.

Li Yu was a little shocked. This didn't happen in the original book. Later, when Prince Jing and the sixth prince were fighting, he was supposed to enter the court through the Ministry of Works. But right now, the sixth prince was still recovering from his injuries.

As far as he could tell, Prince Jing didn't seem to have any intentions of going for the throne yet. Li Yu realized this might just be the emperor having great expectations for Prince Jing.

The Prince Jing of this world would not face too many disasters. He'd try to help him.

"This is a good thing. Congratulations, Your Highness," Li Yu said, smiling. But he had no idea why Prince Jing was showing him the edict.

Prince Jing was actually unhappy that he'd only just started a relationship with Xiaoyu and was now conscripted to go work. *I can't spend a lot of time with you anymore,* he thought, but he was unable to say it.

Li Yu thought it over and realized what he meant. He smiled. "Since Your Highness has a job now, you should do your best. I won't go anywhere. I'll wait for you here in the manor. When you get your...monthly salary, you can buy me a present."

Li Yu was full of words of encouragement, imagining himself as a stay-at-home-boyfriend, walking his boyfriend to work every day and cheering him on. After all, Prince Jing had a lot of serious business to attend to on top of being in a relationship. Prince Jing had to go work at the Ministry of Works now; later on, when he ascended to the throne, he'd have to worry about all sorts of important, national matters.

Unlike him—apart from completing quests, all he had to do was swim around in leisure as a pet fish. It was like he'd entered retirement early. But he was only eighteen... Li Yu rubbed his nose. Maybe he should do his best and try to make his boyfriend a heart bento?

With Xiaoyu's encouragement, Prince Jing gathered himself and started to report to the Ministry of Works on time every morning.

The Ministry of Works was the least important ministry out of the six, responsible for water conservation and civil engineering. Taking into account the fact that Prince Jing would have a hard time communicating, the emperor gave him the job of repairing Zhongcui Palace after it had been damaged in the fire.

The blueprint for Zhongcui Palace was in storage; he just had to fix it according to the plans. It would be difficult to mess up. Prince Jing was a prince, and he would be able to command authority with his personality. But the emperor still found him someone to help him with the task, afraid that he would be overwhelmed with his first job. Deputy Minister Zheng Jing was very capable. He'd already received the emperor's orders ahead of time and was ready to assist Prince Jing at any time.

By doing this, the emperor was making it easy for Prince Jing.

After Prince Jing arrived at the Ministry of Works, the first thing he did was put down a huge pack he was carrying.

Deputy Minister Zheng Jing came to bow at him with a smile. He'd heard a lot about Prince Jing and wanted to have a good relationship with him. "Your Highness," he asked curiously, "what did you bring?"

Wang Xi usually followed Prince Jing, but he wasn't supposed to be in places of business, so Prince Jing picked up the brush on the table and wrote: *lunch*.

Zheng Jing laughed awkwardly. So…it was the prince's lunch. This pack was larger than a basin—what kind of lunch did it hold? But seeing Prince Jing's impassive expression, Zheng Jing could tell his personality was a little aloof and cold, so he probably didn't want him to pry anymore. And so, despite all his questions, he didn't ask anything more.

After Prince Jing finished writing the word "lunch," he paused, but Zheng Jing didn't ask any further. Prince Jing was a little dissatisfied, so he carefully wrote in slightly larger words, under "lunch": *My boyfriend made it.*

With great difficulty, Zheng Jing asked, "Boyfriend?"

Prince Jing nodded. Xiaoyu had specially taught him this word from his home. Xiaoyu said when two people liked each other the way they did, it was called "dating." Xiaoyu was his "boyfriend," and he was also Xiaoyu's "boyfriend." Prince Jing liked this form of address. He guessed that the carp spirit must be from some sort of immortal mountain, and this must mean he now saw him as family. Prince Jing felt very happy.

Zheng Jing thought about it for a while but still didn't know what a boyfriend was supposed to be, so he could only ask Prince Jing. "Your Highness, what does 'boyfriend' mean?"

Prince Jing narrowed his eyes. There was no way he'd let Zheng Jing know about the carp spirit's mountain, but he had an alternate explanation. It was still Xiaoyu, either way. Prince Jing wrote, *My future consort.*

Zheng Jing's expression kept changing. Prince Jing already had a consort? How come he didn't know? Future consort...well, that was easier to understand than "boyfriend." How should he respond?

"W-well...congratulations, Your Highness," he stammered.

Prince Jing finally nodded, satisfied.

Zheng Jing secretly wiped away sweat. Then he saw Prince Jing take something else out of his large sleeves and set it down on the table.

It was a clear bottle, and inside was a silver fish with flecks of gold. It was swimming around in the bottle happily.

Zheng Jing thought his eyes were playing tricks on him. Swallowing, he asked, hesitating, "Your Highness, did you bring a koi with you?"

Prince Jing wrote proudly, *My pet fish.*

What?! Why would anyone bring a fish to work? Zheng Jing couldn't understand. Once he'd seen Prince Jing personally feeding the fish a piece of peach blossom pastry from a white jade box, Zheng Jing shut up completely.

Li Yu, who was currently munching on a pastry, yelled in his head: *I really fell for this asshole's tricks. Walking my boyfriend to work? Why did this jerk have to bring his fish to work too?!*

What happened to being a stay-at-home boyfriend?

Now, in his human form, he had to date Prince Jing and prepare lunch for him, and in his fish form, he had to go to work with him. Sob sob sob, he wanted to start his early retirement where he was always being taken care of!

Touching Fish While on the Clock

THERE WAS NO RUSH on fixing Zhongcui Palace. Prince Jing first followed Zheng Jing around and familiarized himself with the rules and regulations of the Ministry of Works. He needed to reference Zhongcui's Palace's blueprint, so Zheng Jing already had someone find it and bring it to Prince Jing.

Prince Jing spread open the blueprint, and Zheng Jing prepared himself to answer questions at any moment. After all, Prince Jing had never been in charge of anything similar. When Zheng Jing had first come to the Ministry of Works, he also didn't understand anything.

But Prince Jing didn't ask him anything. He just focused on the blueprint and occasionally noted something down on the side.

From Zheng Jing's angle, he couldn't see what Prince Jing was writing, but he noticed that when Prince Jing opened the blueprint, the silver koi inside the crystal bottle had also swum closer, pressing against the side closest to Prince Jing's hand. From this angle, it looked like the koi had stopped right on top of Prince Jing's hand.

Zheng Jing almost felt like the koi was looking at the blueprint with Prince Jing.

...Why would he think that? It's not like the koi was a spirit.

The little carp who'd been mistaken as a spirit thought, *Ah, here it is! I want to see what my boyfriend looks like when he's working!*

Li Yu had seen Prince Jing read, write, and paint, but he'd never seen Prince Jing work. Li Yu was also curious about what ancient blueprints looked like, so he kept trying to inch forward. Prince Jing knew Xiaoyu was getting interested and was afraid the fish had forgotten he was in a bottle and might break it again, so he silently moved the blueprint toward the fish a little and continued to study it, brows knitted together.

My boyfriend is so hot when he's concentrating! Li Yu appreciated Prince Jing's handsome profile for a while, blew him a kiss from afar, then stretched out his neck to look at the blueprint. He was a little excited. What if he picked up on something and could help Prince Jing?

There were many little houses drawn on the blueprint. Li Yu couldn't tell how they were different from each other. Many of them also had notes underneath. The text was smaller than a fish's eyes, which made Li Yu's head hurt.

As it turned out, there was no "what if." The blueprint would learn to read him before he was going to figure this out.

Li Yu sighed. Well, that was that.

When Prince Jing got to the key parts, he suddenly seemed to understand something. Looking back, he saw the fish lying at the edge of the bottle, also staring at the blueprint.

Xiaoyu likes to look at blueprints?

But in the next second, the fish who liked to look at blueprints sank to the bottom of the bottle.

Prince Jing chuckled to himself. Turns out he didn't like it after all. Xiaoyu had fallen asleep again.

He thought back to how Xiaoyu had gotten up early this morning to make him lunch, and his heart felt fuzzy and warm. He couldn't help but reach over to pet the fish. He did this when he was reading in his manor as well, so Prince Jing didn't think it was a big deal.

Xiaoyu blew a bubble. Even though he was sleeping, his tail still drifted over to wrap about his finger, though a little lazily.

Prince Jing couldn't help but smile.

"...Prince Jing."

Zheng Jing, who worked in the same room, and had already witnessed everything, coughed awkwardly.

Prince Jing looked up at Zheng Jing with his deep gaze.

Zheng Jing considered his words carefully and urged him quietly, "Prince Jing, you can't pet your fish on the clock."

Prince Jing glared at Zheng Jing coldly, then went back to studying the blueprint.

He had a habit of writing down notes while he was reading. When there was something he was confused about, he didn't try to ask Zheng Jing immediately, he just made a note. Since he couldn't speak, asking would take a long time. His productivity would go down if he had to constantly interrupt his line of thought and then pick it back up again like that, so Prince Jing read through the whole blueprint first, then collected all his questions for Zheng Jing at the end.

Zheng Jing glanced over at Prince Jing every once in a while. He was quite surprised at the prince's patience. When he'd had to take responsibility and remind Prince Jing not to pet his fish, he'd clearly offended Prince Jing. If the prince really wanted to treat him rudely because of it, Zheng Jing would have to take it, because after all, His Highness was a prince, and he was just a subject.

But Zheng Jing didn't regret it. That was just how he was. He wanted to get along with Prince Jing, but when it came to work, he wouldn't make exceptions for anybody. Zheng Jing disapproved of Prince Jing petting his fish.

Aside from helping Prince Jing, the emperor had given him another job: he had to report back on how Prince Jing was doing in the Ministry of Works. Zheng Jing had already planned out what he was going to say, prepared to ask the emperor for his forgiveness. He didn't think Prince Jing was suitable for this job.

Prince Jing had brought his pet fish to the Ministry of Works, a clear sign the prince wasn't taking this job seriously! Wasting time petting his fish was also definitive proof Prince Jing wasn't really completing his work, Zheng Jing thought.

But after Prince Jing was done with the blueprint, he thrust a bunch of notes at him. When Zheng Jing looked at the dense writing, he was shocked: all the questions Prince Jing had written down were extremely perceptive.

After only a single round of questions, Lord Zheng was sweating bullets. Before, he was a little worried because he was afraid Prince Jing might have just come here to mess around. Now, he was sweating because he was afraid he wouldn't be able to answer Prince Jing's questions.

Zheng Jing couldn't help but recall how the third prince had also been assigned to the Ministry of Works a few years ago. But the Ministry of Works dealt with a bunch of construction workers day in and day out. The third prince thought it was both dirty and not very respectable, so he was very unhappy. It was called a job, but he just drank tea at the Ministry of Works for a few days. In the end, the Minister of Works wrote to the emperor, telling him delicately that the third prince was not suited for this job. As a result, the emperor moved the third prince elsewhere.

In comparison, although Prince Jing's personality was a little odd and he liked to pet fish, just based on how he could sit down and concentrate on the blueprint, he was already leagues ahead of the other princes.

Zheng Jing's opinion of Prince Jing had changed. He decided not to write to the emperor to say Prince Jing wasn't suitable after all. He even thought it was a pity Prince Jing couldn't talk. With this kind of attitude, Prince Jing was someone who could settle down and accomplish something. It was a shame.

"Your Highness," Zheng Jing said gently, "if you have any questions in the future, don't hesitate to ask me. If I can't answer it, you can ask the Minister."

Prince Jing nodded. Since he was done with the blueprint, he could play with his fish now. Despite Zheng Jing's piercing gaze, Prince Jing put the fish into a lotus bowl he'd brought along and started really petting the fish in earnest.

Zheng Jing truly didn't know what to say.

At lunchtime, Prince Jing opened his huge pack and took out an equally huge food box. There were three large bowls inside.

Prince Jing opened each bowl. Zheng Jing, who sat not far away, saw...a bowl of burnt rice, a bowl of dark, black stuff that he couldn't identify, and another bowl...of what looked like soft, wilted cucumber.

Interested, he asked, "Your Highness, what manner of cuisine did you bring?"

As soon as he'd said it, he realized no one would pick up a brush while eating. There was no way Prince Jing would respond. He might even be upset. But Prince Jing was in a good mood. Not only was he not upset, he even took out two pieces of paper from his sleeve and handed them to Zheng Jing.

What? When did Prince Jing prepare these pieces of paper? Did he know he would ask?

There were two dishes, one paper for each. Zheng Jing read the notes that said: *Minced meat and eggplant made by my boyfriend,* and *Smashed cucumber made by my boyfriend.*

Ah. So, the thing he couldn't identify was minced meat eggplant. Were there really eggplants as black as coal?

Zheng Jing refused to comment on the future consort's cooking skills.

But not only had Prince Jing prepared the notes, ready to introduce his boyfriend's cooking at any time, he even ate all three bowls without batting an eye.

Zheng Jing, after witnessing this display of affection, said, "Your Highness...certainly has a good relationship with your consort."

Prince Jing dipped his hand slightly into the bottle, nodding subtly as he touched the little carp's slippery back.

The fish, who had woken up from his nap, was quite delighted. Oh, was he praising him?! He'd gotten up early this morning to make both dishes, and he'd also made the rice. Although the eggplant had turned black for some reason and the rice got a little burnt, it should still taste all right! And the smashed cucumber, Prince Jing's favorite!

Li Yu suddenly thought he should actually taste his own cooking. Maybe there'd been a huge improvement.

While Zheng Jing wasn't paying attention, he swam quietly to the opening of the bottle. Prince Jing's bowls weren't too far away. Li Yu decided to try and steal a little piece of eggplant from Prince Jing's bowl. It was a vegetable, so a fish could eat it, right?

Prince Jing was well aware of the particular flavor of these dishes. Afraid that Xiaoyu would be shocked by the taste, he hurriedly ate all the eggplant in the bowl, as well as all of the cucumber. He didn't even leave behind a single grain of rice.

Li Yu was ecstatic. His cooking must've really improved! Otherwise, why would Prince Jing eat it all so fast and not let him have any?

He started to think about other dishes. He was a useful boyfriend. He couldn't help Prince Jing when it came to blueprints, but he could help Prince Jing by cooking for him.

The fish finally calmed down, and Prince Jing, unaware that increasingly cursed bentos were waiting for him in the future, sighed in relief.

The news of the emperor ordering Prince Jing to begin working eventually made its way to the third prince, making him a little restless. Mu Tianming had asked a few officials to ask the emperor to forgive him and give him something to do. But instead, the emperor ignored the request and went to Prince Jing.

What could a mute do? The emperor would rather rely on a mute than on him?

But no matter how displeased Mu Tianming was, he couldn't act on impulse. The emperor clearly wasn't happy with him right now. Both his injuries and those of the sixth prince were mostly recovered by now. The emperor had let the sixth prince go already, but Mu Tianming still had to go study every day and write down the *Classic of Filial Piety*. He was burning with anxiety. If he continued like this, how was he going to reassure the officials who were on his side?

Going to the Imperial Study Room every day, he could tell the emperor was already starting to train the two young princes. Even their previous teacher had been swapped out for the emperor's own teacher. The emperor was so biased, he was ranking him behind both the two young princes and Prince Jing! Mu Tianming couldn't take it anymore. He complained to the sixth prince, who had come to visit.

"Brother, don't forget what happened to you last time," Mu Tianxiao reminded him in a gentle voice. "You should calm down first. Father wants to see your attitude improve. If you don't make any more mistakes, Father won't ignore you for long. Don't worry, you still have me. I'll keep an eye out for you."

Mu Tianming cheered up immensely. The sixth prince was right. Besides, the sixth prince had been with him for many years now and was extremely trustworthy. Last time he chose not to listen to the sixth prince, he'd suffered a huge setback, which only made the third prince trust the sixth prince even more.

"I feel a lot better with you here," said Mu Tianming. "I can give you authority over a large portion of my people. Help me take care of things."

Mu Tianming took out a token representing his authority, hesitated for a moment, and handed it to the sixth prince. The sixth prince accepted it. No matter how much he wanted this, he couldn't let it show on his face. He thanked the third prince evenly, saying that he appreciated the opportunity and would do anything he could to repay this honor.

Putting away the token, the sixth prince walked out calmly under the third prince's watchful eye.

After leaving the manor, Mu Tianxiao looked up at the sky, his mood soaring. He knew the heavy clouds above his head were about to dissipate. Once he had all of the third prince's people in his control, he could finally stop hiding.

Fishy Love Letters

NOW THAT HE'D RECEIVED Mu Tianming's token, Mu
Tianxiao didn't keep his promise and help the third prince
take care of his business. Instead, he took care of himself.
His injuries from the beating had healed. Mu Tianxiao was
going to the palace to pay his respects to the emperor. Rain or shine,
everything was a gift when it came from the emperor. Even if the
emperor had punished him, he had to smile and thank him anyway.

The emperor met with the sixth prince. The Imperial Guards'
investigation had revealed that the third prince was just using the
sixth prince and he wasn't the main conspirator, but the emperor
still disliked Mu Tianxiao and treated him coldly.

He was like an invisible person to the emperor. He'd only started
appearing before the emperor recently because he was following
the third prince. He'd long since gotten used to the emperor's cold
attitude and responded in turn with respect.

After thanking the emperor, Mu Tiaoxiao said that he planned to
give Prince Jing an extravagant gift with the excuse that he felt bad
for the whole fake monk thing and wanted to apologize. Because
the emperor knew the whole situation, Mu Tiaoxiao wanted to run
it past him first and have him look over the gift list.

Recalling how the second prince had done something similar not
long ago, the emperor's gaze turned suspicious. But he still ended up

looking at the list. It was a set of ink, brush, paper, and inkstone, as well as some calligraphy and paintings, though they were not anything famous.

The emperor suddenly recalled that the sixth prince's mother, Consort Zhang, had been Empress Xiaohui's servant. After Empress Xiaohui passed away, Consort Zhang remained in Changchun Palace. She'd only been given the lowly status of second class attendant after the emperor had shown favor to her one drunken night. Just from that night, Consort Zhang became pregnant with the sixth prince. She'd only ascended to the Consort rank once the sixth prince became an adult. Consort Zhang didn't come from an influential family who could back them, so the sixth prince ended up the poorest of all the princes. The rewards he normally received were just the standard ones given during holidays and the New Year. Things had only gotten a little better for him since he'd been following the third prince these last few years.

The emperor couldn't quite work out what he was feeling, but he felt that the sixth prince had at least put some thought into these gifts, so he nodded and allowed the sixth prince to go ahead.

But he thought about it and decided to mention ahead of time: "If Prince Jing doesn't want to see you, you must not disturb him." He was afraid the sixth prince would bring Prince Jing trouble because he had committed such egregious deeds in the past.

Mu Tianxiao smiled. "Father, please rest assured I will leave as soon as I set the gifts down. I won't bother fifth brother."

Mu Tianxiao bowed and then left. The moment he turned around, his smile seemed to freeze over.

Every day, Li Yu went to work with Prince Jing. Then, every night, he had to keep up with his relationship. He'd been keeping up this schedule for several days now, and although he was a fish for most of it, he was still exhausted. He was sure they had to be "inseparable" by now, but the quest wasn't updating.

The fish-scamming system was scamming him once again. He'd clearly already kissed Prince Jing. With tongue! Prince Jing brought him to and from work and petted him whenever he got the chance. Didn't that count as inseparable?!

‹The quest is determined by the user and the tyrant's relationship,› the system explained. *‹As of now, your relationship hasn't developed since the 'indulging' quest.›*

‹We're already boyfriends and he takes me to work. Doesn't that count as a deeper relationship?›

‹This is ancient China. The concept of 'boyfriends' doesn't exist. Additionally, the tyrant was already in the habit of carrying his pet fish around everywhere, so that doesn't count either.›

‹…›

Made sense. What was he supposed to say to that?

Prince Jing had always doted on the fish. Did that mean it was harder for him to complete his quests now? But if boyfriends didn't count, what was he supposed to do? Was he supposed to marry Prince Jing on the spot?

‹Getting married is one way,› the system replied.

Li Yu scoffed coldly. He should've known the system was going to start scamming him again now that he was continuing his quests. He wanted to turn back into a human. If he didn't, he'd be in constant danger of Prince Jing finding out his secret. That was the reason he'd laid down those rules with Prince Jing in the first place.

He'd hoped he could date Prince Jing while completing his quests, but the fish-scamming system wouldn't let him complete the mission just as boyfriends. If he couldn't complete these quests, then he couldn't become a human. If he couldn't become a human, then he couldn't properly date Prince Jing. How was their relationship supposed to develop?

So he was still blocked from progressing with his tasks. He was stuck in an endless loop...

A light bulb went off in Li Yu's head. He figured it out. The system was once again trying to ship him and Prince Jing. He just hadn't thought that far ahead.

He and Prince Jing had only just started to shyly hold hands like a regular couple, and they even blushed when they kissed. Li Yu couldn't imagine suddenly getting married. He wanted to be with Prince Jing purely because he liked him. It wasn't because he was a prince or would later become the emperor.

Due to Prince Jing's current and future status, he couldn't get married just willy-nilly. In the book, after Prince Jing ascended to the throne, despite all the officials' objections, he was adamant about Chu Yanyu being the empress. The entire Censorate was on their knees, but no one was able to convince him. In the end, Chu Yanyu promising he would only ever be a consort and never the empress was what won the officials over. But for love of him, Prince Jing never picked an empress. As a result, Chu Yanyu remained a consort in name but was treated and honored like an empress.

But Prince Jing still needed an heir, so Chu Yanyu generously found him some consorts. In the original story, Prince Jing was furious over this, which made Chu Yanyu feel unappreciated.

In the past, when he was reading the novel, Li Yu had felt like the delicate little concubine was finally doing something for Prince Jing's sake for once after spending his whole life tricking him—but now that he was the one who was dating Prince Jing, he no longer thought that way.

In the book, Chu Yanyu didn't want to be the empress and even urged Prince Jing to take more consorts. It seemed like he was thinking of the greater good, but one could also interpret this as Chu Yanyu not caring who was with Prince Jing. In other words, he didn't love Prince Jing as much as Prince Jing loved him.

Perhaps Prince Jing had gotten mad because he realized, to Chu Yanyu, he could never compare to the dead sixth prince. That was how love was. Whoever fell first lost.

Prince Jing, who had become a tyrant, could kill the entire world to claim it for himself, but he couldn't kill Chu Yanyu to claim his heart.

At the end of the book, after many years, Chu Yanyu finally started falling for Prince Jing. The tragic love story ended on such an absurd note.

When Li Yu thought of this ending, he felt a little uncomfortable. He really felt bad for the Prince Jing in the book. After ascending to the throne, the tyrant had the entire world, but he didn't have a single person who cared for him wholeheartedly. Even though the delicate little concubine was right next to him all along, he didn't care for Prince Jing for a long time. Prince Jing, who towered above everyone on the throne, had always been very lonely.

But in this world, it was no longer possible for Chu Yanyu and Prince Jing to get together. Li Yu felt bad for Prince Jing, but did that mean it was up to him to change everything? Then, would Prince Jing take him as consort? Would he become the empress after Prince Jing rose to the throne?

Then was he...the Fish Consort? The Fish Empress?

When people had called Li Yu "consort" before, it made him uneasy. "Empress" was a much heavier title. He didn't know if he could carry it with his little fish body.

He was willing to help Prince Jing take the throne, but that was a different matter than becoming a consort or empress. When he imagined being dressed up like a Noble Consort, waiting all alone in his palace for Prince Jing to pay him some attention, goosebumps erupted all over his skin.

Never mind. There was no point dwelling on it so much. He and Prince Jing had only just begun—who knew what would happen in the future? They were just dating, so there was no need to make things too complicated between the two of them. Marriage was the kind of thing they should only consider when they could both view the relationship with a mature state of mind, eighteen-year-old Li Yu thought, as though he were an old man.

But after considering all this, he was still affected. When he transformed to see Prince Jing, he was a little down.

Prince Jing had always been observant. He immediately noticed that Xiaoyu's mood was not as cheerful as usual.

He really looked forward to seeing human Xiaoyu every day. Recently, he'd been busy with work during the day. Though Xiaoyu was with him, there were others there, so they couldn't act too close. It wasn't that Prince Jing feared Zheng Jing; rather, he couldn't let Zheng Jing find out about the carp spirit, so he really only had the time after work to spend with Xiaoyu.

For these two hours, Prince Jing didn't want Xiaoyu to be sad about anything. If there was anything bothering Xiaoyu, he would solve it himself.

What's wrong? Prince Jing seemed to ask while holding Li Yu's hands.

Li Yu pursed his lips. He couldn't mention the original book or becoming the empress. But Prince Jing's careful gaze carried the weight of his care for him; Li Yu could feel it clearly.

It seemed Prince Jing was the first to fall in love this time as well.

Thinking of the confession carved into the walls of the manor, Li Yu started to feel bad for Prince Jing again. No matter what, he decided privately, he'd never let Prince Jing be alone again.

After he'd agreed to Li Yu's rules, Prince Jing never tried to ask Li Yu about the things he didn't want to talk about. He approached Li Yu and held him in his arms so Li Yu could lean against him. Slowly, Li Yu relaxed.

Li Yu blinked. These last few days, he'd gradually started to recognize the patterns in Prince Jing's behavior. For example, when Prince Jing hugged him, that usually meant he wanted a kiss. Prince Jing really liked to kiss him. And Li Yu liked to wait for his kiss: smiling, then returning it. He didn't know if all new couples were as clingy as this, but they both liked it.

This time, though, Prince Jing didn't kiss him. He pulled out a note from his sleeve and handed it to Li Yu.

Prince Jing rarely prepared notes ahead of time to communicate with other people—he usually wrote things down at the time. After he started dating Li Yu, though, he began to cherish every moment they had together, so he'd come up with this method as a compromise to avoid wasting precious time on writing. If he had something to say, it made sense to write it down when he was alone, then give it to Xiaoyu later.

Li Yu accepted the note and looked at it excitedly. The note was already a little worn around the edges, and the sentence written on it was in Prince Jing's handwriting: *I like you.*

This wasn't the first time Li Yu had been confessed to, but he was still delighted. "Your Highness wrote this a long time ago, right?" Otherwise, why would the note be in such a state? And he hid it specifically so he could take it out to make Li Yu happy. He cared for him so meticulously it was a little scary.

Prince Jing nodded, but didn't mention that he'd written this back when Xiaoyu was angry with him and avoiding him. At the time, he'd wanted to show it to Xiaoyu at an opportune moment, but he never got around to using it. Now was the perfect time.

Prince Jing's comforting made Li Yu feel a lot better, and he started to become curious instead. Prince Jing had notes to cheer him up and to show off to Zheng Jing. Could there be others too? Li Yu put his hands on his hips like a bandit and smiled brightly. "Your Highness, you have many more of these notes, don't you?"

It was unusual to see Prince Jing so hesitant. He glanced at Li Yu, then looked away quickly.

Oho, from the looks of this expression, there's clearly something going on. I want to see! Li Yu was now very close to Prince Jing. He smirked, then reached both hands into Prince Jing's sleeves, hugging him. Prince Jing couldn't evade him.

In a flash of awkwardness, Li Yu suddenly thought of the time he'd bitten Prince Jing's nipple. Thank goodness Prince Jing didn't know he was the fish!

Prince Jing, meanwhile, hesitated... He'd also remembered the time the fish bit his nipple, and was a bit flustered.

The two of them each had their own thoughts. Li Yu's eyes shone brightly as he pulled out a bunch of notes from Prince Jing's sleeve. Shocked, he said, "Your Highness, you wrote this many?"

Prince Jing looked at him with a gentle gaze.

Li Yu randomly grabbed one and read: *The food tastes very good— try not to tire yourself out.*

He thought about it carefully. This must be what Prince Jing wanted to say when Li Yu handed him his lunch. But because they had so little time to spend together, Prince Jing didn't let him know what he was thinking most of the time. He must've written it down after the fact.

With emotions swirling in his chest, Li Yu read all the notes and recalled many of the little things that had happened between them. It turned out that despite Prince Jing's cold exterior, his heart was always warm toward Li Yu.

The last note was even more tattered. It was almost worn out.

Prince Jing's expression was suddenly extremely complicated. After a brief internal struggle, he actually tried to snatch it back from him! Li Yu realized something must be up, so of course the curious fishy chose to open it up and see. He thought there'd be some kind of cringy pickup line, but instead it was—

I want to absorb essence.

The Fish Was Hard
to Cast Out

"**A**BSORB ESSENCE?"
Li Yu wasn't quite sure, so he asked quietly, slowly,
"Your Highness, what does this mean?"
Prince Jing had first written that note because he wanted to
express his own emotions. He never thought Li Yu would get his
hands on it. Now that his secret was revealed to Xiaoyu, he was
most worried that Xiaoyu would work out that he already knew
the carp spirit's identity. Prince Jing decided to just shake his head,
expression blank.

If he refused to admit it, then all would be fine.

Li Yu curled his hand into a fist and coughed into it lightly.
"So...Your Highness is saying you also don't know what this means,
and it has nothing to do with you?"

Prince Jing hesitated for a second, then nodded fervently.

Li Yu laughed inside. He and Prince Jing had read a lot of
novels together by now. He knew that in the novels, when yao
wanted to absorb essence, it meant they wanted to do various
indescribable things to the scholar. Did this mean Prince Jing...
also wanted to do those sorts of things with him?

What kind of impure thoughts was this asshole's brain full of?!
And after being found out, he wouldn't even admit it! He never
would've thought Prince Jing had such an immature side.

Li Yu cursed Prince Jing out on the inside, but on the outside he smiled as he said, "You really didn't write this, Your Highness? It's your handwriting."

Prince Jing anxiously did his best to communicate that it really wasn't him!

"Okay, okay, I get it, it wasn't you." Li Yu tried very hard not to laugh out loud and continued to tease him. "Then does Your Highness know what it means to absorb essence?"

Li Yu laughed to himself. *This is what you get for taking advantage of me before! How does it feel now?*

Asking for mercy, Prince Jing brought out a little golden fish from his sleeve and handed it silently to Li Yu. Li Yu liked gold and silver, so Prince had prepared some to keep him happy. This little fish was designed by Prince Jing himself and had been made not long ago.

"This fish is so cute. Is it for me?!" Li Yu was immediately drawn to the little fish. He happily turned the small golden fish over in his hands again and again. It was charming and cute, and its tail was curved. Every part of it looked just like his fish form. There was a braided string attached to the fish's back, and it was in the exact shade of green that Li Yu liked.

Li Yu touched the string gently and asked, despite already knowing the answer, "Where do I hang this?"

Prince Jing smiled as he wrapped his arms around Li Yu and hung the little fish on the colorful silk tie around his waist.

Li Yu played with the fish at his waist for a while, then looked at Prince Jing with bright eyes. "Your Highness, don't change the subject. Tell me what absorbing essence is."

Xiaoyu was a little hard to distract. Prince Jing was both happy and frustrated.

Prince Jing was struggling to find a way to escape answering Li Yu's repeated questioning, when he was saved by Wang Xi's careful knock on the door.

Wang Xi didn't want to interrupt, because his master had requested privacy whenever Li-gongzi was visiting. But the sixth prince was here and had already been waiting for a while in Ninghui Hall. Wang Xi knew the sixth prince had once brought his master harm, so Wang Xi hadn't treated him with the utmost respect, but the sixth prince had said he'd come from the palace, so Wang Xi couldn't make him wait for too long.

"Your Highness, the sixth prince is here from the palace. He says he's here to apologize." Wang Xi spoke apologetically. He didn't want to, but he'd interrupted his master and Li-gongzi again.

Li-gongzi and his master had a pretty big fight last time. Wang Xi and the rest of the servants had all been worried. Finally, things had blown over, and Wang Xi couldn't wait for the two of them to reconcile.

So, were they together now or not?

From Wang Xi's silent observation, his master and Li-gongzi had already slept in the same bed. And they were always touching and hugging each other, so they must be together now... But then, for a while, all Li-gongzi and the master did was converse, read books, and practice calligraphy. They were both very respectful, and it seemed like perhaps they weren't together after all.

After that, Li-gongzi ran away because he didn't want to be intimate with Prince Jing, so Prince Jing ordered the walls to be carved with those words that Wang-gonggong was still too embarrassed to look at. But then Li-gongzi let the master come close again, so they *should* be together now, right?

Then again, every time the master saw Li-gongzi, he'd go take a cold bath. Li-gongzi didn't know about this, but as Prince Jing's closest servant, Wang Xi did. If they were actually together, how could this happen?

And so, to this day, Wang-gonggong could only describe his master and Li-gongzi's relationship as extremely complicated: seemingly there but perhaps actually not.

Wang Xi had been afraid of disturbing Prince Jing, but after he'd managed to bring himself to interrupt, why did it seem like Prince Jing let out a sigh of relief?

Prince Jing patted Li Yu's hand, ready to go throw the sixth prince out. Actually, he was just afraid Xiaoyu would continue asking about essence. He really felt too awkward and couldn't answer, so he wanted to use the sixth prince as an excuse to let it blow over. Xiaoyu liked to play, so maybe by the time he came back, he'd stop asking.

"Your Highness, y-you're going to see the sixth prince?!" As soon as Li Yu heard "the sixth prince," his originally teasing manner became nervous. He automatically grabbed Prince Jing's sleeve.

The sixth prince...was Prince Jing's greatest enemy in the original book. Once the second and third princes were no longer in the running, the emperor began to see the sixth prince in a new light. He'd always hidden behind the third prince, ruthless and calculating. Prince Jing had fallen for many of his traps. And because of Chu Yanyu, Prince Jing had nearly died by the sixth prince's hands. Even after being thoroughly defeated, he still managed to cause a lot of trouble for Prince Jing.

Even if the plot was completely different now, the sixth prince's character traits couldn't have changed much, right?

Li Yu knew the sixth prince's background, but he didn't know how to explain it to Prince Jing.

When Ye Qinghuan had been plotted against, Li Yu said he'd come across the information unexpectedly. It wasn't a particularly good story, but thankfully Prince Jing trusted him and didn't ask too many questions. But if he said the same again when it came to the sixth prince, it would be too suspicious.

Li Yu frowned in thought, trying to think of a reason to tell Prince Jing to watch out for the sixth prince.

Seeing his furrowed brows, Prince Jing reached over and smoothed them out with slightly cool fingertips.

"Your Highness, if I ask you to be careful of the sixth prince..." Prince Jing was so gentle, Li Yu just blurted it out.

Prince Jing glanced at him, then nodded. *Okay.*

"...You don't want to ask why?" Li Yu asked.

Prince Jing pointed at the wall. Next to the painting of the fish, he'd carefully hung up Li Yu's rules. He was afraid he'd forget the conditions he'd agreed to, so he put them up there to remind himself.

Li Yu understood. He was trying to say that according to the agreement, Prince Jing had to believe him. If Li Yu didn't want to say, Prince Jing wouldn't ask. But the agreement only stated that Prince Jing couldn't ask where he was going. He didn't expect Prince Jing to extend that to anything he didn't want to talk about.

...Wasn't that a good thing?

It was good. Very good. This was the best possible outcome.

Li Yu felt reassured, but he still felt like he had to give some sort of reason. "Your Highness, the sixth prince has harmed you before. Please don't trust him." Li Yu didn't know why the sixth prince was visiting, but still, it was better to be safe than sorry.

Prince Jing nodded. He touched Li Yu's face, smiling, asking him not to worry. Then he left with Wang Xi. Li Yu didn't go with them, partially because he didn't want to show up in front of the sixth prince and partially because he was afraid he didn't have much time left. He decided to wait for Prince Jing in his room instead.

Prince Jing's note was still there—he hadn't taken away the "evidence." Li Yu observed the bold, vigorous brushstrokes on his own. They were both men, so he could understand how Prince Jing was feeling. Though Prince Jing had certain thoughts toward him, he hadn't done anything, due to their agreement. At most, he'd say a few flirtatious things on paper.

His Highness was so good to him. He couldn't let someone like that go.

As Li Yu thought this, the corners of his lips raised mischievously.

The sixth prince waited for a long time before Prince Jing finally came out to see him.

Mu Tianxiao approached, wanting to say a few customary pleasantries, but Prince Jing only glanced at the gifts, nodded coldly, and prepared to chase his guest out. He didn't even have any intention of asking the sixth prince to sit.

Mu Tianxiao rubbed his nose and said gently, "I've offended you. I hope you can forgive me, brother." Mu Tianxiao didn't mention the third prince at all. He'd only come for his own sake anyway.

The sixth prince was apologizing to Prince Jing, but the third prince hadn't. The difference between them was clear. Mu Tianxiao wanted to get rid of the third prince as soon as possible. The biggest obstacle between him and the throne had never been the arrogant second prince, or the third prince, who he had in the palm of his hand.

"...Fifth brother, I was deceived before, and nearly had a misunderstanding with you and your fish." The topic suddenly changed. "I heard fifth brother loves this fish so much you take it around with you everywhere. Why don't I see it now?" Mu Tianxiao thought there was something up with Prince Jing's fish, and he wanted to probe a little bit.

Prince Jing glanced at Wang Xi with a stiff expression. Wanggonggong immediately responded, "Fifth prince—His Highness's fish is very precious. It doesn't like to visit irrelevant people."

Mu Tianxiao was randomly slapped in the face by a fish who wasn't even present...

Mu Tianxiao wanted to keep asking questions, but Prince Jing didn't have the patience to listen to him. Since he came to apologize, shouldn't he leave after putting the things down? The sixth prince didn't even get a sip of hot tea. Prince Jing gave Wang Xi another glance, wanting him to see the guest out.

Unbelievable, thought Mu Tianxiao. He bade Prince Jing farewell and left Ninghui Hall. When he was almost out of the manor, someone with disheveled hair threw themselves at him.

"Your Highness, Your Highness!" they sobbed as they threw themselves into Mu Tianxiao's arms.

Mu Tianxiao's first instinct was to push them away, thinking they were part of some plan by Prince Jing. But when this person looked up, face tear-streaked, Mu Tianxiao was shocked.

"Does Your Highness not recognize me anymore?" he cried.

"Are...are you Yu-er?"

Mu Tianxiao could not believe that this person before him—with his ashen complexion and eyes as swollen as peaches—was Chu Yanyu, who used to be so bright and open. If he didn't still look somewhat similar, Mu Tianxiao would never have recognized him.

"Yu-er, how did you come to be in this state?"

It was very hard for Mu Tianxiao to contact Chu Yanyu. It got harder and harder each time he tried to send a note to Prince Jing's manor. Chu Yanyu had only mentioned briefly that Prince Jing barely showed him any attention, but Mu Tianxiao never expected this.

Chu Yanyu bit his lip, crying without answering. He didn't know how to tell the sixth prince that Prince Jing had never even looked him in the eye. He'd failed to drug Prince Jing, and in the end, he was the one who had been drugged.

Nobody defiled him. He was tied up, unable to move. He screamed and cried, losing his mind, trying all he could to get relief. He couldn't have been in a sorrier state. He was tied up for three days before the drug finally subsided. But his body was ruined.

Even worse, everyone in Qingxi Garden had heard his mindless screaming. Now, they looked at him with blatant contempt.

Chu Yanyu forced himself not to think about those memories as he knelt before the sixth prince. "Your Highness, I really can't stay at Prince Jing's manor any longer. Please take me back!"

He didn't want to stay in Qingxi Garden in Prince Jing's manor anymore. He never wanted to see Prince Jing again. Now that the sixth prince was here—he liked the sixth prince, and the sixth prince liked him back. He still wanted to be with the sixth prince!

In the past, if Mu Tianxiao had been faced with such a weeping beauty, he definitely would've comforted him gently—but this was Prince Jing's manor. Mu Tianxiao was afraid this was part of Prince Jing's plans.

As he scanned their surroundings, he thought there were eyes all around them. Chu Yanyu's appearance shocked him. Mu Tianxiao worried that Prince Jing had created this scene to reveal that he and Chu Yanyu were involved. He'd only just felt a glimmer of hope that the emperor might value him—he couldn't let Chu Yanyu ruin his reputation now. He had to distance himself from Chu Yanyu!

"Chu-gongzi, you and I have never met. As you have entered my brother's manor, you belong to him. Why are you saying all this to me?" Mu Tianxiao yelled loudly, pretending to be angry as he pushed Chu Yanyu away. "If you continue like this, don't blame me for what will come after!"

The sixth prince ruthlessly slapped Chu Yanyu in the face, then turned to leave with a wave of his sleeve.

Chu Yanyu had barely managed to sneak out because he heard the sixth prince was coming. He never thought the sixth prince, who'd always cared for him the most, would hit him. That slap left Chu Yanyu completely dazed, and he heard the sound of his heart shattering.

Prince Jing watched all of this silently from a distance.

"Your Highness, th-this..."

Wang Xi was afraid to speak up. His Highness had never cared about Chu Yanyu, but why did he ask him to lead Chu Yanyu to the sixth prince this time? The sixth prince had hit Chu Yanyu, but from Chu Yanyu's reaction...he could tell that the two of them definitely knew each other!

Prince Jing glanced at him. Wang Xi understood his master wanted him to continue as ordered, so he nodded and got busy.

Because of this, Prince Jing was delayed in getting back to Xiaoyu. He walked faster.

The room was dark. Half of the candles were extinguished, leaving only a dim, warm light by the bed. There was no one by the bed, or in the room.

Xiaoyu had probably transformed already. Prince Jing was very frustrated. Perhaps he shouldn't have tried to confirm the relationship between Chu Yanyu and the sixth prince.

When Prince Jing saw Chu Yanyu and the sixth prince, a weird feeling welled up in his heart. He didn't know why he felt a flicker of gratification when Chu Yanyu was hit. But it was a shame he couldn't see Xiaoyu again. He'd probably have to wait until tomorrow.

As this disappointing thought crossed his mind, though, the tightly shut curtains around the bed twitched open, and Xiaoyu poked his head out, rubbing his eyes blearily. "Your Highness, you took so long to get back, I'm about to fall asleep," he giggled.

Prince Jing was surprised and delighted. He stared at Li Yu unblinkingly.

The youth got up, pulling his robe up around his shoulders. He turned up one of the oil lamps by the bed to make it brighter, and also brightened the only hint of warmth in Prince Jing's heart.

"Your Highness, you…" Li Yu blushed, a little sneakiness creeping in behind his shyness. "You still haven't told me what absorbing essence is."

Fishy Reads a Novel

PRINCE JING REALLY DIDN'T KNOW what to do with this fish. He smiled and reached over to pet Li Yu on the head.

Hm... Did this mean the same thing as when he patted the fish's head, Li Yu wondered... Oh, whatever!

Li Yu pulled Prince Jing down to sit by him. Prince Jing was a little cautious because he didn't know what Xiaoyu wanted, but he still sat down.

Before he sat down all the way, the fish quickly shut the curtains with a whoosh.

A faint glow from the oil lamp outside filtered through the curtains. The fabric was embroidered with cotton roses, and their shadows played over the youth's snowy white undershirt. His star-like eyes shone with the jumping flame.

Prince Jing's breath hitched. His desire for Xiaoyu surged unstoppably within his heart, but remembering their agreement, he did his best to suppress it.

"Your Highness, why are you sitting so far away? Come closer." Li Yu patted the jade pillow next to him.

Prince Jing didn't dare get too close. He only moved over a little bit.

Li Yu urged him a few times, then giggled. "I'm not a fierce beast, Your Highness. Are you afraid of me?"

Prince Jing thought silently, *You aren't a fierce beast, but you are a seductive little yao, which is much more dangerous.* But he couldn't just stay there when the seductive little yao had asked so many times. After hesitating for a while, he sat down next to Xiaoyu. There was only a finger's width between them.

Li Yu was just waiting for him to get close enough, and he immediately wrapped his arms around Prince Jing and pulled him in. Now there was no more space between them.

"Your Highness, Your Highness, look!" Li Yu pulled out a few books from behind him as if he was performing a magic trick. By the light from outside the bed, Prince Jing saw it was the *Legend of the White Snake*, which he hadn't read in a long time.

Li Yu shoved the book into his hand and stuffed himself back into his arms. He couldn't be more pleased on the inside, but on the outside, he said very seriously, "Since Your Highness wouldn't tell me what absorbing essence meant, I thought I would be able to find the answer in one of your many books, so I looked through them."

Prince Jing didn't know what to do with the soft, warm body that was suddenly pressed against his. He didn't even know where to put his limbs. He felt like he'd fallen into the carp spirit's gentle trap as soon as he'd entered the canopy of the bed. But he was happy to fall.

As he mentally recited the Pure Heart Mantra, he quietly watched the carp spirit in his arms put on a performance.

"And then guess what—I found it! It's in these books! Look, Your Highness, look at what the white snake spirit said to Scholar Xu." Li Yu lay back into Prince Jing's chest, flipping to a certain page in the book. He pointed to a line and read it out loud. "'Husband, we yao need to absorb essence.'"

Prince Jing was shocked. Something was going to happen if they continued like this. He quickly covered the fearless carp spirit's mouth. Li Yu shook like he'd pulled a muscle, then burst into laughter. Prince Jing didn't want him to say it, but he was going to anyway. He freed his mouth and stubbornly flipped to another page.

"Here it is again... 'Husband, we yao must absorb essence every day.'" Li Yu blinked and looked up at Prince Jing. "Your Highness," he asked as if he didn't know, "is this what you were talking about?"

Li Yu calling him "husband" was really testing Prince Jing. He could barely keep himself under control. After some internal struggle, he nodded his head lightly.

Li Yu thought he finally had Prince Jing hooked and said smugly, "Your Highness, it also explains how exactly they went about 'absorbing' in the novel. If you're still not sure, let's read it together."

If they read it together, perhaps something could happen. At least that was Li Yu's plan. But, keeping their agreement in mind, Prince Jing adamantly shook his head, wanting to put the book away.

This wasn't going quite as Li Yu had thought it would.

While Prince Jing was gone, Li Yu had already skimmed through the whole book. Although there were a lot of ancient words he couldn't read, he could still make out most of it. His comprehension skills were shockingly adept.

Prince Jing took good care of him, and he loved and cared for Prince Jing. He'd always had the intention of becoming more intimate with Prince Jing, but the book had really stoked the flames in his heart. He'd been lying down for a while, but he couldn't calm down, so he decided to wait for Prince Jing on the bed. No matter what, he had to get Prince Jing to agree. But now, at such a crucial moment, why wasn't Prince Jing cooperating?

...And the reason Prince Jing wasn't cooperating seemed to be the agreement he himself had laid down?

Li Yu suddenly felt like he'd shot himself in the foot.

N-no, Li Yu suddenly thought, *What I want right now doesn't* exactly *contradict the agreement.*

When he'd first laid the rules down, it wasn't because he didn't *ever* want to do those things. It was mostly because he was afraid he'd lose track of time and turn into a fish in the middle of it. There was no way he could recover from that. But he'd forgotten there were things they could do where he didn't need to be afraid of turning into a fish! Why did they have to restrain themselves?

The novel was useless, unable to seduce his boyfriend for him. He had to do it himself.

Li Yu was busy for a while, even kicking the books off the bed. He looked up with a mysterious smile. "Your Highness, I-I have a friend who told me boyfriends can do other things together besides merely spending the night..."

Prince Jing was just about to get jealous over this friend when a sweet pair of lips pressed against his. Xiaoyu put Prince Jing's hand on the string of pearls at his waist, smiling shyly.

The leaf green blanket with the gold edge was scrunched up into a ball, then spread back out. Occasionally, sweet laughter would come from underneath it.

Li Yu felt like he could drown in this tenderness. Blushing, he asked in a small voice, "Your Highness, let's do it together, okay?"

Prince Jing didn't really understand, but Xiaoyu made him understand with his body. There were many ways for a carp spirit to absorb essence. Prince Jing was just a bit inexperienced. Of course, Prince Jing listened to Xiaoyu. Listening to Xiaoyu meant he got to be absorbed, as well as dine on fish. He'd never experienced such joy.

"Your Highness, how long do you normally last?" Li Yu peeked out from the warm blanket with his hair in a mess. His exposed neck was covered in indecent red marks. Prince Jing couldn't look away.

Li Yu rubbed his toe against Prince Jing's leg.

The sixth prince had come at the wrong time. He didn't have much time left. After he got his answer, he could prepare for the next step.

Prince Jing, whose hair was just as messy, felt like he'd only just gotten a taste...

No man would be modest at a time like this. He silently held up one finger.

"Ten minutes? That fast?"

Furious, Prince Jing pinched his butt... With just a little pressure, Li Yu was already yelping.

Realizing his mistake, Li Yu smiled apologetically, "Sorry, I-I got it wrong, not that fast, i-it's..."

If it wasn't ten minutes, then an hour? Either way, there wasn't enough time.

Li Yu stood up and kissed him on the corner of the lips apologetically. "Sorry, Your Highness, I-I have to leave again."

Prince Jing understood. He ruffled his hair.

"Oh, right." Li Yu laughed. "You shouldn't take so many cold baths in the future."

Although they couldn't take it all the way to the end, like other couples, they could try all the steps that came first.

After Li-gongzi left, Prince Jing always took a cold bath. Though he could hide it from Li-gongzi, Xiaoyu saw everything.

Prince Jing froze, then nodded, wanting to kiss Li Yu again. But his gentle little fish suddenly pushed him away and yelled, "Ahhhhh, there's no time!"

Xiaoyu, who'd finished absorbing essence, hastily pulled on some clothes, then immediately ran off.

As Prince Jing lay there, it felt like he could still feel that captivating tenderness.

The little carp in the fish tank was skulking around, behaving as if he'd done something wrong. He waited for a while to confirm that the person on the bed was asleep, and then he finally pulled out the cute, little golden fish. Now he had a new gift! Prince Jing was always giving him things. Li Yu kissed it happily, then entered the system, feeling uplifted.

As expected, while he and Prince Jing were tussling about in the blankets, the quest had updated. But at the time, Li Yu's hands and mouth had been very busy, so he had no time to check.

This really meant his relationship with Prince Jing was progressing quite well. So much so that he didn't even really care about the quests.

Unexpectedly, the quest that he thought had been stuck in a logic loop was cleared just like that. Getting married was one way to progress in a relationship—so was being intimate. As he and Prince Jing grew closer and closer, perhaps he'd be able to breeze through the next quest too.

Li Yu thought his current mindset was a good one. He had to keep it up. He could strategically disregard the system, but in terms of actual goals…he had to figure out how to fully become a human.

The reward for the "Inseparable" quest was another one of Prince Jing's secrets. Li Yu thought that after the main questline of "Priceless Pet Fish," the system had gotten a lot stingier. Each quest only rewarded him with a single secret. But perhaps "Priceless Pet Fish" was just the tutorial level. It needed the fish to level up quickly. Now that he had a good foundation of skills, it was time to get more in-depth by learning secrets.

Like last time, there were four choices. The three he hadn't chosen from the "Indulging" quest were still there, but the one Li Yu had already seen had been replaced by another one, showing the vague shine of a sword.

Li Yu looked at it. There was no chance the system would show him all of the tyrant behavior Prince Jing had tried to keep hidden from him, right? He was afraid of violent, bloody scenes, so he rejected the sword instinctively. As for the rest...

Li Yu chose the dark palace that he didn't recognize. He had already mentally prepared himself and immediately entered the memory.

This was the corner of some unknown palace, in a dark room. There was a sewing box on the table, and in the box was a half-sewn toy tiger. A slightly chubby woman in her thirties sat next to the table. This woman had a melancholy expression, occasionally picking up the tiger to add a few stitches. She looked like she was waiting for someone.

Before long, a servant came in. Li Yu was confused; he had no memory of this person. If this was someone serving Prince Jing, he would be very familiar with them by now.

The servant handed a small, paper package to the woman. She was terrified and distressed, kneeling down on the ground to beg for mercy, but the servant ignored her. Eventually, perhaps because he ran out of patience, he kicked the woman.

With no other choice, the woman poured out the powder with shaking hands.

Li Yu thought perhaps she was being forced to drug Prince Jing, but in the next moment, the woman swallowed the powder, tears streaming down her face.

That was the end of the secret, only leaving him with more new questions than answers.

He knew this secret was related to Prince Jing's past, but in the memory of the prince almost drowning, he'd been able to see Prince Jing and even himself—he could even hear. But this memory had no sound, and no Prince Jing.

If Prince Jing wasn't there, how could it be Prince Jing's secret? What relation did the woman and servant have to Prince Jing?

And that powder... Most of the powders in the palace were either aphrodisiacs or poisons. Why did the woman take it herself? It couldn't be that she was another Chu Yanyu, plotting to drug Prince Jing and thus being forced to take it herself? The woman seemed a little on the older side, so it didn't seem likely. Besides, there weren't many people in the world like Chu Yanyu...

Li Yu didn't understand, but he had experience now. If he didn't understand something from the system, he could usually just set it aside for the time being.

Now that the "Inseparable" quest was complete, Li Yu was both nervous and excited about the next quest. What kind of dumbass task would require them to be even closer than they were now?

Li Yu was feeling suspicious. He took a deep breath and clicked open the main quest. The next step was—

"Stay with the Tyrant Through Thick and Thin."

Fish Buying Antiques

LI YU THOUGHT the next quest would be something more shameless, something that would push him and Prince Jing closer, but in the end it turned out to be "Stay with the Tyrant Through Thick and Thin." Did this mean they were going to face some sort of hardship together?

Even if they were, it would be fine. Every moment with Prince Jing was a happy one. Now that they were lovers, he couldn't expect everything to go smoothly all the time. No matter what, he'd continue onward with Prince Jing, side by side.

Li Yu was fully confident he could complete this step.

The reward for "Thick and Thin" was another secret. It seemed like sooner or later, he'd get to peek at all of Prince Jing's secrets.

Li Yu smiled and exited the system, then glanced at the bed, worried. Prince Jing was probably resting and not paying attention to the fish tank, so he swam to the silver rock bed and covered himself with the leaf blanket.

Thinking back to what had happened under the real blanket with Prince Jing, the usually shameless fish was suddenly a little shy. His heart beat quickly in his chest, and he waved his tail in agitation, as though that would help chase away the embarrassment.

...Never mind, they'd already done it. And they'd be going further in the future! What did he have to be embarrassed about?!

Li Yu kept comforting himself, but it still took many more flaps of his tail before he managed to slowly fall asleep.

Meanwhile, the person on the bed waited until the fish was completely silent before opening his eyes to watch over the fish with a gentle gaze.

Ye Qinghuan's wedding to the Princess of Jinjue drew closer. The little princess had invited Li Yu to the wedding, and Li Yu had agreed. By now, it was soon enough that Li Yu thought it was about time to prepare a wedding gift. He couldn't just show up empty-handed.

But during the day, he had to go to work with Prince Jing as a fish, and at night, he had to spend time with Prince Jing as a human. He couldn't avoid Prince Jing, so he picked a day to drag Prince Jing out to pick a gift.

Prince Jing didn't really understand it. Wang Xi usually took care of these things, and Prince Jing had never paid attention to what Ye Qinghuan liked. Why did Xiaoyu have to go buy it himself? Couldn't he just pick something random from the storeroom?

"Your Highness, it's the thought that counts," Li Yu explained. "You have to prepare a gift yourself to show your sincerity."

Prince Jing was extremely unhappy with Xiaoyu bustling about busily for other people's sake. But he was happy about going out with Xiaoyu. The whole time, he stuck by Xiaoyu's side, never straying far.

Xiaoyu liked shiny gold things, so he also gave gifts along this theme. Considering Ye-shizi and the princess's status, after all, there was no need to buy them anything practical. With his boyfriend there to support him, Li Yu took a look at many high-end antique stores, wanting to give the couple something sophisticated and classy.

But Li Yu had no eye for antiques. At first, a violet gold incense pot caught his interest. Because Prince Jing had said they should try to hide who they were, the two of them were on their own without any guards. Prince Jing was new to shopping, and it showed, so the owner exaggerated wildly in praise of his store, thinking it would be easy to make some money off these rich young men. Li Yu fell in love with the glittering, gold incense pot engraved with complicated patterns. He was ready to pull out the money when Prince Jing couldn't take it anymore. He silently knocked a hole into the pot, revealing the actual color of the stone underneath. The gold was just a thin layer on the outside.

...*Sob sob sob, so the pretty antique incense pot was fake?!* That couldn't be blamed on him. As a fish, he had no experience, so he couldn't tell. But he supposed antiques were called antique for a reason. They should be dusty and old. If they were shining and glittering, there was definitely something suspicious going on, so they shouldn't buy those!

Wang-gongong and the guards, who were following from a distance, took the store owner who'd been selling fakes to be dealt with by the relevant authorities.

Li Yu quickly learned his lesson. He decided to try again and went to another store. This time, an accessory box caught his eye. The owner said it used to belong to a princess from the previous dynasty. Li Yu thought the box had a vintage feel to it and it did look very old, so it had to be the real thing. The former belongings of a princess would definitely suit a princess. Li Yu was just about to buy it when Prince Jing coughed lightly and glanced out the window. Li Yu followed his gaze and saw that the little peddler on the side of the road was selling a whole row of the exact same "antique from the previous dynasty."

Li Yu's confidence had taken a serious hit. He thought he just wasn't suited to buying antiques and decided to look at gold and silver decorations instead.

He decided on a gold and jade folding screen, thinking there would be no problems this time. But the eagle-eyed Prince Jing spotted a very subtle crack on the back. As soon as he touched it, the whole thing split in two.

Then, Li Yu spotted a pair of green jade necklaces, one carved with a dragon and the other with a phoenix. Prince Jing casually threw a cup of cold tea on it, and it turned out they were made with fake jade. The dark green on the jade was painted on, and with the cold tea, it all washed off.

They looked through store after store. Anything that caught Li Yu's eye was either fake or damaged. Wang Xi also caught owner after owner, but Li Yu remained giftless.

I'm supposed to be a koi! What kind of luck is this?!

Li Yu was very unhappy. He kept being fooled by a bunch of fakes. Didn't that mean he was as good as blind? Furious, he turned to leave with a huff. Prince Jing stopped him and tucked something into his hand.

Li Yu wasn't mad at Prince Jing. But he felt really dumb, always picking out fakes, so he was a little embarrassed. For the sake of his boyfriend, he tried to calm down. Looking down at the thing Prince Jing had put into his hand, he saw it was a little golden fish. It was in the same style as the previous one, with the same cute charm. But this time, it was in a different pose. The one before had its tail curled, but this one had its lips pursed, like it was blowing bubbles.

Li Yu furrowed his brows and glanced at Prince Jing, who was looking back at him. Li Yu knew he was trying to make him feel better and ended up bursting into laughter. Holding the fish in his hands, he no longer felt so angry.

How many of these little golden fish did he have?

Li Yu moved closer so Prince Jing could tie the fish to his waist for him. Prince Jing hung it on his waist with a smile, then grabbed Li Yu's hand and took him to the biggest jewelry store in the city. The owner often did business with the nobility, so he recognized Prince Jing. He hurried to greet them and exchange some pleasantries.

That was when Li Yu found out all the little golden fish were made here.

He was so stupid. Why did he have to go look for a store on his own? Why didn't he ask Prince Jing for his opinion? Then he could've avoided being scammed so much on this wild goose chase.

All because he never thought Prince Jing would come to a jewelry store.

Prince Jing watched from the side as the owner brought out all the highest quality wares for Li-gongzi to choose from. Li Yu went all out and chose a pair of silver vases, a pair of gold ruyi, and a pair of lifelike jade dolls. Prince Jing put down a few bills, and the owner quickly ordered some people to wrap up the goods to be delivered to the manor.

He didn't get many chances to visit this store, so Li Yu decided to also buy an oval silver bead.

The bead was the size of his thumb, and the design was like a modern globe, which was what caught Li Yu's eye. Prince Jing had given him so many gifts, but it seemed like he hadn't properly given Prince Jing anything back yet.

Li Yu asked the owner for a red string. He strung the bead through the string and presented it to Prince Jing.

"This is for you, Your Highness," said Li Yu, smiling. "Thank you for taking care of me."

Prince Jing had paid for everything else; Li Yu should pay for this! He rushed to pull out a light gold money pouch that was stuffed full. Actually, Wang Xi had given him this before they left the manor, so it wasn't his money either, but it was coming from his hand, so that meant he bought it!

A bead like this from this store had to be quite expensive, Li Yu thought.

The owner wasn't sure what to say, too afraid to tell the truth, which was that this was just a little bead used for decorating. It wasn't worth much. In fact, he could just give it away for free. But faced with Prince Jing's icy stare and the young gongzi's anticipation, after some careful consideration, the owner weakly gave a price. Li Yu paid for it happily.

The bead was indeed a little expensive. Li Yu felt bad when he was taking the money out, but the price did reflect the quality, he supposed. When Prince Jing put the bead on right away, Li Yu couldn't be happier. He thought his taste wasn't quite bad to the point of being hopeless.

At least, he sure had a good eye when it came to boyfriends!

After buying the gifts and returning to the manor, Prince Jing ordered someone to rewrite the gift list to include the ones Li Yu just bought.

"Why do our gifts have to be together?" Li Yu knew his gifts couldn't compare to Prince Jing's.

Prince Jing wrote Li Yu's name next to his own, giving him a deep glance.

Li Yu suddenly understood and went bright red. The space next to a prince was for his consort. Why did Prince Jing want to put their names and gifts together? Because Li Yu was his family, his consort.

But they were just dating. Did he actually want to be his consort or not?

Li Yu thought it over, but the rejection never left his lips.

On the day of the wedding, Li Yu wore the coral red robes Prince Jing had made for him. They were made of brocade and embroidered with silver lotuses. With a jade hairpin and a string of little golden fish tinkling at his waist, he looked dashing and vibrant.

Prince Jing wore a set of matching robes in black, edged with crimson. He had a red ribbon in his hair and looked ethereally handsome. Every time he snuck a glance at him, Li Yu felt delighted. They seemed to be wearing matching outfits. Wouldn't they steal the show from Ye-shizi?

Prince Jing wrapped an arm around his waist to reassure him. Prince Jing didn't care what Ye Qinghuan thought.

Once they were both ready, the carriage headed off. Li Yu sat in the carriage with Prince Jing, but as soon as he was in the carriage, he realized something was off.

Last time, when they went to the market, the carriage was very small and cramped. But this time, it was very spacious. It had more than enough room for the two of them. There was even a table, tea, and a few of his favorite pastries.

Prince Jing smiled as he held Li Yu's hand, and they sat down together.

Li Yu glared at Prince Jing. *An asshole is an asshole, after all!*

On this trip to the Cheng'en Manor, just in case Xiaoyu had to transform in the middle of the wedding, Prince Jing brought his "pet fish" again. The fish plush was floating quietly in a corner of the bottle, staring at the two of them.

When the carriage started moving, Prince Jing handed Li Yu a book (but not one featuring yao). He had noticed that Li Yu liked reading. The carriage he'd selected this time was very large, so Li Yu lay down comfortably with his head resting on Prince Jing's knee and flipped through the book as he chatted with the prince. Prince Jing picked up a piece of peach blossom pastry and broke it into several pieces. He fed one to the "fish" in the crystal bottle, and the rest all went to the real carp spirit, who was waiting with his mouth wide open.

Soon, they arrived at Cheng'en Manor.

Today, Cheng'en Manor was bustling with people and draped in color and lanterns. The King of Jinjue had come to attend the wedding, as well as friends and relatives of the Duke of Cheng'en and plenty of court officials. Head Eunuch Luo brought the emperor's edict along with large amounts of gifts. It took a while just to read the list of gifts. The King of Jinjue loved this daughter of his, and her wedding procession was over five kilometers long. Her dowry was at least a hundred boxes.

Prince Jing and Li Yu were welcomed by the groom, Ye-shizi.

Prince Jing nodded at the Duke of Cheng'en, who was sitting on the main seat. The current Duke of Cheng'en was Empress Xiaohui's brother, Prince Jing's uncle. On meeting, the two of them communicated a great deal with just a glance.

Prince Jing's aunt, the Duchess of Cheng'en, was also attending to the guests. When she saw Prince Jing had brought a young man with him as his partner, her eyes were full of smiles.

Soon, a servant girl came and handed Li Yu a pair of jade butterflies. Smiling, she said, "My lady thanks you for coming to attend the celebration and also wishes the two of you happiness together forever."

Wow... Li Yu accepted the butterflies, then saw the Duchess of Cheng'en smiling at him from a distance. He was confused—wasn't it Ye Qinghuan's wedding today? Why were they saying that to him and Prince Jing?

Unless—

Li Yu suddenly realized. Did Prince Jing bring him along today so he could meet his family? He covered his face. It was too sudden— he wasn't prepared at all!

This was such a happy surprise!

Meeting the Family

YE QINGHUAN WORE scarlet wedding robes, a smile bright on his face. The Princess of Jinjue was draped in a veil embroidered with mandarin ducks playing in the water,[8] and she was holding a jade vase and ruyi. Although her face was hidden, while the couple took their bows, there was just a glimpse of her bright red lips smiling.

Li Yu watched as the young couple performed their wedding bows, feeling emotional. Partly thanks to his help, these two were able to break through the original plot of the novel and be together. He hoped they could be happy and at peace, safe and healthy.

This was a good sign. The other pair from the book was now different too. He couldn't help but sneak a glance at Prince Jing, only to find that he was already looking at him. The two of them felt for each other's hands underneath their sleeves.

Li Yu made a wish in his heart.

The wedding proceeded smoothly, with the Duke of Cheng'en hosting. Soon after, an older servant came to tell Prince Jing that there was an old acquaintance who wanted to see him. As soon as Prince Jing saw who the servant was, he knew who was summoning him. His hand tightened around Li Yu's.

---

8   *"Two mandarin ducks playing in water" (鸳鸯戏水) is a proverb used to describe loving couples. Mandarin ducks are a traditional symbol of romantic love and fidelity.*

Did this mean Prince Jing wanted him to come along?

As Li Yu followed, Prince Jing had one hand on his and one hand on the crystal bottle. Even though Li Yu knew it was ridiculous, he still felt a little jealous. Who did Prince Jing like better? Him or the fish?

If he had to compete against any other human, he wouldn't be worried at all. But against the fish...

After all, Prince Jing had turned his entire manor into a huge tank for the fish. He'd done many things he'd never done before for the fish's sake. And as Li-gongzi, he was tasked with taking care of the fish. Even all the accessories he was given were of fish...

When he thought of it like that, it was a little terrifying. Could it be that all those fish gifts weren't because his name meant "fish," but because he came second to the fish?

No, he had to know for sure. If Prince Jing dared like the fish more, he'd never let him hear the end of it!

In an instant, it was like Li Yu had been overtaken by the god of jealousy. He'd completely forgotten that his new nemesis was in fact himself.

Prince Jing had no idea what Xiaoyu was thinking about next to him. The two of them held hands as they walked into the back garden of Cheng'en Manor. In the depths of the flower bushes, an elderly man with snowy white hair was warming a pot of wine on a little stove made of red clay. Prince Jing pursed his lips and walked forward with Li Yu.

"You're here?" When the elder saw the two of them, he wasn't at all surprised. He casually pointed to two chairs before him and said, smiling, "Come sit."

Prince Jing bowed respectfully and sat down with Li Yu.

Li Yu was just pondering who this elderly man might be, when he suddenly smelled the scent of green plum wine. He'd heard all the green plum wine in Cheng'en manor was made by the old Duke of Cheng'en, so who else could this be? It was Ye Qinghuan's grandfather, Prince Jing's grandfather, the old Duke of Cheng'en!

Suddenly excited, Li Yu got up to bow. "H-hello!"

In the book, this elderly man was the backbone of the House of Cheng'en, but due to his health, he never officially appeared. After disaster had befallen Ye Qinghuan, he'd passed away from illness. Now that Ye Qinghuan and the princess were getting married, however, the old Duke of Cheng'en was fine too. Li Yu never thought he'd get to see the man in person.

He truly was meeting Prince Jing's family!

Ye Qian glanced at the youth, smiling, and then at Prince Jing. "What a nice young man." Ye Qian gestured for Li Yu to sit. He considered himself to be very good at reading people. It was easy to see what kind of personality a youth at this age had with just a glance.

"You've decided, Your Highness?" Ye Qian asked Prince Jing.

Prince Jing nodded, expression serious. Ye Qian didn't ask him to justify himself. "Then I've made my decision too," he said, still smiling. "I will do everything I can to help Your Highness."

They looked at each other for a while. With both calmness and gratitude in his eyes, Prince Jing poured more wine for Ye Qian and some for himself. They both drank, as though they'd come to some sort of agreement.

Li Yu didn't know what they were talking about, and this wasn't the kind of situation where he could just butt in, so instead he pushed his own bamboo cup in front of Prince Jing. Fish couldn't think about things that were too complicated, but he could at least taste the wine, right?

Ye Qian and Prince Jing both paused.

Ye Qian held back his laughter, ready to sit back and watch. Prince Jing glanced at Li Yu, then filled Li Yu's cup. But just when Li Yu had happily picked up the cup to have a sniff, Prince Jing stole the bamboo cup from his hand and drank all of it.

"Your Highness, that's my wine!" Li Yu objected quietly. The prince had poured it into the cup he'd claimed, so it was his.

Prince Jing shook his head, smiling. He couldn't let the carp spirit get drunk outside. Just a whiff of the scent was enough.

Li Yu mumbled in complaint. Meanwhile, Ye Qian drank leisurely, keeping out of it. A calm, silent youth with a lively and enthusiastic one. He was happy to see this couple together. He'd seen Ye Qinghuan with the Princess of Jinjue as well. They were also good kids, just like these two.

When he saw the pair of jade butterflies Li Yu was holding, Ye Qian smiled even wider and got out the jade pendants he'd been given when he got married.

Meeting your boyfriend's family isn't hard at all, Li Yu thought, clutching the jade pendant and butterflies.

To be honest, he'd always been worried that Prince Jing's family would be against them. After all, he and Prince Jing were in a gay relationship. Weren't they worried about Prince Jing's future?

He was friendly with Ye Qinghuan and the princess already, so they didn't count. But the old Duke of Cheng'en and Duchess of Cheng'en had all seemed to take a shine to him immediately, giving him gifts. When Prince Jing wasn't paying attention, the old Duke of Cheng'en had even secretly told Li Yu that he'd give him a few jugs of good wine next time.

Sob, what's with this huge sense of responsibility I'm feeling right now?

After meeting the family and being treated well, he had to treat Prince Jing even better now!

Seeing Xiaoyu's sudden serious expression, Prince Jing really wanted to pinch his cheeks. Naturally, no one in the House of Cheng'en would disapprove of them. Prince Jing was long past the age to get married and have a child, but there still hadn't been a single person he was close to. Now that he finally had someone he liked, they were all delighted and wished everything could be made official for Prince Jing right away.

But Prince Jing's marriage had to be approved by the emperor. Taking Xiaoyu to see his family at Cheng'en Manor was the most he could do for now.

Ye Qinghuan's marriage made Prince Jing, who was never jealous, feel a little jealous.

Prince Jing had no hesitations—of course he would marry Xiaoyu. But he had to think about when to let the emperor know and when to ask the emperor for Xiaoyu. Especially now that the old Duke of Cheng'en was on his side.

He was the noble di son and constantly faced judgment and questioning throughout his life—sometimes even assassination attempts. He was used to this and did what he had to in order to survive, but after the House of Cheng'en had almost come to harm, and then several of the princes had tried to do something to his fish, Prince Jing realized he couldn't protect the people around him by keeping to himself.

He couldn't trust any of the other princes. If he wanted to protect the people he wanted, then he had to become the emperor.

Due to the disability he was born with, he still had a long way to go, and the path might be filled with danger. Before he could finally achieve a safe, peaceful life, he'd have to do anything he could to avoid involving Xiaoyu, as he couldn't bear to think of risking him.

So for now, he could only date Xiaoyu. He couldn't confirm Xiaoyu's status.

But one day, he'd give Xiaoyu everything he deserved.

Li Yu tucked the jade butterfly and pendant away in his robes. "Your Highness, I want to walk around by myself for a bit, then I'll head back on my own," he said.

Since they'd made their agreement, Li Yu was putting much less effort into his excuses. It didn't matter, Prince Jing wasn't ever going to ask.

Prince Jing watched as he walked to the edge of the garden and behind some trees.

Li Yu quickly transformed back to a fish, then slid back over on his tail. The crystal bottle was just behind Prince Jing. With Prince Jing blocking his line of sight, the old Duke of Cheng'en wouldn't see anything.

Li Yu jumped quietly into the crystal bottle. Although Prince Jing wasn't looking directly at the fish, he knew Li Yu had made his way back safely when he heard the quiet splash behind him.

Ye Qian was in high spirits and ordered someone to bring over a weiqi set. "Last time I played against Your Highness, you hadn't moved out of Jingtai Hall yet," he said, smiling. "I was ordered to go see you by the emperor... So many years have passed in the blink of an eye."

Prince Jing nodded, gesturing for his grandfather to play white and that he would play black.

Li Yu swam to the mouth of the bottle, carefully leaning against the side. Perhaps the two of them had spoken so mysteriously before because he was there. But even now that he was "gone," the two focused on the game instead and Li Yu learned even less.

Li Yu only knew how to use Go sets for games that weren't Go, so he didn't understand what was going on at all. Very quickly, he became sleepy.

Prince Jing kept an eye on his fish. As soon as he saw the fish drifting off, about to tip over back into the bottle, Prince Jing quickly found a way out of the difficult match. Soon, the winner and loser were clear.

Ye Qian rubbed his chin. "Your Highness, your aura is very different from before. Is it because of *him*?"

Prince Jing just smiled casually in response. Protecting oneself was different from protecting someone else.

Ye Qian rarely got a chance to see Prince Jing and wanted to continue their conversation, but a servant suddenly came to announce that the emperor was here. Ye Qian immediately went to greet him with Prince Jing.

The emperor was wearing a set of casual robes, and he was only accompanied by the Head of the Imperial Guard as he came to Cheng'en Manor in person.

Originally, there had been no need for the emperor to show up to Ye-shizi and the princess of Jinjue's wedding—he just had to make sure his gifts arrived. But due to the mess the second prince had created, the emperor had to reassure and comfort the King of Jinjue, so he came to visit personally to show how much he cared about this marriage.

The Duke and Duchess of Cheng'en and all the officials kneeled down, greeting the emperor.

The emperor waved an arm cheerfully. "Continue with the wedding. I'm just here for a cup of wine." Joyfully beaming, he sat down to speak with the King of Jinjue for a while. Gradually, the guests started to relax.

Ye Qian and Prince Jing walked into the main hall one after the other and bowed to the emperor.

Ye Qian's health had been declining these past few years, so he rarely entered the palace. Seeing Ye Qian as well as Prince Jing beside the new young couple at their wedding, the emperor couldn't help thinking about his past with Empress Xiaohui.

Since Ye Qian had already agreed to help Prince Jing, he needed to fully utilize the advantages Prince Jing had. "The empress's rooms are still maintained here at the manor," he said. "Does Your Majesty want to take a look?"

The emperor rarely came to Cheng'en Manor since Empress Xiaohui had passed away, mostly because he was afraid it would hurt too much. But at that moment, he couldn't help but nod. And as Prince Jing was Empress Xiaohui's only son still left in this world, the emperor asked him to come along.

Prince Jing still carried the bottle with him. When he took a glance, the emperor was briefly speechless. "It's only been a short while, and your fish has changed this much?"

The emperor recalled the letter Prince Jing had sent, specifically reporting the changes in his fish. But reading it in a letter was completely different from seeing it. The last time the emperor saw the fish, it was still black with flecks of gold. Now the entire fish was a different color. No wonder the emperor took a while to react.

"It looks like Liao Kong was right," he said. "It really is part koi."

The emperor walked closer, looking at the fish in the bottle. Afraid the emperor would find something amiss, Li Yu was too afraid to even blow a bubble. He put on an elegant mien, trying to pretend to be an emotionless koi.

Good thing the fish wasn't the main character today. Soon, the emperor followed the old Duke of Cheng'en to Empress Xiaohui's old rooms.

The rooms Ye Qian spoke of had belonged to Empress Xiaohui before she got married. The emperor led Prince Jing inside. Seeing all the decor that was so similar to Changchun Palace's, the emperor's vision started to go blurry. He sat down and began to tell Prince Jing a few stories about Empress Xiaohui.

Li Yu was in the crystal bottle, so he had a lower angle than everyone else. While the emperor saw many familiar decorations, Li Yu saw a portrait of a servant girl on the wall. Because this was Empress Xiaohui's room, Li Yu guessed she must have painted it herself.

Prince Jing was good at painting too. Did he inherit the skill from his mother? It wasn't impossible.

Li Yu looked at the painting for a while before his gaze landed on an unobtrusive wardrobe beneath where it hung. At the corner of the wardrobe an old plush was sticking out. Li Yu thought it looked a bit familiar. After he'd staring at the black and yellow plush for a while, Li Yu realized with a start—wasn't this the cloth tiger he'd seen in the secret the system had showed him?

Although there was no way to confirm if it was the exact same one, it was very similar. And the tiger in the memory had only been half sewn, but this one was clearly already completed.

Did the secret have something to do with Empress Xiaohui?

But Li Yu was very sure the room in the secret wasn't this one but one in the palace.

...Could it be Empress Xiaohui's Changchun Palace? Li Yu had never been, so he had no way of knowing. All he could do was stare at the tiger in frustration.

Suddenly, he had an idea. The fish tapped at the glass in the direction of the tiger. Prince Jing noticed Li Yu's urgency at once, and he walked over and found the cloth tiger in the wardrobe. He thought about it, then took it out.

The emperor smiled. "Your mother loved things like this. She made some for you back then too. There are many in Changchun Palace—do you still remember?"

Prince Jing nodded slightly.

The emperor's words were like fireworks, instantly exploding inside Li Yu's head.

The secret was Prince Jing's secret. Even Prince Jing remembered the tiger plush—it really must be at Changchun Palace. What kind of secret was this?!

Fishy Messing up Plans

TRYING TO FIGURE OUT MORE about the secret, Li Yu pressed against the walls of the bottle, but that was all the emperor had to say about it. Everything else he said was about Empress Xiaohui's other interests and hobbies.

Li Yu knew that due to Empress Xiaohui, the emperor always had a soft spot for Prince Jing. He'd even given Prince Jing a job recently, and it seemed he intended to rely on him. If Li Yu couldn't figure out the secret right now, maybe it was because it wasn't time yet. Right now, the emperor and Prince Jing were alone together. It was a good opportunity to kindle their father-son relationship.

As a result, Li Yu tried to be unobtrusive, listening quietly as the emperor told stories to Prince Jing.

Without realizing it, the emperor went on for a while. When he emerged from his reminiscence, he smiled and said, "Tianchi, do you think I talk too much?"

The emperor's mouth was upturned, but his eyes were distant. As an emperor and father, he rarely showed such a sorrowful side to his sons.

Prince Jing shook his head, reached out hesitantly, and patted the emperor on the back of the hand. This was also very rare, but Prince Jing's gaze showed how much he cared for the emperor. The emperor was very comforted by this gesture.

"Tianchi, I know...you're very good. Zheng Jing has told me all about your performance at the Ministry of Works. You're doing well."

The emperor patted Prince Jing on the shoulder. He was about to say something else when a guard came to report, "Your Majesty, the sixth prince is here to congratulate the couple."

The emperor glanced at Prince Jing, who was standing next to him. The House of Cheng'en was Prince Jing's family. It was natural that he attend Ye-shizi and the Princess of Jinjue's wedding. But what did this marriage have to do with the sixth prince? The sixth prince wasn't family or friend, nor was he an important official of the court. What was he doing here?

Not to mention, if the sixth prince really was here to celebrate, why didn't he come earlier like the rest of the guests? Why did he only arrive when the wedding was about to end? The emperor only came so late because he didn't want to alarm anyone. Why did Mu Tianxiao come even later?

Coming to celebrate was probably an excuse. The real reason was that he wanted to show himself in front of the emperor.

The emperor saw through the sixth prince and said impassively, "The Duke of Cheng'en will take care of him. Let him be." He wasn't in the mood to see the sixth prince.

The emperor spoke a bit more with Ye Qian, then decided to return to the palace. This time, the sixth prince sent word that he'd like to escort the emperor back. The emperor agreed this time.

He took Prince Jing along with him. When Mu Tianxiao saw that Prince Jing was with the emperor, he froze.

Li Yu was with Prince Jing as always. When Li Yu saw the sixth prince's shock, he happily shook his tail. *So what? We're not going to just let you have the emperor!*

With sharp eyes, Li Yu noticed a slender woman standing next to the sixth prince, wearing a pomegranate-colored pleated dress. The woman was wearing a veiled hat that covered her face, but even through the veil, one could see her eyes that sparkled like water. Her hands, peeking out from her sleeves, were like jade. Although no one could see what she looked like, everyone wondered what kind of beauty was under that veil.

Li Yu didn't know who this woman was, but the sixth prince had already tried using the third prince to shove people into someone else's homes. This was clearly Ye-shizi's wedding, but he brought a beautiful woman. And he came right after the emperor, so that was clearly why he was here. Perhaps the sixth prince wanted to give this woman to the emperor...

Li Yu remembered that in the original book, when the fight for the throne had gotten to a boiling point, the sixth prince had given the emperor an unknown beauty as a concubine. She'd said a lot of good things about the sixth prince to the emperor in private, which Prince Jing couldn't compete with.

The plot was in complete shambles—were they here already?

...He had to find a way to mess it up! That was what the fish was good at!

As Li Yu was thinking of a plan, he heard Mu Tianxiao say, "Royal Father, it's a long trip back to the palace. I just so happen to have brought a servant talented at massages, and she would be honored to serve you."

Seems like Mu Tianxiao still had some shame. He didn't announce in broad daylight that he'd brought a beauty for his dad and ask him to accept her. He just said she was a servant who could give him a massage. Whether or not he wanted to keep or use her was up to the emperor. He was a lot smarter than that stupid third prince.

Li Yu was with Prince Jing, right next to the emperor. He had a little bit of reservation in front of the emperor—he couldn't just burst out of the bottle. He thought perhaps he could flip over again. Prince Jing would definitely ask the emperor to summon someone to see to the fish if he did, and perhaps if there were more people here, the emperor would forget about the beauty that the sixth prince had brought.

Deciding on his plan, Li Yu decided to put it to action. But as a koi, he wasn't the same as before; he was being taken care of a little too well now, so it was more difficult to flip over than to just slide around everywhere.

Li Yu was huffing with frustration as he tried to lean to the side. He'd yet to flip completely over when the emperor said in shock, "Tianchi, why is your fish a little tilted to the side?"

Actually, Prince Jing had noticed as soon as the fish started moving. But Xiaoyu hadn't had anything to drink, nor had anyone touched him. Nothing was wrong. Prince Jing suspected Xiaoyu was doing this on purpose to get his attention, the same way he kept knocking on the bottle in Empress Xiaohui's room, so he thought Xiaoyu wanted him to notice something.

But unexpectedly, the emperor was also staring at his fish. Before Prince Jing could react, the emperor already said, "There seems to be something wrong with Prince Jing's fish. Guards—"

The emperor ordered the imperial guards to fetch the imperial physician they'd brought along. Li Yu was taken aback. Why did it feel like the emperor was more worried than Prince Jing? Now he was afraid to flip over completely. He had to maintain this angle. Unfortunately, that was even harder than flipping over.

The two imperial physicians rushed over. Regardless of whether or not they knew how to take care of a fish, they had to try in front of the emperor. They looked at the fish for a while, and then they discussed it amongst themselves even longer.

After the sixth prince had made his offer, his smile remained plastered on his face. Even though he was more capable than the third prince, he was still experiencing the same neglect and awkwardness the third prince had gone through.

In the end, the physicians said Li Yu might've eaten too much and there was nothing wrong with him. With that, Li Yu cooperated and straightened out his body. He pushed through the water with his fins slowly, puffing up his cheeks, looking like he really was too full, to corroborate with the physicians' diagnosis.

"Since the fish is fine," said the emperor, "I'll be returning to the palace. I just need Prince Jing to accompany me." His expression was a bit dark. The sixth prince? The massage servant? He only mentioned Prince Jing and no one else.

Li Yu thought the emperor was mad, but at who? He was a little worried. When no one noticed, Prince Jing put a finger in the bottle, petting the fish's back to calm him down.

...True, Li Yu thought. Prince Jing was right here with him. What was there to worry about?

The emperor returned to the palace in his imperial carriage. Prince Jing rode behind him on a horse. Before they entered the palace, the emperor stopped and looked into the crystal bottle. "Tianchi, I must thank your fish for today."

Li Yu had been listening in this whole time. Huh? Why was the emperor thanking him? So the emperor *was* mad, but who was he mad at? The sixth prince? Why?

The sixth prince had only come to do one thing: present a beauty to the emperor. But when he thought about the time and place he chose to do it, Li Yu suddenly understood.

If the sixth prince was just trying to curry favor with the emperor like normal, the emperor might not have gotten angry. Any other time, the emperor might have accepted the servant. But the sixth prince shouldn't have done it at Cheng'en Manor—Empress Xiaohui's family home. Even worse, he did it when the emperor had just been reminiscing about Empress Xiaohui with Prince Jing. He'd basically just slapped the emperor in the face!

The sixth prince's mother was not favored by the emperor, so he'd wanted to present a beauty to the emperor for a long time. But he was afraid that giving the emperor someone directly would result in a lot of trouble, and the emperor might not accept it. That's why he thought he would wait until the emperor left the palace in casual clothes and give him a peek at a half-covered beauty. If the emperor himself was interested, it would make things easier for him. But he'd failed to predict that the emperor would reminisce about the empress while attending a wedding, or else he would never have picked such a time.

The emperor must've been incredibly irritated, but he couldn't reject the sixth prince outright when the sixth prince hadn't offered outright. With so many people looking on, the emperor needed an excuse to get out of the situation the sixth prince had put him in.

All the emperor had at his disposal was the fish. So the moment the fish started to tilt, the emperor insisted on summoning the physicians to stir things up a bit.

Li Yu thought he'd successfully messed up the sixth prince's plan, but it was actually the emperor who'd seized the opportunity and messed up the sixth prince's plan himself.

Thinking back to his original plan, Li Yu realized there were plenty of holes. After he flipped over, perhaps Prince Jing wouldn't notice in time, or if he did and the emperor didn't call for any physicians, or Prince Jing asked the emperor and the emperor ignored him...

If the emperor was in the mood for a new concubine, there would be no helping it. This time, his luck had actually won out. He'd somehow managed to run into a situation where even the emperor needed a bailout.

Hold on, Li Yu thought belatedly. Was this the luck the system had given him?

He remembered the system had increased his luck stat on the following categories: "slapping villains in the face," "well-fed and well-clothed," and "one-shot KO."

He'd always worked hard at feeding and clothing himself. His luck wasn't obvious, and slapping villains in the face was easy to understand. This was the kind of situation where they came into play, right? It seemed like a koi's traits really did come in handy.

After Prince Jing escorted the emperor back to the palace, he returned to Cheng'en Manor. It was dark now, and after sending the newlyweds to their room, most of the guests had left. But the sixth prince was still there.

"Fifth brother, we meet again."

Mu Tianxiao had never shown his temper to outsiders. He smiled as he greeted Prince Jing with a bow.

Li Yu noticed that the veiled beauty was still with the sixth prince. The sixth prince probably didn't know why the emperor had treated him so coldly, so he wanted to find out from Prince Jing. The little carp immediately turned into a fighting fish. He swiped his tail at the sixth prince furiously. *Master, husband, don't pay him any attention!*

Prince Jing nodded at the sixth prince, unperturbed. The sixth prince was just about to turn the subject to the emperor when Prince Jing looked straight past him.

...He wasn't able to stop Prince Jing, but his gaze fell to the crystal bottle Prince Jing always carried around with him, and the fish that wouldn't stop moving.

Li Yu quickly realized that Mu Tianxiao's icy cold gaze was aimed at him. Li Yu froze up for a moment and quickly went to hide where Prince Jing's sleeve covered the bottle a little bit. As long as he didn't look at the sixth prince, the sixth prince probably wouldn't look at him either.

After waiting patiently for a while, Li Yu peeked out again. The sixth prince had already turned around.

Li Yu wanted to look some more, but the crystal bottle was suddenly covered by something. Prince Jing had stopped moving and turned the bottle so the fish could only look at him.

Sheesh.

Fishy Plan

LI YU THOUGHT he should warn Prince Jing that the sixth prince was his adversary in the original book. Now that the second prince was out of the way and the third prince had lost favor with the emperor, the sixth prince wasn't to be underestimated in this fight for the throne.

Li Yu had once urged Prince Jing to be wary of the sixth prince, but he knew they had to be more proactive than that with someone like Mu Tianxiao. Prince Jing and the House of Cheng'en had suffered so much because of him in the book. It would be best if they could take him down before he got too powerful. But how should he convince Prince Jing to make a move?

He was a young gongzi who always stayed in the manor and never went out. Even if he was dating Prince Jing and Prince Jing cared for him, he didn't think he had enough sway to convince Prince Jing... Honestly, he had to admit he had no sway at all.

He wasn't a good strategist, and analyzing a situation wasn't one of his strengths. All he understood was that being vigilant was the same as staying defensive, and it wouldn't change the situation. But actively doing something would be changing to the offensive, which would mean Prince Jing had to let go of the way he'd always done things. Plus, that would catch the sixth prince's attention. As things currently stood, Prince Jing probably didn't have any intention to fight for the throne yet. If he really started clashing with the sixth prince, he'd have to fight for the throne whether he wanted to or not...

Okay, frankly, it was harder to think of a reason to get Prince Jing to agree to fight for the throne than to just get him to deal with the sixth prince. Prince Jing could keep his guard up against the sixth prince without needing to know why, but there was no way he'd just fight for the throne without a really good reason.

Li Yu was also worried that Prince Jing would think he had some sort of ulterior motive and was using him if he started to nudge the conversation toward the throne.

Sob sob, how do I convince Prince Jing? wept Li Yu, completely unaware Prince Jing already had his own plans.

No matter what, he had to at least try. It was over for the third prince, but the sixth prince was now champing at the bit. He even dared present the emperor with a beauty—this meant the sixth prince was already preparing to position someone in the back palace to help him. They couldn't let him succeed.

So, when he got the opportunity, Li Yu turned into a human and said to Prince Jing, "Your Highness, the sixth prince..."

Li Yu concentrated. He wanted to use both emotion and reason to convince Prince Jing to take the throne; he needed to argue for him to consider his duty, given his position and status.

When Prince Jing heard him say "the sixth prince," his eyes narrowed dangerously. Prince Jing didn't like the sixth prince, but Li Yu didn't notice anything unusual. He continued on, not catching on to Prince Jing's mood, and ended up pushed onto the bed. A pair of lips covered his roughly.

Ever since the two of them had gotten together, Prince Jing had always let Li Yu take the lead when it came to more intimate acts. They did whatever Li Yu wanted, however he wanted. Even if they couldn't go all the way, Prince Jing waited patiently and never tried to force him. In fact, he cared a lot about how Li Yu felt and had never gotten mad at him. Although Li Yu never said anything, he was very happy to get closer with Prince Jing. So much so, he'd almost forgotten he was dating a tyrant.

With this push, all of Prince Jing's hidden cruelty and fierceness were released.

Li Yu's cries were muffled as he hit Prince Jing in the chest over and over. He liked it when they acted lovingly, sweetly, but he didn't like it rough—plus, he had important things to talk about!

But it was like Prince Jing couldn't hear and didn't care. He just continued to press into his lips roughly, easily stripping away all of Li Yu's defenses.

Li Yu was used to enjoying moments like these, so he very quickly lost the will to fight and relaxed into the bed. His eyes were shimmering, and all that came out of him were small moans.

Prince Jing only calmed down once the two of them were covered in a light layer of sweat. After Li Yu recovered some energy, he smoothed out Prince Jing's hair and said hoarsely, "Wh-what's gotten into you, Your Highness?"

To be honest, he wasn't really angry. Prince Jing had just kissed Li Yu too hard in the beginning and frightened him. Li Yu's lips were swollen.

After Prince Jing was done, all of his viciousness seemed to evaporate. Lightly kissing Li Yu's face, he stuffed a slightly sweaty note into his hand.

Li Yu opened it to see: *Do not look at other men.*

...Fuck, why did it feel like he'd somehow wronged this powerful master of his?! Li Yu rubbed his temples. "Your Highness, did you misunderstand? I didn't look at other men, I just—"

Li Yu's heart missed a beat. He'd only briefly mentioned the sixth prince this time. He might've mentioned him a few times before as well. Did Prince Jing think he felt something for the sixth prince?! This note had been pre-prepared as well. How long had this asshole been jealous?

Li Yu thumped the bed angrily. "I'm trying to tell you he's your enemy in life, not in love!"

Prince Jing stared at him.

Li Yu sighed and took the opportunity. "I might as well just say it. Your Highness, if the sixth prince were to ascend to the throne, it would be very bad for you. Can you stop him?"

Prince Jing slowly looked at Li Yu, a peculiar expression on his face. It seemed like he didn't understand Li Yu, but it didn't seem like he was suspicious either. No matter. Li Yu hadn't thought he could convince Prince Jing in just a few sentences anyway. The misunderstanding just now had given him an idea. Li Yu thought that other than appealing to the prince's emotions and reason, he could use another tactic: himself.

After he'd diligently, sincerely used himself a few times, and nearly passed out from exhaustion in the process, Prince Jing finally smiled and "reluctantly" agreed to stop the sixth prince from getting the throne.

The two other adult princes were clearly out of the picture. After the sixth prince was gone, Prince Jing would be the only one left. This basically meant Prince Jing was agreeing to join in on the fight for the throne!

Except he wasn't stealing, because he was the di son. The throne should've been his to begin with!

The fish who had sacrificed so much for all of this thought, *Sob sob sob, it's so hard getting the tyrant to do things he should be doing by himself! Why did the duty of carrying the protagonist's halo fall onto this fish?!*

But if not him, who would consider the tyrant's future for him?

Li Yu had finally taken care of something that had been weighing heavily on his mind, so now it was time to take care of a few smaller things.

One of which was: since he and Prince Jing were constantly tangled together, he was no longer very good at estimating his transformation time. Although the system would always give him a countdown, the system's warning consistently came at the last minute. There were several times when he'd nearly blown his cover and basically had to roll off the bed to escape. Prince Jing was having about as good a time as his fish, so Li Yu wanted something like a clock to remind himself more effectively.

There were no clocks in ancient times; people either kept track of the time through sundials or water clocks, neither of which was very accurate nor convenient to use. Li Yu remembered hourglasses, though, and tried to explain them to Wang Xi. After Li Yu gestured for a while, Wang Xi finally understood. "Li-gongzi, do you want an hourglass? This old servant knows where to get one and can acquire it for you."

...So hourglasses existed!

Li Yu thanked him many times, then shoved a few boxes of peach blossom pastries at Wang Xi. Then he turned around and considered the second small thing.

Before, Li Yu had gone to buy a wedding gift for Ye Qinghuan and the princess. He'd already given the gifts, but he still remembered all the fake goods he'd tried to buy. His luck was so good when it came to slapping the sixth prince in the face, but why did he keep running into fakes when he went shopping? Was it his taste or his luck?

Li Yu didn't want to admit to either option, so he asked Wang Xi, "Wang-gonggong, are there a lot of merchants selling fake goods around the manor?" If there were lots around, then it would be normal for him to run into them.

Wang Xi had gone with them that day, and he was the one who led the guards to arrest all the shop owners that were selling fakes. He immediately understood what Li Yu meant and burst into laughter. "There weren't many before, but gongzi, your luck..." He coughed. "Your luck is just too good, and you ran into all of them. The administrative office can't wait to thank you."

That was the truth. Li-gongzi going shopping was much more effective than someone from the administrative office investigating personally.

"Since there are people selling fakes, then buying fakes happens fairly often too, right?" Li Yu's expression stiffened, and he tried to recover a little dignity. "I think the rocks in the fish tank even look pretty real."

Wang Xi started laughing again. "Gongzi, please stop joking. All of the gems in the fish tank are completely genuine. They were all selected from the prince's storage and polished."

"What?" Li Yu was shocked. "The entire tank?" The red and blue stones he loved to toss around when he was bored, and the pile of purple ones he liked to kick—they were all real???

"Every single stone." Wang Xi nodded seriously. "And they're all top-quality gemstones. It wouldn't be an exaggeration to say they could buy a whole city."

Li Yu didn't know he'd been playing with gems that could buy a whole city... He thought the silver rock bed and gold embroidered blanket that Prince Jing had given the fish were already quite excessive, but he was actually swimming on top of a pile of real gemstones.

They weren't very sparkly, so Li Yu never realized at all. He thought they were just ordinary rocks.

It seemed he hadn't run into so many fakes because of his luck. His taste really was terrible.

Li Yu put a hand on the wall weakly. "Wang-gonggong, I need a sec."

Wang-gonggong was under Prince Jing's orders to give Li-gongzi anything he wanted. But if Li-gongzi mentioned anyone else...

In the past, Li-gongzi had brought up a chubby man and Prince Jing ordered Wang Xi to look into it. Wang Xi thought this chubby fellow sounded somehow familiar, but he'd never found out who it was. Now there was someone else named..."Aseck"?

An alarm went off in Wang Xi's head. He immediately asked on behalf of his master, Prince Jing, "Li-gongzi, please be clearer. Who is Aseck, and why do you need him?"

...It was so hard to communicate with ancient people.

Two days later, Wang Xi brought Li Yu a silver hourglass.

Li Yu tried the hourglass out in accordance with his transformation time. The hourglass was roughly two hours, so it worked perfectly. Li Yu put the hourglass away in his inventory and took it out whenever he turned into a human, so he didn't always have to guess at the time.

What he didn't know was that after he'd gotten a sec to mourn his bad taste in peace, Wang Xi recounted to Prince Jing how Li-gongzi wanted an hourglass. There was no way Prince Jing could take any of Xiaoyu's requests lightly. Though hourglasses weren't expensive, they were mostly used as decorations here and weren't always accurate. The one that Li Yu received was different. Prince Jing had specially asked the skilled craftsmen in the palace for a rush order, and he had carefully checked the timing, so it was much more accurate than ordinary hourglasses. On the base, in a spot that wasn't too obvious, was a lightly etched fish.

Prince Jing was used to taking care of Xiaoyu. He was very happy seeing Xiaoyu bring the hourglass with him everywhere he went in his human form.

He wanted everything that Xiaoyu owned, from the things he ate with to the things he used, to have him stamped all over them.

Fishy Offering Himself Up

O N THE FIRST REST DAY after his wedding, Ye-shizi brought his new wife to visit.

Since Prince Jing worked at the Ministry of Works, the couple specifically picked a day when Prince Jing was home and asked Wang Xi to pass along the message in advance so that they could see Li-gongzi too. When Li Yu found out, he was very happy. Ye Qinghuan and the princess were some of the only friends Li Yu had in these ancient times, and he liked spending time with them.

On the day, Li Yu deliberately waited until Wang Xi came to announce their arrival before transforming, so he could go see the couple in human form.

It was the first time the Princess of Jinjue came to Prince Jing's manor. When she saw the confession carved into the wall, she gave Ye Qinghuan a meaningful look. Ye Qinghuan turned red, wondering how he was still losing to Prince Jing even though he'd gotten married first.

When the princess saw the ponds connecting into a large fish tank, she was so shocked she couldn't speak.

With the princess gazing around enviously, Li Yu led them around the manor.

Everyone said getting married was like getting a fresh start. It had been a while since Li Yu last saw them, and he thought they really had changed quite a bit.

There was still a hint of redness on Ye-shizi's cheeks and a soft smile on his lips as he looked gently at his wife. The Princess of Jinjue was as sweet and beautiful as always, absolutely radiant, but when she looked into Ye Qinghuan's eyes, it seemed like the happiness inside was going to spill out.

"You guys really have changed," Li Yu teased.

Ye Qinghuan didn't retort for once, while the princess blinked and laughed. "Li-gongzi has as well."

Li Yu snuck a glance at Prince Jing beside him, thinking, *There's no way I'm that obvious.*

Ye Qinghuan also brought Xiongfeng along, and he and the princess held Xiongfeng's leash together. It had been a long time since Xiongfeng last saw the fish, so as soon as he saw Li Yu, he wagged his tail at him. Li Yu remembered Xiongfeng liked to eat fish food, so he pulled out the box and fed Xiongfeng a few pieces.

As Li Yu fed him, he suddenly remembered all the things he'd said about having a second master. Now that Ye Qinghuan was married to the Princess of Jinjue, wasn't the princess Xiongfeng's second master?

Heh heh heh, Xiongfeng, have you gotten used to it yet?

Li Yu scratched Xiongfeng's chin, then rubbed his belly. The dog was large and strong, with smooth, silky fur. It seemed like Xiongfeng was getting along with his second master and living well, just like the fish. The only difference was Xiongfeng's second master was a good person and loved pets, while the fish's second master was himself.

If he combined the happiness of all the pets in the world, the fish probably took up eighty percent all on his own.

"Oh right, Li-gongzi, I brought a fish today too!" After some pleasantries had been exchanged, the Princess of Jinjue clapped her hands, beaming. A female servant carefully brought over a quartz fish tank.

This fish tank was made from smooth, pink rose quartz. There were many different koi inside, all different colors. They waved their beautiful tails, swimming around in a lively group.

"Not bad." Li Yu smiled at Ye Qinghuan. The little princess had liked him as a fish—was she trying to appeal to his interests?

Ye Qinghuan stuttered uncharacteristically. "This was the princess's idea. I-I just help feed them once in a while."

Li Yu giggled while covering his mouth. "They're just fish, Ye-shizi. Why are you blushing?"

Aren't you just admitting that you like fish? There's no need to be embarrassed!

All of the princess's fish were very healthy, but the princess herself was a little disappointed. She had a hand on her chin as she stared at the fish and said, "All the servants say these are the smartest fish, but how come they can't compare to Your Highness's...?"

After getting some herself, the little princess came to the realization that not all fish were equal.

Prince Jing and Li Yu glanced at each other, thinking, *Of course not.*

Since they were talking about fish, the princess mentioned she wanted to see Prince Jing's fish.

Li Yu was in an awkward position. Li-gongzi and the fish couldn't both exist at the same time. Because he was afraid the princess would want to take a good look, he hadn't brought the fish plush out... Thank goodness Prince Jing's expression remained dark after the princess brought it up. Since the owner wouldn't say yes, there was nothing the princess could do.

Ye Qinghuan tried to smooth things over, and Li Yu used all his tactics, talking to the princess about food for a while. Soon, it was time for him to transform again.

Li Yu excused himself as always, saying he had something important to attend to. After Li Yu left, Prince Jing waited another fifteen minutes before ordering Wang Xi to bring out the fish in the crystal tank.

Li Yu, who'd had to rush back to swap between his human and fish form, was quickly scooped out of the water by Wang-gonggong using a large jade spoon. For some reason, Prince Jing had been very possessive lately and refused to let anyone else touch his fish. As a result, Wang-gonggong had to use the spoon. Then, Wang Xi put Li Yu into a brand new lapis lazuli tank. This tank wasn't the usual simple box shape; instead, it was shaped like a house. Jade bells hung from the eaves, tinkling whenever the wind blew. For ease of viewing, all the windows and doors were filled with a layer of crystal.

Li Yu had never seen this tank before. Prince Jing, the fish lover, probably just had it made. Such a large piece of lapis must have been really expensive—Li Yu was too scared to swim around once he was inside.

Wang Xi came out holding the lapis fish tank. As soon as Ye Qinghuan saw this new tank, the corners of his mouth twitched. Sky-blue lapis lazuli was rare and hard to find, and only the royal family was allowed to use it. This time, he and the princess had totally lost.

The princess hadn't seen the fish in a long time. Last time, at the market, she'd only managed to get a brief glimpse at the plush from a distance. Now, seeing the real thing, the princess was shocked. "How...how did it get like this?"

Even though Ye Qinghuan had already warned her, she still remembered that little black fish at the banquet, eating from Prince Jing's hand.

Prince Jing glanced at Wang Xi, who'd already memorized the explanation. He retold it to the princess, and the princess, eyes wide, couldn't stop exclaiming, "Oh, oh!"

The servants placed the two fish tanks together. Prince Jing's fish tank was clearly bigger than the princess's. Through the crystal windows, Li Yu looked at the fish across from him.

The emperor had also gifted Prince Jing fish before, but at the time, Li Yu didn't have an opportunity to observe them so up close.

Slowly, he had a scary thought. Humans couldn't understand fish, no matter how many bubbles he blew. But what about other fish?

Fish... How did they say hi?

Li Yu tried to swim a little closer and yelled toward the other tank, "Hi, can you hear me?"

No reaction from the other side.

Li Yu thought he might be thinking too much. After all, he wasn't a normal fish. He was a transmigrated fish. Even fish-to-fish, they couldn't communicate in language, right?

Suddenly, scales flashed before his eyes. All the fish in the tank across started to swim toward him. They raised their heads, blowing bubbles at Li Yu. None of them made the same kind of noise as Li Yu, but somehow, Li Yu could understand them.

The fish were saying: *Hello, what do you want?*

...What an unexpected surprise!!

Li Yu swung his tail, and the fish lined up in a line. Li Yu swung again, and they lined up in a cross.

Li Yu laughed. What should he do next? Then he had another, more devious thought.

"Tianchi, what...what's going on with these fish?"

Ye Qinghuan was completely blown away. His and the princess's fish all swam to Prince Jing's fish and were blowing bubbles together. What a sight! If it were just one or two fish, that could be a coincidence, but if the whole group was doing it, that was too uncanny.

Prince Jing watched from the side. He knew exactly what was going on. Xiaoyu's true form was a koi. He was probably communicating with the other fish. But he couldn't hear what they were saying.

Prince Jing watched the fish, annoyance and bitterness rising in his heart. Eventually, he walked up and picked up his own fish tank. The other fish suddenly lost their conversation partner and looked around, confused.

Prince Jing threw a warning glance toward Ye Qinghuan. *You didn't see anything.*

Ye Qinghuan randomly found an excuse and said, as though suddenly coming to a realization, "Tianchi, is your fish female?" Other than a female fish attracting a bunch of male fish, Ye-shizi couldn't think of any other explanation.

Li Yu and Prince Jing both separately felt complicated about this.

Anyway, Li Yu's new, devious thought had to do with the other fish. It was almost time for the emperor's birthday celebration. In the original book, that was when the sixth prince took the opportunity to show himself off. If Prince Jing wanted to fight for the throne, he could take advantage of this celebration and use the sixth prince's tricks better than he could. That way the sixth prince would be left with nothing!

In the book, because the sixth prince couldn't afford expensive gifts, he'd projected the word "longevity" onto the golden bricks of Qianqing Palace. The clever idea had pleased the emperor greatly.

Of course, not being able to afford an expensive gift was only an excuse. The sixth prince had thought of such a gift a long time ago. It would gain the emperor's sympathy and make him happy.

Li Yu wouldn't urge Prince Jing to ruin the sixth prince's gift; he'd just think of something better and win against the sixth prince. The emperor's birthday was a chance to show off everyone's skills and creativity anyway!

Li Yu first asked Wang Xi to get a tank of fish. Then, he worked with the fish for a while. After he was confident, Li Yu looked for an opportunity to ask Prince Jing about the details of the celebration.

In past years, Prince Jing would always give his own calligraphy as his gift. It was standard and expected.

But now that he had his eyes on the throne, he couldn't be too careless. The emperor had given Prince Jing a job, so Prince Jing should show his thanks. Other than writing something of his own, Prince Jing had also found a painter that the emperor really liked and commissioned him to paint a scene of cranes and flat peaches[9] to celebrate. This painter had a quirky personality and didn't like to take commissions, so it was already a miracle that he'd agreed to paint for Prince Jing.

By the time Li Yu came to ask Prince Jing, Prince Jing already had his entire gift planned out. But he still wanted to hear Xiaoyu's idea. He knew Xiaoyu wanted the best for him, and he liked it when Xiaoyu was busy doing things for him.

Li Yu asked tentatively, "Your Highness, do you have any ideas for the emperor's birthday?"

Prince Jing shook his head, only to see Xiaoyu's dark eyes shine abnormally brightly. Prince Jing looked at him, smiling. *What do you have in mind now?*

---

9   Cranes (仙鹤) and flat peaches (蟠桃) both symbolize longevity.

Li Yu rubbed his hands together. "Your Highness, let's try to arrange some fish into the word 'longevity' and present it to the emperor!"

The sixth prince's projection was static; how could it compare to Li Yu's living, breathing arrangement? Besides, koi were auspicious. There was no way his koi arrangement would lose to the sixth prince's light projection! Besides, he'd tested it out over the last few days. He was able to have simple communications with the other fish. Arranging them into the word "longevity" would be a piece of cake! Then, during the performance, he could join the group of fish to prevent any mistakes.

Li Yu thought his idea was very good. "I feed fish every day," he said smugly. "I know how to arrange them into a word. Just let me try, Your Highness."

Prince Jing raised a brow. He'd seen Xiaoyu interact with the other fish with his own eyes and couldn't help but consider the possibility. Li Yu was afraid he wouldn't agree, though, so he grabbed his hand, swinging it back and forth and acting spoiled and cute.

This was the first time Xiaoyu had shaken his arm like this. Inside, Prince Jing was already smiling. He showed no outward reaction to Li Yu's cute actions, seemingly still contemplating the idea, but his eyes kept drifting to his own lap.

Li Yu immediately flushed. What an asshole, taking advantage at every opportunity! Oh well, he was a flexible fish. He'd do whatever it took. They had to go "through thick and thin" together...

In order to be given this extremely important job, Li Yu swallowed his embarrassment and sat down on Prince Jing's legs obediently.

Fifteen minutes later, Li Yu emerged victorious, his legs shaking. Offering himself to the tyrant, bite by bite, the tyrant finally agreed to let him try in the end. Now, it was all up to him.

Fishy Celebration

I N ORDER TO ACHIEVE the best effect, Li Yu used only red carp in his arrangement. That was his only requirement, other than not allowing anyone to watch while he trained the fish. Prince Jing let him do whatever he wanted. The fish that were purchased weren't as precious as the koi in the palace, but they did look celebratory and jubilant.

It wasn't enough just to practice. Li Yu had asked Prince Jing to write down the word "longevity" as reference. Originally, the prince didn't expect much; he was just trying to make Xiaoyu happy. But seeing how meticulous the arrangement was—exactly the same as his own handwriting—Prince Jing was both shocked and deeply moved. Xiaoyu was the only person in the world who could achieve this.

After that, in order to practice, the little fish didn't sleep or eat. Prince Jing thought his fish had lost a lot of weight, and he prepared plenty of feed. He'd also fed human Xiaoyu lots of nutritious foods, but Li Yu would only eat a little bit each time.

Unfortunately, Li Yu had to join in on the performance, so he couldn't look too different from the rest of the fish. In the past, Li Yu had never paid much attention, but now that he was with the other fish, he realized what a celebrity fish should look like. But even though Li Yu didn't eat much, he really wanted to. All the food

Prince Jing fed him was too delicious. Maybe he could wait until after the emperor's birthday to make up for it.

While Li Yu was practicing his fish arrangement, the spy Prince Jing sent to keep an eye on the sixth prince came back to report that the sixth prince had bought many paper lanterns. Li Yu immediately understood what that meant. It was just as he expected: when it came to these plot points that didn't affect much of what came before or after, the sixth prince really did follow the original plot. He was indeed preparing a light show.

But if they were keeping an eye on the sixth prince, was the sixth prince keeping an eye on them too? Li Yu remembered the sixth prince's icy cold gaze and couldn't help the shiver creeping up his spine. He decided he had to be careful. He couldn't underestimate that person no matter what.

Considering the fish arrangement might not go according to plan, Li Yu made some contingency plans.

The emperor's birthday arrived in no time at all.

Prince Jing had to go to the palace early in the morning. Li Yu was afraid that if he transformed into a human now, something might happen later and he wouldn't be able to transform again, so the day before, he'd told Prince Jing that Li-gongzi was asking for the day off. Prince Jing would take the crystal bottle and Xiaoyu into the palace first, and Wang Xi and the guards would bring the rest of the fish afterward.

In order to avoid suspicion, all the fish were in fish tanks covered in cloth. They would just tell anyone who asked that these were gifts for the emperor.

The emperor was holding his birthday banquet in Baohe Palace and would be receiving birthday wishes from all of his court officials.

Gifts from various states and counties had already started coming in a month earlier, and there were plenty of common people who'd traveled to the capital to celebrate and witness the festivities. As a result, the emperor had colorful tents set up all over for the occasion.

Li Yu was there with Prince Jing for the celebration at Baohe Palace, and the whole thing really opened his eyes. If he had to choose one word to describe it, it would be "lavish." There were so many gifts from court officials and other members of the aristocracy that the rooms in Baohe Palace weren't enough to hold them all. The gifts were all priceless. Any random piece could be a family heirloom.

The emperor was very happy. He had a few drinks with some of the officials and each of the six ministers, and then it was time for the princes to present their gifts. They lined up according to age, which meant the one at the very front was the Marquis of An, the second prince. The emperor had allowed him into the palace to celebrate on such a special day, but Mu Tianzhao still wasn't in his right mind. He didn't manage to recognize the emperor when he saw him. And when the emperor saw the Marquis of An and thought back to the personable second prince of the past, he couldn't help but feel melancholy.

Very quickly, though, this feeling was washed away by the other princes. The third prince, Mu Tianming, had also been allowed to enter the palace. The emperor nodded as he saw how much humbler the third prince was now. The third prince brought forth the gift he'd carefully selected: a sarira[10] he'd purchased for a fortune. The emperor was touched at the third prince's filial piety, but such relics were found in places of worship. Buddha probably wasn't pleased at the trouble he'd gone to.

---

10   A sarira is a typically pearl-like object purported to be found in the ashes of cremated Buddhist masters.

But because it was a celebration, the emperor didn't let his dissatisfaction show on his face. However, he did think about it a bit more deeply. The third prince was still on house arrest. All he could do was study and copy books. How did he get his hands on such a precious thing? But he decided to leave that question for later. The third prince insisted that he was now regretful of his mistakes, but the emperor wanted to check the third prince thoroughly.

From inside his bottle, Li Yu saw the third prince present the relic. It was pitch-black, and he couldn't quite tell what shape it was. Regardless of whether or not the third prince managed to get the real thing, most sarira were made when monks were cremated. Li Yu instinctively feared such things.

Feeling Li Yu's nervousness, Prince Jing covered him up with his sleeve. Li Yu felt a lot safer peeking out from behind the fabric.

The two young princes, the seventh and eighth princes, had each copied sutras for the emperor and came to kowtow to the emperor with their mothers. The emperor liked seeing his young sons' faces. It made him feel like he was still young, not yet old.

When it was the sixth prince's turn, Mu Tianxiao first had his head lowered, asking for forgiveness. He said he was poor, unable to prepare a proper gift. All he could do was prepare a light show for the emperor.

The way he said it provoked intrigue and sympathy. The emperor was also curious what exactly the sixth prince was planning and asked him to do his best.

Li Yu screamed mentally, *It's here, it's here!* He immediately swam to the edge of his crystal bottle.

Following the sixth prince's request, half of the candles in Baohe Palace were extinguished. Then, six lanterns that the sixth prince had brought were hung up. The emperor looked up at them, and thought the lights were quite ordinary, but the sixth prince asked him to look at the floor.

On the gold bricks of Baohe Palace, many vague shadows appeared. With closer examination, each shadow read "longevity." The emperor was shocked. "Tianxiao, how did you do this!"

Mu Tianxiao smiled and explained it to the emperor in detail. After the sixth prince had purchased the lanterns, he'd stuck many cut-outs of the word "longevity" on the inside. When the lanterns were lit and hung up high, the words inside would be projected onto the ground.

Mu Tianxiao said humbly, "It's but a simple trick, not anything impressive."

The emperor clapped delightedly, "I know it wasn't easy. It's the thought that counts."

When the sixth prince was presenting his gift, the third prince was right on the side. Mu Tianming originally had a lot of confidence in his relic, hoping it would allow him to make a comeback. But he saw the difference in how the emperor treated him and the sixth prince. So, to the emperor, the relic he'd spent a fortune on was nothing compared to a few lanterns?

The third prince was incredibly frustrated—and also confused. Wasn't the sixth prince always helping him out? Why did he try to steal the show during such an important occasion, the emperor's birthday?

The third prince turned his confusion to the sixth prince. The sixth prince said quietly, "Third brother, don't be angry. You're still on house arrest now. I was thinking that if I can get a word in front of our royal father, I could help you out of your situation."

The third prince froze. That seemed to make sense. But was that really how it was?

After the sixth prince left, Head Eunuch Luo came to whisper to the emperor. Prince Jing's Wang-gonggong had asked him to announce Prince Jing's gift last. It was a very small thing for Luo Ruisheng, but Prince Jing would owe him a favor in the future. Why not? So, after the emperor praised the sixth prince's gift over and over, Luo Ruisheng found the opportunity to bring up Prince Jing.

The emperor smiled, then glanced at Prince Jing, a little surprised. "Tianchi, I heard you prepared a unique gift this time?"

Prince Jing usually gave him his own calligraphy. If even he had prepared a surprise, that would truly be unusual.

Prince Jing walked out of the lineup and presented his own calligraphy and a painting scroll. When the emperor saw the prince's calligraphy, he smiled. Doing something every single year was a kind of perseverance. Then, as he unrolled the scroll, the emperor's expression was full of delight. "You managed to get your hands on a painting from Tang Yin for my birthday?"

Tang Yin was the name of the painter. Many people praised him as the "painting immortal," and the emperor really enjoyed his works too, wanting to bring him into the palace. But Tang Yin was a little strange. He didn't like money or power and rarely painted for anyone else. How unexpected that he made an exception for the emperor's birthday!

The sixth prince spoke of his hardships, but Prince Jing said nothing of how he'd persuaded Tang Yin to paint this for him. He only brought the painting out. But as soon as the emperor saw it, he knew how much effort Prince Jing had put in.

After the emperor finished examining the crane and peach painting, he asked Luo Ruisheng to hang it up in Qianqing Palace, satisfied. He wanted to see this painting every day. In comparison, the sixth prince's lighting projection was a lot cruder. The emperor no longer paid the shadows any mind.

After Prince Jing had presented the painting, he stood there unmoving. The emperor said, curious, "Do you have something else?"

Prince Jing nodded lightly and gestured for the emperor to follow him. The emperor was quite happy and was willing to do as Prince Jing said. He followed Prince Jing, and they arrived at Taiye Pool.

Luo Ruisheng held the emperor's arm, and they looked into the pool together, only to see patches of red jumping here and there. There were many red carp swimming within.

The carp were constantly moving and seemed to be increasing in number. They lingered before the emperor, not leaving.

Luo Ruisheng understood that this was why Prince Jing asked the emperor to come. He chuckled, "Your Majesty, look, the fish are congratulating you."

Pleased, the emperor nodded.

The sixth prince followed behind the emperor. The smile remained on his face, but he felt disdain on the inside. What was this? All he had to do was toss some fish feed in before the emperor came. Of course the fish would all gather. This couldn't even be considered a trick! How was it comparable to his lanterns?

The emperor looked at the fish in the pool, then suddenly realized the fish seemed to be in formation. Some were horizontal, some were vertical. They looked like strokes of a brush.

Luo Ruisheng saw it too and exclaimed in a low voice, "Do these fish form a word?"

The emperor took a step back so he could see all the carp at once. Connecting the patches of red, they formed a spectacular, proper word.

—Longevity.

The precise "longevity" that Prince Jing had written many times throughout the years.

Luo Ruisheng was stunned, nearly to tears. "Your Highness, the carp are celebrating your birthday!"

First the emperor had received Tang Yin's crane and peach painting, now he had the red carp "longevity." He couldn't be more pleased. Luo Ruisheng spewed out a bunch of auspicious, congratulatory messages. And after all that, the red carp were still in formation!

No one had ever seen such a thing. Everyone rushed forward to look.

The emperor liked Prince Jing's gift the best. He showered the prince with praise but never asked how he did it. There was no need to reveal the secret behind such a beautiful scene. The emperor would just pretend it was a miracle.

Mu Tianming stared at all this in fury. Seeing Mu Tianxiao, he said passive aggressively, "I might not be as smart as you, but you can't even compare to a mute."

But the sixth prince just smiled. "Fifth brother's gift is truly extraordinary. I really cannot compete."

Mu Tianming saw that either way, his gift couldn't come close to the others', so he left in a hurry. Mu Tianxiao kept smiling. No one would be able to criticize him.

The emperor admired the red carp for a long time. They were somehow still holding their formation. The sixth prince suddenly thought of something.

Prince Jing must've done something to the water to make the carps spell out "longevity." But he didn't know how Prince Jing did it. If he could ruin the formation, Prince Jing wouldn't feel so smug anymore.

Very quickly, he thought of a plan and asked a servant nearby, "Is there fish feed? I've never seen a sight like this before. I want to reward these fish."

The sixth prince wasn't stupid—he wouldn't poison these fish in front of the emperor. He just wanted to feed them. There must be a reason these fish spelled out "longevity." But fish were fish. How smart could they be? If he threw down a handful of feed, the fish would start fighting.

When faced with such a sight, most people would want to feed them. The sixth prince's actions weren't suspicious. Even the emperor heard. "That's right, I want to reward them too."

In an instant, Prince Jing's heart flew into his throat. But remembering how Xiaoyu had promised him, he couldn't ruin Xiaoyu's plan, so Prince Jing forced himself to calm down, staring at the fish.

The sixth prince smiled smugly. He took the fish feed from the servant and threw a huge handful down.

The carps really did rush toward the food. The huge "longevity" dissipated in an instant!

The emperor suddenly realized something and felt a little disappointed. But just as the red carp were dispersing, he saw a silver koi speckled with gold swim up slowly from below.

The koi was holding a lotus flower in its mouth, its gold fins illuminating the azure waves of Taye Pool. It swam to the emperor and spun in an elegant circle.

The emperor had never experienced so many surprises in a row!!!

He quickly recognized his son's pet fish. "Tianchi, this is... your fish!"

Prince Jing nodded, giving the fish in the water—who was trying to do a seaweed dance—a doting glance.

The sixth prince had played a dirty trick, but Xiaoyu had something up his sleeve. He was prepared.

Prince Jing was so proud of his love.

Through Thick
and Thin

THE EMPEROR WAS VERY HAPPY with Prince Jing. At the banquet, he thought a lot, and often looked toward Prince Jing.

After the banquet, the emperor summoned Prince Jing to speak to him alone.

Li Yu had just returned from Taiye Pool to the crystal bottle. He didn't have time to come along, so he had to wait outside Qianqing Palace with Wang Xi.

While they waited, Wang Xi brought out lots of red fish food and peach blossom pastries to feed him. Prince Jing's gift had never been so successful, and Wang-gonggong thought it was all thanks to Master Fish. It really needed to be appreciated for its hard work.

Just now, when the sixth prince had thrown the fish feed into the water, Li Yu hadn't eaten a single bite. The proud fish didn't even glance at the food, only focusing on swimming in front of the emperor, not tiring at all. With Wang-gonggong feeding him now, however, Li Yu could finally feel his hunger. He hurriedly started gobbling it down until both cheeks were stuffed.

"Master Fish, eat slowly," Wang Xi chuckled.

Li Yu was still busy eating when he suddenly heard footsteps. Delighted, Li Yu turned to look with a piece of food still in his mouth, then realized the footsteps were coming from outside, so it must not be Prince Jing.

Soon, Li Yu saw Mu Tiaoxiao's gentle, amiable face.

...The sixth prince? Li Yu was a little disappointed. Why hadn't he left yet? Probably because he was waiting for the emperor to summon him. *I bet he wasn't expecting to see Wang Xi here with the fish.*

Mu Tiaoxiao saw the fish too. The sixth prince examined the fish for a long time and was about to take a step forward.

"Your Highness, Sixth Prince, please stop!" Wang Xi called out with his brows knit together.

"I can't take a look at my fifth brother's fish?" The sixth prince seemed to smile.

What did he want? Li Yu was so nervous, he forgot to eat his food. He sneakily gathered all his strength into his tail. If the sixth prince tried anything, he'd slap him!

"Sixth prince." Wang Xi held the crystal bottle protectively in his arms. "This is His Highness's fish. Without his permission, no one is allowed to approach."

Mu Tianxiao's expression went cold. "You dare to look down on me too?"

"This servant is not looking down on Your Highness," said Wang Xi, neither too self-deprecating nor too arrogant. "Although I'm just a servant, I know taking without asking is stealing. Why does Your Highness have to come look at the fish while our prince is gone?"

Li Yu would have clapped for Wang Xi if his fins could reach. Sob sob sob, Wang-gonggong was standing up to the sixth prince for him, how touching!

Wang Xi refused to give in, putting Mu Tianxiao in an awkward position. Realizing that getting into a fight with Prince Jing's most trusted servant in front of Qianqing Palace would be a bad look, Mu Tianxiao quickly smoothed out his expression and said, "There's no need to be so nervous. I just want to take a look. If that's not okay, then never mind."

Mu Tianxiao had walked into the palace without asking, and very quickly he was politely asked to leave by the servants inside. He glared at Wang Xi and left.

It looked like the sixth prince was unable to ask for an audience with the emperor. The emperor didn't want to see him.

Now that he was finally gone, Li Yu relaxed a little.

At last Luo Ruisheng walked Prince Jing out. Wang Xi hurried to greet him with Li Yu.

"Your Highness, you're finally done!" Wang Xi handed the crystal bottle over, smiling. Prince Jing always wanted to see the fish first. It had become a habit.

Prince Jing accepted the crystal bottle and smoothed a hand over the fish's smooth back. Li Yu rubbed up against him happily.

The emperor had spoken to Prince Jing for ages. It would be great if the emperor had been so pleased that he made Prince Jing the crown prince right then and there. Garbage like the third prince and the sixth prince could all stand to the side! Li Yu nearly laughed at himself. How could it be so easy? He knew he was only dreaming, but he wanted to think about it just for fun.

But even if he wasn't made crown prince, he should at least be rewarded, right? Li Yu snuck a glance at Prince Jing's expression. He didn't look happy or sad. It seemed like the reward this time was different.

Prince Jing glanced at Wang Xi: *Go to Changchun Palace.*

Wang Xi made a noise in response and led the way. This was the first time Li Yu had gone to Changchun Palace. It made him think of a certain mysterious secret related to the place... He'd once tried to ask Prince Jing, but it had become clear that Prince Jing had no such memory. If he wanted to figure out the secret, he'd have to do it himself.

Li Yu had wanted to ask Prince Jing if he could take him to Changchun Palace before, but he was never able to find a good excuse. After all, Changchun Palace was where the empress had lived. It would be rude if he randomly asked to go see it. Besides, if he wanted to come in human form, he'd have to pay attention to the time. If Prince Jing agreed to take him and then he "disappeared," there was no possible way to explain that. But if he was a fish, he couldn't ask Prince Jing to take him anywhere.

Li Yu had been planning on waiting until Empress Xiaohui's birthday. The original story mentioned that Prince Jing would go to Changchun Palace every year on that day. Prince Jing usually brought the fish around with him everywhere. If he didn't, the fish just wouldn't leave him alone—he'd get to Changchun Palace somehow. Then, while he was there, he would figure out the secret.

Unexpectedly, before the empress's birthday, on the emperor's birthday, Prince Jing was going for some reason. He'd just met with the emperor—was it because the emperor ordered him to?

Li Yu observed Prince Jing's expression carefully. Prince Jing should've been rewarded, so why was his expression so solemn...?

Soon, they arrived at Changchun Palace.

As soon as Li Yu saw the landscaping around the palace, he grew more and more sure that the secret had happened here. The decorations on the eaves were very similar to the ones he saw in the system, and Wang Xi was muttering that after the empress's death, no other concubines had lived here, and that it had been a long time since it was fixed up.

Changchun Palace was engulfed in darkness. Wang Xi ordered someone to light the candles. There were funeral cloths hanging all over the place, and Empress Xiaohui's memorial tablet rested on the table.

Prince Jing put the crystal bottle on a side table. Wang Xi took out three sticks of incense, and Prince Jing lit them himself. Then he approached the tablet and kowtowed three times.

Li Yu entered the palace with Prince Jing. He looked around everywhere for the tiger plush, but he didn't see it. Because he couldn't do anything as a fish, he had no choice but to give up.

He watched as Prince Jing paid respects to Empress Xiaohui and couldn't help but think back to the family that Prince Jing had taken him to see in Cheng'en Manor. Now he'd brought Li Yu to Changchun Palace. Empress Xiaohui was Prince Jing's mother... Realizing, Li Yu hurriedly bobbed his fish body, following along with Prince Jing's movements. Because this was all so sudden, Li Yu wasn't prepared. All he could do was say silently, "Your Majesty, if you can hear me, please protect Prince Jing..."

From the corner of his eye, Prince Jing caught sight of Li Yu bobbing his head and tail. He immediately understood Li Yu's intentions and smiled, at peace.

After the fish was done "bowing," Prince Jing sat down to touch the fish. Li Yu could feel Prince Jing's heavy heart even through the bottle. What was it? Was he not rewarded? Did he get scolded instead?

"Your Highness, what's wrong?" Wang Xi was a little worried too.

Prince Jing shook his head lightly and glanced outside. Wang Xi immediately understood what he meant. This was the palace; it wasn't a place to talk.

Prince Jing sat long enough for a cup of tea, then led Wang Xi and Li Yu out of the palace.

It wasn't until they were back at the manor that Wang Xi and Li Yu found out that not only did the emperor not reward Prince Jing, he ordered Prince Jing to go live on the western border for a while.

Or in other words, the emperor's "reward" for Prince Jing was for him to leave the city.

How could that be?

Li Yu didn't understand it. The emperor was clearly very happy when he saw the "longevity" made of fish, and had even mentioned hanging Tang Yin's painting up in Qianqing Palace. Why had he suddenly gotten mad at Prince Jing? He couldn't find anything wrong. Was there a problem with his fish arrangement? Was it that he shouldn't have gone the extra mile to give the emperor the lotus?

But if he hadn't, and the fish had just scattered, the emperor would've been upset...

Sob, it was too hard to guess at an emperor's thoughts as a fish!

Li Yu was self-reflecting; Wang Xi also thought it was unfair. After he voiced a few complaints, Prince Jing ordered him to leave.

Once Wang-gonggong had left, the more Li Yu thought about it, the more he thought it was his fault. He could no longer stomach any more fish feed or pastries, and he couldn't help replaying all the details of the banquet in his head.

He just didn't understand. While he was blaming himself, Li Yu saw Prince Jing had left a little lamp on by the window and was sitting there. The dark night made his young, handsome face seem slightly hazy.

It was already dark. He'd had such an exhausting day, but Prince Jing wasn't resting. Perhaps just like Li Yu, he couldn't figure it out and couldn't fall asleep.

He couldn't continue like this.

Li Yu shook his head and turned into a human where Prince Jing couldn't see. He walked to the window and called out apologetically, "Your Highness."

Prince Jing looked up at him, eyes full of smiles, and waved at him. Li Yu suddenly realized Prince Jing was there because he was waiting up for him, not because he was upset about today.

"Your Highness, I'm sorry, I-I tried my best, I don't know why things ended up like this..." Li Yu mumbled an explanation, feeling very sorry for himself. Didn't all the novels say that fighting for the throne meant making the emperor happy? Why was it that he made the emperor happy but it only backfired? Did the emperor suspect Prince Jing because he tried to get his favor?

Why couldn't Li Yu share some of his luck in specific, slightly weird places with Prince Jing?

Prince Jing saw that he'd misunderstood and shook his head. He patted Li Yu's hand, then pointed at the painting on the wall.

Li Yu tried to guess for a while before he understood what Prince Jing meant. Prince Jing was saying it wasn't Li Yu's fault; Prince Jing had given a painting as well, after all.

Li Yu sniffled and said uncertainly, "You don't blame me, Your Highness?"

Prince Jing shook his head again, holding Li Yu's hands tighter. It was hard to say what he wanted through a few brief actions. Prince Jing kissed Li Yu on the lips, then put him on his lap.

Li Yu was shocked. Prince Jing wanted to do that *now*?

Unless he was afraid he wasn't coming back anymore, so he had to eat his fill?

...Just like how he suddenly went to Changchun Palace? Was he afraid he wouldn't be able to pay his respects anymore?

Li Yu's heart was aching. Either way, the fish had nothing to give but himself. It wasn't a big deal to let Prince Jing have some fun. He steeled himself, wrapping his arms around Prince Jing's neck.

Prince Jing paused a little at Li Yu's sudden initiative, then laughed like something had just occurred to him. He pushed Li Yu away from him slightly, held Li Yu's hand, and spread out a sheet of paper.

Li Yu suddenly went bright red. So he didn't want to eat him, he wanted to...write.

Prince Jing wrote, with his hand over Li Yu's, *You've worked hard. You're very good, don't worry. Father isn't mad at me.*

"Really?" Li Yu didn't quite believe him. "Then why does the emperor want Your Highness to leave?"

In the book, the western border was a desolate, dangerous place, and quite poor. There was no way the emperor wanted Prince Jing to go on a vacation there, right?

Father hasn't taken away my title yet. Prince Jing wrote down roughly, hinting at something.

Li Yu mulled those words over in his head. His eyes brightened. "Hasn't taken away my title yet," what did that mean?

The emperor was thoroughly disappointed with the second prince, not even leaving him the title of Prince, only calling him the Marquis of An. None of the other princes were given proper titles either. Prince Jing's title was given to him out of regret and reassurance. If the emperor was really angry and sent Prince Jing away in a fit of rage, he wouldn't let him keep his title.

"So...the emperor ordered you to go to the western border, not as punishment, but as—"

Li Yu was just about to say it, when Prince Jing put a finger to his lips hurriedly and shushed him.

The emperor hadn't said anything. He just told him to go to the western border. He'd receive more specific instructions when he got there.

Prince Jing himself didn't get it either. He'd just inferred this from the fact that the emperor still asked Luo Ruisheng to see him out. He felt like he had the right idea, but he couldn't say it out loud. If the emperor wanted him to go to the border, he had no choice but to go.

Li Yu covered his mouth cooperatively, but his heart immediately started to jump.

Since ancient times, if a father was kicking his son out not for punishment, then it was to test him. But why did the emperor want to test Prince Jing?

It must be because he had new hopes for him. In the past, the emperor rarely interfered with Prince Jing's life because he didn't expect much from him, so he didn't care what Prince Jing did.

So now, he was hopeful. Going to the western border might not be a bad thing.

Now that he'd figured it out, Li Yu's dismay turned to joy. "Your Highness, wh-when are you leaving?"

Prince Jing wrote: *Soon, in a few days. You stay here. Wang Xi will take care of you.*

Though Prince Jing was fairly confident he'd figured out what the emperor was thinking, the western border was a desperate place. He didn't want Xiaoyu to come with him. Besides, he was afraid the trip would be too much for Xiaoyu, so he wanted him to stay in the city. He hadn't pampered Xiaoyu enough yet. How could he let Xiaoyu go through such hardship with him?

Li Yu couldn't believe he was going to be left behind! Holy shit, if Prince Jing was going to the western border, didn't that mean they were about to "go through thick and thin"?

"No, Your Highness," he declared loudly, "I'll go where you go. If you're going, we're going together!"

Fake Fishy Pregnancy

LI YU WASN'T AFRAID of hard times. He'd been prepared to go through thick and thin with Prince Jing for a long time. Since he'd transmigrated, apart from the very beginning when he'd nearly been eaten by that cat, he'd been taken care of by Prince Jing. So what if now he had to follow Prince Jing to a desolate place?!

He didn't have a home in this time period. It was Prince Jing who gave him somewhere to stay.

Li Yu thought of a very touching line. "I... To me," he said, smiling, "home is wherever Your Highness is."

Prince Jing didn't expect him to say something like that. He touched Li Yu's cheek tenderly, his eyes flickering with emotion.

Li Yu thought Prince Jing would feel touched and allow him to go to the western border with him. That way, he could complete the "Through Thick and Thin" quest that he'd nearly forgotten about. But though Prince Jing was touched, he still refused.

This was way too hard! He couldn't convince Prince Jing even with such beautiful language? He couldn't always use his body every single time...

Oh, he got it! Li Yu suddenly had an idea. His man was someone with a sense of responsibility!

Li Yu sniffled, "Your Highness, I-I'm already with your child, you're still going to leave me here alone?"

No matter how resolute Prince Jing had been before, he was now thoroughly shocked by Li Yu's words. Looking at the person in his arms pretending to be demure, Prince Jing thought his soul was floating away.

If he remembered correctly, he and Xiaoyu had not made it to the last step. Besides, Xiaoyu was male. If this were any other occasion, he'd just laugh—how could men get pregnant? But the problem was that Prince Jing knew Xiaoyu was not human. He was a carp spirit. Perhaps carp spirits were just different, and a male fish could get pregnant?

Prince Jing wanted to believe Li Yu. If Xiaoyu said he was, then he was. But Xiaoyu was a fish. He was human. So, was he pregnant with a fish or a human?

A human would be easier... If it were a fish...

Prince Jing placed his palm carefully on Li Yu's belly. No matter what, that was his child in there, he wouldn't deny it!

Li Yu had just been joking. Even though they'd never gone all the way, they'd done everything else, so they'd been quite intimate already. He refused to let Prince Jing leave him here, but he didn't think Prince Jing would take his joke seriously and touch his belly. Li Yu didn't know whether to laugh or cry.

Who would believe such nonsense? But Prince Jing did. If this misunderstanding continued, Prince Jing might even pick a name. Li Yu hurriedly apologized, "Your Highness, I'm sorry, I was lying, I'm not pregnant, I was just kidding!"

There was only fish feed and pastries in the fish's belly, no babies!

Prince Jing looked up, gaze lost: *You're not?*

Li Yu's heart ached at the emotion in his eyes, and he hugged him tightly. "Your Highness, I'm a man, how could I...I'm sorry, I shouldn't have joked about something like that. I just want to be together with you, I don't want to be apart from you for even a second. Please don't be mad at me."

...It was a joke? Prince Jing smiled helplessly. If he didn't let the fish come with him, he'd pretend to be pregnant? He really didn't know what to do with this fish. Although he'd gotten his hopes up for nothing, Prince Jing wasn't angry. He patted the top of Li Yu's head.

Oh well, the situation in the capital was complex. If he left Xiaoyu behind by himself, he wouldn't be able to take care of him so far away at the western border. Besides, if Xiaoyu didn't mind going with him, what did he have to worry about?

Prince Jing stopped rejecting Li Yu, but he didn't nod either. Despite that, Li Yu knew he had succeeded because the system, which had been silent the last few days, gave him a new notification.

‹The main quest "Through Thick and Thin" is in progress. Please beware of your safety.›

It seemed like he was on the right track with going to the western border. He probably had to go there to complete the main quest.

Because of the notification, Li Yu remembered the protagonist halo the system had mentioned in the past. These last few days, he'd been too busy worrying about Prince Jing, and he'd forgotten that Prince Jing would definitely ascend to the throne one day.

"Your Highness, no matter how dangerous it gets or how many obstacles stand in your future, don't worry." Li Yu chuckled, very confident. "You will definitely achieve what you want, and I'll stay with you every step of the way."

Prince Jing looked at him deeply, nodded, and pulled the fish that had changed his entire life into his arms.

In Qianqing Palace, the emperor, dressed in bright yellow robes embroidered with dragons, stared at the crane and peach painting on the wall expressionlessly. He was thinking about something.

After a while, he looked up at the person beside him. "How is he?"

Head Eunuch Luo had always been at the emperor's side, so of course he knew who the emperor was speaking of. "Prince Jing seemed calm and went to Changchun Palace," he replied. "He paid his respects to the empress with three sticks of incense, then went home... This servant heard Prince Jing's manor has already started packing up the prince's belongings."

The emperor nodded, happy with Prince Jing's attitude. This son of his had never traveled far from home, and the emperor was worried about his safety. He told Luo Ruisheng, "Send two troops to follow him and secretly protect him."

Luo Ruisheng agreed.

The emperor stared at Head Eunuch Luo for a while, then said, "Do you think I'm being too harsh, sending him to the western border despite being the happiest with his gift?"

That was exactly what Luo Ruisheng was thinking, but there was no way he'd be brave enough to admit it. He said hurriedly, "This servant doesn't dare have an opinion on the emperor's decision. You must have your reasons. This servant just has to do as you say."

"Good." The emperor smiled. So what if other people misunderstood his intentions? He didn't care.

He liked Prince Jing's gift the most. And because of this gift, the emperor saw a bit of Prince Jing's ambition.

After all, Prince Jing had given him his own calligraphy for many years now. He'd always been slightly cold toward the emperor; it was like an unspoken agreement between the two of them. But now, suddenly, Prince Jing was trying to appeal to the emperor. What did that mean? The emperor didn't even need to think about it. After all, this was something he had gone through himself. How could he not understand that Prince Jing was starting to make a bid for the throne?

The emperor hadn't chosen a crown prince for a long time. It was only expected for his adult princes to have such thoughts. The emperor was at least aware of that much. If the second and third princes hadn't made mistakes, he had been willing to give them the chance. But this was Prince Jing. Aside from being surprised, the emperor felt a bit of sadness and bitterness.

In terms of status, no one deserved it more than Prince Jing. But because of his muteness, Prince Jing had lost his chance long ago. He always thought Prince Jing had accepted this fate.

But now it seemed he hadn't.

Didn't this brat know he couldn't choose a mute prince to be the crown prince? Why was he still fighting?

If this were before, the emperor would've thought this was a huge joke. But during his birthday banquet, the emperor realized the second prince had gone mad and the third prince was still colluding with officials while he was on house arrest. They'd both crossed the line. The only adult prince he could consider was the sixth prince. Though the emperor said he wasn't planning on picking a crown prince for now and wanted to see how the seventh and eighth princes fared in the future, they were still too young. It was hard to say what the future would hold. If the sixth prince wasn't suitable...

Then would he not consider Prince Jing at all?

Prince Jing was mute, but compared to the idea of having no sons to choose from at all, that problem no longer seemed so important. As for his children, though the imperial physicians said it was very possible Prince Jing would pass his muteness on to his children, it wasn't certain. It was still possible for Prince Jing to have children without that disability.

The emperor thought silently. He had eight sons, and only one of them was mute. If it came down to it, if Prince Jing had eight sons, at least one of them would *not* be mute, right?

And so Prince Jing wasn't completely out of the question. If he took the muteness out of the equation, Prince Jing certainly didn't lose to the sixth prince, or even the second prince from before.

Now he'd thought this all through, the emperor was a little excited. He wanted to see exactly how far Prince Jing could go. But he had to do better than simply not losing to the other princes. If he was going to pick a mute son to be the crown prince, this son had to have other qualities that elevated him above the competition.

The western border was messy with battles and constantly plagued with disasters. The emperor had always wanted to test the future crown prince there. Well, there wasn't a crown prince now. If Prince Jing wanted to fight for the throne, then Prince Jing could go. If he hit a wall, then he could give up and live his life peacefully. But if Prince Jing managed to solve such a mess…

"Your Highness, Prince Jing has already set out," Luo Ruisheng said quietly.

The emperor was deep in thought and didn't answer. Luo Ruisheng thought he'd spoken too quietly and repeated himself. The emperor jolted out of his thoughts and ordered Luo Ruisheng to find the sixth prince. He had a job for him too.

FAKE FISHY PREGNANCY   393

If one of the princes was able to control the western border, he'd consider making them the Crown Prince. If Prince Jing could do it, he would be considered as well!

Prince Jing had already agreed to bring Li Yu along with him. The guards, carriage, and luggage were all ready. He'd even prepared ten crystal bottles. Fish food and fish tanks took up several carts. He said it would be a tough time, but no matter what, Prince Jing wasn't going to let his fish starve.

With all of this prepared, Li-gongzi was still quite anxious and on edge.

This time, he wasn't just going shopping with Prince Jing or going to buy antiques, where he could maintain his human form just long enough. Prince Jing had calculated this trip. If they were quick, it'd take nearly a month. If they traveled at a normal pace, it'd take them around two and a half months. For most of that time, Li Yu would have to be crammed into the carriage, eating and sleeping in the same space as Prince Jing.

Squeezing together in the carriage, living and eating together— he could do all of those things as a fish, but he couldn't as a human. He could only maintain his human form for two hours a day. If he was going to be stuck with Prince Jing, how was he going to transform? Even if he managed to figure out how to transform, how was Li-gongzi going to suddenly vanish every day?

When they were on the road, they were going to be surrounded by guards. If Li-gongzi really were to leave, he'd be spotted by them. But in reality, Li-gongzi was only pretending to leave. There was no way he could actually leave. As soon as that was found out, Li Yu's disguise would be revealed.

So the only way was to try to stay as a fish for as long as possible on the journey and only interact with Prince Jing as a fish. But Li Yu, the dumbass, didn't think things through when he was faced with the possibility of completing his quest, so he asked Prince Jing to take him along as a human. He was overconfidently shooting himself in the foot.

Li Yu was so anxious. He'd asked for it himself, so he couldn't suddenly change his mind at the last moment. Prince Jing was definitely bringing Li-gongzi on this trip, he was definitely going to be living with Li-gongzi every day, taking bites out of Li-gongzi. That meant revealing his identity was an inevitability for Li-gongzi, sob!

Li Yu wasn't able to find a solution, right up to the moment they were about to leave. Wang Xi prepared the carriage and helped Li Yu into it. Li Yu climbed into the carriage holding the crystal bottle, his heart heavy with worry, and nearly stumbled over his own feet. It was a good thing Prince Jing was quick enough to steady him. Prince Jing was about to get in the carriage as well, and Li Yu couldn't have been more nervous if he was seeing a countdown to his demise.

Soon, Prince Jing entered the carriage too and looked at Li Yu, confirming there was nothing wrong. Li Yu couldn't hide what he was feeling. Prince Jing smiled at the way he was trembling, then left.

What?

Prince Jing didn't get into the carriage again, only following along beside the carriage on his horse.

Li Yu was confused. Was Prince Jing not going to get in?

He lifted a corner of the curtain, wanting to ask someone, when he saw Wang Xi just outside.

"Wang-gonggong, Wang-gonggong, what's going on?"

Wang Xi was going to the western border too. Wang-gonggong wasn't getting into the carriage either; he was riding on a donkey on the other side. When he saw Li Yu peeking out, he hurried to ask him to sit down.

"Gongzi, sit properly!" He tried not to laugh. "His Highness was afraid it'd be too cramped for you since you're pregnant now. That carriage is for you alone. Please get some rest and take care of Master Fish. If you need anything just call for me! This old servant is right outside."

Wang Xi said all that, but he was laughing on the inside the entire time. How could a man get pregnant? This must be part of the gongzi and Prince Jing's relationship, and Wang-gonggong was happy to play along.

Li Yu glared at Prince Jing for a while. Prince Jing returned the gaze, smiling. Why was this smile so offensive to his eyes? The huge asshole strikes again!

To be honest, Prince Jing really did take care of him. Was he worried Li Yu would get bored and claustrophobic with an extra person in the carriage?

Well, his identity certainly wouldn't be revealed if he had this carriage all to himself!

The only way for Li-gongzi not to be discovered...was to pretend to be pregnant.

THE STORY CONTINUES IN
The Disabled Tyrant's Beloved Pet Fish
VOLUME 3

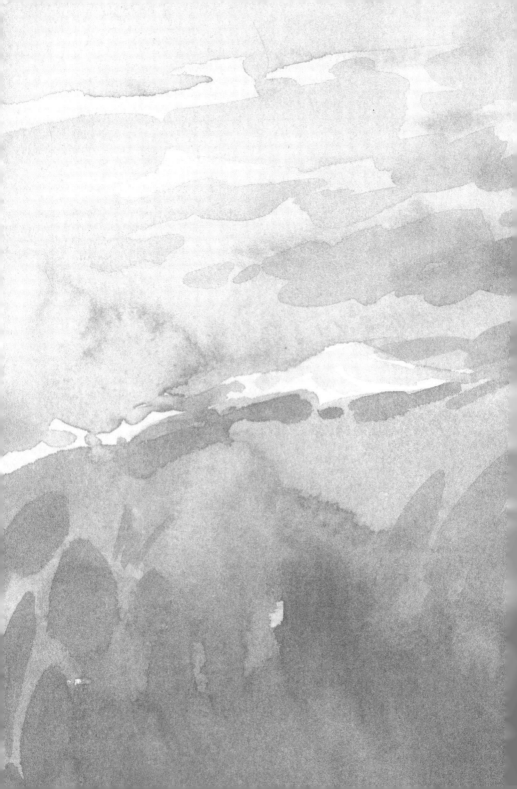

APPENDIX

Characters,
Names, and
Pronunciations

Characters

MAIN CHARACTERS

LI YU 李鱼: A modern-day webnovel reader who has been transmigrated into a fish.

MU TIANCHI 穆天池: The mute fifth prince, also known as Prince Jing.

THE ROYAL FAMILY

THE EMPEROR: Prince Jing's father.

EMPRESS XIAOHUI: Prince Jing's mother; deceased.

CONCUBINE QIU 仇贵妃: Mother of the second prince, Mu Tianzhao. Previously a noble consort.

CONSORT QIAN 钱妃: Mother of the third prince, Mu Tianming.

CONSORT ZHANG 张妃: Mother of the sixth prince, Mu Tianxiao.

SECOND PRINCE MU TIANZHAO 穆天昭: The oldest prince, since demoted to Marquis of An.

THIRD PRINCE MU TIANMING 慕天明: The second prince's rival for the role of crown prince.

SIXTH PRINCE MU TIANXIAO 穆天晓: Supports the third prince.

SEVENTH PRINCE: Unnamed, yet to come of age.

EIGHTH PRINCE: Unnamed, yet to come of age.

LUO RUISHENG: Head eunuch and the emperor's personal servant.

PRINCE JING'S MANOR

WANG XI 王喜: A eunuch; Prince Jing's personal servant.

CHU YANYU 楚燕羽: Prince Jing's love interest in the original webnovel, gifted to Prince Jing by the third prince.

CHENG'EN MANOR

YE QIAN 叶骞: The previous duke of Cheng'en and the current Duke's father. Prince Jing's grandfather.

THE DUKE OF CHENG'EN 承恩公: Ye Qinghuan's father.

YE QINGHUAN 叶清欢: Prince Jing's cousin, heir to the House of Cheng'en.

THE PRINCESS OF JINJUE 金绝公主: Engaged to be married to Ye Qinghuan.

XIONGFENG 叶清欢 ("FIERCE WIND"): Ye Qinghuan's dog.

JINJUE ROYAL FAMILY

KING OF JINJUE 金绝王: Ruler of the neighboring country of Jinjue.

PRINCESS OF JINJUE 金绝公主: The king's daughter, whom he seeks to marry into the emperor's family.

Name Guide

Diminutives, Nicknames, and Name Tags:

A-: Friendly diminutive. Always a prefix. Usually for monosyllabic names, or one syllable out of a two-syllable name.

DOUBLING: Doubling a syllable of a person's name can be a nickname, e.g., "Mangmang"; it has childish or cutesy connotations.

XIAO-: A diminutive meaning "little." Always a prefix.

-ER: An affectionate diminutive added to names, literally "son" or "child." Always a suffix.

Family:

DI/DIDI: Younger brother or a younger male friend.

GE/GEGE/DAGE: Older brother or an older male friend.

JIE/JIEJIE/ZIZI: Older sister or an older female friend.

Other:

GONGZI: Young man from an affluent household.

-GONGGONG: A respectful suffix for eunuchs.

-SHIZI: Denoting the heir to a title.

Pronunciation Guide

Mandarin Chinese is the official state language of mainland China, and pinyin is the official system of romanization in which it is written. As Mandarin is a tonal language, pinyin uses diacritical marks (e.g., ā, á, ǎ, à) to indicate these tonal inflections. Most words use one of four tones, though some are a neutral tone. Furthermore, regional variance can change the way native Chinese speakers pronounce the same word. For those reasons and more, please consider the guide below a simplified introduction to pronunciation of select character names and sounds from the world of *The Disabled Tyrant's Beloved Pet Fish*.

More resources are available at sevenseasdanmei.com

GENERAL CONSONANTS

Some Mandarin Chinese consonants sound very similar, such as z/c/s and zh/ch/sh. Audio samples will provide the best opportunity to learn the difference between them.

X: somewhere between the **sh** in **sh**eep and **s** in **s**ilk
Q: a very aspirated **ch** as in **ch**arm
C: **ts** as in pan**ts**
Z: **z** as in **z**oom
S: **s** as in **s**ilk
CH: **ch** as in **ch**arm
ZH: **dg** as in do**dg**e
SH: **sh** as in **sh**ave
G: hard **g** as in **g**raphic

GENERAL VOWELS

The pronunciation of a vowel may depend on its preceding consonant. For example, the "i" in "shi" is distinct from the "i" in "di." Vowel pronunciation may also change depending on where the vowel appears in a word, for example the "i" in "shi" versus the "i" in "ting." Finally, compound vowels are often—though not always—pronounced as conjoined but separate vowels. You'll find a few of the trickier compounds below.

IU: as in **ewe**

IE: **ye** as in **ye**s

UO: **war** as in **war**m

CHARACTER NAMES

Lǐ Yú: Li (as in *ly* from merri*ly*), yu (as in you)

Mù Tiānchí: Mu (as in moo), t (as in tea), ian (as in Ian), chi (as in *ch* from *ch*ange)

* *Note:* With chi, the i is not pronounced like ee, the way Li is pronounced. With chi, it is a sort of emphasized ch noise without any vowel sound. This applies to z, c, s, zh, ch, sh, and s.

Yè Qīnghuán: Ye (as in *ye*sterday), qing (as in *ching* from tea*ching*), h (as in *h* from *h*ello), uan (as in one)

* *Note:* The difference between ch and q is that chi is a sound produced more with the front of the teeth with a puckered mouth, while q is a sound produced more at the back, with a wider mouth.

Xióngfēng: Xi (as in *sh* from *sh*eep), ong (like *own* but with the *ng* from ring), feng (as in *fung* from *fung*us)

APPENDIX

Glossary

Glossary

CONCUBINES 妻妾: In ancient China, it was common practice for a wealthy man to possess women as concubines (妾) in addition to his wife (妻). They were expected to live with him and bear him children. Generally speaking, a greater number of concubines correlated to higher social status, hence a wealthy merchant might have two or three concubines, while an emperor might have tens or even a hundred.

DI AND SHU HIERARCHY 嫡庶: Upper-class men in ancient China often took multiple wives, though only one would be the official or "di" wife, and her sons would take precedence over the sons of the "shu" wives. "Di" sons were prioritized in matters of inheritance.

ANCIENT CHINESE IMPERIAL HAREM 后宫: Emperors would take multiple wives, and as a whole, they were referred to as the "back palace." This term can also be used to refer to the physical location where the concubines lived, which was the inner half of the palace. The concubines were separated into ranks, and their ranking directly correlated to how well they were treated, how much respect they were afforded, and how much money they were given. The ranks of the concubines changed throughout the dynasties, but these remain fairly consistent and are often used in modern media:

◇ Empress 皇后
◇ Imperial Noble Consort 皇贵妃
◇ Noble Consort 贵妃
◇ Consort 妃
◇ Concubine 嫔
◇ Noble Lady 贵人

ANCIENT CHINESE ARISTOCRACY: It was unusual for a prince to be demoted to a lower rank, but a title like "Marquis" was still a very impressive one. In order, the five highest titles after those of the emperor and princes were as follows:

- ◇ Duke 公
- ◇ Marquis 侯
- ◇ Count 伯
- ◇ Viscount 子
- ◇ Baron 男

GRAND SECRETARIAT 内阁: The Grand Secretariat was a part of the government responsible for coordinating the rest of the government. Because they controlled communications to and from the emperor, they eventually became more powerful than the Six Ministries. The Grand Secretariat was headed by six Grand Secretaries (大学士).

SIX MINISTRIES 六部: The central government system in ancient China. It consisted of the Ministries of Personnel, Revenue, Rites, War, Justice, and Works. Each of the Ministries was headed by a Minister (尚书) and two Deputy Ministers (侍郎).

IMPERIAL ASTROLOGICAL BUREAU 钦天监: An official branch of the government responsible for things like creating calendars and observing the skies. It was believed that the stars held messages from the heavens, and so the Imperial Astrological Bureau was trusted by the emperor to predict incoming disasters or auspicious events.

TAELS 两: A unit of measurement for weighing gold and silver, used as a standard form of currency.

GOLDEN FINGER 金手指: A protagonist-exclusive overpowered ability or weapon. This can also refer to them being generally OP ("overpowered") and not a specific ability or physical item.